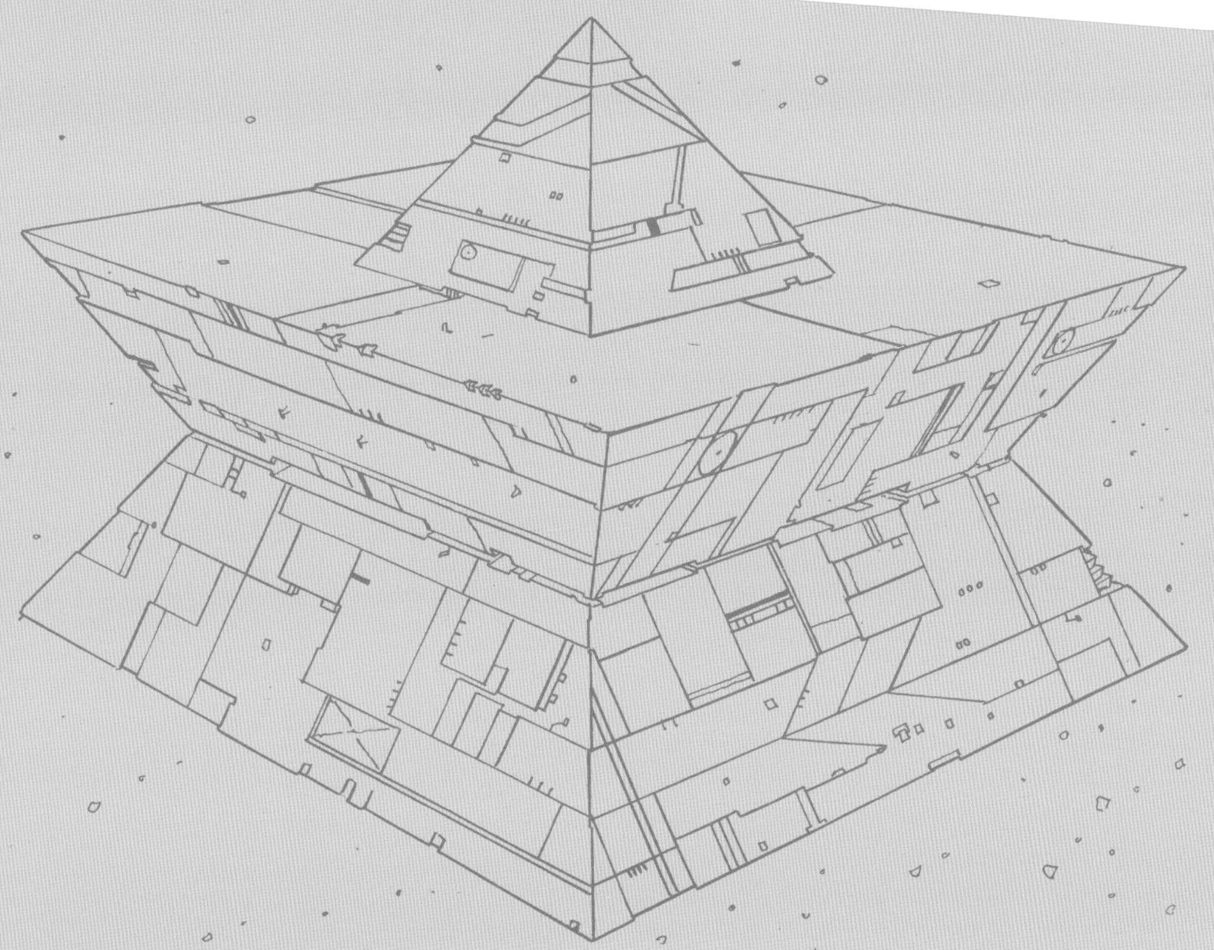

JODOROWSKY & MŒBIUS

THE INCAL

HUMANOIDS

ALEJANDRO JODOROWSKY
Writer

MŒBIUS
Artist

YVES CHALAND
ISABELLE BEAUMENEY-JOANNET
& **ZORAN JANJETOV**
Colorists

This edition contains the colors used in the original publication of this series by Yves Chaland (book 1), Isabelle Beaumeney-Joannet (books 2, 3 & 4), and Zoran Janjetov (books 5 & 6), under the supervision of Mœbius, completely restored and corrected in some minor instances.

•

SASHA WATSON & **JUSTIN KELLY**
Translators

•

ALEX DONOGHUE
US Edition Editor

BRUNO LECIGNE
Original Edition Editor

JERRY FRISSEN
Senior Art Director

FABRICE GIGER
Publisher

Rights and Licensing - licensing@humanoids.com
Press and Social Media - pr@humanoids.com

This edition of THE INCAL collects all six volumes of the series UNE AVENTURE DE JOHN DIFOOL, originally published in French by LES HUMANOÏDES ASSOCIÉS between 1981 and 1988.

THE INCAL. This title is a publication of Humanoids, Inc. 8033 Sunset Blvd. #628, Los Angeles, CA 90046.

BY THE SAME CREATORS

ANGEL CLAWS

THE EYES OF THE CAT

MADWOMAN OF THE SACRED HEART

OTHER TITLES IN THE JODOVERSE

from Alejandro Jodorowsky

THE INCAL SERIES:

BEFORE THE INCAL
with Zoran Janjetov

THE INCAL
with Mœbius

FINAL INCAL
with Ladrönn

•

DECONSTRUCTING THE INCAL
with Mœbius, Zoran Janjetov, Ladrönn,
Jean Annestay, Christophe Quillien

THE METABARONS SERIES:

THE METABARONS, FIRST CYCLE
with Juan Gimenez

(individual editions)
VOLUME 1:
OTHON & HONORATA

VOLUME 2:
AGHNAR & ODA

VOLUME 3:
STEELHEAD & DONA VICENTA

VOLUME 4:
AGHORA & THE LAST METABARON

•

METABARONS GENESIS: CASTAKA
with Das Pastoras

WEAPONS OF THE METABARON
with Travis Charest, Zoran Janjetov

THE METABARONS, SECOND CYCLE
(previously THE METABARON series)
with Jerry Frissen, Valentin Sécher,
Niko Henrichon

(individual editions)
VOLUME 1:
THE TECHNO-ADMIRAL & THE ANTI-BARON
with Jerry Frissen, Valentin Sécher

VOLUME 2:
THE TECHNO-CARDINAL & THE TRANSHUMAN
with Jerry Frissen, Niko Henrichon

VOLUME 3:
THE META-GUARDIANESS AND THE TECHNO-BARON
with Jerry Frissen, Valentin Sécher

•

DECONSTRUCTING THE METABARONS
with Juan Gimenez, Christophe Quillien

THE EXPANDED JODOVERSE:

MEGALEX
with Fred Beltran

THE TECHNOPRIESTS
with Zoran Janjetov, Fred Beltran

•

HUMANOIDS PRESENTS: THE JODOVERSE
(excerpts from multiple series)

Foreword by Brian Michael Bendis

Listen to me right now!

If you are a storyteller from any visual medium on the planet Earth and if you are even thinking about nicking something out of this Incal graphic novel collection stop!! Stop it! Stop the madness!!

Even if you think you are creating an homage... stop! It!

Be the first writer or artist on the planet Earth to have read this material and not ripped it off.

There- got that out of my system. Kind of.

I agreed to write this introduction specifically because it gave me an excuse to reread this material that I had not read in years... but material that meant everything to me.

See, like almost everybody who is ever read The Incal I read it first in college. And like everybody who's ever read it... it blew my mind. It blew my mind to the point where I then went and found every piece of graphic novel literature with these authors' names on it that I could possibly find.

And this is Mœbius. This is expensive stuff. I literally bought Mœbius graphic novels in lieu of buying things that would somehow help me get ladies. I didn't buy clothes so I could buy graphic novels by Mœbius. I didn't buy food and some of the graphic novels weren't even in English. And I only speak English. Well, a little Hebrew but that ain't gonna help me here.

Hey, listen; I knew that Mœbius and his peers heavily influenced much of modern science fiction in America and certain movies. I always prided myself on "really" knowing what that meant. I could lean over to my wife and tell her what graphic novel this movie or that show we were watching had a Mœbius influence. (If you are like that too and happen to find a woman that actually finds it cute... marry her.)

But after rereading this material specifically to write this introductior I became infuriated. Shocked. Angered.

There is literally whole sections of this work that have been liftec whole cloth and put into major motion pictures where neither the writer nor the artist has been credited. Not just little bits here anc there. Whole sections! This is stunning to me. We're talking pane after panel, page after page lifted and put in other people's work I had forgotten about some of the sequences here and now I see then with fresh eyes I see the depths in which certain storytellers had sunk. I do not want to name names (really I do, but, I know, no cool).

Listen, I'm sure both of our authors are men of means at this point ir their life. One would have to imagine that they are doing okay fo themselves. I've never met them and I hope one day to, but, one has to imagine it's flattering on some level but I will be angry for the authors that I've never met and say: shame on you, you grifters, you charlatans. Shame!

I get the impulse. Sure I do. But if you want to be inspired by wha you read here today... Do what they did. Invent. Imagine. Build. Be inspired by their inspiration. Don't take it for yourself.

To the authors of this material: thank you. Thank you for literally decades of inspiration and showing all my peers and me what the graphic novel is capable of.

To the publishers: congratulations on a magnificent presentation.

To those of you who are about to read this for the very first time: I'm truly jealous.

Bendis!

March, 2011
Portland, Oregon

THE BLACK INCAL

NIGHT AT THE CRIMSON RING

THIS IS A COMMON SIGHT IN SUICIDE ALLEY. YOU DON'T HAVE TO BE AN UPPER LEVEL CITIZEN TO WATCH BLOOD FLOW.
GO ON! KILL HIM!
TALK!
HELP!
OWWMMF!

THE POOR SAP IS JOHN DIFOOL. A CLASS "R" LICENSED PRIVATE INVESTIGATOR.

NO! NOT THAT!
HIS ATTACKERS ARE MASKED MEN, FACELESS AND MYSTERIOUS.

AH! BRAVO!
QUICK! TO THE RACER!
HOURA!
OUAIIS!
AAAHHHA
1

SUICIDE ALLEY, IT'S A DIRECT NONSTOP FALL STRAIGHT DOWN TO THE GREAT ACID LAKE, WHICH DISSOLVES EVERYTHING IT TOUCHES.
WHOOA! THERE'LL BE MORE!
LOOK! A SUICIDE!
BEEN A LONG TIME...
AARGHHHHH
42
KOSKICH! GET ME MY WEAPON! GOTTA BAG ME A FALLING ONE!
GET OUT YOUR GUNS!
IBIS

HIS FATAL PLUNGE DOWN SUICIDE ALLEY TRIGGERS THE USUAL WAVE OF SUICIDES.

THAT'S NOT HIM! IT'S A SUICIDE!
THAT'S HIM, THERE!
PILOO
7CK

AW, DAMN. I MEAN-- OH, NOOO...!
ARE YOU READY TO TALK?

LESS THAN THIRTY SECONDS BEFORE THE ACID LAKE!
I-I'LL TELL YOU EVERYTHING!

GOT HIM!
04

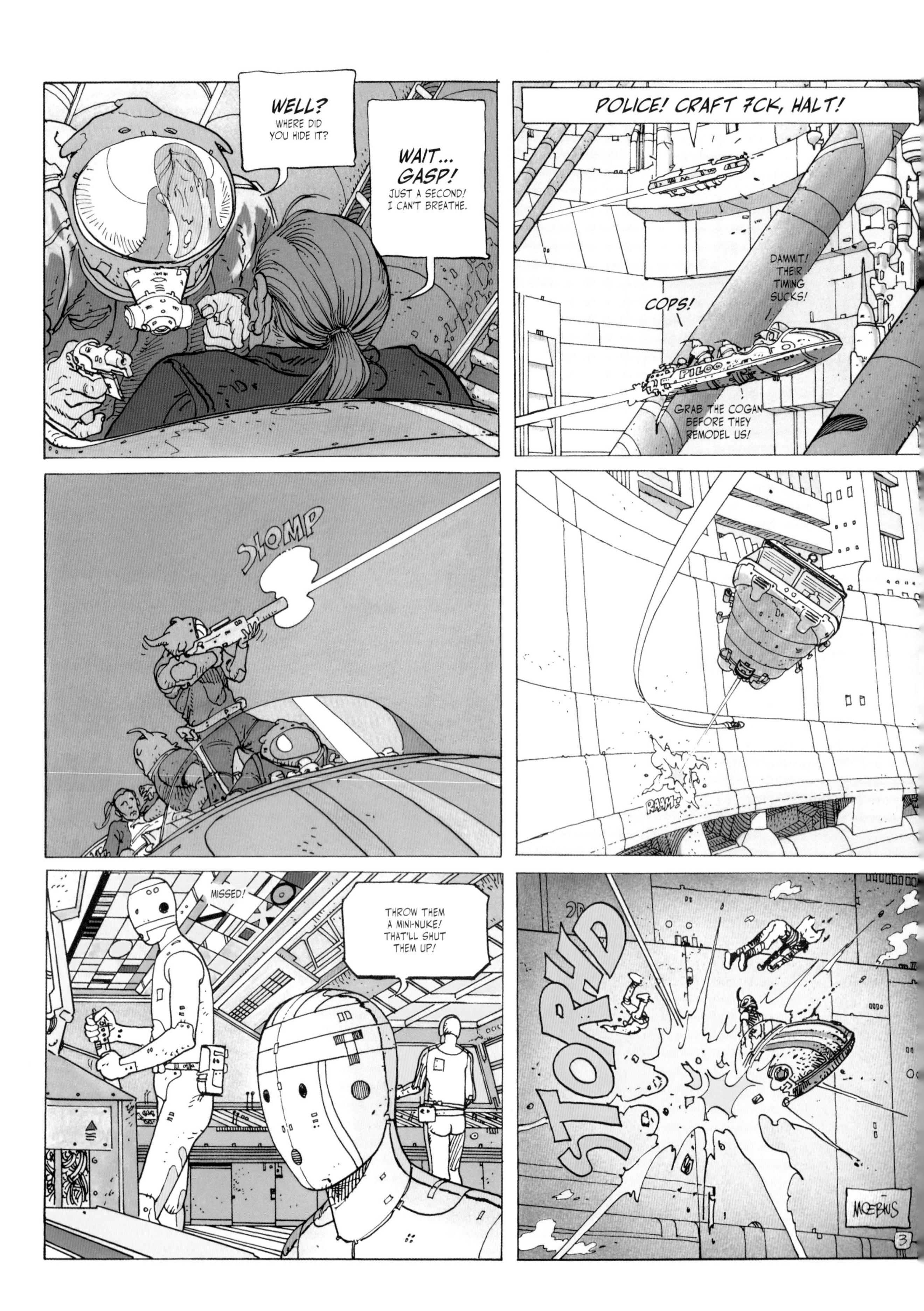
WELL?
WHERE DID YOU HIDE IT?
WAIT... GASP!
JUST A SECOND! I CAN'T BREATHE.
POLICE! CRAFT 7CK, HALT!
COPS!
DAMMIT! THEIR TIMING SUCKS!
GRAB THE COGAN BEFORE THEY REMODEL US!
SLOMP
RAAM!
MISSED!
THROW THEM A MINI-NUKE! THAT'LL SHUT THEM UP!
STORHD
MŒBIUS
3

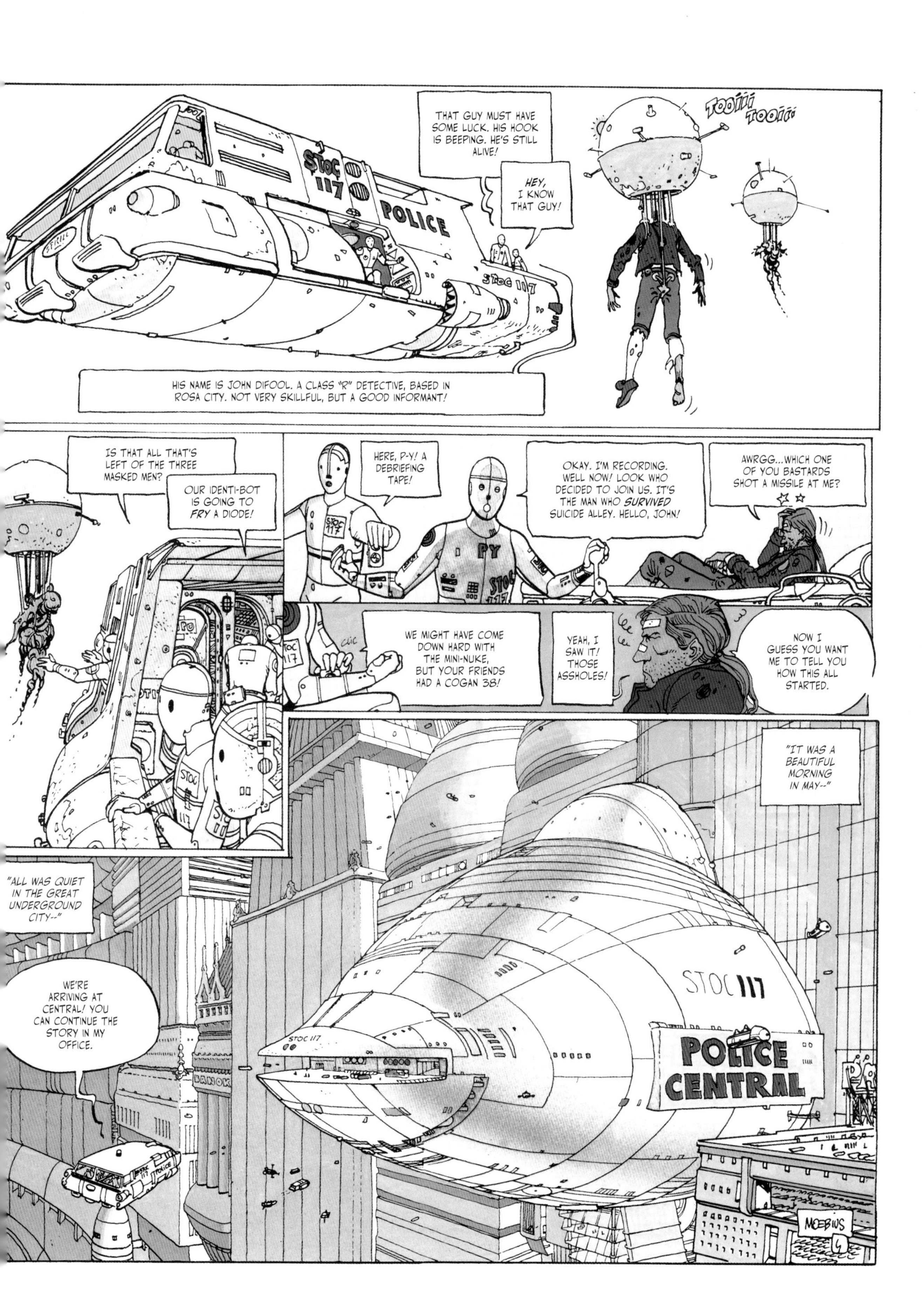
THAT GUY MUST HAVE SOME LUCK. HIS HOOK IS BEEPING. HE'S STILL ALIVE!
HEY, I KNOW THAT GUY!
TOOÏÏÏ TOOÏÏÏ
HIS NAME IS JOHN DIFOOL. A CLASS "R" DETECTIVE, BASED IN ROSA CITY. NOT VERY SKILLFUL, BUT A GOOD INFORMANT!
IS THAT ALL THAT'S LEFT OF THE THREE MASKED MEN?
OUR IDENTI-BOT IS GOING TO FRY A DIODE!
HERE, P-Y! A DEBRIEFING TAPE!
OKAY. I'M RECORDING. WELL NOW! LOOK WHO DECIDED TO JOIN US. IT'S THE MAN WHO SURVIVED SUICIDE ALLEY. HELLO, JOHN!
AWRGG...WHICH ONE OF YOU BASTARDS SHOT A MISSILE AT ME?
CLIC
WE MIGHT HAVE COME DOWN HARD WITH THE MINI-NUKE, BUT YOUR FRIENDS HAD A COGAN 38!
YEAH, I SAW IT! THOSE ASSHOLES!
NOW I GUESS YOU WANT ME TO TELL YOU HOW THIS ALL STARTED.
"IT WAS A BEAUTIFUL MORNING IN MAY--"
"ALL WAS QUIET IN THE GREAT UNDERGROUND CITY--"
WE'RE ARRIVING AT CENTRAL! YOU CAN CONTINUE THE STORY IN MY OFFICE.
STOC 117
POLICE CENTRAL
MOEBIUS

...ON THIS GREAT POLITICAL HOLIDAY, C-DAY MINUS ONE OF PREZIDENTIAL CLONAGE, WE...
"ALL THE COMMOTION AT CENTRAL STOC117 DOESN'T HELP KEEP MY HEAD CLEAR."
IT ALL STARTED LAST NIGHT...
"...SURROUNDED BY EMOTIONLESS CYBO-COPS..."
"I WAS CALMLY WASHING DOWN A STEAK SANDWICH WITH SOME FAKE BOURBON, WHEN SUDDENLY--"
CROTT!
QUIET, DEEPO!
DONG
ARE YOU JOHN DIFOOL? I'LL EXPECT YOU IN AN HOUR... FOR AN URGENT ASSIGNMENT... IT'S UNIT 771636.
...SECTOR 28, BELLEVUE CIRCUIT... OUT!

"THAT'S RIGHT. LESS THAN TEN MINUTES LATER, I WAS TREADING THE CRIMSON CARPET OF HER CONAPT."
ACCORDING TO MY DATA, YOU WERE SPEAKING TO LADY NIMBEA S. QINQ!

"WITH HER HALO, AND HER ACCENT, I COULD TELL SHE WAS AN ARISTO FROM THE UPPERMOST LEVEL. SOMETHING SMELLED FISHY ABOUT HER, BUT THE FRESH SMELL OF MONEY WAS BLOCKING MY NOSE."
HI, I'M JOHN DIFOOL. THE CLASS "R" DETECTIVE YOU--
I KNOW. COME IN AND SIT DOWN.

I AM NIMBEA SUPRA QINQ. I NEED A GUIDE AND BODYGUARD FOR AN OUTING TO THE CRIMSON RING. I BELIEVE YOU'RE FAMILIAR WITH THE AREA.
THE CONTRACT IS ON THE TABLE.
WHAT? THE CRIMSON RING? BUT...
"FIFTY KUBLARS! I WOULD HAVE TAKEN HER TO HELL FOR THAT KIND OF MONEY!"
MIDNIGHT PRECISELY, OR YOU FORFEIT YOUR FEE.
FIFTY KUBLARS! BUT I HAVE TO BRING YOU BACK EXACTLY BY MIDNIGHT?
MOEBIUS
5

SO I TOOK HER TO THE CRIMSON RING... AND EVEN LOWER! SHE WAS INSATIABLE. LET ME TELL YOU, SHE FOUND SOME PLACES EVEN I HADN'T SEEN BEFORE. ANYWAY, EVERYTHING WAS GOING GREAT 'TIL SHE WANTED TO END THE NIGHT IN STYLE AT THE "DAREDEVIL!" THAT'S WHERE SHE MET KILL WOLFHEAD.
YUMM! KILL, YOUR DARK BLACK MUZZLE MAKES ME RED HOT! GIGGLE!
MY WOLF!
MY QUEEN!
"IT'S NOT TOO OFTEN KILL GETS HIS HANDS ON A HIGH-CLASS ARISTO. SO HE WAS MAKING THE MOST OF IT!"
LESS THAN TEN MINUTES...
IT'S ALMOST MIDNIGHT, MILADY! TIME TO GO!
"I HAD NO CHOICE! IF THE CRAZY WOMAN KEPT IT UP, I COULD KISS MY FIFTY KUBLARS GOODBYE."
I HAVE TO THINK OF SOMETHING, BUT WHAT...?
OOUUUUUU
"ESPECIALLY SINCE, WITH KILL'S LEGENDARY STAMINA, THIS COULD HAVE GONE ON ALL NIGHT."
"DESPERATE TIMES CALL FOR DESPERATE MEASURES."
"IT WAS MOMENTS BEFORE MIDNIGHT! THE SHOT HAD TO BE PRECISE!"
I WISH HE WASN'T MOVING SO MUCH!
STONN!
YOU LITTLE BASTARD! YOU SHOT A HOLE IN MY EAR!
LET ME EXPLAIN, KILL! THE LADY AND I HAVE A CONTRACT. LOOK--
THAT ROTTEN BASTARD! I WAS FINALLY ABOUT TO HAVE AN ORGASM! TEAR HIM APART, KILLY!
MŒBIUS 6

YES, MY WOLF! SLAUGHTER HIM! I WANT HIS HIDE! I WANT-- HACK! COUGH, COUGH!
GRRRR!
LOOK AT THAT!
LOOK AT WHAT?
YIPES!
OUCH

"IT TURNED OUT NIMBEA QINQ WAS AN OLD WOMAN, WHOSE HOLO-MASK WORE OFF AT MIDNIGHT!"
YOU'RE ALL A BUNCH OF BASTARDS!
"KILL WOLFHEAD'S ARDENT PASSION HAD MADE THE SORDID CINDERELLA FORGET ALL ABOUT THE TIME!"

I DON'T SEE THE CONNECTION BETWEEN YOUR STORY AND SUICIDE ALLEY?
WELL, WOLFHEAD WENT CRAZY. HE GOT IT INTO HIS HEAD THAT I WAS THE ONE RESPONSIBLE FOR NIMBEA'S TRANSFORMATION. HE STARTED CHASING ME THROUGH THE CROWD AT THE "DAREDEVIL."
ONE MORE THING. HE WAS YELLING, "I'M GOING TO RIP OFF YOUR EARS AND MAKE YOU EAT THEM!

"I FINALLY MANAGED TO ESCAPE HIM BY ENTERING A VENTILATION SHAFT. KILL WAS TOO BIG TO FOLLOW ME."

"AN HOUR LATER, I WAS HOPELESSLY LOST."

"WHEN SUDDENLY THE SOUND OF RUNNING FOOTSTEPS ECHOED THROUGH THE FILTHY TUNNEL."
COULD IT BE KILL...?
MOEBIUS
7

WHAT IS THAT THING??

"I'D NEVER EVEN HEARD OF SUCH A CREATURE. HE WAS CHARGING AT ME AS HARD AS A PALEO-BULLDOZER, AND LOOKED JUST AS FRIENDLY!"

"BUT BY EXTRAORDINARY LUCK, THE HUGE BEAST HAD ONLY COME THAT FAR TO FALL DOWN AND DIE."
"I ONLY HAD TIME TO SEE A STRANGE BLADE EMBEDDED IN THE CREATURE'S BACK."
"BEFORE THE VIOLENT IMPACT KNOCKED ME UNCON-SCIOUS."

WHEN I CAME TO, I WAS AT SUICIDE ALLEY, AND THOSE THREE HOTHEADS WERE BEATING ME UP. YOU KNOW THE REST.
AND OF COURSE, YOU DON'T HAVE THE SLIGHTEST IDEA WHO THEY WERE, OR WHAT THEY WANTED FROM YOU.
OF COURSE NOT! THEY HAD MASKS, AND...

DON'T WEAR YOURSELF OUT. WE'VE IDENTIFIED THEM. PETTY KILLERS, AND MEMBERS OF "AMOK." IMPOSSIBLE TO FIND OUT WHO THEIR COMMANDER IS. OKAY, YOU'RE FREE TO GO, DIFOOL. BUT SOMETHING ABOUT THIS CASE STINKS, AND YOU SHOULDN'T HIDE THE TRUTH FROM US! THE ONLY PLACE IT'LL GET YOU IS--
BUT I TOLD YOU THE TRUTH! I'VE GOT NOTHING TO HIDE! IT ALL CHECKS OUT: THE OLD LADY, WOLFHEAD, THE CREATURE'S BODY, ET CETERA.
THAT "ET CETERA" IS PRECISELY WHAT STINKS, DIFOOL!

"IT SURE DOES. P-Y IS RIGHT! OH WELL, RIGHT NOW THE MOST IMPORTANT THING IS TO BUILD MYSELF A WOMAN AND FIND SOMETHING TO SMOKE, SO I CAN RELAX AND WET MY WHISTLE IN THE COMPANY OF SOMETHING SOFT, PINK, AND TENDER!"
LATER, AT A HOMEO-BROTHEL IN THE FRENCH QUARTER.
AHH, NOW HERE'S WHAT I NEED!
8
MOEBIUS

DANCE OF THE INCAL

"PARIS LEVEL SEXUAL CREDIT UNION." JUST THE TYPE OF UPPER-CLASS ESTABLISHMENT I WAS LOOKING FOR.
COME IN, SIR. THE CREDIT UNION IS AT YOUR SERVICE.
CREDIT CART
CRRM
I'M GOING TO GO AHEAD AND TREAT MYSELF TO A DELUXE MODEL! AFTER WHAT I'VE BEEN THROUGH, I *DESERVE* IT!
LATER...
AHH...A BOTTLE OF WHISKY, A BOX OF SPV*, A CIGAR AND A HOT BATH... WHAT MORE COULD I WISH FOR?
* LIGHT HALLUCINOGEN FOR MAINSTREAM CONSUMPTION.
COOTCHIE COOTCHIE!
ALL RIGHT! NOW THAT'S WHAT WAS MISSING!
BUT TODAY, THE HOMEO-WHORE'S CARESSES CAN'T COMPLETELY CHASE AWAY THE THOUGHTS RUSHING THROUGH JOHN'S HEAD.
DAMN IT!
OR THE IMAGES THAT KEEP RETURNING... EVERYTHING HE HID FROM THE ROBOT POLICEMAN.
WHAT IS THIS CREATURE?
IT'S PINNED LIKE A BUTTERFLY.
DAMN! WHAT A STORY!
VDAM
10

OUTSTA!
"DAMN! I NEVER KNEW THE CITY'S VENTILATION SHAFTS WERE SO POPULAR!"
LET'S SEE... I'LL BET THESE ARE THE FUN-LOVING GUYS WHO PLANTED THE DAGGER IN ITS BACK!

OUTSTAAAAAA
"EACH ONE OF THOSE CHARMING CREATURES MUST HAVE WEIGHED EIGHT HUNDRED POUNDS."

TTOMPPP!!
CAN'T I GET SOME PEACE AROUND HERE?

"LUCKILY, I HAD SOMETHING TO CALM THEM DOWN. I SET MY INHIBITOR TO 'EMOTION-SEEKING PARALYSIS SWEEP!' I DIDN'T EVEN HAVE TO AIM."

VE NEVER EEN SUCH ORRIBLE REATURES BEFORE! ERHAPS A EW RACE MUTANT?
"THEY'D SLEEP FOR ABOUT AN HOUR, THEN WAKE UP WITH A MASSIVE HANGOVER."
OR MAYBE A STILL UNCLASSIFIED EXTRATERRESTRIAL LIFEFORM? WHAT A CRAZY WORLD!
EEEK! EEEK!

"THE SURPRISE CAME WHEN MY PINNED BUTTERFLY WAS STILL ALIVE. HE EVEN SPOKE CITIZEN, LIKE YOU AND ME."
WITH A SLIGHT LOWER-LEVEL TWANG.
11

JOHN DIFOOL... WAIT! LISTEN! I HAVE SOMETHING FOR YOU!
?
YEAH, OKAY, SURE. BUT HOW DO YOU KNOW MY NAME?
GUARD IT VERY CLOSELY! THE FATE OF NOT ONLY THE PLANET, BUT THE FATE OF THE WHOLE UNIVERSE DEPENDS ON THAT OBJECT!
THE UNIVERSE?
"TO TOP I ALL OFF, T MUTANT WA MELTING. B I WAS FE UP, SO I PRETENDE NOT TO S ANYTHING.
TAKE THIS, JOHN...DIFOOL! IT'S IMPORTANT!
SO THIS CREATURE.... KNOWS MY NAME! ISN'T THAT NICE!
HURRY!
"IT WAS A SMALL BOX, UNREMARKABLE EXCEPT FOR A CURIOUS SENSATION."
SO WHAT'S IN THIS DAMN BOX?
THE INCAL? I WONDER WHAT THAT IS?
AAARGH! THE INC- THE INCAL!
THERE! IT'S OPEN.
?
12

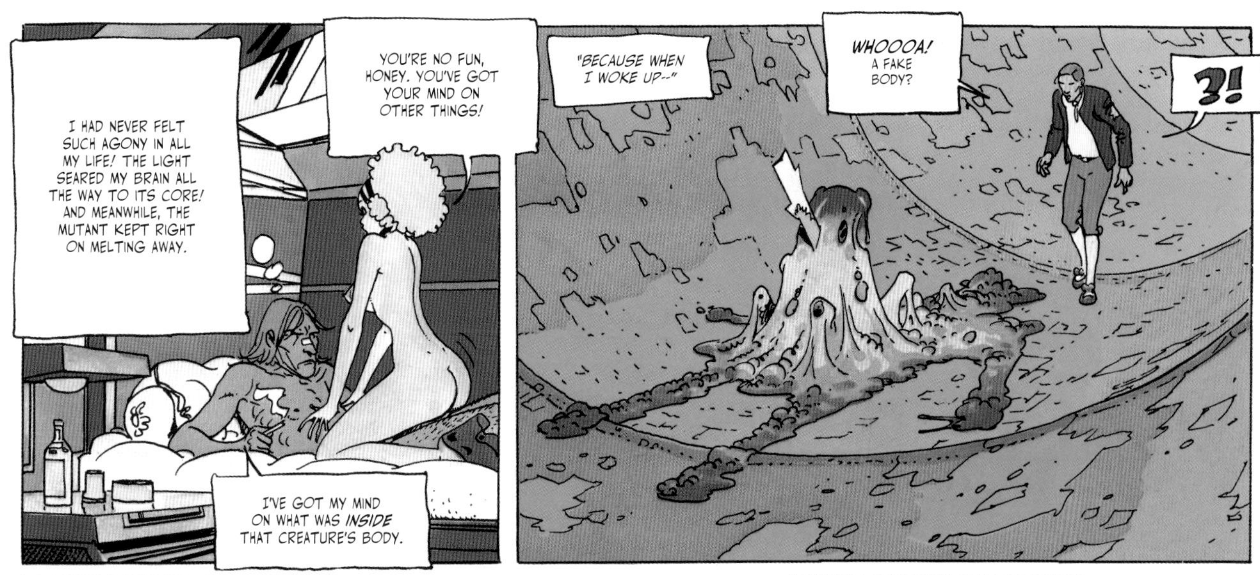
I HAD NEVER FELT SUCH AGONY IN ALL MY LIFE! THE LIGHT SEARED MY BRAIN ALL THE WAY TO ITS CORE! AND MEANWHILE, THE MUTANT KEPT RIGHT ON MELTING AWAY.
YOU'RE NO FUN, HONEY. YOU'VE GOT YOUR MIND ON OTHER THINGS!
I'VE GOT MY MIND ON WHAT WAS *INSIDE* THAT CREATURE'S BODY.
"BECAUSE WHEN I WOKE UP--"
WHOOOA! A FAKE BODY?
?!

"AND, INSIDE THE FAKE, MELTED BODY--"
A BERG!

"THIS WAS TOO MUCH! I WAS INVOLVED IN A MESS OF GALACTIC PROPORTIONS!"
"FINALLY, AFTER TWO LONG HOURS OF WAN-DERING--"
YESSS! AN EXIT!

"FOR YEARS THE AIRWAVES HAD BEEN POUNDING US WITH NEWS OF A SO-CALLED BERG EMPIRE, WHICH WAS APPARENTLY SWARMING OUT OF THE SWAN CONSTELLATION INTENDING TO WIPE US OFF THE FACE OF THE GALAXY! BUT WHAT I'D SEEN NOW WAS A LOT MORE CONVINCING THAN SOME BLURRY SATELLITE SNAPSHOTS!"
SO THOSE DAMN BERGS REALLY DO EXIST! IT'S NOT JUST PROPAGANDA!
13

YEAH, THAT WAS GREAT, SUGAR. REALLY!
COOTCHIE, COOTCHIE.
"THEN NOTHING ELSE HAPPENED, 'TIL I GOT BACK TO MY CONAPT!"
HI DEEPO! IT SURE IS NICE TO BE SAFE AND SOUND AT HOME!
CROOTT!
ROCK CONCERT
"SAFE AND SOUND. THAT WAS TRUE FOR ABOUT FIFTEEN SECONDS."
SDOOM SDOOM
OPEN UP!
WHAT SHOULD I DO WITH THIS THING? I WONDER IF I CAN SELL IT?
DAMN! WHAT NOW?!
I HAVE ABOUT TWO SECONDS TO HIDE IT WHERE THEY'LL NEVER FIND IT.
CROODU!
SDOOM SDOM
ROCHT!
"I COULD SEE THEY WERE EQUIPPED WITH EMOTION-SEEKING PARALYSIS-SWEEP BLOCKERS! MY INHIBITOR MIGHT AS WELL HAVE BEEN JUNK! AND I KNEW JUST WHAT THEY WERE LOOKING FOR!"
AMOK KILLERS!
THAT'S HIM! WHATEVER YOU DO, DON'T SHOOT! WE NEED HIM ALIVE AND CONSCIOUS!
14

WHERE DID YOU HIDE IT? TALK!!
ET'S TOSS
S CONAPT!
IT'S IN... OH... I DON'T KNOW.
THE STRANGE THING IS THAT I TRIED TO TELL THEM SEVERAL TIMES, BUT EVERY TIME, THE WORDS GOT STUCK.
ANYWAY, THE ONLY THING THOSE BASTARDS GOT FOR THEIR TROUBLE WAS DEATH, AT THE BOTTOM OF SUICIDE ALLEY!
HEE HEE! I GUESS I FOUND A PRETTY GOOD HIDING SPOT AFTER ALL!
DIFOOL, AFTER TAKING FIVE KUBLARS FROM HIS ACCOUNT TO PAY THE HOMEO-WHORE, NOW USES PUBLIC TRANSPORT TO GET BACK TO HIS LEVEL. HOT AND SMELLY, BUT CHEAP.
IT'S A SHAME I HAVE TO GO BACK TO THE CONAPT, NOW.
INDEED, LADIES AND GENTLEMEN, THE NINTH PREZIDENTIAL CLONAGE IS SURE TO BE A GALA EVENT...
OH NO! FEELS LIKE I'M BEING FOLLOWED. THE COPS? OR THE KILLERS?
SOMEONE ELSE?
WELL NOW, IF EVERYONE WANTS THIS THING THEY CALL...
...THE INCAL...
...THERE'S GOT TO BE A PILE OF KUBLARS IN IT!
Q.E.D.... THIS COULD BE THE CASE OF MY LIFE!
DAMMIT! WHY DO MY SMOKES TASTE FUNNY TODAY?
PTEW!
NOW WHAT? WHAT ARE ALL THESE IDIOTS DOING BLOCKING THE DOOR TO MY CONAPT!?
STOP PUSHING!
I'M SICK, PAL!
WE CAN'T SEE BACK HERE!
15

HEY, STEP ASIDE! LET ME THROUGH! THIS IS MY PLACE!
THIS IS NUTS! WHAT'S GOING ON?
THEY SAY THERE'S A BIRD WHO'S BEEN PREACHING SINCE MORNING, PERCHED ON TOP OF A WARDROBE. HE'S BEEN DOING CURES, EACH ONE MORE MIRACULOUS THAN THE LAST, IF YOU GET MY DRIFT!
ALL THE SICK PEOPLE ON THIS LEVEL HAVE BEEN SHOWING UP NON-STOP!
THE SACRED BIRD!
A MIRACLE!
WE CAN'T SEE!
IT'S MY TURN!
LOOK! I'M CURED!
IT CAN'T BE REAL!
I BELIEVE IN IT!
AFTER A HALF-HOUR OF PUSHING...
STEP ASIDE! GET OUT OF MY HOUSE, DAMN IT!
I WANT TO BE HEALED TOO! LET ME CLOSER, YOU BASTARDS!
SHOVE OFF!
HE'S BEAUTIFUL! LIKE AN EAGLE!
NO! LIKE AN ANGEL OF HEAVEN!
REPENT!
CODES
I'M DREAMING! THIS CAN'T BE!
AMEN! YOU MUST FULLY REPENT, AND PURIFY YOURSELVES, SO THAT YOU MAY BE GRANTED TRUE--
GLORY TO THE BIRD, OUR PROPHET!
HEAL ME!
HE GLOWS LIKE AN ARISTO!
DEEPO!?
--TRUE FORGIVENESS! MY FRIENDS, I TELL YOU THE ARCHANGEL IS COMING SOON, TO DESTROY THIS WICKED CITY!
O BIRD!
HOLY BIRD! I SUFFER SO MUCH!
AND I HAVEN'T HAD A BOWEL MOVEMENT IN THREE MONTHS!
FOR THIS DEN OF SIN WILL SOON BE REDUCED TO ASHES, AND THE ARCHANGEL WILL--
PSSST, DEEPO! IT'S ME, JOHN!
I'M CURED! IT'S A MIRACLE!
HEY! WHAT'S THAT GUY DOING ON THE WARDROBE?
GET BACK, DIFOOL! LEAVE ME ALONE! MY REVELATIONS ARE NOT YET COMPLETE!
DEEPO!
WILL YOU CUT THE CRAP! WE HAVE TO GET OUT OF HERE!
STOP HIM!
16

NOT YET! THE PEOPLE MUST LEARN THE FATE OF THEIR CITY!
YOU LEAVE ME NO CHOICE, DEEPO.
ACRILEGE!
STOP HIM! HE'S CRAZY!
SPIT IT OUT, YOU DUMB ANIMAL.
FIRE AND BR-- ACK!
HEY, WAIT!
LET HIM GO, JERK!
ROOH!
AH! AT LAST!
?
?
?
CROOOK
CROOT CRRT!
YOU'RE IN FOR IT NOW, PAL!
KILL HIM!
RIP HIS GUTS OUT!
KILL HIM!
SICK BASTARDS! LET ME GO!
THE BIRD HAS BEEN PROFANED!
I'M BLIND, AND I CANNOT SEE!
SUDDENLY --
STAC STAAK STAAK
ARGH!
?
?
WELL?*
AKARAR! THERE IT IS! I SAW THE GLOW BETWEEN HIS FINGERS!
EEEK! HE'S DEAD! THEY'RE ALL DEAD!
WHO ARE THESE MON- STERS?
IT'S... IT'S THE
OH, CRAP! A BERG ASSAULT SQUAD JUST BLASTED THROUGH THE WALL WITH LASERS!
BERGS!
IMPOSSIBLE!
THEY'VE COME FOR THE INCAL!
WHAT DO WE DO NOW, CHIEF? WE CAN'T GET TO HIM THROUGH THIS CROWD!
NEVER MIND THAT! FOLLOW MY LEAD!
17
INSTANTANEOUS TRANSLATION

YAAAAAKK YAKK!
ATTACK!
CROOT CROT
ROTT
CROOT!
AARGH
I MUST BE DREAMING!
HELP ME!
MOMMY!
NOOO...

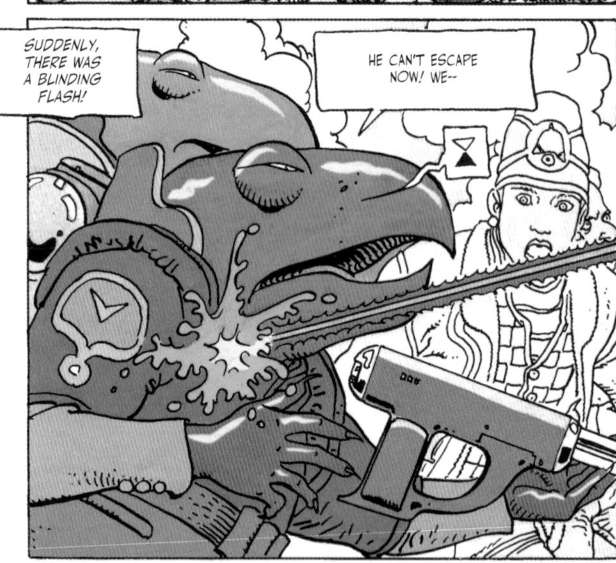
SUDDENLY, THERE WAS A BLINDING FLASH!
HE CAN'T ESCAPE NOW! WE--

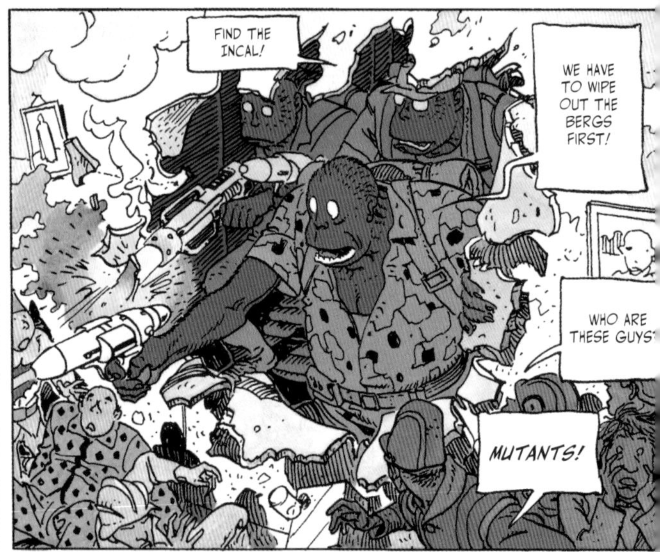
FIND THE INCAL!
WE HAVE TO WIPE OUT THE BERGS FIRST!
WHO ARE THESE GUYS?
MUTANTS!

THE BATHROOM! IT'S MY ONLY HOPE.

SOON THE COPS JOIN THE PARTY--
THEY'RE WREAKING HAVOC! SEND THREE ANTI-EMOTION SQUADS TO THE "HILL 210" SECTOR!
SAVE US!
BOOM
HERE COME THE COPS!
DEAR TELEFRIENDS! WATCH WITH US, AS ALL HELL BREAKS LOOSE!
--ALONG WITH THE LOCAL TV REPORTERS.
18

FOLLOWED BY ANOTHER PARTY-CRASHER: THE MOST DANGEROUS YET, FROM THE DEPTHS OF THE CITY.
CCRASH
KBANG
STOMP!
THIS IS INSANE!
MOVE ALONG!
LOOK AT THAT! IT'S A COMBAT ROBOT!
DEAR TELEFRIENDS! WE'RE WITNESSING A FIERCELY PITCHED BATTLE. THE "HILL 210" SECTOR HAS BECOME A SLAUGHTERHOUSE. RUMORS ABOUND THAT A BERG ASSAULT SQUAD...I REPEAT, A BERG ASSAULT SQUAD HAS--
OH! SOMETHING'S HAPPENING! A COMBAT ROBOT JUST SURGED UP FROM PARTS UNKNOWN.
MEANWHILE...
REUH KOF KOFF
ALL RIGHT! I'M IN THE CLEAR!
FREEZE!
OH NO!

THE PREZIDENT'S HUNCHBACKS! WHAT...WHAT DO YOU WANT FROM ME?
NO QUESTIONS! GET IN THE SLIDERCRAFT!
HURRY! SOMEBODY'S COMING!

DON'T TELL ME THE PREZIDENT'S INVOLVED IN THIS TOO. FORGET IT, I GIVE UP! IF HE WANTS THE INCAL, HE CAN HAVE IT!
19

HIS SUPREME HIGHNESS

DEAR TELEFRIENDS, WE ARE NOW LIVE INSIDE THE FLOATING PALACE, ABOUT TO WITNESS THE PREZIDENTIAL CLONAGE... THE NINTH, OF COURSE. WITH THE FABULOUS TECHNO-TECHNO EQUIPMENT STANDING BY, BOTH THE SOURCE BODY AND THE DESTINATION BODY HAVE BEEN MOVED INTO PLACE.

"AND WHAT A MAGNIFICENT BODY IT IS! SEVEN FEET TALL, TWO HUNDRED POUNDS OF FIRMLY TONED MUSCLE."
...25...24...
23...22...

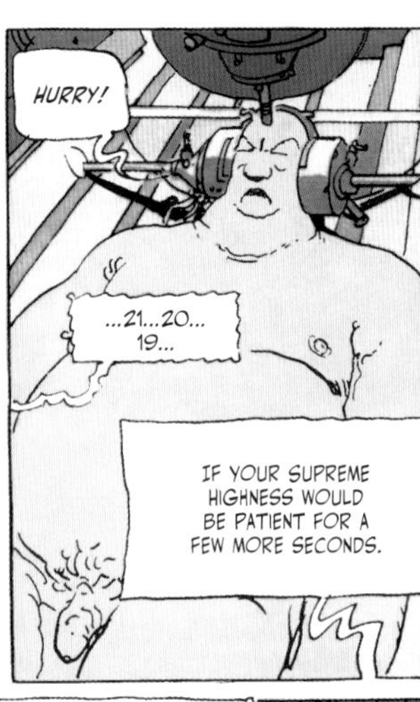

HURRY!
...21...20...
19...
IF YOUR SUPREME HIGHNESS WOULD BE PATIENT FOR A FEW MORE SECONDS.

KABOS, ANY NEWS OF JOHN DIFOOL AND THE INCAL?
...18...
17...
16...

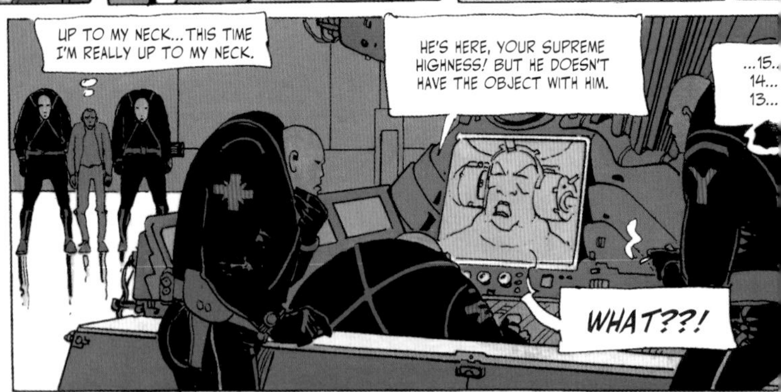

UP TO MY NECK... THIS TIME I'M REALLY UP TO MY NECK.
HE'S HERE, YOUR SUPREME HIGHNESS! BUT HE DOESN'T HAVE THE OBJECT WITH HIM.
...15..
14...
13...
WHAT??!

SEARCH THE SECTOR FROM TOP TO BOTTOM. AND MAKE HIM TALK.
...9
...8...
UNDERSTOOD. I'LL SEE TO IT PERSONALLY, YOUR SUPREME HIGHNESS.

...7...6...
5...4...
THREE MORE SECONDS!
"AS TECHNO-TECHNO SPECIALISTS, UPPER-LEVEL ARISTO GUESTS, AND MILLIONS OF CITIZENS GLUED TO THEIR 3D-TVs ALL WATCH BREATHLESSLY, THE MIRACLE OF THE TRANSFER IS ABOUT TO TAKE PLACE IN THE CLONING CHAMBER."
20

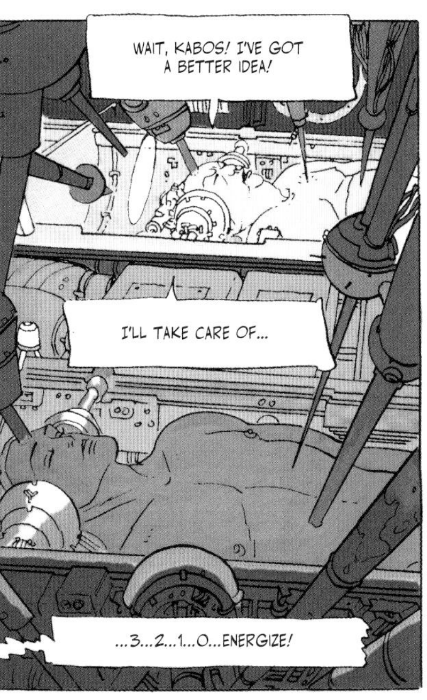
WAIT, KABOS! I'VE GOT A BETTER IDEA!
I'LL TAKE CARE OF...
...3...2...1...0...ENERGIZE!

COMMENCING IMMEDIATE MUMMIFICATION PROCESS.
...THE YOUNG JOHN DIFOOL MYSELF!
TAKE HIM TO THE ORGY CHAMBER, AND WAIT FOR ME THERE.
HOORAY! THE PREZIDENTIAL CLONAGE WENT WITHOUT A HITCH!
NOW, DEAR TELEFRIENDS, WE LEAVE THIS EXTRA-ORDINARY POLITICAL EVENT TO RETURN TO YOUR REGULARLY SCHEDULED GAME SHOW, PISS AND FECES!
YEAH!

INCREDIBLE! HIS SUPREME HIGHNESS DISPLAYED TREMENDOUS COURAGE IN THE FACE OF DISCOMFORT.
LONG LIVE HIS SUPREME HIGHNESS!
WHAT A MIRACLE OF TECHNO-TECHNO SCIENCE!
HIS SUPREME HIGHNESS HAS SUCH A BEAUTIFUL BODY NOW!
UP WITH TECHNO-TECHNO SCIENCE!
21

SLOW DOWN, YOUR SUPREME HIGHNESS! HUFF, PUFF!
I'M ANXIOUS TO BEHOLD THIS JOHN DIFOOL! IS HE HANDSOME, AT LEAST?
UHH...WE COULDN'T REALLY SAY, YOUR SUPREME HIGHNESS!
I WONDER WHY I DIDN'T JUST HAND THE DAMN INCAL THING OVER TO THEM, SINCE IT'S BROUGHT ME NOTHING BUT...NOTHING BUT...
AND DON'T FORGET TO CALL THE PREZ "YOUR SUPREME HIGHNESS." GOT IT?
WHATEVER YOU SAY.
HERE HE COMES!
WELL, WELL WELL! JOHN DIFOOL, AM I RIGHT?
NOTHING BUT TROU-BLE!
YEAH, THAT'S RIGHT... JOHN DIFOOL!
"YOUR SUPREME HIGHNESS," IDIOT!
AÏÏE!
CROO
TAKE IT EASY, BOYS. JOHN DIFOOL IS MY SPECIAL GUEST TODAY. YOU MUST TREAT HIM GENTLY, WITH MERCY AND INDULGENCE.
LATER, AS THEY RECLINE IN COMFORT ON CUSHIONS OF LIGHT.
COUGH, COUGH! THIS CIGARETTE'S BURNING MY LUNGS! UHH...THE OBJECT YOU SAY I HAVE IN MY POSSESSION? I DON'T KNOW WHAT YOU'RE REFERRING TO, YOUR SUPREME HIGHNESS?
LOOK AT THAT LIGHT.
GOOD HEAVENS
JOHN DIFOOL, MY PATIENCE HAS ITS--
--ITS LIMITS?
CROOO
CROO
LOOK, YOUR SUPREME HIGHNESS! HE'S GLOWING!
THAT'S ILLEGA HE'S NOT AN ARISTO!
SCANDALOUS!
22

IT'S TRUE! I'M GLOWING LIKE A NEON SIGN.
NOT ONLY THAT, BUT I FEEL A STRANGE FORCE PULLING ME INTO THE AIR.
UNBELIEVABLE!
AMAZING!
BUT...I'M FLYING!
HE'S FLYING!
?
CROT
YEARGGH! I'M BURNING.
IT'S ALL BURNING! THE WHOLE FLOATING PALACE IS ON FIRE!
IN THE NAME OF THE EMPIRE, SHUT HIM UP!
AND YOU! OUR MIGHTY LEADER, I SEE YOU WALLOWING IN MUD! I-- ARGH!
22BIS

THIS...THIS ALCOHOL! I FEEL...I FEEL SICK! OOOH!
SUMMON MY HUNCHBACKS!
OHH?!
DDDGLLARG
HIS SUPREME HIGHNESS
THIS IS SCANDAL-OUS!
THE INCAL!

BRING PERFUME!
AND TOWELS!
THE INCAL! IT'S THE INCAL! HE SWALLOWED IT!
GRAB HIM! QUICK!
HUH?!
DON'T LET HIM ESCAPE!
BLOCK THE EXITS!

SEARCH THE CORRIDORS!
NOW WHAT?
THAT WAY! I SAW HIM!
THERE HE IS!
HE WENT THROUGH THERE!

JUST WHAT THE TECHNO-DOCTOR ORDERED!
23

THERE HE IS!
WE'VE GOT HIM NOW!
HE'S SURROUNDED!
IT'S HIM!
HE'S TRAPPED! HIS SUPREME HIGHNESS'S SHIP IS CALIBRATED TO HIS PERSONAL BRAIN SIGNATURE!
HOW DO YOU START THIS THING?
I'LL JUST HIT SOMETHING AT RANDOM! I SENSE... SOMEHOW...
YES, THIS IS IT!
WITH A LOW WHISTLE, THE CRAFT SUDDENLY LAUNCHES AT THE AIRLOCK.
IT'S WORKING!
ZZIIIIFFFFFFFFFFFFFFFF...
WHAT!? HOW COULD HE--
IT'S IMPOSSIBLE!
GET DOWN!
WATCH OUT!
FIND HIM! KILL HIM IF NECESSARY, BUT DON'T DAMAGE THE INCAL! BE CAREFUL, HIS METABOLISM HAS CHANGED, HIS LIFE FORCE INCREASED TENFOLD BY THE INCAL'S POWER INSIDE HIM! HE'S NOT THE SAME MAN HE WAS BEFORE!
WE'VE SPOTTED THE CRAFT, YOUR SUPREME HIGHNESS.
AN INTERCEPTOR SQUAD! HE'S PULLING OUT ALL THE STOPS! FINE, YOUR SUPREME HIGHNESS, I'M READY TO PLAY IF YOU ARE.
24

THAT FOOL THINKS HE CAN HIDE IN THE CLOUDS!
HE'S FLYING AT GROUND LEVEL, BELOW OUR RADAR!
BUT THE PILOTS HAVE A SURPRISE WAITING.
THERE HE IS!
THE SHIP'S FLYING ON AUTO-PILOT! WHERE DID HE GO?
DAMN IT! THE COCKPIT'S EMPTY!
HIS SUPREME HIGHNESS WILL BE FURIOUS. THE POLICE WILL HAVE TO TAKE OVER THE SEARCH!
GOOD LUCK TO THEM!
THEY'VE GIVEN UP! I'M SAVED!
CROOOT!
HMM...SAVED? MORE LIKE TRAPPED! INSIDE A TRAIN THAT'S PROBABLY TAKING ME STRAIGHT TO MY DOOM! ALTHOUGH... I SOMEHOW FEEL I'M HEADED THE RIGHT DIRECTION.
25

LET'S TAKE A LOOK AT THIS
ODD LITTLE THING! SOMETHING'S
CHANGED...IT'S DIMMER.

IT'S JUST A GLASS PYRAMID!
NOTHING REMARKABLE, EXCEPT
THE GLOW. AND YET...
AND YET, EVER SINCE I HAD IT
INSIDE ME, I FEEL LIKE...LIKE...

LIKE THE ANSWERS TO ALL
MY QUESTIONS ARE INSIDE
THIS LITTLE PIECE OF GLASS!
WHO ARE
YOU, INCAL?

WHOA!

YOU FINALLY
ASKED A
QUESTION.
?
I WAS MADE THUS...
I CAN NEVER SPEAK
UNLESS CALLED UPON.
NOW, WE HAVE VERY
LITTLE TIME!

AND THERE
IS MUCH
FOR US TO
ACCOMPLISH.
NOW, I UNDERSTAND.
IT'S A MINIATURE
PHOTONIC COMPUTER.
AMAZING!

NO, JOHN
DIFOOL, YOU
UNDERSTAND
NOTHING! I
AM NOT A
COMPUTER.
I AM ALIVE,
JUST LIKE YOU!
AND DESTINY
HAS BROUGHT
US TOGETHER
TO RESTORE
JUSTICE TO
THE UNIVERSE.

WHOOOAA! SLOW DOWN, BUDDY!
I'M JUST A CLASS "R" PRIVATE DETECTIVE.
I'VE GOT NOTHING TO DO WITH JUSTICE!
BESIDES, I'VE GOT THE
POLICE, THE PREZIDENT'S
HUNCHBACKS, AND MUTANTS
FROM THE VENTILATION
SHAFT HOT ON MY TRAIL!

BUT YOU DO NOT KNOW WHO YOU TRULY ARE.
IF YOU KNOW SO MUCH, WHY DON'T YOU TELL ME HOW TO ESCAPE THE PREZ AND EVERYONE ELSE! TELL ME WHERE YOU CAME FROM, AND WHERE THIS TRAIN IS GOING! TELL ME. TELL ME!

WE MUST HURRY. ALL YOUR QUESTIONS WILL BE ANSWERED IN DUE TIME.
FOR NOW, WE MUST ASK: "WHO IS THE REAL JOHN DIFOOL?" BUT FIRST, WE MUST KNOW HOW MANY JOHN DIFOOLS THERE ARE?

THAT'S THE DUMBEST QUESTION I'VE EVER HEARD!
THE ANSWER MIGHT SURPRISE YOU. ALLOW ME TO--

HEEYY!!
--SHOW YOU!

ERKK!

MY GOD!

ONE PART OF THE ANSWER IS REVEALED!
YOU SEE MY QUESTIO WAS NO SO DUMB AFTER ALL! THERE'S TWO OF YOU.

AND NOW THERE'S THREE OF YOU.
ONLY NOW CAN WE TRULY ASK--

AND THE LEGS MAKE FOUR.
WHO IS THE REAL JOHN DIFOOL?

ME!
ME!
NO, ME!
IT'S ME!
27

LET'S NOT PANIC! THERE MUST BE A RATIONAL EXPLANATION FOR THIS!
O INCAL! TRYING TO LOVE MY SINFUL SELF HAS MADE ME MISERABLE!
WHO?
YOU WIMPS!
I'M NOT GOING TO LET THIS LITTLE LIGHT BULB DECIDE WHO I AM!
I DON'T UNDERSTAND! I'M HUNGRY, AND COLD, AND TIRED!
HMM...
SOB! SNIFF.
I CAN GIVE LIFE TO ONE OF YOU.
BUT ONLY ONE. WHO?
ME, OF COURSE!
HMPH! WITHOUT ME, THEY'RE NOTHING.
ME!!!
MEE!!!
IT'S ME!
ME!
NO! ME!
ME!
ME!
IT'S MINE!
FFLAMM
28

TIME PASSES, AND JOHN DIFOOL SLOWLY COMES TO HIS SENSES.
OWW. HOW LONG WAS I OUT FOR?

THE INCAL! WAS IT ALL A DREAM? MY HEAD!
MY...MY HEAD! MY LEGS! I'M BACK IN ONE PIECE!
CROOT

DON'T BE SCARED, DEEPO! IT'S ME, JOHN DIFOOL.
CROOOT ROOOTKKK

BUT AM I REALLY JOHN DIFOOL? I HAVE THE STRANGEST SENSATION. AS IF MY HEART WERE...BURNING.
CROOT! THAT'S THE INCAL!

?
BELIEVE ME, I KNOW! I HAD IT INSIDE OF ME TOO, REMEMBER!

DEEPO? YOU CAN TALK!
REALLY? OH YEAH, I CAN TALK! IT JUST CAME TO ME. SO TELL ME, WHERE ARE WE? AND WHERE ARE WE GOING?
I DON'T KNOW. WAIT, I DO!

WE'RE INSIDE A FUNERAL TRAIN, HEADED FOR TECHNOCITY! WHOA! TECHNOCITY! EVEN THE PREZIDENT CAN'T GET IN THERE!
SOUNDS LIKE FUN!

AND ONCE WE GET INSIDE THAT THING, WHAT HAPPENS THEN?
THAT'S WHAT I'M WONDERING, DEEPO. ALL I KNOW IS, WE'RE NOT GOING TO LIKE IT. WAIT. THERE'S A THOUGHT COMING TO MY MIND... "THE BLACK INCAL!"
JODO-MOEBIUS
MOEBIUS

TECHNO SCIENCE

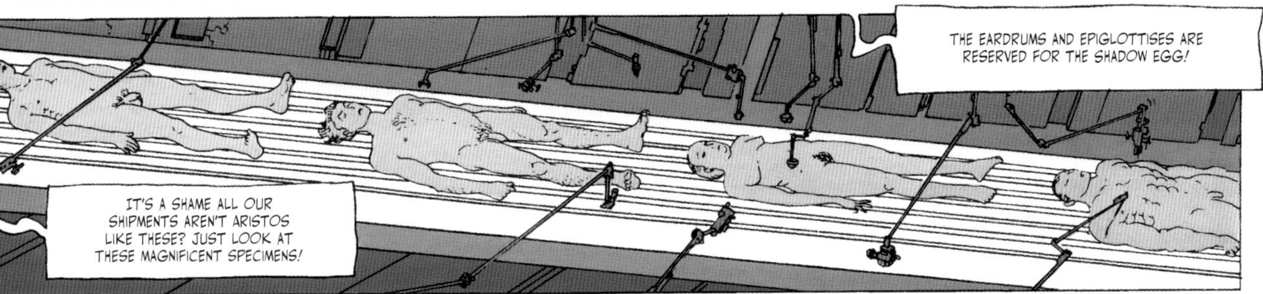

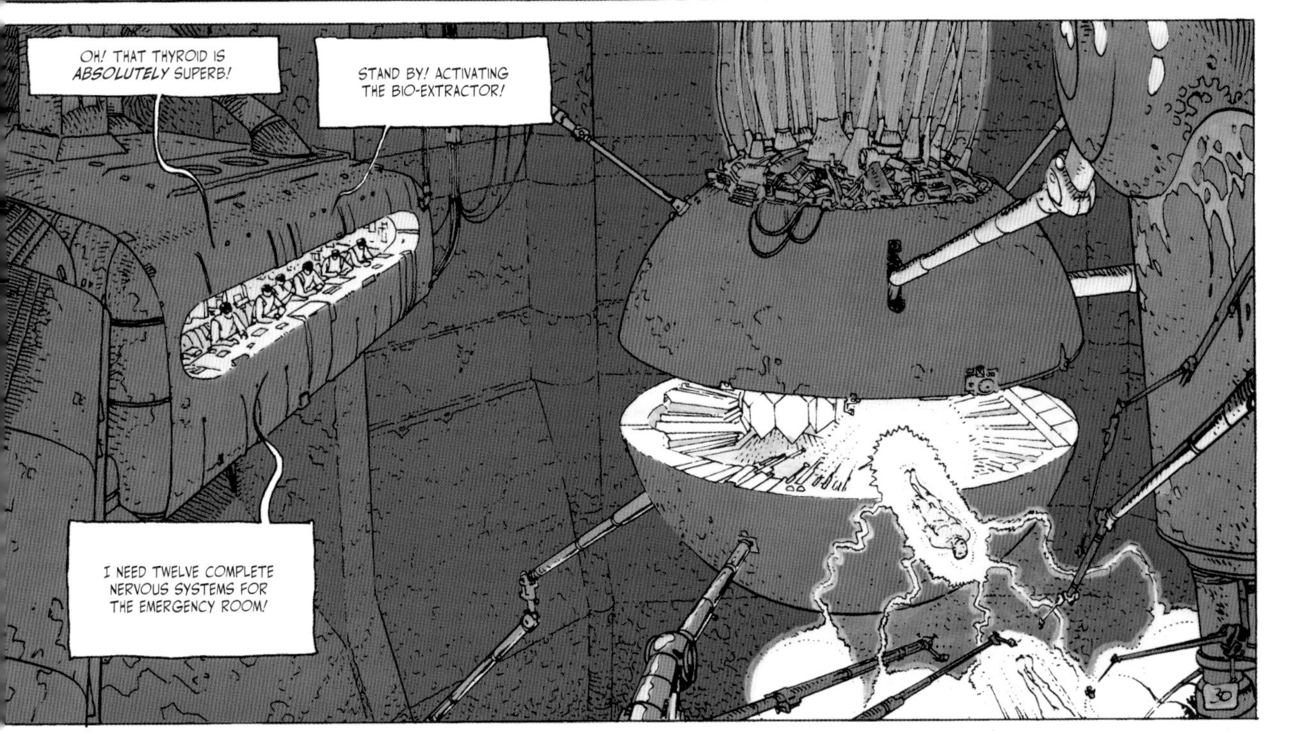

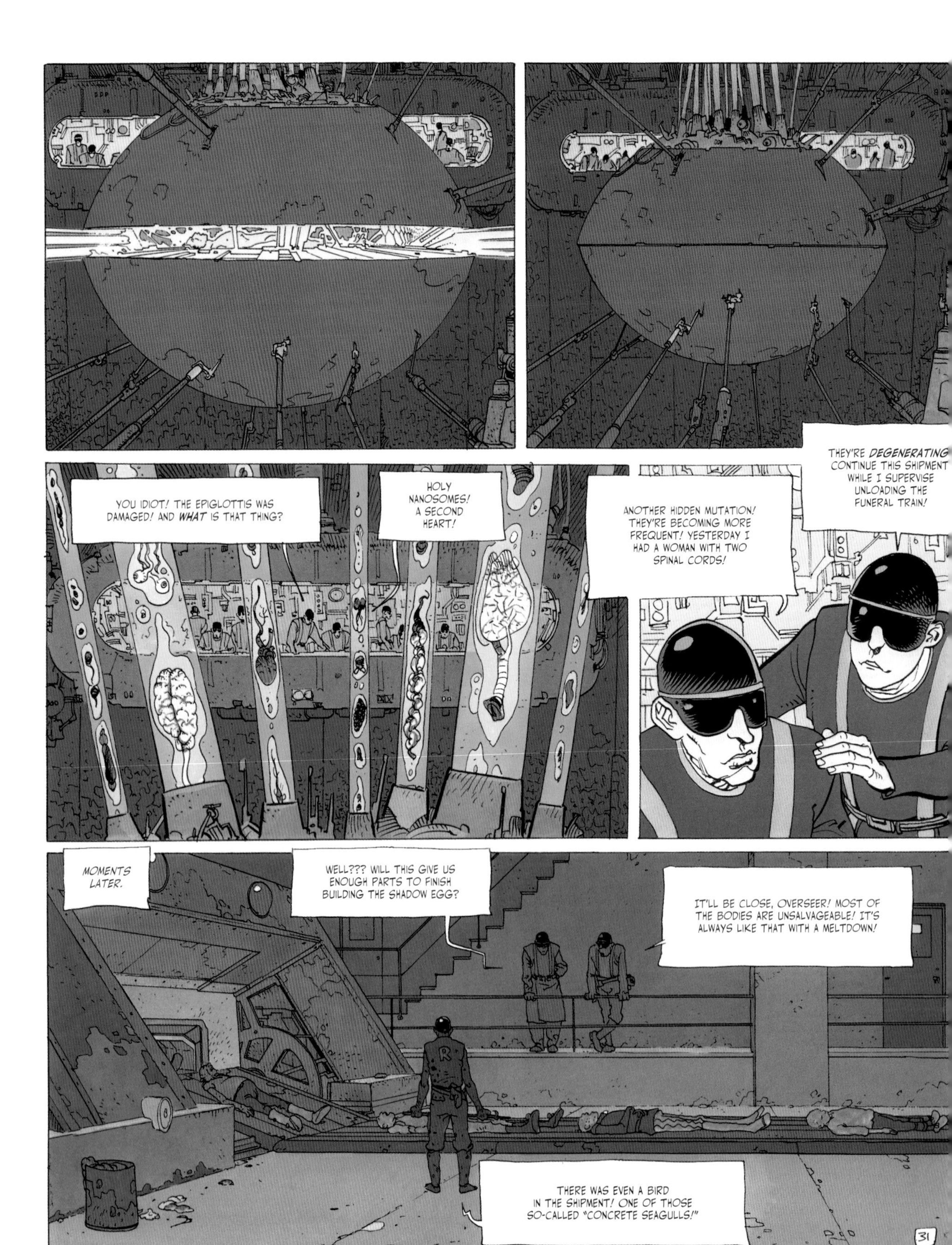
YOU IDIOT! THE EPIGLOTTIS WAS DAMAGED! AND WHAT IS THAT THING?
HOLY NANOSOMES! A SECOND HEART!
ANOTHER HIDDEN MUTATION! THEY'RE BECOMING MORE FREQUENT! YESTERDAY I HAD A WOMAN WITH TWO SPINAL CORDS!
THEY'RE DEGENERATING CONTINUE THIS SHIPMENT WHILE I SUPERVISE UNLOADING THE FUNERAL TRAIN!
MOMENTS LATER.
WELL??? WILL THIS GIVE US ENOUGH PARTS TO FINISH BUILDING THE SHADOW EGG?
IT'LL BE CLOSE, OVERSEER! MOST OF THE BODIES ARE UNSALVAGEABLE! IT'S ALWAYS LIKE THAT WITH A MELTDOWN!
THERE WAS EVEN A BIRD IN THE SHIPMENT! ONE OF THOSE SO-CALLED "CONCRETE SEAGULLS!"
31

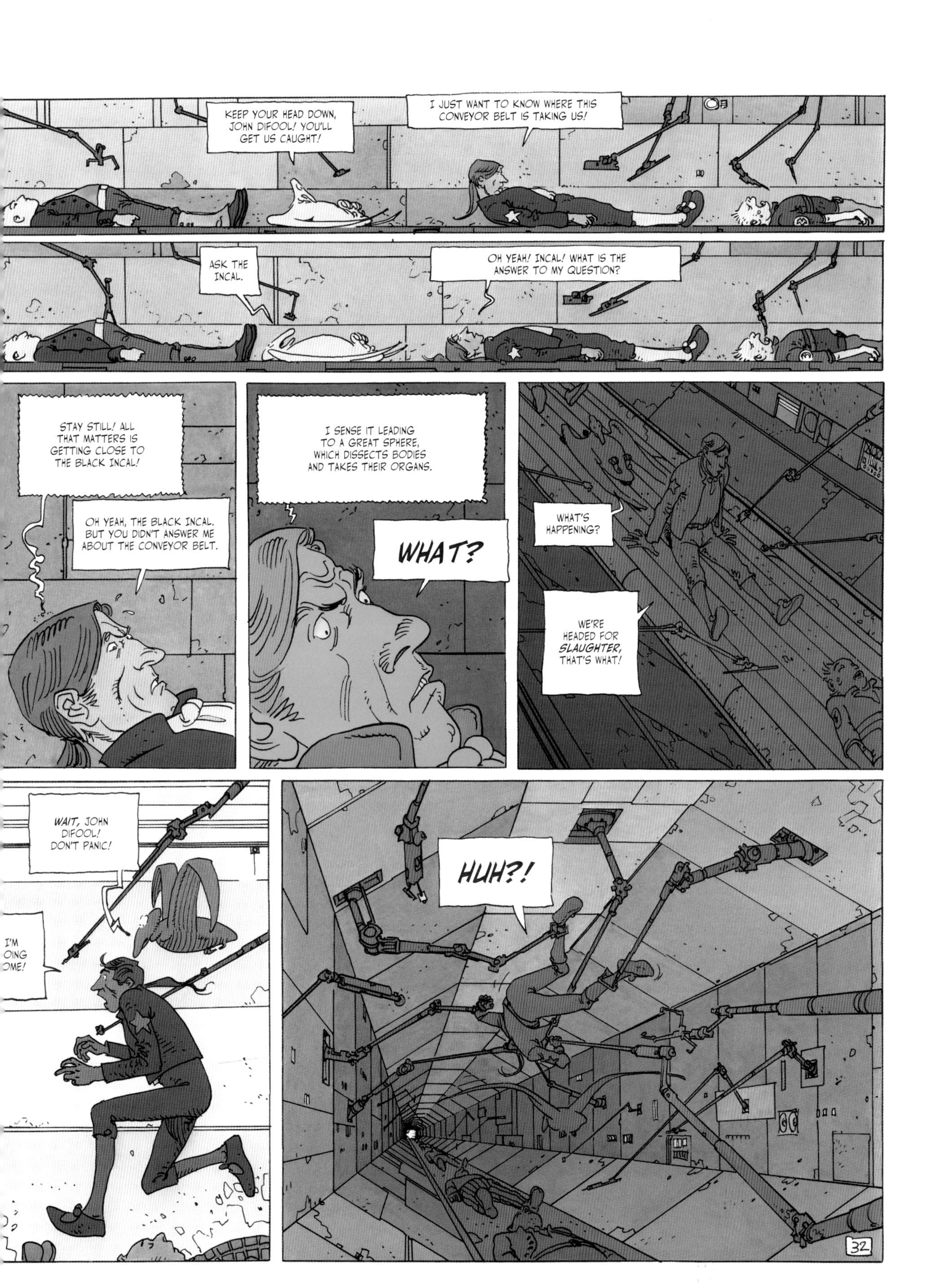
KEEP YOUR HEAD DOWN, JOHN DIFOOL! YOU'LL GET US CAUGHT!
I JUST WANT TO KNOW WHERE THIS CONVEYOR BELT IS TAKING US!
ASK THE INCAL.
OH YEAH! INCAL! WHAT IS THE ANSWER TO MY QUESTION?
STAY STILL! ALL THAT MATTERS IS GETTING CLOSE TO THE BLACK INCAL!
OH YEAH, THE BLACK INCAL. BUT YOU DIDN'T ANSWER ME ABOUT THE CONVEYOR BELT.
I SENSE IT LEADING TO A GREAT SPHERE, WHICH DISSECTS BODIES AND TAKES THEIR ORGANS.
WHAT?
WHAT'S HAPPENING?
WE'RE HEADED FOR SLAUGHTER, THAT'S WHAT!
WAIT, JOHN DIFOOL! DON'T PANIC!
I'M OING OME!
HUH?!
32

WE'VE PINPOINTED HIM, MR. OVERSEER! CORRIDOR C403, SECTION X9...HE STOWED AWAY WITH THE JUNK-BODIES FROM CITYSHAFT MARGARITA.
LET GO OF ME!
ODD THAT OUR INSTRUMENTS DIDN'T PICK HIM UP RIGHT AWAY. ALERT TECHNOCOMMAND, IMMEDIATELY.
IDIOT! YOU LET FEAR GET THE BEST OF YOU!
LET'S SEE YOU DO BETTER.
THE INCAL SAID THAT WHENEVER YOU LOSE FAITH, ONE OF YOUR FOUR PARTS WILL TAKE CONTROL.
HEY, I DON'T WANT TO BE CHOPPED UP INTO PIECES AGAIN!
THE LIFE-SIGNS SEEM TO MATCH, O BELOVED TECHNOPOPE.
OF COURSE IT'S HIM. THE DARKNESS IS POWERFUL. IT TUGS THE THREADS OF DESTINY, DRAWING ITS UNWITTING VICTIMS TO THE CENTER OF ITS WEB. I'D EVEN WAGER, DEAR HECTOR, THAT THE WHITE INCAL IS NEARBY. ***HA HA HA!***
PRESENTLY...
AFFIRMATIVE. I AM SCANNING VIBRATIONS EXCEEDING 14 ON THE KENTZ SCALE!
WELCOME TO OUR MIGHTY TECHNOCITY, JOHN DIFOOL.
ON BEHALF OF THE PRECIOUS DARKNESS, THANK YOU FOR BRINGING THE INCAL WITH YOU. OR IN YOU, I SHOULD SAY. ***HA HA HA HA!***
COME HERE, BIO-CREATURE.
HOW DO YOU KNOW MY...? UHH... I DON'T KNOW WHAT YOU'RE TALKING ABOUT.
33

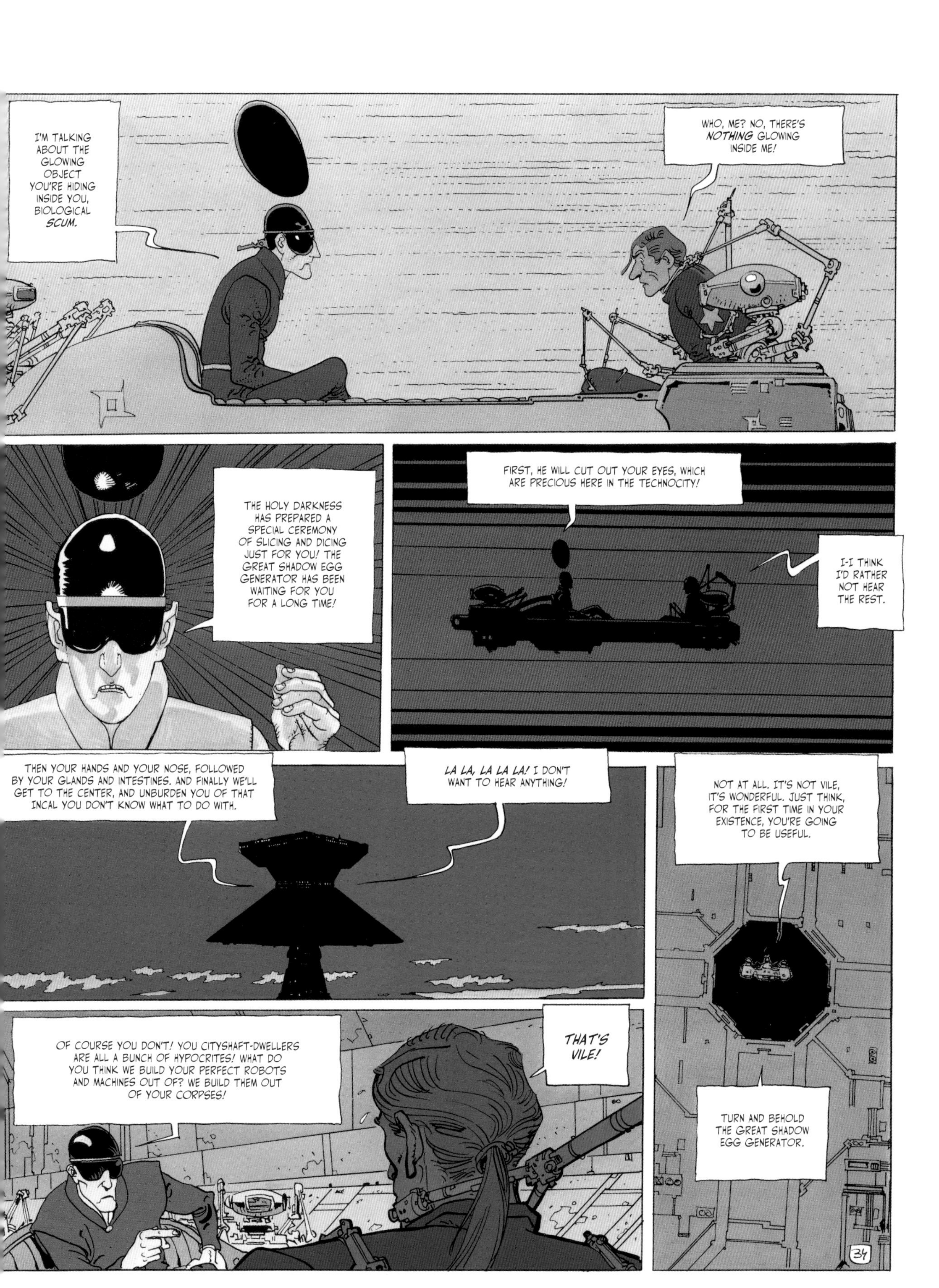
I'M TALKING ABOUT THE GLOWING OBJECT YOU'RE HIDING INSIDE YOU, BIOLOGICAL *SCUM.*
WHO, ME? NO, THERE'S *NOTHING* GLOWING INSIDE ME!
THE HOLY DARKNESS HAS PREPARED A SPECIAL CEREMONY OF SLICING AND DICING JUST FOR YOU! THE GREAT SHADOW EGG GENERATOR HAS BEEN WAITING FOR YOU FOR A LONG TIME!
FIRST, HE WILL CUT OUT YOUR EYES, WHICH ARE PRECIOUS HERE IN THE TECHNOCITY!
I-I THINK I'D RATHER NOT HEAR THE REST.
THEN YOUR HANDS AND YOUR NOSE, FOLLOWED BY YOUR GLANDS AND INTESTINES. AND FINALLY WE'LL GET TO THE CENTER, AND UNBURDEN YOU OF THAT INCAL YOU DON'T KNOW WHAT TO DO WITH.
LA LA, LA LA LA! I DON'T WANT TO HEAR ANYTHING!
OF COURSE YOU DON'T! YOU CITYSHAFT-DWELLERS ARE ALL A BUNCH OF HYPOCRITES! WHAT DO YOU THINK WE BUILD YOUR PERFECT ROBOTS AND MACHINES OUT OF? WE BUILD THEM OUT OF YOUR CORPSES!
THAT'S VILE!
NOT AT ALL. IT'S NOT VILE, IT'S WONDERFUL. JUST THINK, FOR THE FIRST TIME IN YOUR EXISTENCE, YOU'RE GOING TO BE USEFUL.
TURN AND BEHOLD THE GREAT SHADOW EGG GENERATOR.
34

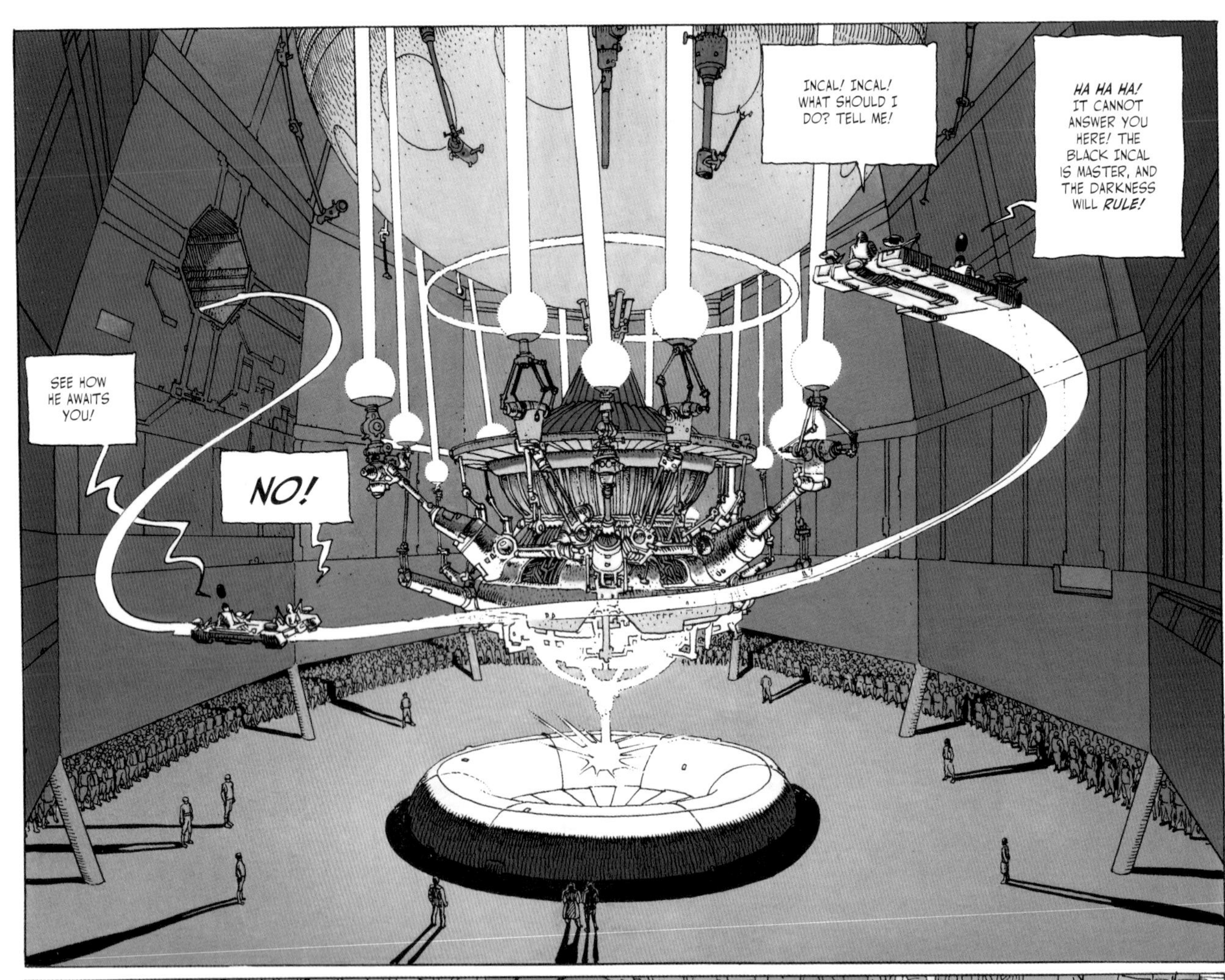
INCAL! INCAL! WHAT SHOULD I DO? TELL ME!
HA HA HA! IT CANNOT ANSWER YOU HERE! THE BLACK INCAL IS MASTER, AND THE DARKNESS WILL RULE!
SEE HOW HE AWAITS YOU!
NO!

MEANWHILE, DEEP IN THE GREAT CITYSHAFT, JUST ABOVE THE NOXIOUS ACID LAKE.
HURRY!
35
MOEBIUS

THE METABARON

SO, THIS IS YOUR FILTHY RATHOLE!

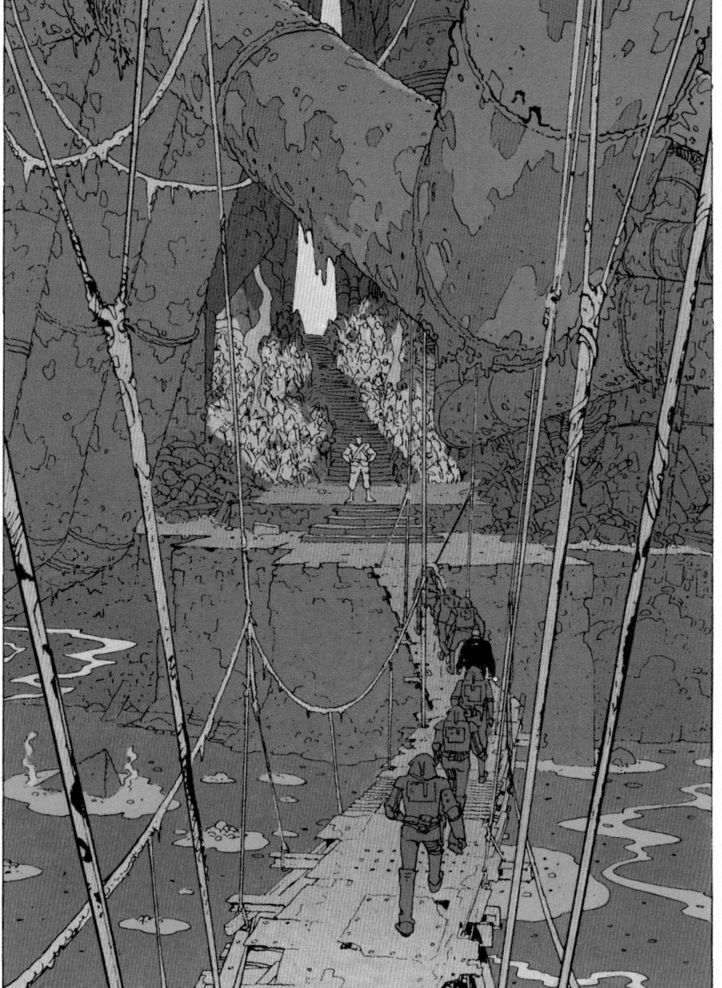

WELCOME TO THE LAIR OF AMOK, *METABARON!*
THE...THE METABARON?
36

ENOUGH TALK! WHERE IS HE? HAS HE BEEN HARMED?
LET GO, METABARON!
HEH HEH! WOLFHEAD'S GOT HIM UPSET!
CALM DOWN, METABARON! I SWEAR BY THE HOLY MOTHER, YOUR SON IS SAFE!
THAT'S THE METABARON!
IT'S HIM! THE GREAT KILLER!
THE GREATEST MERCENARY IN THE WHOLE SYSTEM!
HURRY! THE QUEEN OF AMOK AWAITS!
HE DOESN LOOK SO TOUG
HE'S FINALLY COME OUT OF HIS METABUNKE
THEY SAY HE ONCE KILLED SEVEN MEN IN ONE SECOND.
SOON, AFTER WALKING THROUGH A LONG, DAMP STONE CORRIDOR.
WE'RE HERE! BOW BEFORE THE HOLY MOTHER, POWER OF THE DEPTHS, MISTRESS OF THE NETHERWORLD... QUEEN OF AMOK!
3

SO, YOU'RE THE QUEEN OF AMOK? UP ON THE SURFACE, THEY TELL *MANY* DARK AND STRANGE TALES ABOUT YOU.
AND ABOUT YOU AS WELL. LET THEM GOSSIP! SOON, I WILL GIVE THEM REAL REASON TO FEAR ME.
COME CLOSER, SO WE CAN TALK. YOU'VE BEEN RETIRED FOR TEN YEARS. I HAD TO USE *DRASTIC* MEASURES TO LURE YOU FROM YOUR LAIR. I AM SORRY...

PLEASE, HOLY MOTHER...TELL HIM TO BRING HIM BACK ALIVE. I WANT HIM!
SIT, WOLFHEAD! STOP PANTING IN MY EAR!
WOLFHEAD DEMANDS *REVENGE!*

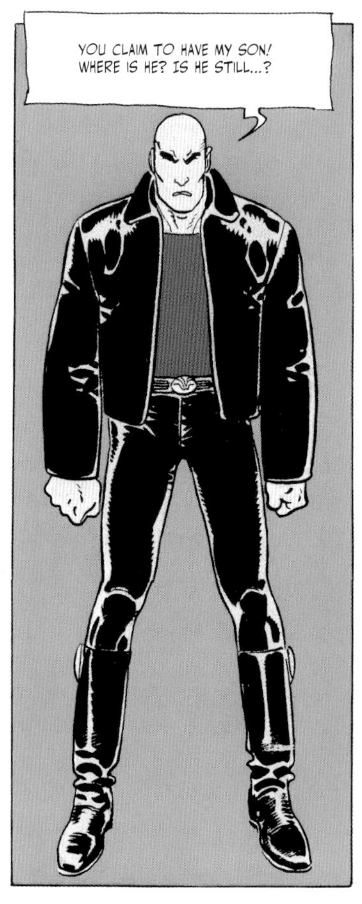
YOU CLAIM TO HAVE MY SON! WHERE IS HE? IS HE STILL...?

STILL ALIVE? BUT OF COURSE, DEAR METABARON... IF NOT, WHAT POWER WOULD I HAVE OVER YOU?
OPEN THE CURTAIN, AND LET HIM SEE!
38

FATHER! HELP!
YOU SEE? YOUR BELOVED SON IS AS SAFE AS A BABY IN ITS MOTHER'S WOMB.
OF COURSE, HIS COMPANIONS IN THE AQUARIUM AREN'T EXACTLY FRIENDLY. BUT THEY DO MAKE GOOD GUARDIANS! **HA HA HA HA!**

QUICK AS LIGHTNING, THE METABARON ATTACKS THE NEAREST GUARD.
?

ZZAF

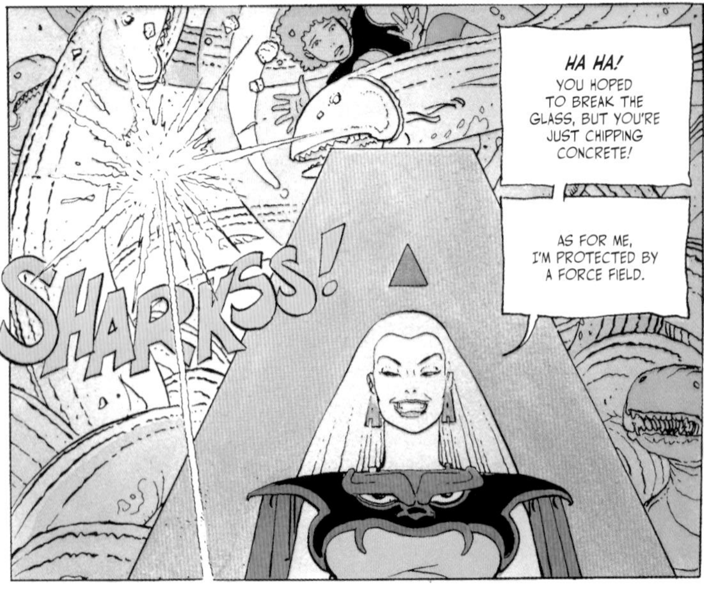
HA HA! YOU HOPED TO BREAK THE GLASS, BUT YOU'RE JUST CHIPPING CONCRETE!
AS FOR ME, I'M PROTECTED BY A FORCE FIELD.
SHARKSS!

FOOL! IT'S NOTHING BUT A HOLOGRAPHIC PROJECTION! DO YOU THINK I'M STUPID?
YOUR SC IS FAR FR HERE, AND SOON E DEVOURED MY RAVENC FRIENDS
UNLESS...

WELL?
UNLESS YOU BRING ME JOHN DIFOOL!
THIS IS HIS FILE! I WANT HIM HERE IN 24 HOURS, DEAD OR ALIVE!
WOLFHEAD!
HAND THESE PAPERS TO THE METABARON!
JOHN DIFOOL? HMM... HIS FACE LOOKS FAMILIAR.
AH YES! IT'S THAT TRIVIAL PRIVATE DETECTIVE ALL THE CYBO-COPS ARE SEARCHING FOR. WITH ALL THE RIOTS GOING ON, IT WON'T BE EASY.
THAT'S NOT A PROBLEM. HE'S NOT IN THE CITY AT THE MOMENT.
HE'S UP NORTH. IN THE HEART OF THE TECHNOCITY.
SILENCE, WOLFHEAD!
BRING HIM BACK ALIVE! I'VE GOT A SCORE TO SETTLE WITH HIM!
THE TECHNOCITY. THAT WON'T BE EASY EITHER.
A NEST OF EVIL. NOW I SEE WHY YOU CHOSE TO BLACKMAIL ME.
NO FEE IN THE UNIVERSE WOULD MAKE ME ACCEPT THIS CONTRACT, BUT NOW YOU LEAVE ME NO CHOICE. I ACCEPT! BUT BEWARE! IF ANYTHING HAPPENS TO SOLUNE, I'LL DESTROY YOU ALL!
MOEBIUS

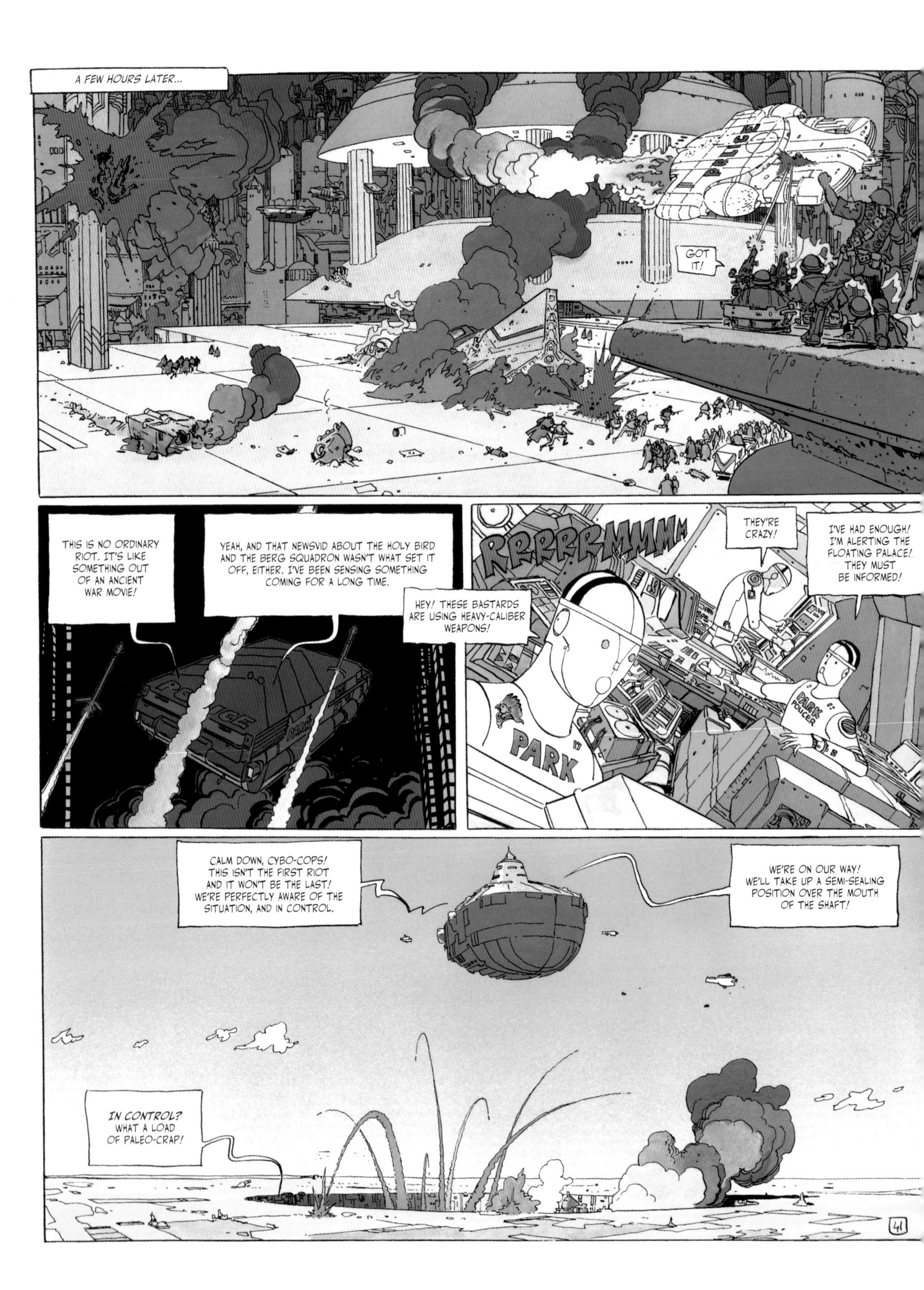
A FEW HOURS LATER...
GOT IT!
THIS IS NO ORDINARY RIOT. IT'S LIKE SOMETHING OUT OF AN ANCIENT WAR MOVIE!
YEAH, AND THAT NEWSVID ABOUT THE HOLY BIRD AND THE BERG SQUADRON WASN'T WHAT SET IT OFF, EITHER. I'VE BEEN SENSING SOMETHING COMING FOR A LONG TIME.
RRRRRMMMM
HEY! THESE BASTARDS ARE USING HEAVY-CALIBER WEAPONS!
THEY'RE CRAZY!
I'VE HAD ENOUGH! I'M ALERTING THE FLOATING PALACE! THEY MUST BE INFORMED!
PARK
PARK POLICER
CALM DOWN, CYBO-COPS! THIS ISN'T THE FIRST RIOT AND IT WON'T BE THE LAST! WE'RE PERFECTLY AWARE OF THE SITUATION, AND IN CONTROL.
WE'RE ON OUR WAY! WE'LL TAKE UP A SEMI-SEALING POSITION OVER THE MOUTH OF THE SHAFT!
IN CONTROL? WHAT A LOAD OF PALEO-CRAP!
41

LOOK! ANOTHER ONE OF THOSE NEO-URBANITES TRYING TO BREAK THROUGH OUR LINES!
HE'S DEAD!
IT'S ABOUT TIME!
KAB BOOO
THE METABARON'S PRECISELY CONTROLLED BODY MOVEMENTS USE THE FORCE OF THE EXPLOSION TO PROPEL HIM TO HIS PREDETERMINED TARGET.
OPEN THE SOUTHERN AIRLOCK! IS THE METACRAFT READY?
READY, METABARON!
HELLO, TONTO!
STATUS?
YOU'LL VE SOME ROUBLE ETTING UT. THE ZIDENTIAL ALACE IS SEALING OSITION!
ALREADY? HMM...NO, FIRST THEY'LL TAKE UP A SEMI-SEALING POSITION, TO SPARE THE ARISTO LEVELS. I'M MORE CONCERNED ABOUT THESE VIBRATIONS. THE METABUNKER WON'T LAST LONG.
I KNOW! THERE'S AN INTER-LEVEL WAR GOING ON, AND WE'RE TRAPPED IN THE MIDDLE! I'VE NEVER SEEN ANYTHING SO VIOLENT. IN MY OPINION, YOU HUMANS ARE COMPLETELY...
YES...? COMPLETELY WHAT?
WHRRGL! AHEM... I MUST ADMIT THE EXACT WORD ISN'T IN MY DATABANKS!
42

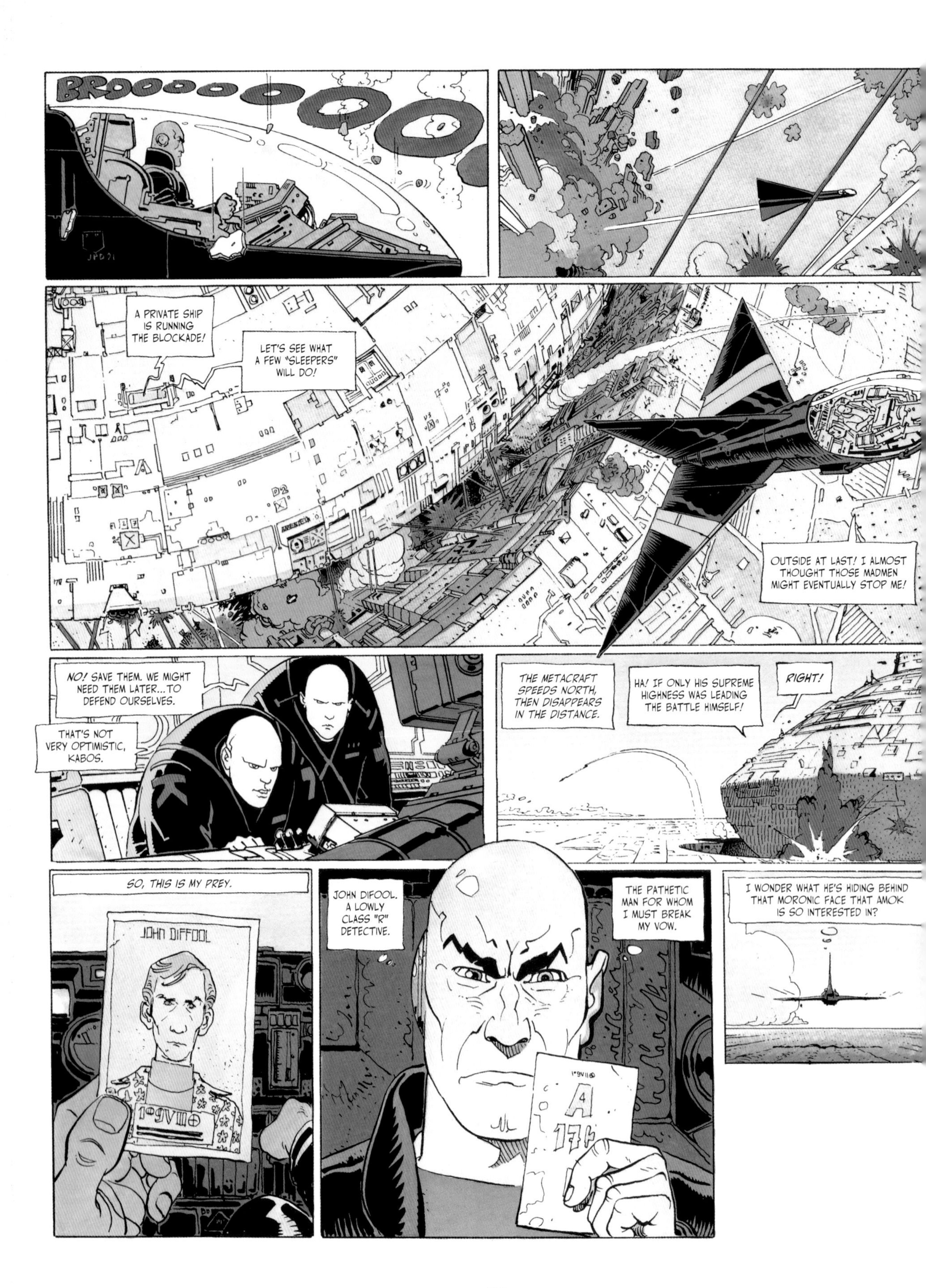
BROOOOOOOOOO
A PRIVATE SHIP IS RUNNING THE BLOCKADE!
LET'S SEE WHAT A FEW "SLEEPERS" WILL DO!
OUTSIDE AT LAST! I ALMOST THOUGHT THOSE MADMEN MIGHT EVENTUALLY STOP ME!
NO! SAVE THEM. WE MIGHT NEED THEM LATER...TO DEFEND OURSELVES.
THAT'S NOT VERY OPTIMISTIC, KABOS.
THE METACRAFT SPEEDS NORTH, THEN DISAPPEARS IN THE DISTANCE.
HA! IF ONLY HIS SUPREME HIGHNESS WAS LEADING THE BATTLE HIMSELF!
RIGHT!
SO, THIS IS MY PREY.
JOHN DIFFOOL
JOHN DIFOOL. A LOWLY CLASS "R" DETECTIVE.
THE PATHETIC MAN FOR WHOM I MUST BREAK MY VOW.
I WONDER WHAT HE'S HIDING BEHIND THAT MORONIC FACE THAT AMOK IS SO INTERESTED IN?

MOEBIUS 81

THE LUMINOUS INCAL

OVE TENEBRAE

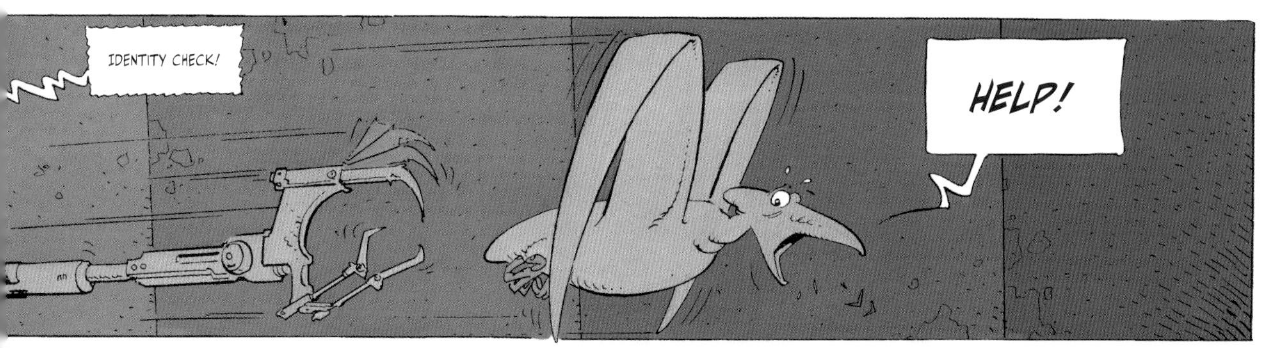

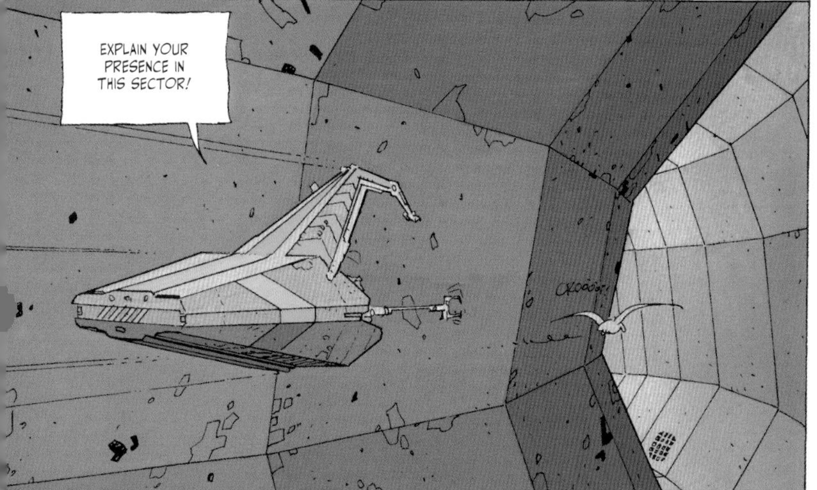

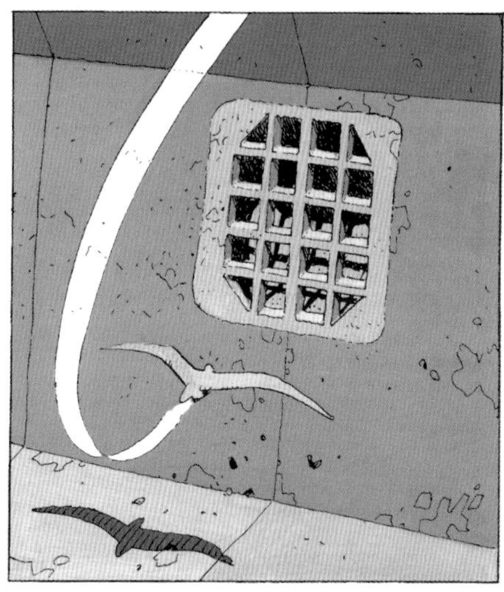

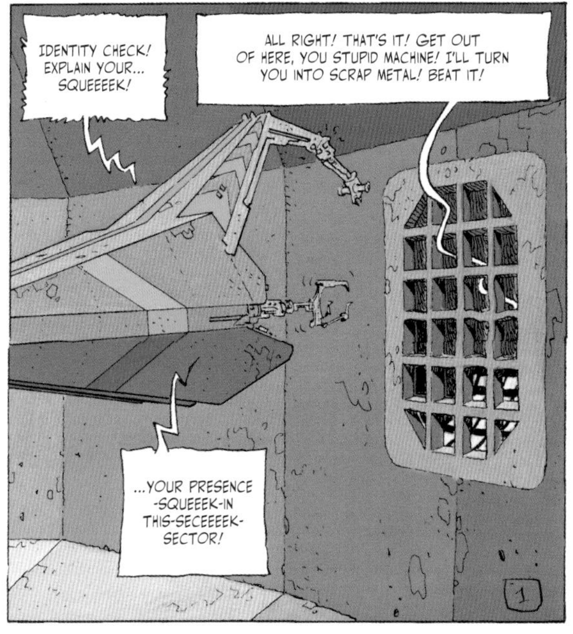

KRASK
CROOOT!?

SQUEEK! ...YOUR PRESENCE IN THIS SECTOR!

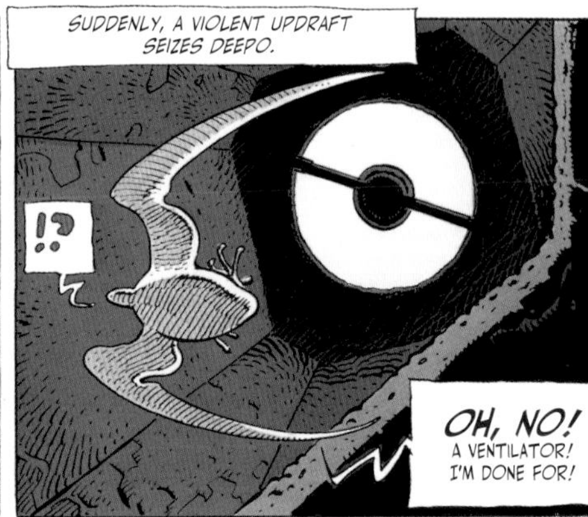
SUDDENLY, A VIOLENT UPDRAFT SEIZES DEEPO.
!?
OH, NO! A VENTILATOR! I'M DONE FOR!

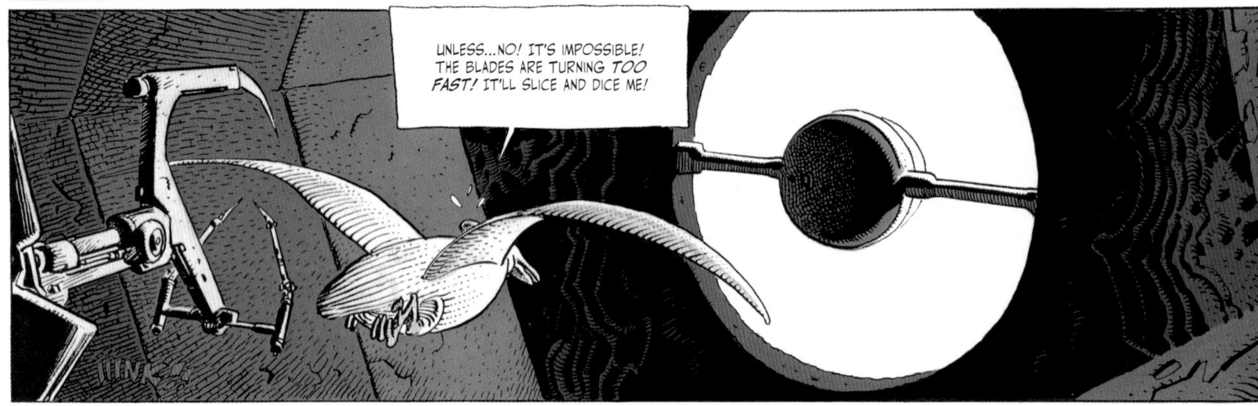
UNLESS...NO! IT'S IMPOSSIBLE! THE BLADES ARE TURNING TOO FAST! IT'LL SLICE AND DICE ME!

CHECKEEEK

I HAVE TO DO IT! I USED TO BE GOOD AT THIS! BACK WITH THAT FLOCK OF HATCHLINGS AT THE STARPORT, I USED TO FLY RIGHT BETWEEN THE PROPELLER'S BLADES...

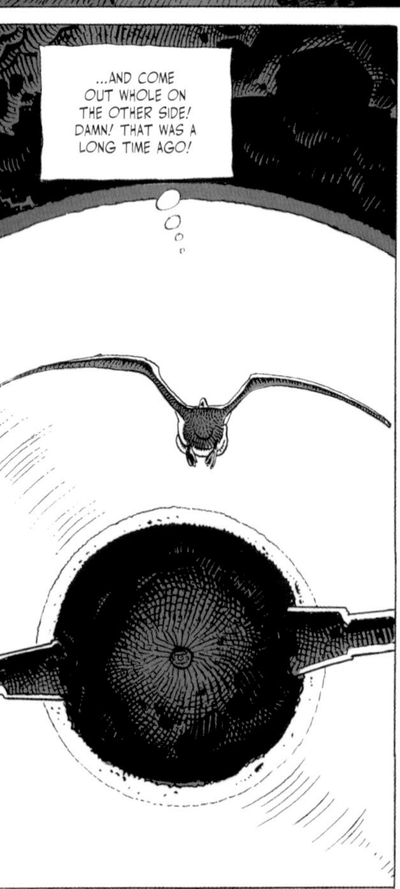
...AND COME OUT WHOLE ON THE OTHER SIDE! DAMN! THAT WAS A LONG TIME AGO!

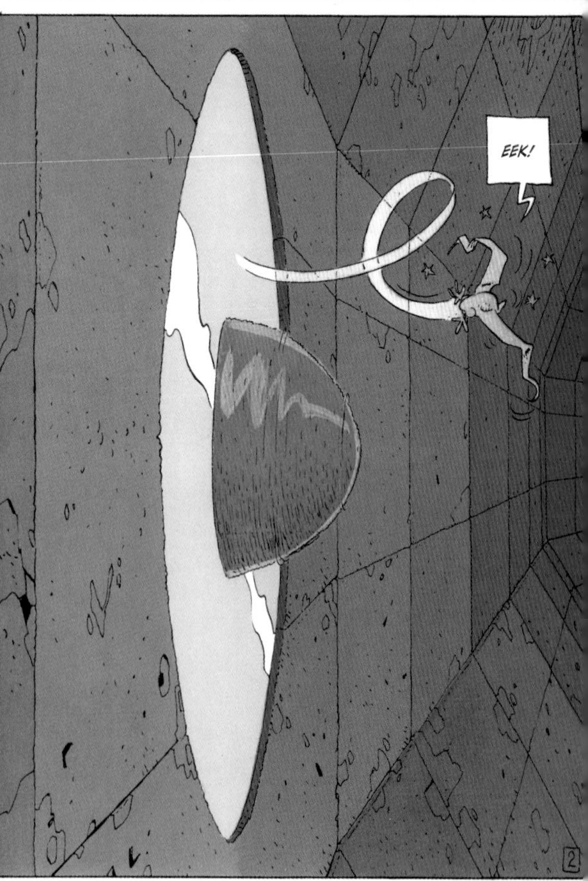
EEK!

WHEW!
A LITTLE BATTERED, BUT I MADE IT!
JUST LIKE THE GOOD OLD DAYS!

AND I LOST THAT HUNK OF SCRAP METAL! WHAT AN ESCAPE!

SO, NOW I JUST HAVE TO FIGURE OUT WHERE I AM. I'VE GOT TO EVALUATE THE SITUATION AND THEN FIND JOHN DIFOOL!

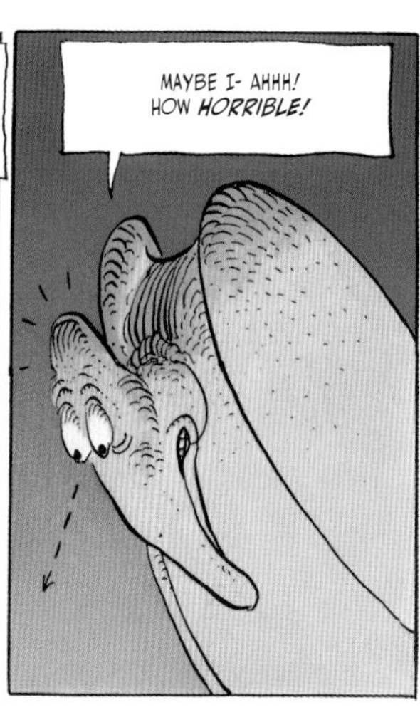
MAYBE I- AHHH! HOW HORRIBLE!

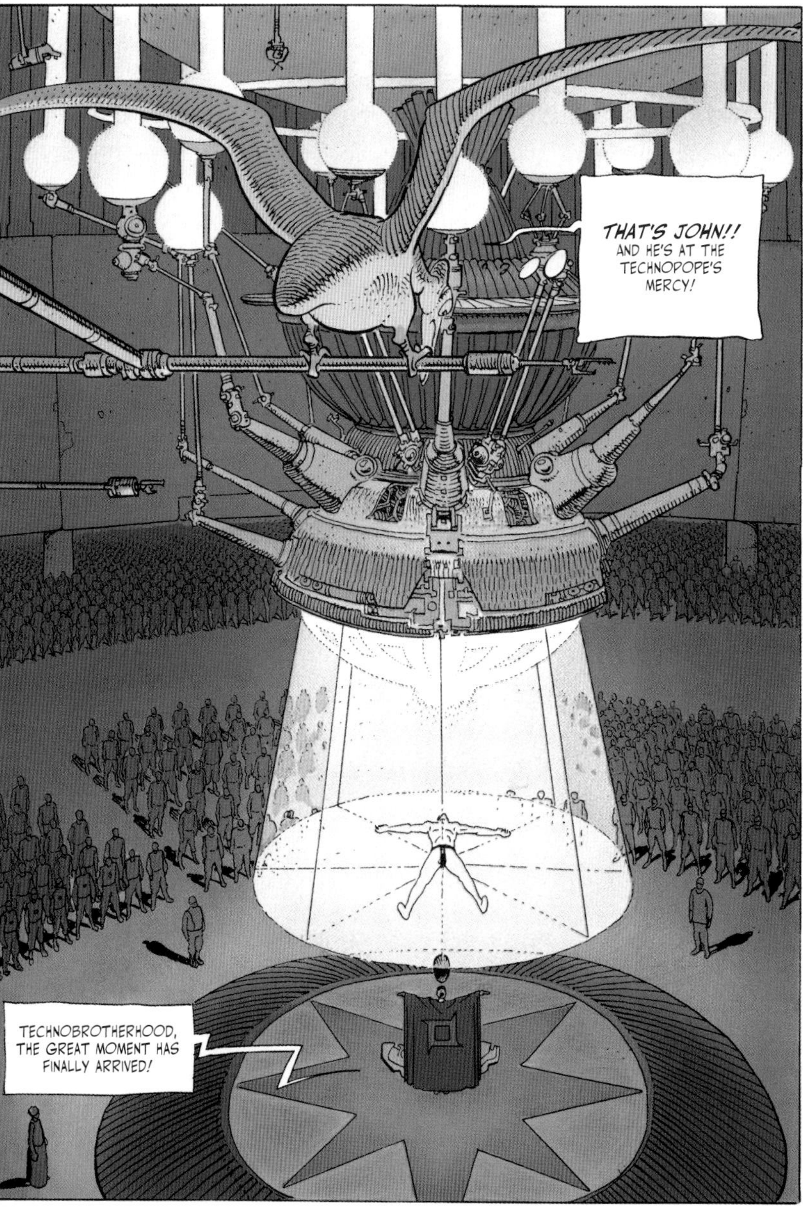
THAT'S JOHN!! AND HE'S AT THE TECHNOPOPE'S MERCY!
TECHNOBROTHERHOOD, THE GREAT MOMENT HAS FINALLY ARRIVED!

PLEASE, INCAL, DON'T LET ME DOWN!
OUR UNION WITH THE GREAT DARKNESS WILL BEAR ITS DARK FRUIT TONIGHT!

OVÉ!
OVÉ!
OVÉ!
RAISED FISTS! CHANTING CHORUS! TECHNOMADNESS!
OVÉ!
OVÉ!
OVÉ!

TODAY IS THE DAY OF VICTORY! THE LUMINOUS INCAL IS OUR ENEMY. THOUGH IT PRETENDS TO ILLUMINATE, IT ONLY BLINDS US.
OVE!
OVE!
OVÉ!
OVÉ!
OVÉ!

HOLY CONCRETE! THE TECHNOPOPE AND ALL THE TECHNOS HAVE GONE INSANE!
...BLINDS US WITH ITS EVIL LIGHT. THAT ENEMY IS HERE NOW...AND IT IS POWERLESS!
OVÉ!

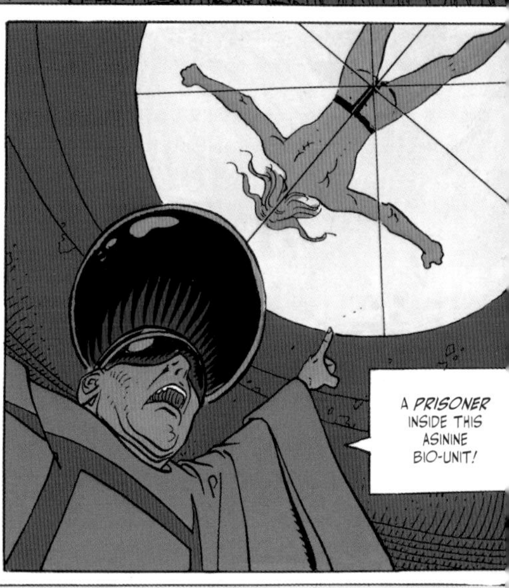

A PRISONER INSIDE THIS ASININE BIO-UNIT!

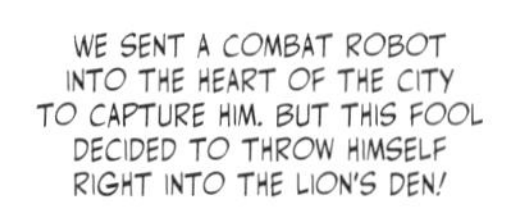

WE SENT A COMBAT ROBOT INTO THE HEART OF THE CITY TO CAPTURE HIM. BUT THIS FOOL DECIDED TO THROW HIMSELF RIGHT INTO THE LION'S DEN!

INCAL! YOU CAN DO ANYTHING, PLEASE, SEND US BACK IN TIME TO MY GOOD OLD CONAPT. WITH A NICE FULL BOTTLE OF WHISKEY AND MY FAITHFUL BOX OF FIRST CLASS SPV! OH, INCAL!

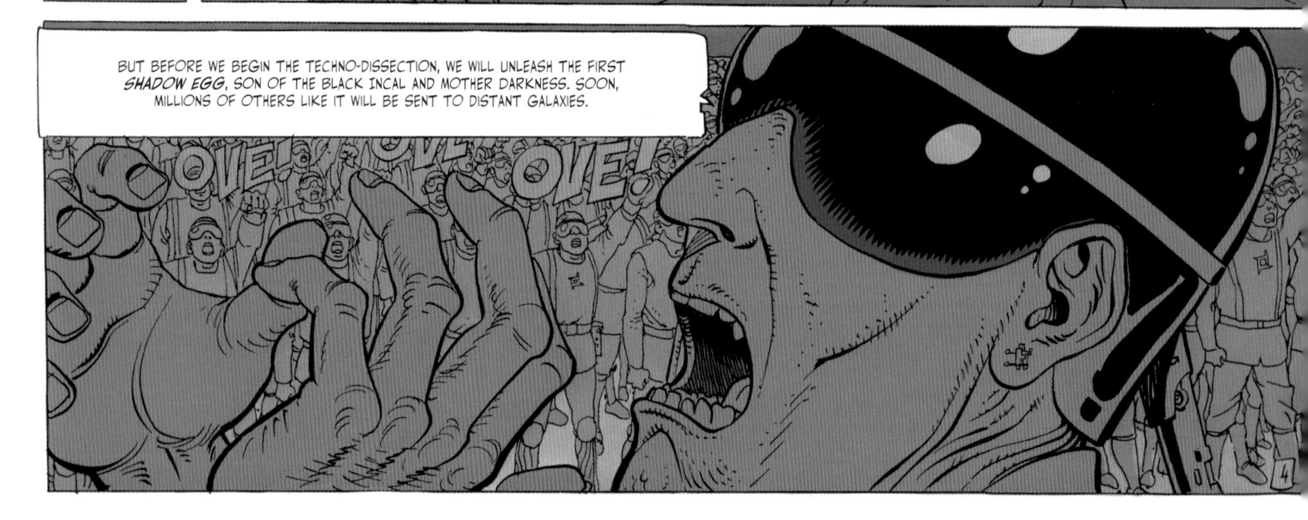

BUT BEFORE WE BEGIN THE TECHNO-DISSECTION, WE WILL UNLEASH THE FIRST SHADOW EGG, SON OF THE BLACK INCAL AND MOTHER DARKNESS. SOON, MILLIONS OF OTHERS LIKE IT WILL BE SENT TO DISTANT GALAXIES.
OVE! OVE! OVE!

THERE THEY WILL SWALLOW ENTIRE SUNS DOWN TO THE LAST PHOTON, RETURNING THE COSMOS TO IMMACULATE NIGHT. AT LAST THE REIGN OF *THE GREAT DARKNESS* WILL BEGIN!
OVE TENEBRAE!

HOW CAN I HELP JOHN DIFOOL GET OUT OF THIS MESS?
BBBRRRRRRRRR
OVE TENEBRAE
SUDDENLY, A MUFFLED RUMBLING SHAKES THE ENORMOUS ROOM AND AN ICY WIND PIERCES DEEPO'S HEART.

WHAT HAVE THEY DONE?
OVE TENEBRAE

IT-IT'S HORRIBLE!!! INCAL! DO SOMETHING!
PLEASE!

GO, SHADOW EGG!
FILL THE UNIVERSE WITH YOUR DARKNESS!
5

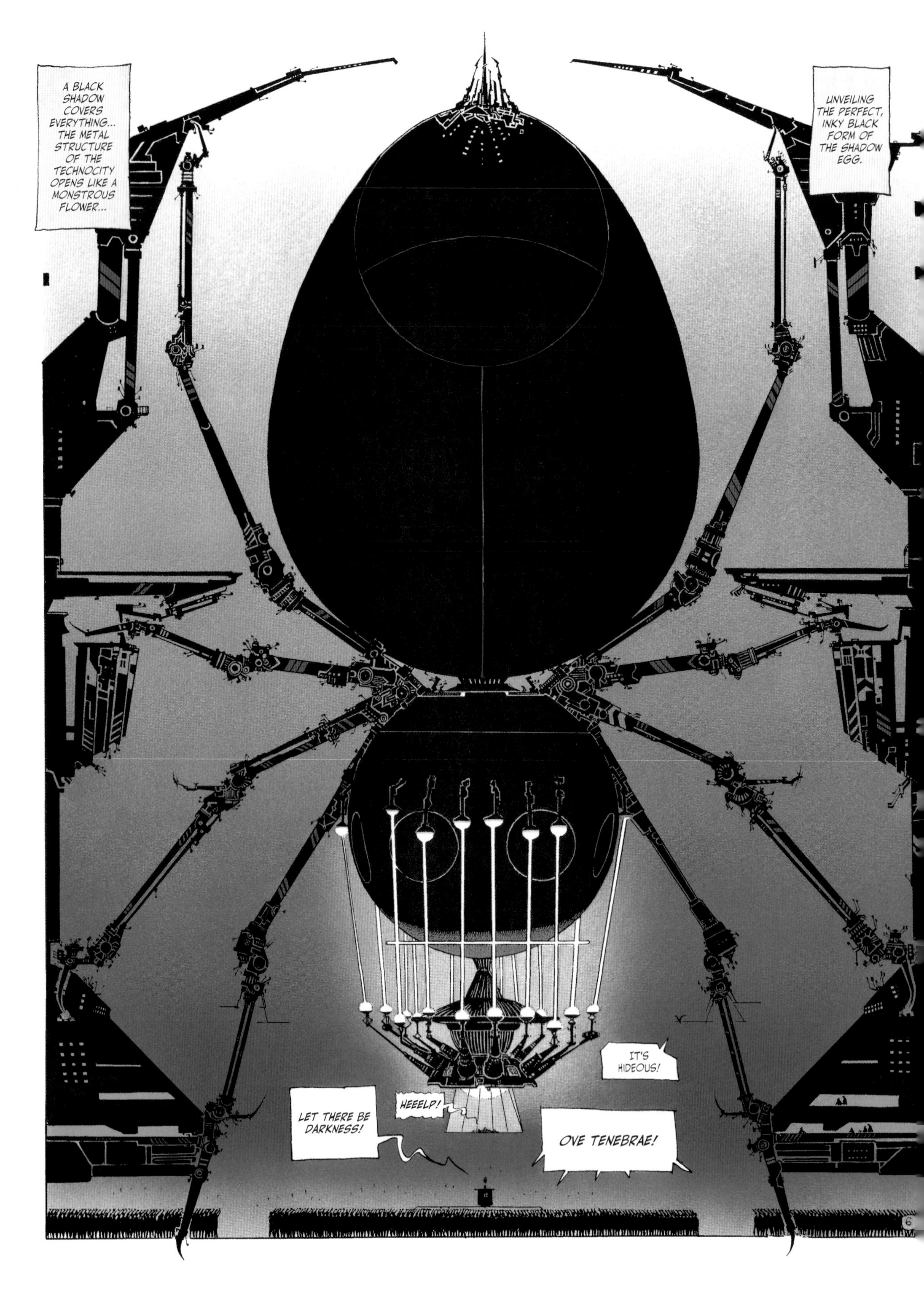
A BLACK SHADOW COVERS EVERYTHING... THE METAL STRUCTURE OF THE TECHNOCITY OPENS LIKE A MONSTROUS FLOWER...
UNVEILING THE PERFECT, INKY BLACK FORM OF THE SHADOW EGG.
IT'S HIDEOUS!
HEEELP!
LET THERE BE DARKNESS!
OVE TENEBRAE!

RRRRRRRRROOOOOOOORRRRRR...

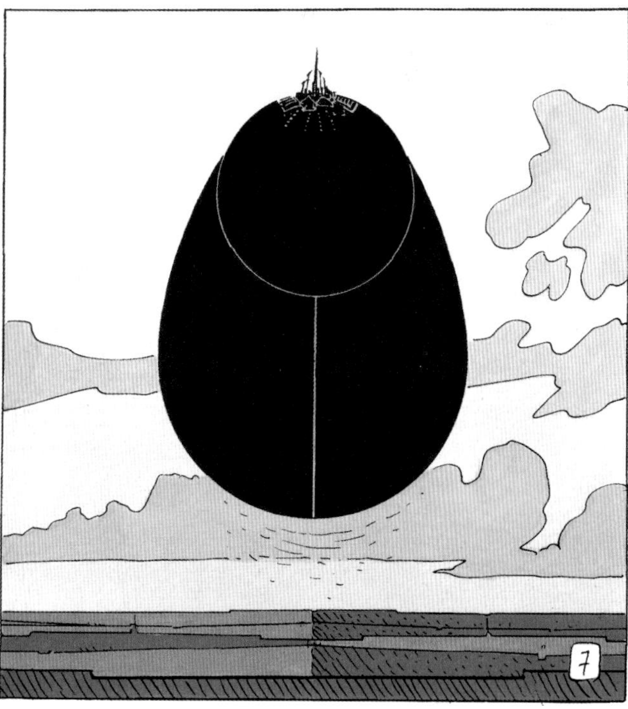
7

OVE TENEBRAE!...

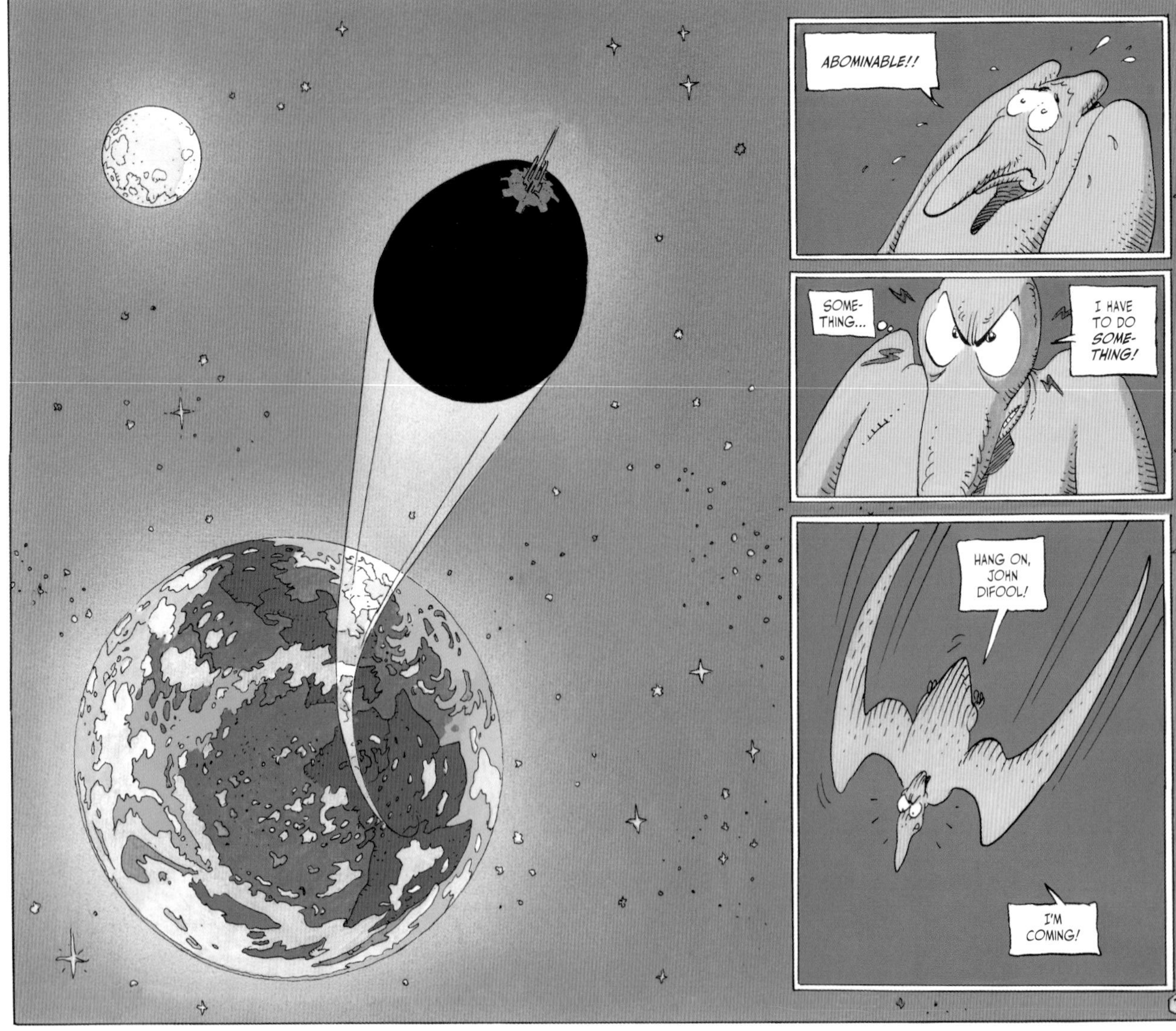
ABOMINABLE!!
SOME-THING...
I HAVE TO DO SOME-THING!
HANG ON, JOHN DIFOOL!
I'M COMING!

PANIC ON THE INSIDE/OUTSIDE

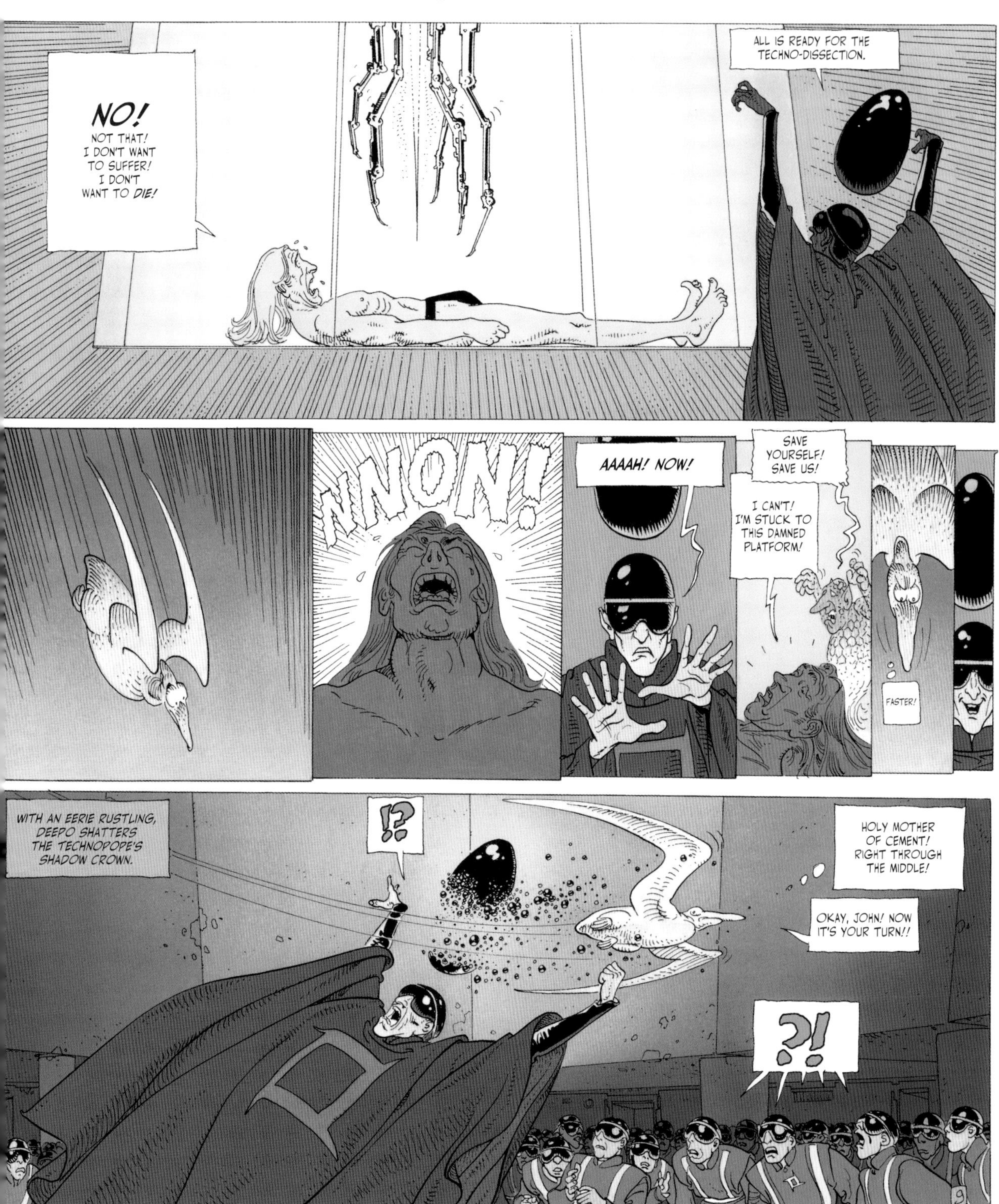

THE TECHNOPOPE'S "PSYCHO-ABDOMEN" BURSTS INTO MILLIONS OF GLISTENING MARBLES, NULLIFYING HIS POWER.
GARGGH
JOHN! HURRY UP AND TAKE MENTAL CONTROL OF THE TRANSPARENT PLATFORM!
SACRILEGE!
PROFANITY!
?!
MY CROWN! CURSES! DARKNESS! HELP ME! I'M BLIND!
GET THE BIRD!
INCAL! I'M FREE! ARE YOU FREE? CAN YOU TALK TO ME?
JUST FOR A FEW SECONDS, JOHN! THE PSYCHO-ABDOMEN IS ABOUT TO REFORM! YOU HAVE TO ACT NOW!
ACT!? WHAT... WHAT DO YOU MEAN?
JOHN! HURRY!!! UP HERE!
10

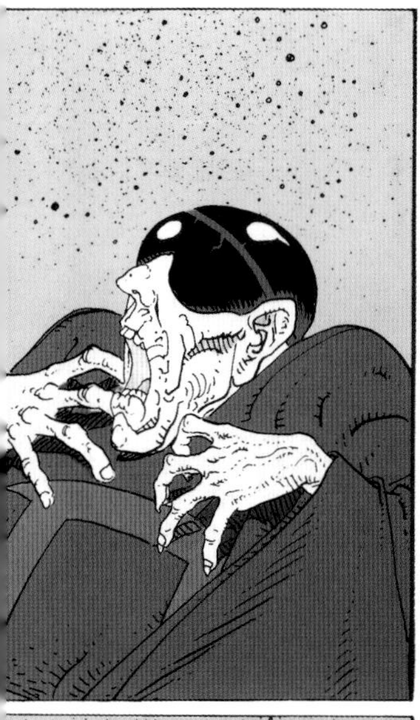

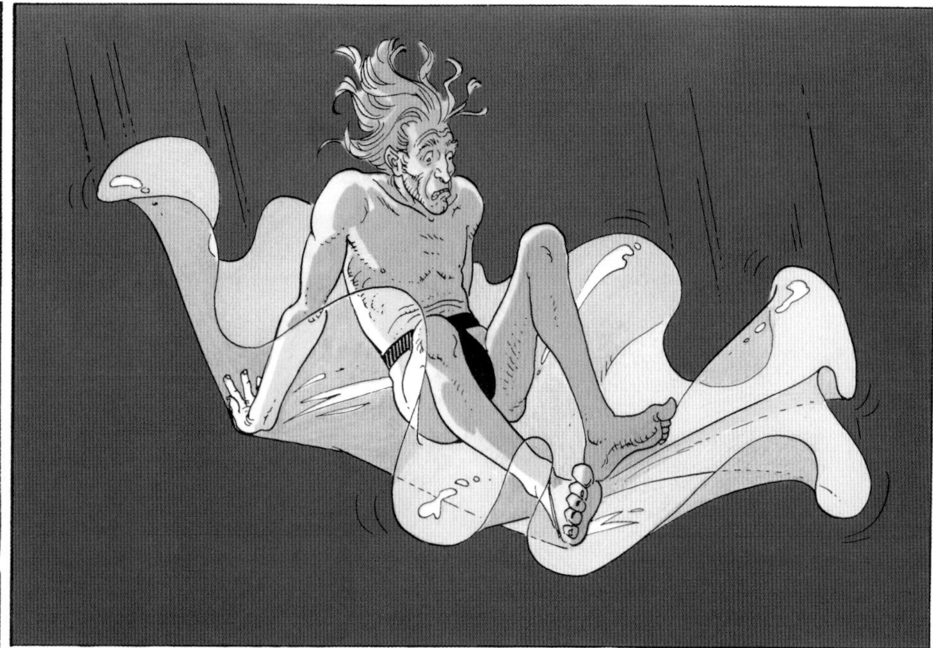

UNLEASH YOUR TECHNO-POWERS!

UP THERE! AT THE TOP OF THE SPHERE! THERE'S A TRAPDOOR!
OH, GREAT! THE KEY WORD BEING, "TRAP."
THEY'RE GETTING AWAY!

THE PEGAZ! RELEASE THE PEGAZ!

QUICK!

IT LOOKS LIKE A NEW KIND OF HELL IN THERE!
IF YOU DON'T CLOSE THAT TRAP DOOR, WE'LL BE SOMEPLACE EVEN WORSE!

CLAC!
TOO LATE!

IT DOESN'T MATTER. HE'S SEALED HIS FATE BY CLOSING THAT DOOR! THERE'S NO WAY BACK FROM THE INSIDE/OUTSIDE! AND SOON HE WILL MEET THE TERRIBLE AND HOLY GUARDIAN OF THE BLACK INCAL! THE CARDIOCLAW!
THE CARDIOCLAW!
THE CARDIOCLAW!
12

MEANWHILE, NOT FAR AWAY...
DETECTION IS CONFIRMED! WHAT WE'RE LOOKING FOR IS INSIDE THAT BUILDING.
HUH... IT LOOKS LIKE A REAL FORTRESS, CHIEF.
HAVEN'T WE ALREADY LOST ENOUGH MEN, CHIEF?
YOU WHIMPERING MOURGS! DON'T FORGET THAT THE EMPEROR HIMSELF IS SUPERVISING THIS SQUADRON BY COSMOVIDEO! THIS HILL WILL MAKE AN EXCELLENT OBSERVATION POST...
...AND FOR GOD'S SAKE, ACT LIKE REAL BERG HEROES!
NO NEED TO SWEAR, CHIEF.
STOP! SILENCE! CEASE MOVEMENT!
WHAT'S GOING ON, CHIEF?
IT'S AN INDIGENOUS HUMAN...
ALONE!?
WHAT DO WE DO?
HE'LL RAISE THE ALARM.
WE HAVE TO ELIMINATE HIM! FIRE ON MY SIGNAL! READY. AIM.
13

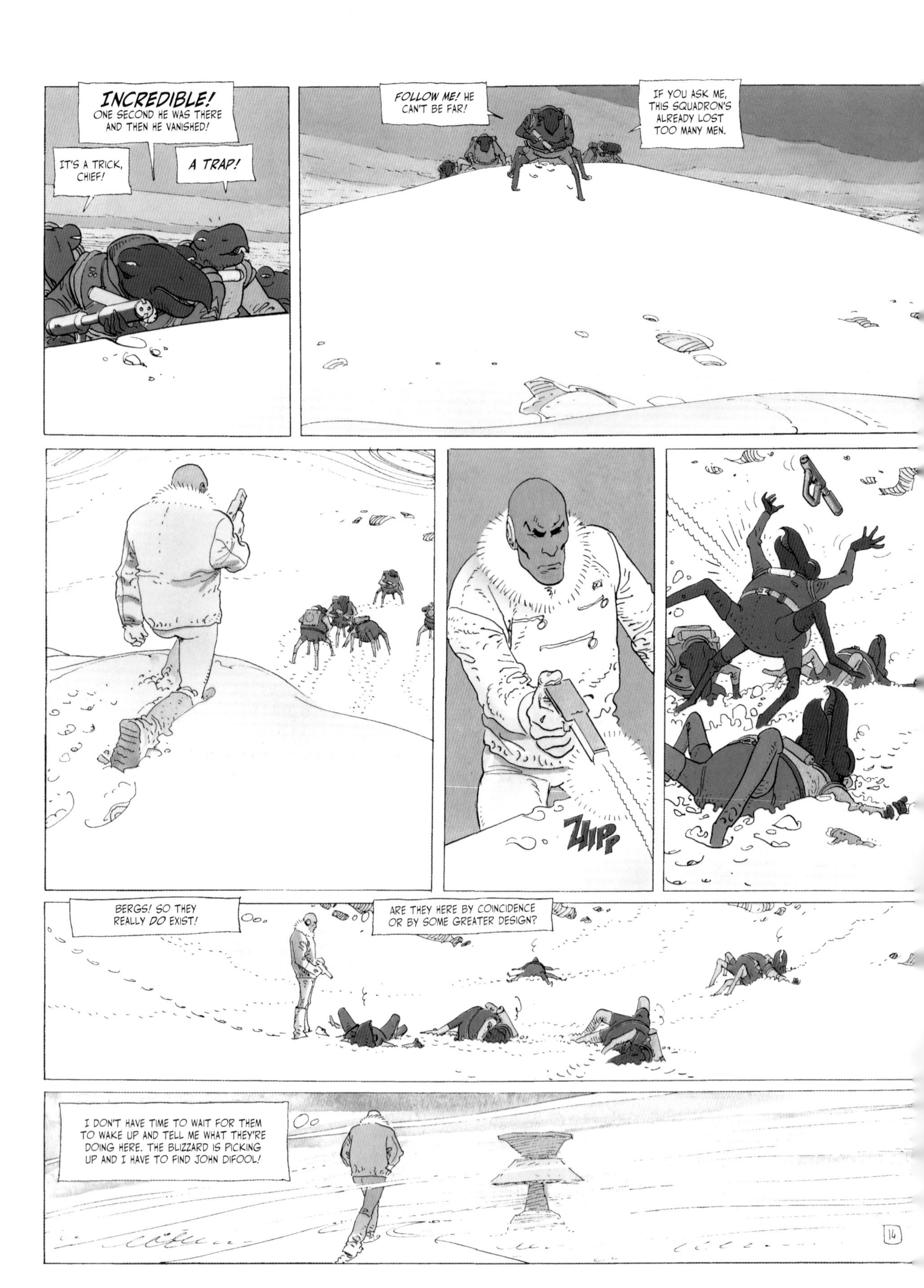
INCREDIBLE! ONE SECOND HE WAS THERE AND THEN HE VANISHED!
IT'S A TRICK, CHIEF!
A TRAP!
FOLLOW ME! HE CAN'T BE FAR!
IF YOU ASK ME, THIS SQUADRON'S ALREADY LOST TOO MANY MEN.
ZIIPP
BERGS! SO THEY REALLY DO EXIST!
ARE THEY HERE BY COINCIDENCE OR BY SOME GREATER DESIGN?
I DON'T HAVE TIME TO WAIT FOR THEM TO WAKE UP AND TELL ME WHAT THEY'RE DOING HERE. THE BLIZZARD IS PICKING UP AND I HAVE TO FIND JOHN DIFOOL!
14

MEANWHILE, DEEP WITHIN THE TECHNO-CITADEL...
HOLY CONCRETE, THIS IS AMAZING! WE WENT INSIDE THE SPHERE AND NOW WE'RE OUTSIDE A SPHERE!
THEY-THEY'RE NOT FOLLOWING US! DEEPO! WE'RE *SAFE!*
JUST THINK, *I* BEAT THE TECHNOS! *BY MYSELF!* ME! JOHN DIFOOL...PATHETIC CLASS R DETECTIVE...ME...HA HA HA!
RIGHT! AND ALL I DID WAS SMASH HIS PSYCHO-ABDOMEN WITH MY BEAK...
THIS PLACE IS CREEPY! IF I HAD HAIR IT'D BE STANDING ON END!
HOW DO WE GET OUT? I DON'T SEE THE TRAPDOOR ANYWHERE!
PFFF!
WHAT, GET OUT JUST SO WE CAN FACE THOSE LUNATICS AGAIN? NO THANKS!
LET'S EXPLORE THE SPHERE! THERE MUST BE A WAY OUT SOMEWHERE!
JOHN, WHY DON'T YOU ASK THE INCAL WHAT WE SHOULD DO?

THE INCAL! ALWAYS WITH THE INCAL! I THINK I CAN LIVE TEN MINUTES OF MY LIFE WITHOUT THE INCAL!
JOHN! THERE'S SOMETHING COMING!
15

HOW CAN WE FIGHT A MONSTER LIKE THAT WITHOUT WEAPONS?
OH, IT'S PROBABLY JUST A TECHNO-ILLUSION. IT'LL POP IF YOU PRICK IT WITH YOUR BEAK.

I DON'T THINK SO, JOHN! THIS IS SERIOUS! WE'RE GOING TO NEED THE INCAL'S HELP!
NOW!
YOU'RE RIGHT! UM...INCAL?

INCAL! YOU BELONG TO ME! HELP ME KILL THIS MONSTER!
THAT'S AN ORDER!

INCAL! INCAL! PLEASE! ANSWER ME! QUICK!
16

ANIMAH!

INCAL!
ANSWER ME!
WE DON'T HAVE TO ASK NOTHING FROM NO ONE!

?
WE ALREADY WON! THE INCAL MUTATED US INTO THIS NEW FORM!
GO AHEAD! FIGHT THAT PANSY! DISINTEGRATE IT! WE HAVE SUPER POWERS NOW!

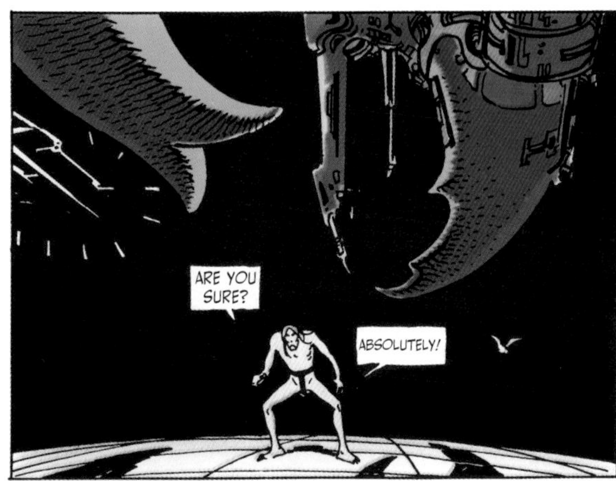
ARE YOU SURE?
ABSOLUTELY!

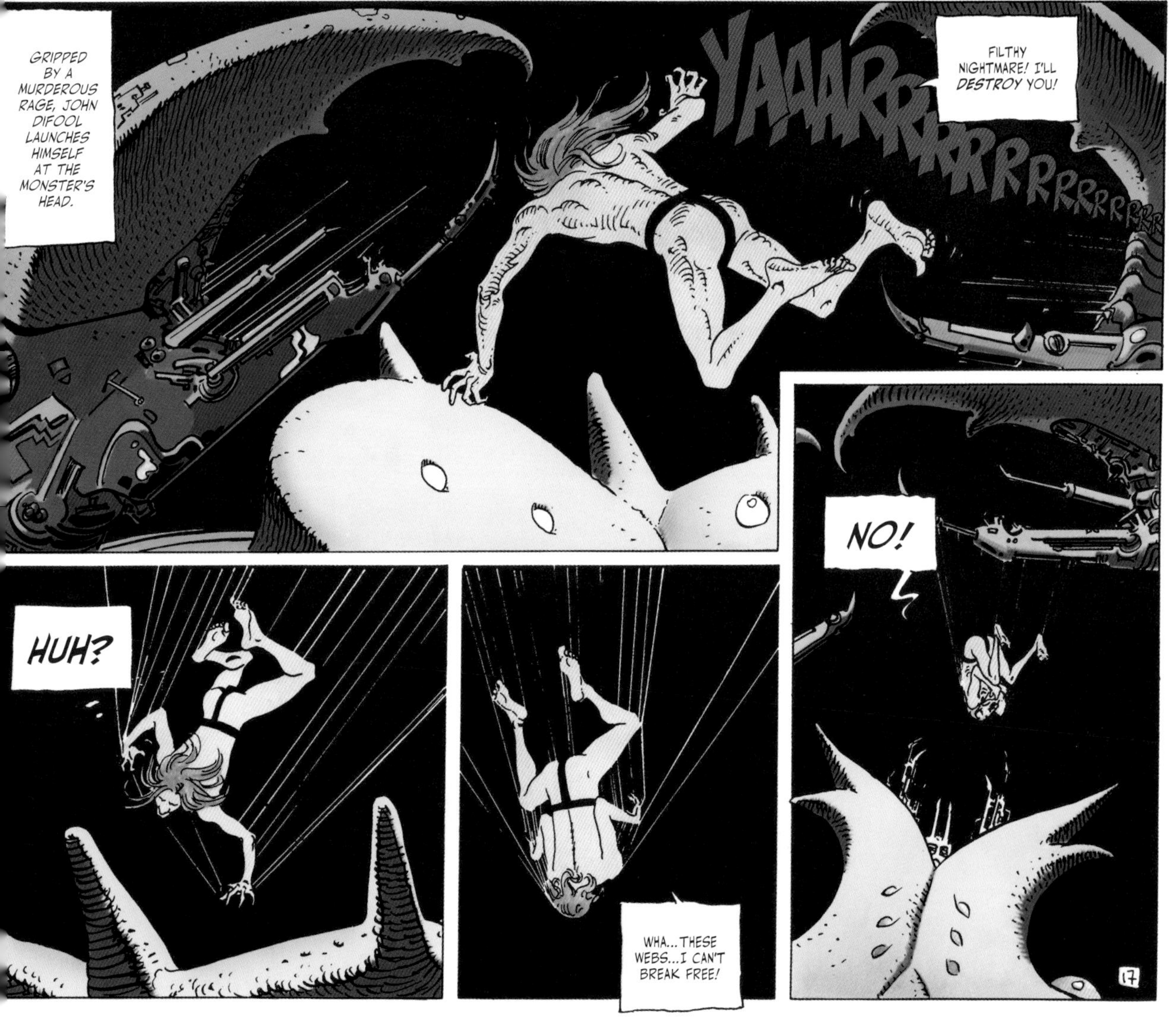
GRIPPED BY A MURDEROUS RAGE, JOHN DIFOOL LAUNCHES HIMSELF AT THE MONSTER'S HEAD.
YAAARRRRRRRRRRRRRR
FILTHY NIGHTMARE! I'LL DESTROY YOU!
NO!
HUH?
WHA...THESE WEBS...I CAN'T BREAK FREE!
17

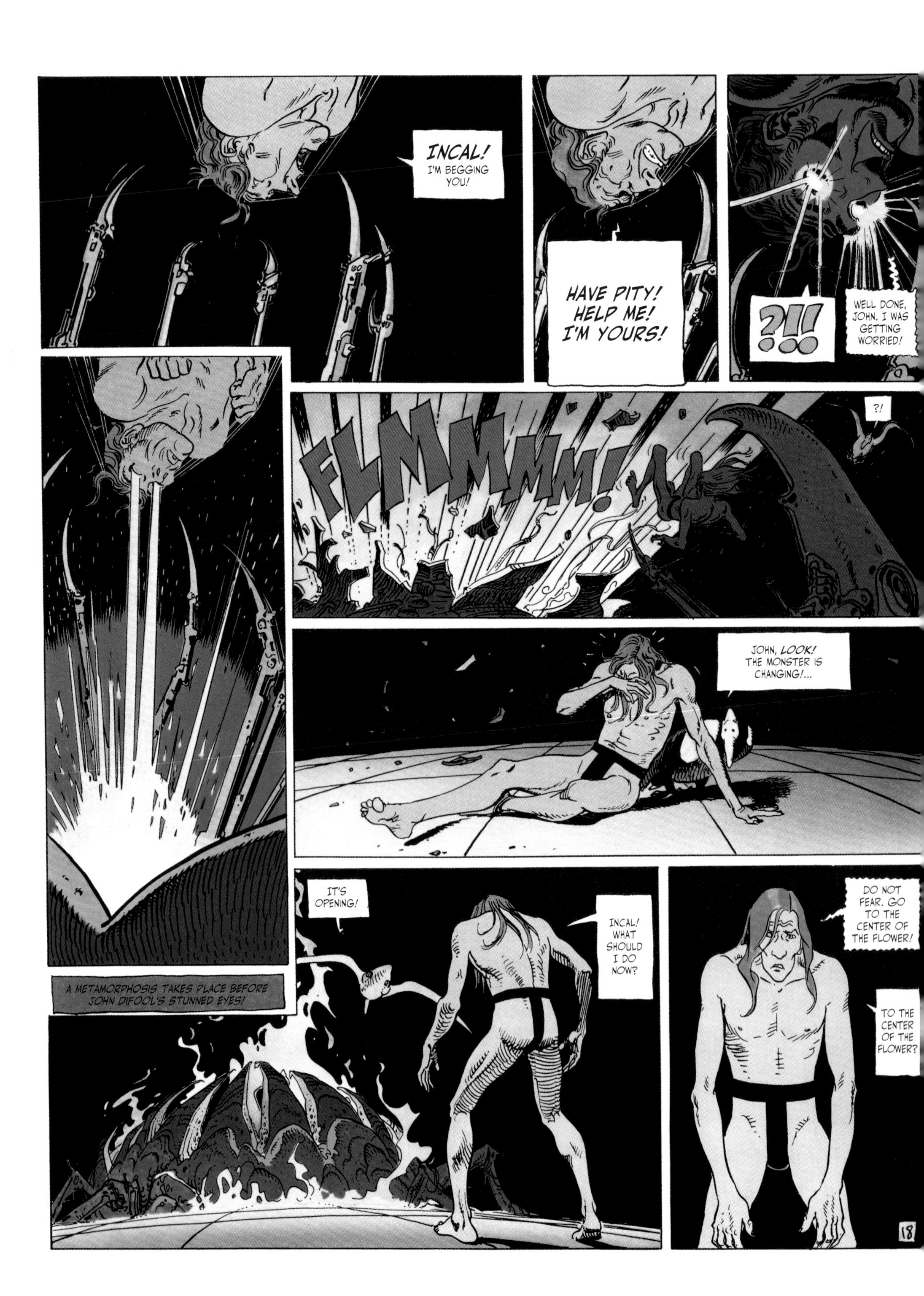
INCAL! I'M BEGGING YOU!
HAVE PITY! HELP ME! I'M YOURS!
?!!
WELL DONE, JOHN. I WAS GETTING WORRIED!
FLMMMM!
?!
JOHN, LOOK! THE MONSTER IS CHANGING!...
A METAMORPHOSIS TAKES PLACE BEFORE JOHN DIFOOL'S STUNNED EYES!
IT'S OPENING!
INCAL! WHAT SHOULD I DO NOW?
DO NOT FEAR. GO TO THE CENTER OF THE FLOWER!
TO THE CENTER OF THE FLOWER?
18

THE REMAINS OF THE GIANT FLOWER WHEEZES, CRACKS, THEN OPENS...
THE BLACK INCAL IS THERE! TAKE IT!
PHEW! IT STINKS!
THE BLACK INCAL! I SEE IT IN THE MIDDLE OF THE ROSE.

MOMENTS LATER IN THE CENTER OF THE TECHNO-TEMPLE.
SSSPROKM
MOTHER DARKNESS! I CAN'T BELIEVE IT! THEY'VE DEFEATED THE CARDIOCLAW!

THE BLACK INCAL IS LOST!

THE END IS UPON US!

19

OUT OF THE WAY! COMING THROUGH!

YOUR SUPREME HIGHNESS! THERE'S BEEN A *DISASTER!* TECHNOCITY HAS JUST BEEN DESTROYED!
WHAT'S THAT, MY GOOD KABOS?

HOW AM I SUPPOSED TO *ENJOY* MYSELF WITH ONE CRISIS AFTER ANOTHER? WHAT A PAIN IN THE ASS!
RIOTS! PLOTS! BERG ASSAULTS! SPIES! THE TECHNOCITY *DESTROYED!*

AND THAT *JOHN DIFOOL* IS STILL ON THE LOOSE! IF I DON'T DO SOMETHING, I'LL END UP LOSING MY GOOD LOOKS! BUT *WHAT* CAN I DO? *WHAT?*
YOUR SUPREME HIGHNESS...I--

BROOOMMMMMM

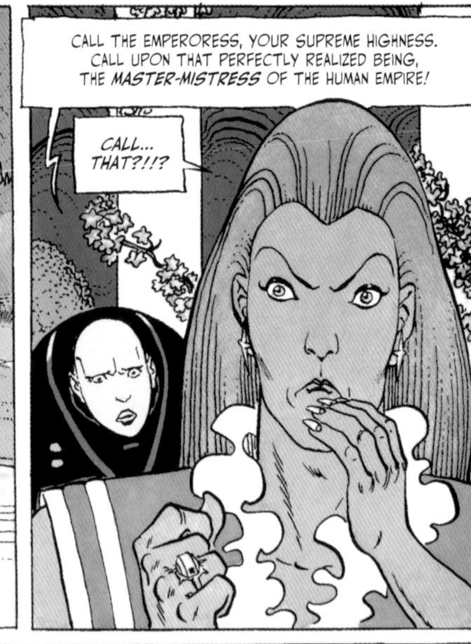
CALL THE EMPERORESS, YOUR SUPREME HIGHNESS. CALL UPON THAT PERFECTLY REALIZED BEING, THE *MASTER-MISTRESS* OF THE HUMAN EMPIRE!
CALL... THAT?!!?

MEANWHILE, FAR AWAY IN THE FROZEN LONELINESS OF THE BLIZZARD-SWEPT ICE PLAINS...
20

WE WERE SO CLOSE. THE PLANET WOULD HAVE BEEN OURS! THE SUN...THE GA-GALAXY! THE UNIVERSE! OUR SACRED UNION WITH THE DARKNESS!
AAARGH...

WHAT...

IT'S...IT'S HIM! AND HE'S ALIVE.
HE IS RESPONSIBLE FOR THIS MISERY!

WE LOST EVERYTHING BECAUSE OF YOU! DIE!

THE TECHNOPOPE!

JOHN DIFOOL!
?!
21

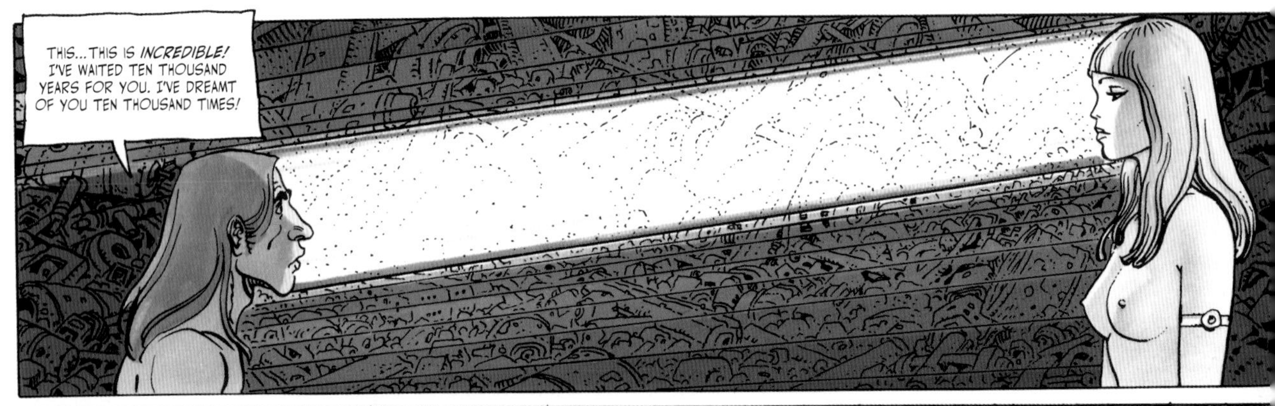
THIS... THIS IS *INCREDIBLE!* I'VE WAITED TEN THOUSAND YEARS FOR YOU. I'VE DREAMT OF YOU TEN THOUSAND TIMES!

22

WHAT IS YOUR NAME?

ANIMAH!

WHEN WILL I SEE YOU AGAIN?

YOU IDIOT! NEVER! YOU CHUMP! YOU GAVE HER THE BLACK INCAL! JUST LIKE THAT! A PRECIOUS TREASURE THAT NEARLY COST US OUR LIVES!
YOU HEARTLESS MONSTER! YOU LET ANIMAH GET AWAY! NOW WE MIGHT AS WELL JUST LIE DOWN AND DIE, BROKEN-HEARTED.

GIVE ME BACK MY INCAL, BITCH!
MY BELOVED! COME BACK! DON'T LEAVE ME ALONE!

COME BACK!

OOPS!

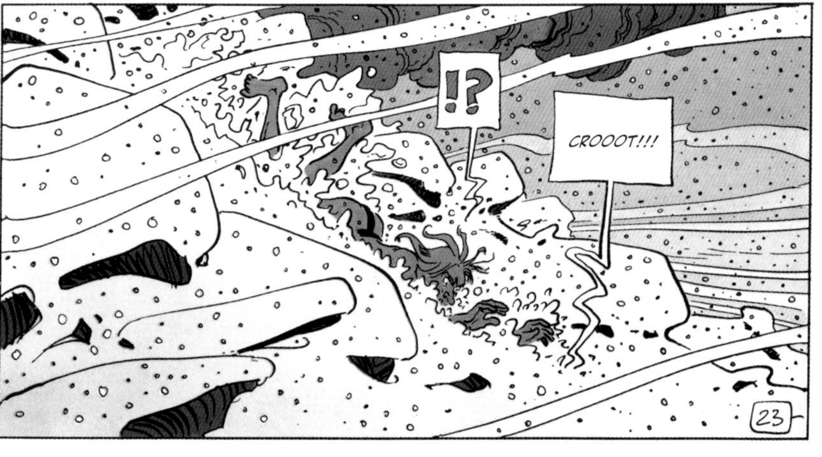
!?
CROOOT!!!
23

NO! POOR OLD DEEPO!
SO THAT'S WHERE YOU WERE!
CROOT...
YEAH, I WAS RIGHT HERE...
HOLY CONCRETE, JOHN!!! I THINK WE ACTUALLY SURVIVED AGAIN!
I'LL TAKE YOU BACK INSIDE WHERE THERE'S SHELTER. YOU'RE NOT HURT? NOTHING'S BROKEN?
I'M OKAY, I'M OKAY! I JUST NEED TO CLEAN THIS MUD OFF.
SHE SAVED US. SHE'S THE ONE.
JOHN!
BEHIND YOU!
?!
WHAT IS IT NOW?
I AM THE METABARON AND I HAVE BEEN SENT TO KILL JOHN DIFOOL!
JODO-MOEBIUS
24

DEPREZZIVE CLASS STRUGGLE

SCRIPT: JODOROWSKY
ART: MŒBIUS
MEANWHILE...
THE REBELS ARE PLOTTING SOMETHING, BOSS!
AND HIS SUPREME HIGHNESS CAN'T DECIDE IF HE SHOULD CALL THE EMPERORESS!
ARE YOU READY FOR THE NUCLEO-TACTICAL?
READY!
OKAY...FIRE!
EVERYTHING'S SHAKING!
ACTIVATE THE GYROSCOPES!
GROBOUM!
DAMN THEM! THEY USED A NUCLEO!
THEY'VE VIOLATED THE TREATY!
VICTORY! WE'VE BREACHED THE HULL!
ATTACK!
KEEP FILMING, FOR GOD'S SAKE!
FOR AMOK!
25

DEAR TELEFRIENDS, TODAY WE BEAR WITNESS TO SOME TRULY SPECTACULAR CARNAGE. OVER A MILLION RIOTERS ARE RUSHING THE GAPING HOLE THAT THE NUCLEO BLAST HAS RIPPED INSIDE OF THE FLYING PALACE.
WHY DON'T WE TAKE THE PALACE BACK UP?
IMPOSSIBLE! THAT DAMN BOMB DAMAGED OUR STABILIZERS!

ONWARD FOR THE BLUE SEDENTARISTS!

IONIST PHALANXES, FOLLOW ME!

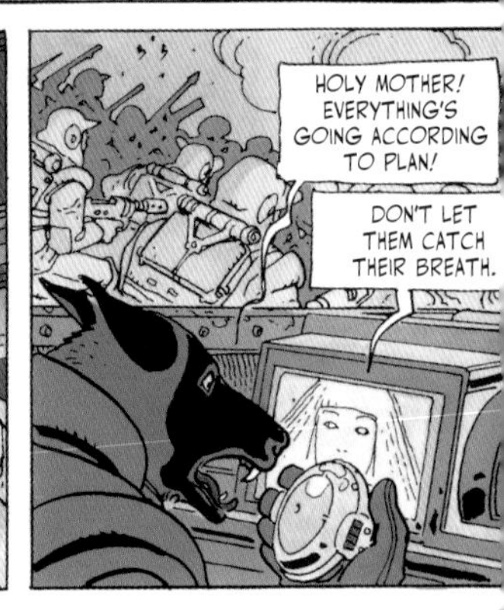
HOLY MOTHER! EVERYTHING'S GOING ACCORDING TO PLAN!
DON'T LET THEM CATCH THEIR BREATH.

GET A TIGHTER SHOT OF THE BOMBING!
GIVE HIM SOME TEARS!
DON'T FORGET THE FAKE BURNS!

DEAR TELEFRIENDS! YOU'RE LUCKY TO BE SAFE AND SNUG IN YOUR CONAPTS AS YOU WATCH THIS INCREDIBLY MASSIVE RIOT ON YOUR HOLOVIDS!

BUT OUT HERE MEN ARE FIGHTING... FOR THEIR FREEDOM, FOR THEIR RIGHT TO RISE TO THE SURFACE...FOR THEIR RIGHT TO FREE SPV...AND EVEN FOR THEIR RIGHT TO RIOT!
NOW LET'S GO TO A DIRECT BROADCAST OF OUR RIOTERS' ATTEMPT TO TAKE THE PREZIDENTIAL PALACE! THE BROADCAST WILL, OF COURSE, INCLUDE SEVERAL ADVERTISING POPUPS FROM OUR SPONSORS!
26

LONG LIVE THE ARISTOS!
CRIMINALS!
BASTARDS!
SCUM!
HOUU HOUU!
WHADDA WE DO WITH THESE ARISTO PRISONERS, BOSS?
CUT OFF THEIR HEADS IN THE NAME OF THE POLYFINALIST FRONT!
HEY, ANDREBER, WHY DON'T WE SEND IN SOME MORE TROOPS FROM THIS SIDE?
HMMM...NO... AMOK HOLDS THAT SECTOR! WE SHOULD GO IN FROM THE HOSPITAL-INCUBATOR SECTOR INSTEAD!

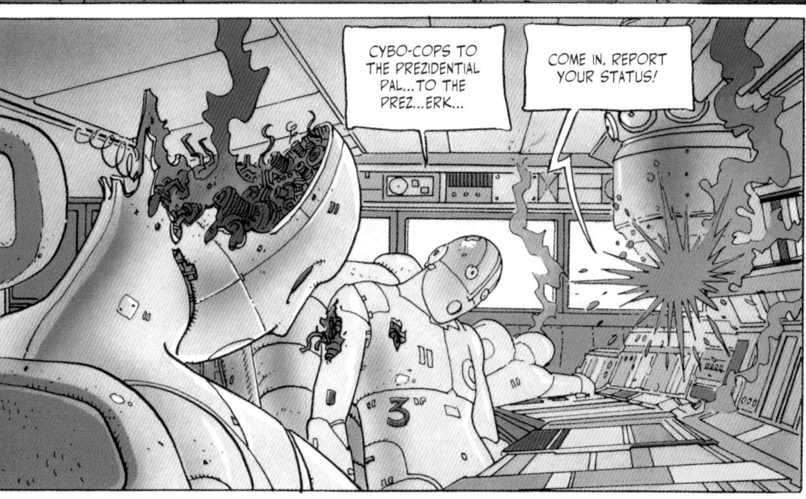
CYBO-COPS TO THE PREZIDENTIAL PAL...TO THE PREZ...ERK...
COME IN. REPORT YOUR STATUS!

NO LUCK! THE CYBO-COPS' CONNECTION IS DEAD!
BY MY HUMP, LOOK! THERE'S A RED ALERT ON EVERY SCREEN!

BY THE ALL POWERFUL! THE VERMIN HAVE DESTROYED THE SHIELDS AND THE LASER BATTERIES. THEY'RE COMING IN!
LAUNCH THE GRAPPLE LINES!
27

THEY'RE USING TECHNO-TECHNO EQUIPMENT!! WE'VE BEEN BETRAYED!
ALERT HIS SUPREME HIGHNESS! THIS SITUATION IS BEYOND CRITICAL!

WE'LL HAVE TO USE THE HYPER-HALO!
BUT...IT WILL BE HORRIFIC!

WHAT'S THAT GLOWING DISK SPINNING DOWN FROM THE BASE?!
ZGBZZZGB
SHIT! THE HYPER-HALO! WE'RE DEAD!
GET BACK!
RUN!
NO! KEEP GOING! AMOK IS PREPARED FOR THIS!

AMOK SOLDIERS! PREPARE FOR BATTLE! ACTIVATE YOUR PERSONAL INVERTERS!
28

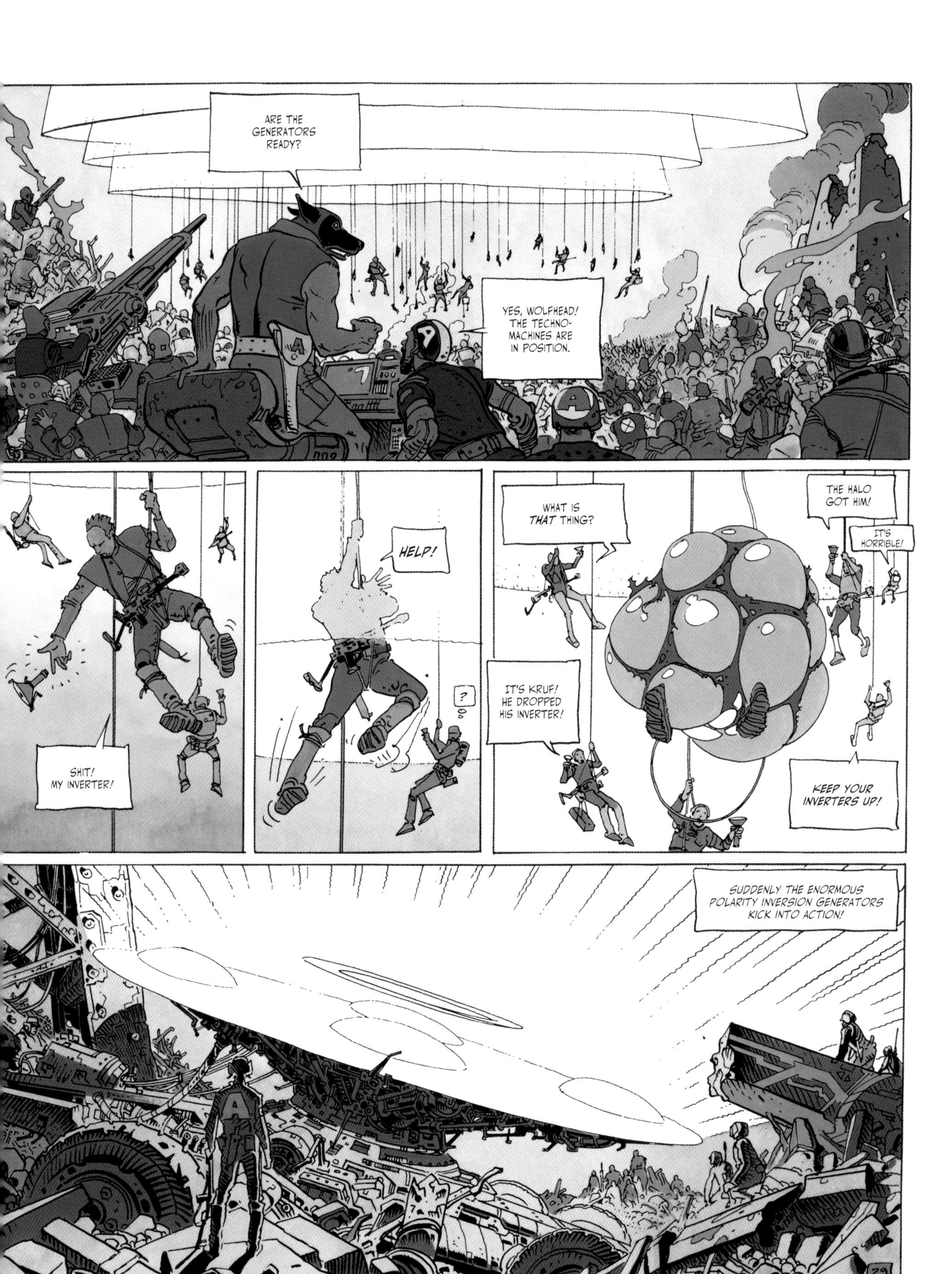
ARE THE GENERATORS READY?
YES, WOLFHEAD! THE TECHNO-MACHINES ARE IN POSITION.
SHIT! MY INVERTER!
HELP!
?
WHAT IS THAT THING?
IT'S KRUF! HE DROPPED HIS INVERTER!
THE HALO GOT HIM!
IT'S HORRIBLE!
KEEP YOUR INVERTERS UP!
SUDDENLY THE ENORMOUS POLARITY INVERSION GENERATORS KICK INTO ACTION!
29

MEANWHILE... NEAR THE TOP OF THE FLYING PALACE.
HA HA HA!
HEE HEE! YOU'RE TICKLING ME!
ANOTHER DRINK! HA HA! ANOTHER!
LET'S SMOKE THIS GRASS!
LET'S SNORT THIS POWDER!
MMM...THIS DRAGONFLY SOUFFLE IS SUBLIME!
PERFECT!
OOH! THE KILLINGS ON HOLOVID RIGHT NOW ARE ABSOLUTELY DIVINE!
IF RIOTS DIDN'T EXIST, WE'D HAVE TO INVENT THEM!
YOUR...YOUR SUPREME...
YOUR SUPREME HIGH-HIGHNESS!
THE REBELS HAVE DEFEATED THE HA-THE HALO!
WHO TOLD YOU TO INTERRUPT MY TEA PARTY, DOG!
30

MOVE YOUR FAT ASS, PIG...AND WARN THE EMP...
OOH! SACRILEGE!
...PEROR...
GLUG
HE THREW SOMETHING ON THE TABLE!
THE HALO SICKNESS!
!?!
AAAH! OOOH!
THAT INSOLENT HUNCHBACK IS FLYING!
HEE HEE! HOW FUNNY!
?
DAMN!
THE ROYAL TRANSMITTER IS RINGING!
TRIPLE DAMN! HIS/HER HIGHNESS, THE EMPERORESS IS CALLING ME. HE/SHE'S DEMANDING MY PRESENCE!
MEANWHILE...
WELL, THEY'VE REALLY DONE IT NOW. THEY HIT THE PALACE WITH A NUCLEO. A PAGE HAS TURNED.
HMM...IT WON'T BE EASY TO GET IN THERE, BUT I HAVE TO BRING THESE BODIES BACK TO THAT CRAZY BITCH FROM AMOK!
31

LET'S SEE WHAT MY SCANNERS SAY.

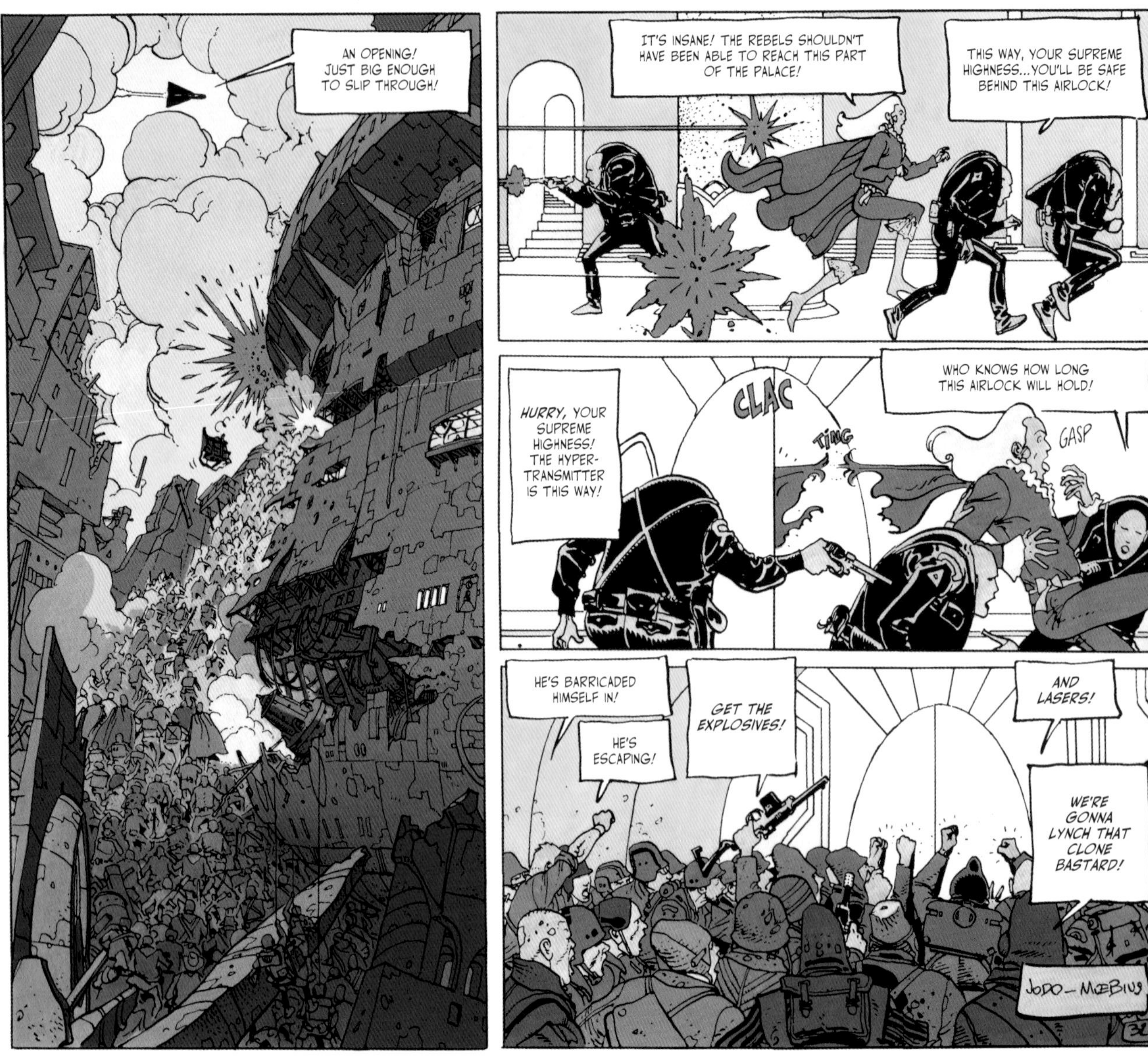
AN OPENING! JUST BIG ENOUGH TO SLIP THROUGH!
IT'S INSANE! THE REBELS SHOULDN'T HAVE BEEN ABLE TO REACH THIS PART OF THE PALACE!
THIS WAY, YOUR SUPREME HIGHNESS...YOU'LL BE SAFE BEHIND THIS AIRLOCK!
HURRY, YOUR SUPREME HIGHNESS! THE HYPER-TRANSMITTER IS THIS WAY!
CLAC
TING
WHO KNOWS HOW LONG THIS AIRLOCK WILL HOLD!
GASP
HE'S BARRICADED HIMSELF IN!
HE'S ESCAPING!
GET THE EXPLOSIVES!
AND LASERS!
WE'RE GONNA LYNCH THAT CLONE BASTARD!
JODO — MŒBIUS

EMPERORESS

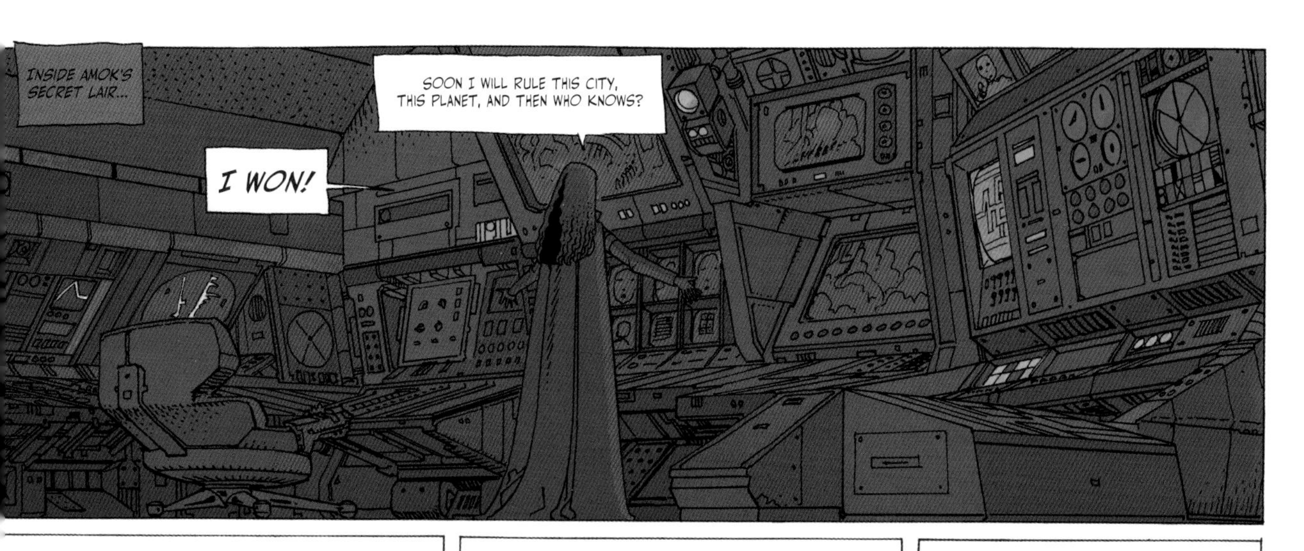
INSIDE AMOK'S SECRET LAIR...
SOON I WILL RULE THIS CITY, THIS PLANET, AND THEN WHO KNOWS?
I WON!

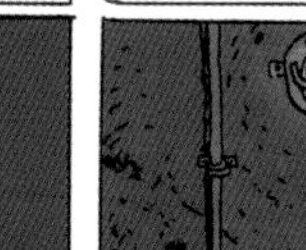
THAT PUPPET PRESIDENT IS POWERLESS IN HIS FLYING CASTLE AND SOON MY REBEL PAWNS WILL BOW AT MY FEET.

AND NOW I HAVE THE LUMINOUS INCAL. ALL I HAVE TO DO IS REUNITE IT WITH THAT MORONIC TECHNOPOPE'S BLACK INCAL.

AND MY POWER WILL KNOW NO BOUNDS!

LIFE SIGNS ARE TOTALLY FLAT, SIR.
THE MAN IS DEAD, HOLY MOTHER!
TOO BAD! WOLFHEAD WILL MISS OUT ON HIS REVENGE.
OPEN THE BODY IMMEDIATELY.
23

?
STOP!
FIRST AMOK MUST RESPECT OUR AGREEMENT. GIVE ME MY SON, SOLUNE!

YOU STILL HAVEN'T BREACHED THAT DAMN DOOR?
NOBODY IS PENETRATING THE IMPERIAL ALLOY!

THE METAL IS HEATING UP, BUT IT'S STILL HOLDING!
THEY'LL FIND A WAY! AT LEAST HIS SUPREME HIGHNESS IS FINALLY TALKING TO THE EMPERORESS!

IDIOT!

YOU FOOL! THIS MISERABLE SECTOR OF THE GALAXY HAS ALWAYS BEEN THE SHAME OF THE EMPIRE! AND NOW, BECAUSE OF YOU, YOU PIG...

...IT'S TURNED INTO A DOOR! A WIDE OPEN DOOR...
...FOR THE DARK HORRORS, THE INTRACOSMIC FORCES OF PUTREFACTION AND DESTRUCTION! WHAT DO YOU HAVE TO SAY FOR YOURSELF?
UH...
34

LET THE ULTRASONIC BAZOOKA THROUGH. IT'LL OPEN THIS DAMN DOOR!
WOW! THE ULTRASONIC BAZOOKA!
CKNOWLEDGE L MY FAULTS! YOUR EGAHOLINESS IS RIGHT A THOUSAND TIMES OVER, BUT HURRY!
WHAT SHOULD I DO? TELL ME BEFORE THE REBELS BREAK THROUGH THE DOOR AND LYNCH ME!
IMPOTENT WORM! YOU'LL LISTEN TO ME UNTIL I'M DONE! YOU'RE RIGHT, YOU NEED TO DO SOMETHING! BUT FIRST, THINK ABOUT THE HARM YOU'VE CAUSED WITH YOUR INFINITE FOOLISHNESS!
"FIRST, THE BERG ARMADA FINALLY DECIDED TO ATTACK THE EMPIRE. WE DETECTED ITS HYPERSPACIAL FLIGHT ONLY ONCE ITS EMERGENCE INTO NORMAL SPACE WAS ALREADY A NEAR CERTAINTY. IT WAS A THIRD OF A LIGHT YEAR FROM YOUR SOLAR SYSTEM! COINCIDENCE? WE THINK NOT."
"WE WATCHED THE DESTRUCTION OF YOUR TECHNOCITY! WE WATCHED THE RIOTS! BUT THERE'S WORSE! MAJOR DISTURBANCES IN YOUR SUN'S CORONA. SUNSPOTS AND UNUSUALLY VIOLENT ERUPTIONS."
"WE BELIEVE THEY HAVE BEEN CAUSED BY A STRANGE OBJECT THAT HAS JUST BEEN PLACED IN SOLAR ORBIT."
"HOW? WHY?..."
...WHO LAUNCHED IT? HOW DO WE DESTROY IT?
THAT'S WHAT YOU HAVE TO FIND OUT, BUT DO NOT FEAR! I WILL GIVE YOU THE MEANS!

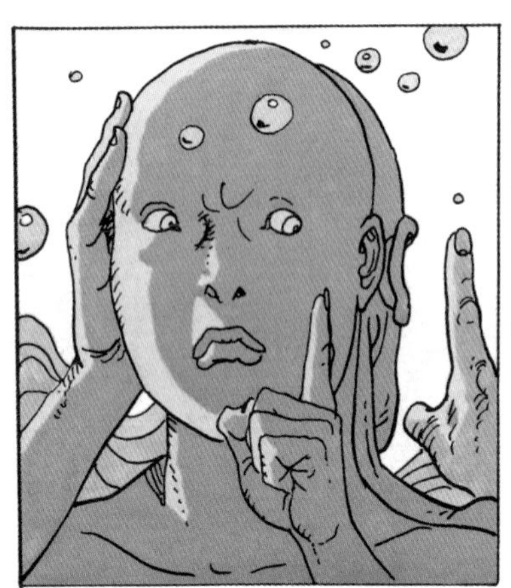

WAIT! SOMETHING IS HAPPENING THAT I DON'T UNDERSTAND! I FEEL AN UNFAMILIAR ENERGY IN YOUR SECTOR. A DEVELOPING CONSCIOUSNESS SUPERIOR TO OUR OWN!
HE/SHE FEELS THE INCAL!

SIGH...ANOTHER RIOT SHOW! THIS IS GETTING BORING.
THE BAZOOKA ISN'T WORKING! BRING IN SOME ANTIMATTER BOMBS!
MEANWHILE, IN THE CONAPTS...
THAT WOLFHEAD'S HYSTERICAL!
NO IT ISN'T, NAD! IT'S REALLY INTERESTING. THEY'RE TRYING TO LYNCH THE PREZIDENT NOW!

GIVE HIM TO YOU? NEVER. FIRST OF ALL, HE'S NOT YOUR REAL SON AND YOU KNOW IT! BESIDES, HE'S A MONSTER!...
SOLUNE!

...ONCE HIS POWERS FULLY DEVELOP, HE'LL GET IN MY WAY SOONER OR LATER.
SO, YOU UNDERSTAND, MY ONLY ALTERNATIVE...
...IS TO KILL YOU! GUARDS!

...KILL THE METABARON! KILL SOLUNE! SLICE OPEN THAT CORPSE!
36

STOFFFF
STFFFFF
STOOTF

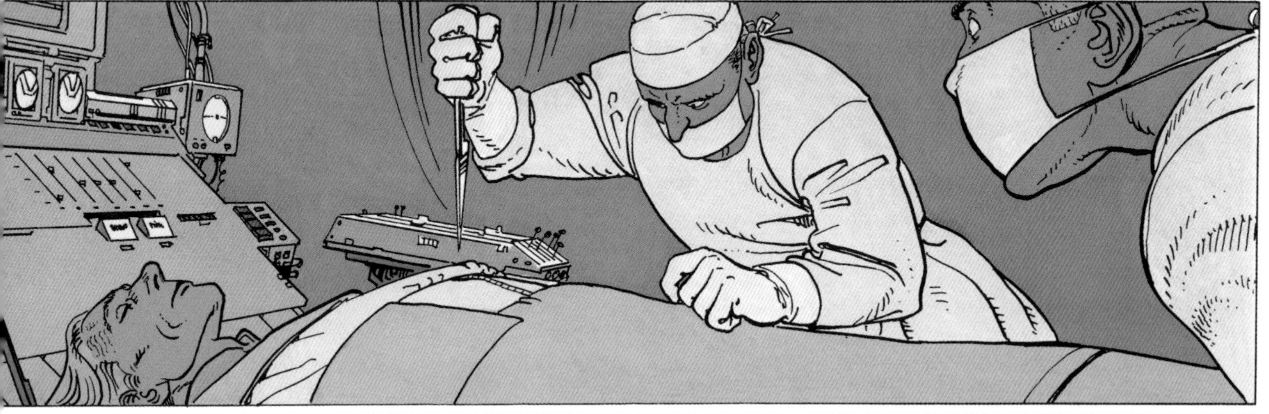

"THE IMPERIAL FLEET IS ON ITS WAY TO WIPE OUT THE BERGS AND THE MYSTERIOUS BLACK EGG...THIS IS THE END OF THE LONG PERIOD OF UNIVERSAL PEACE. WE ARE NOW ENTERING OUR FIRST GREAT INTERGALACTIC WAR."

NOW LISTEN, THIS IS WHAT YOU'RE GOING TO DO...
37

SOON AFTER...
BMM
ATTACK!
WATCH OUT FOR THE HUNCHBACKS!
DIE!
AAAARGH!

THIS WAY!
IT'S THE ONLY PLACE HE COULD BE HIDING!

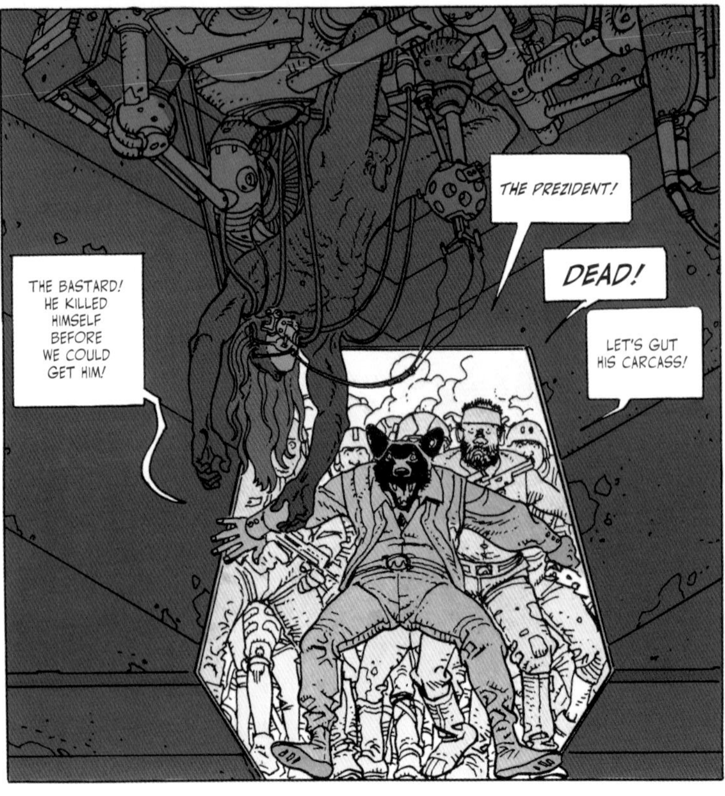
THE PREZIDENT!
DEAD!
THE BASTARD! HE KILLED HIMSELF BEFORE WE COULD GET HIM!
LET'S GUT HIS CARCASS!

QUIET!!! THERE'S SOMETHING HERE...SOMETHING I DON'T LIKE!

DEAR TELEFRIENDS! YOU MAY BE SNUG AS A BUG IN YOUR CONAPT'S RUG, BUT HERE'S A MOMENT OF GREAT SUSPENSE. WOLFHEAD'S NOSE IS POINTING EVERY WHICH WAY. HE SMELLS TROUBLE!

SUDDENLY...
CLCLCRR..
AT LAST! VERMIN!
HA HA HA!!
VERMIN FOR ME TO EXTERMINATE!
A TRAP!
RUN FOR YOUR LIVES!
THE...THE NECRODROID! THE LEGENDARY, INVINCIBLE KILLING MACHINE! SO, THIS IS THE ULTIMATE PREZIDENTIAL CLONE! HIDE IN YOUR CONAPTS, DEAR TELEFRIENDS, IF YOU WANT TO STAY ALIVE!
AT THAT VERY MOMENT, DEEP IN THE CITY-SHAFT.
ARGH!
THE... THE BODY!
GACK!
?
I'VE BEEN BETRAYED! JOHN DIFOOL IS ALIVE!
INCREDIBLE!
?!!
HE'S GETTING AWAY!
STOOTF!!
STOTF
ROOMMMMM
HEY! WHERE'S THE BRAT?
I HAD HIM A SECOND AGO.
THERE!
?!
39

KILL THEM! EVERY EXIT IS SEALED! THERE'S NO ESCAPE!
JOHN DIFOOL, IT'S TIME TO PROVE THAT THE INCAL HAS TRULY MUTATED YOUR BIO-SYSTEM!
BUT FATHER, WHAT CAN WE DO AGAINST AN ARMY?
WE CAN FIGHT THEM. AND PERHAPS WE CAN WIN...
PERHAPS...
MEANWHILE...
KILL! KILL!
I'VE ALREADY EXTERMINATED OVER A HUNDRED THOUSAND! SOON EVERY REBEL WILL BE DEAD! HA HA HA! THEN I'LL TAKE CARE OF THE INCAL. I CAN FEEL IT MOVING DOWN THERE. HA HA! THIS NEW BODY DOESN'T LACK SENSUALITY AFTER ALL!
HOLY MOTHER!
40

HOLY MOTHER! ALL IS LOST. THEY'VE UNLEASHED THE NECRODROID!
THE NECRODROID !?!?
!!?

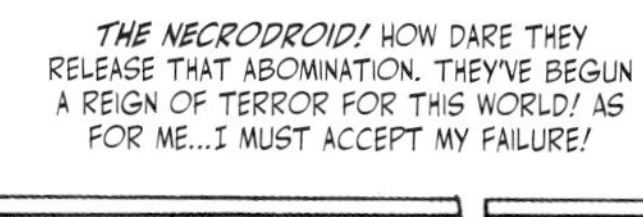
THE NECRODROID! HOW DARE THEY RELEASE THAT ABOMINATION. THEY'VE BEGUN A REIGN OF TERROR FOR THIS WORLD! AS FOR ME...I MUST ACCEPT MY FAILURE!

WHAT HAPPENED TO THE AMOK GUARDS?
THEY MET THREE WARRIORS!

BUT WE'VE STILL GOT ONE CARD LEFT TO PLAY... JOHN DIFOOL. YOU SHOULD HAVE BOTH OF THE INCALS IN YOUR POSSESSION. HERE'S WHAT WE'RE GOING TO DO...

I DON'T HAVE THE BLACK INCAL ANYMORE.
?
WHAT? WHERE IS IT?

I GAVE IT TO A WOMAN.
"GAVE IT TO A WOMAN?"
?
?
?

?
HER NAME IS ANIMAH.
HER! I THOUGHT SO! NICE MOVE! SO, I HAVE NO CHOICE NOW.
ANIMAH! MY MOTHER... AT LAST!
ANIMAH! THE RAT QUEEN!

SO!
WITHOUT THE BLACK INCAL, YOUR LUMINOUS INCAL IS POWERLESS AGAINST THE NECRODROID. IF YOU WANT TO LIVE, THERE'S ONLY ONE OPTION: WE JOIN FORCES AND RUN!
FOLLOW ME!

WE'RE MOVING FURTHER AWAY FROM THE SURFACE?
OUR SALVATION LIES BELOW!
HEY! THE GROUND IS SHAKING!

BUT THERE'S NOTHING THIS DEEP EXCEPT THE ACID LAKE!
SO EVERYONE BELIEVES...
WATCH OUT FO FALLING ROCKS

IN TRUTH, THERE IS A VAST WORLD AT THE CENTER OF THE PLANET, BENEATH THE ACID LAKE. THE GREAT CRYSTAL CAVERNS...PYRAMID ISLAND... ANIMAH AND I CAME FROM THIS SECRET WORLD.
ARE YOU SISTERS, THEN?

PERCEPTIVE! YES, WE ARE. WE ARE ALSO THE GUARDIANS OF THE TWO INCALS. BUT DARKNESS LURED ME DOWN ANOTHER PATH! I STOLE THE BLACK INCAL AND CAME TO THE SURFACE TO GAIN POWER!

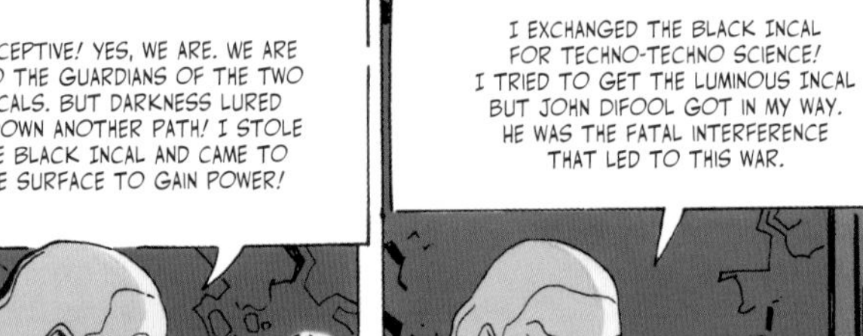
I EXCHANGED THE BLACK INCAL FOR TECHNO-TECHNO SCIENCE! I TRIED TO GET THE LUMINOUS INCAL BUT JOHN DIFOOL GOT IN MY WAY. HE WAS THE FATAL INTERFERENCE THAT LED TO THIS WAR.

AMOK'S SECRET BUNKER!
I THOUGHT I COULD WIN BUT, ULTIMATELY, I FAILED! NOW I HAVE TO RETURN BELOW. WHATEVER THE COST...

...THE TWO INCALS *MUST BE* REUNITED!
LOOK! THAT'S THE NECRODROID! IT'S DESTROYING OUR ARMY SINGLE-HANDEDLY!

CRRRK
ARE YOU THERE, MY FAITHFUL SERVANTS?

WHO GOES THERE?
IT IS I, TANATAH!
HOLY MOTHER, LOOK OUT!

SCCROOMM!
?
THE... THE ROOF IS CAVING IN!

THE COLLAPSE OPENED THE WALL!
CROOT!
THERE! THE ACID LAKE!
AND THE METACRAFT!
MY POOR SERVANTS!

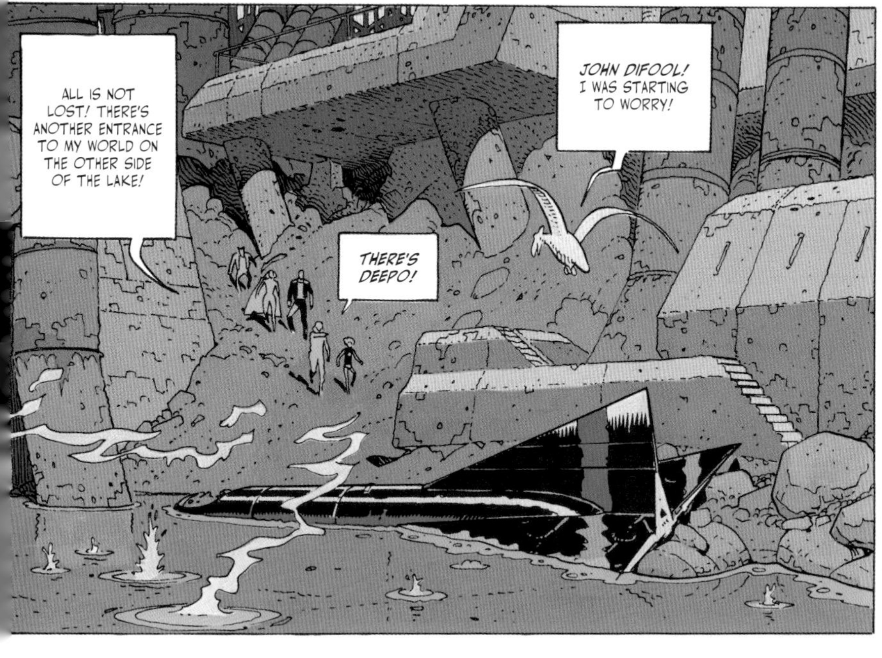
ALL IS NOT LOST! THERE'S ANOTHER ENTRANCE TO MY WORLD ON THE OTHER SIDE OF THE LAKE!
JOHN DIFOOL! I WAS STARTING TO WORRY!
THERE'S DEEPO!

A BUNCH OF ROCKS FELL ON THE METACRAFT. IT REALLY SHOOK ME UP.
DAMN! THE ENGINE IS RUINED!
43

HELP ME PUSH!
WITH NO ENGINE?

WE'LL FIRE MAGNETIC GRAPPLING HOOKS INTO THE SUPERSTRUCTURE, THEN PULL OURSELVES ACROSS!

SOON...

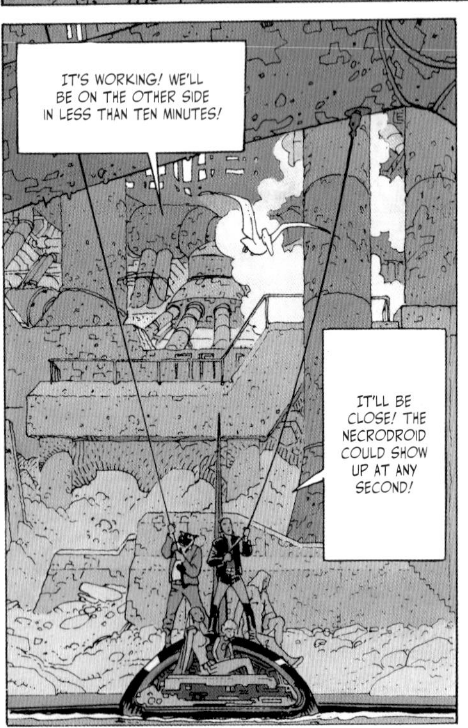
IT'S WORKING! WE'LL BE ON THE OTHER SIDE IN LESS THAN TEN MINUTES!
IT'LL BE CLOSE! THE NECRODROID COULD SHOW UP AT ANY SECOND!

FASTER!
DAMMIT! THE ACID IS EATING AWAY AT THE METACRAFT'S HULL.
THAT'S NOT ALL. I FEEL A CURRENT PULLING US!
IMPOSSIBLE! THE ACID LAKE DOESN'T HAVE...
LOOK OVER THERE!

A-A WHIRLPOOL!
THERE'S NO WAY TO FIGHT IT!
THIS TIME...
THERE'S NOTHING WE CAN DO! THE CURRENT IS TOO STRONG!
THIS TIME WE'RE DOOMED!
CROOOT!
THIS IS AWFUL!
INCAL!
45

INCAL! DON'T ABANDON ME!
INCAL !!!

WHAT LIES BENEATH

PSYCHORATS

I THINK THE INCAL'S REALLY ABANDONED ME THIS TIME! WE'RE DEAD!
THIS WHIRLPOOL HAS TO LEAD SOMEWHERE!

IT'S A HUGE UNDERGROUND RIVER!

I JUST HOPE THE SHIP CAN WITHSTAND THE ACID!

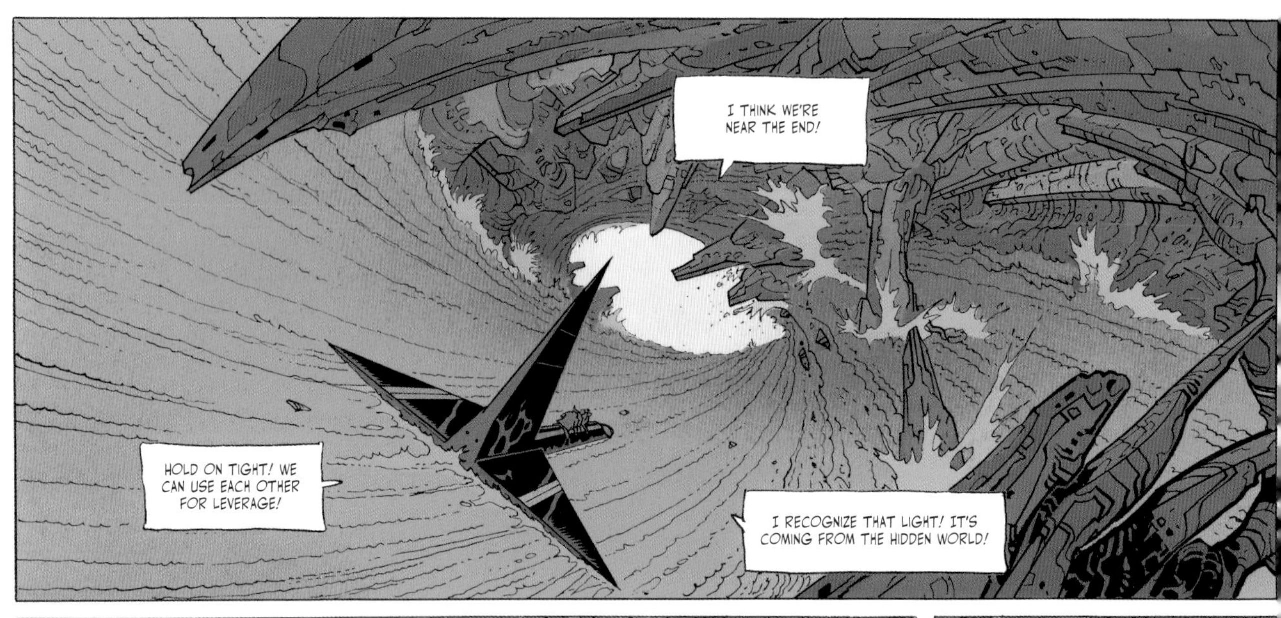
I THINK WE'RE NEAR THE END!
HOLD ON TIGHT! WE CAN USE EACH OTHER FOR LEVERAGE!
I RECOGNIZE THAT LIGHT! IT'S COMING FROM THE HIDDEN WORLD!

WE MADE IT!
I WOULDN'T BE SO SURE OF THAT...
NOW WHAT?
THIS IS IT! WE'RE GOING TO CRASH!

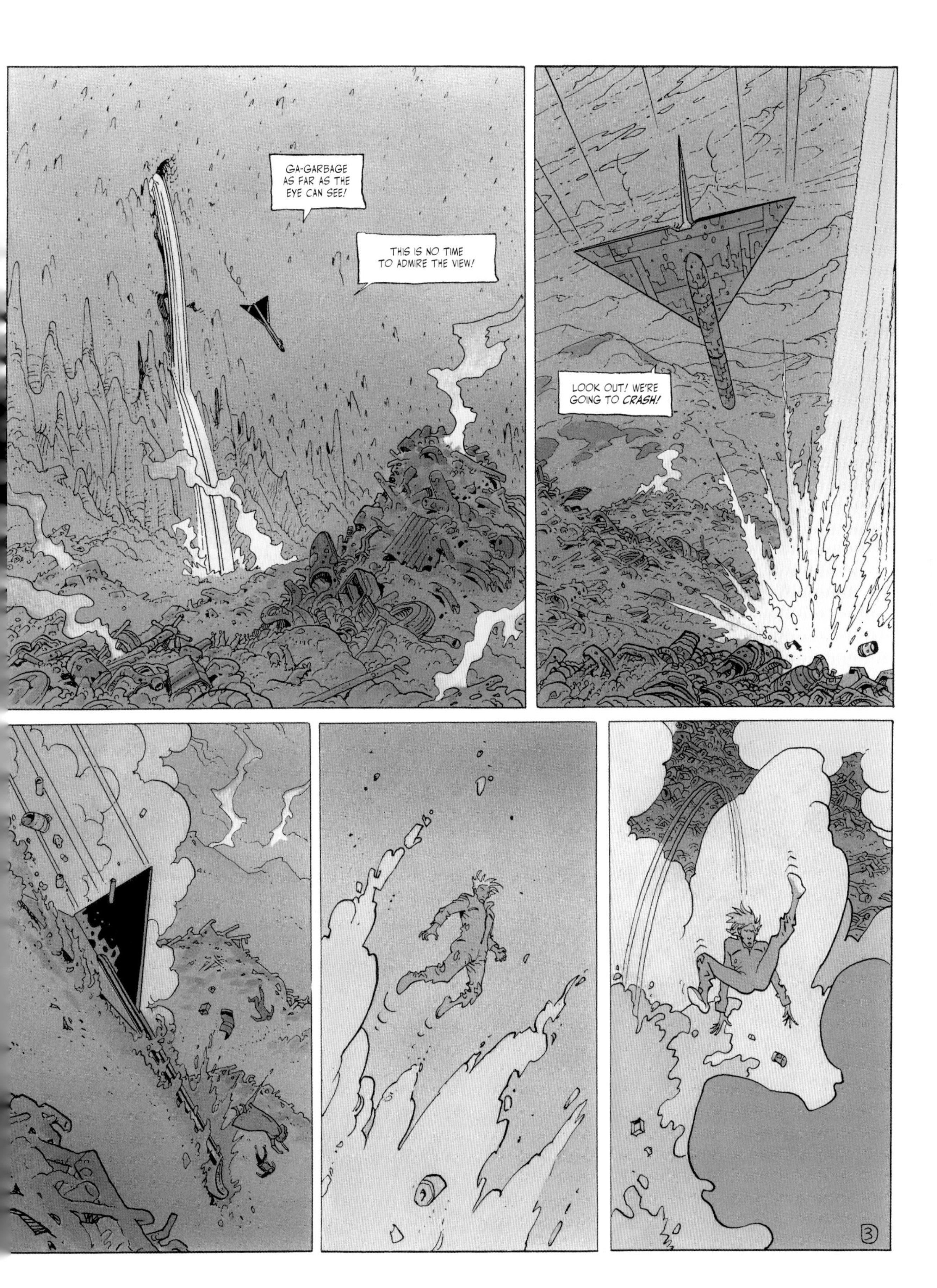
GA-GARBAGE AS FAR AS THE EYE CAN SEE!
THIS IS NO TIME TO ADMIRE THE VIEW!
LOOK OUT! WE'RE GOING TO CRASH!
3

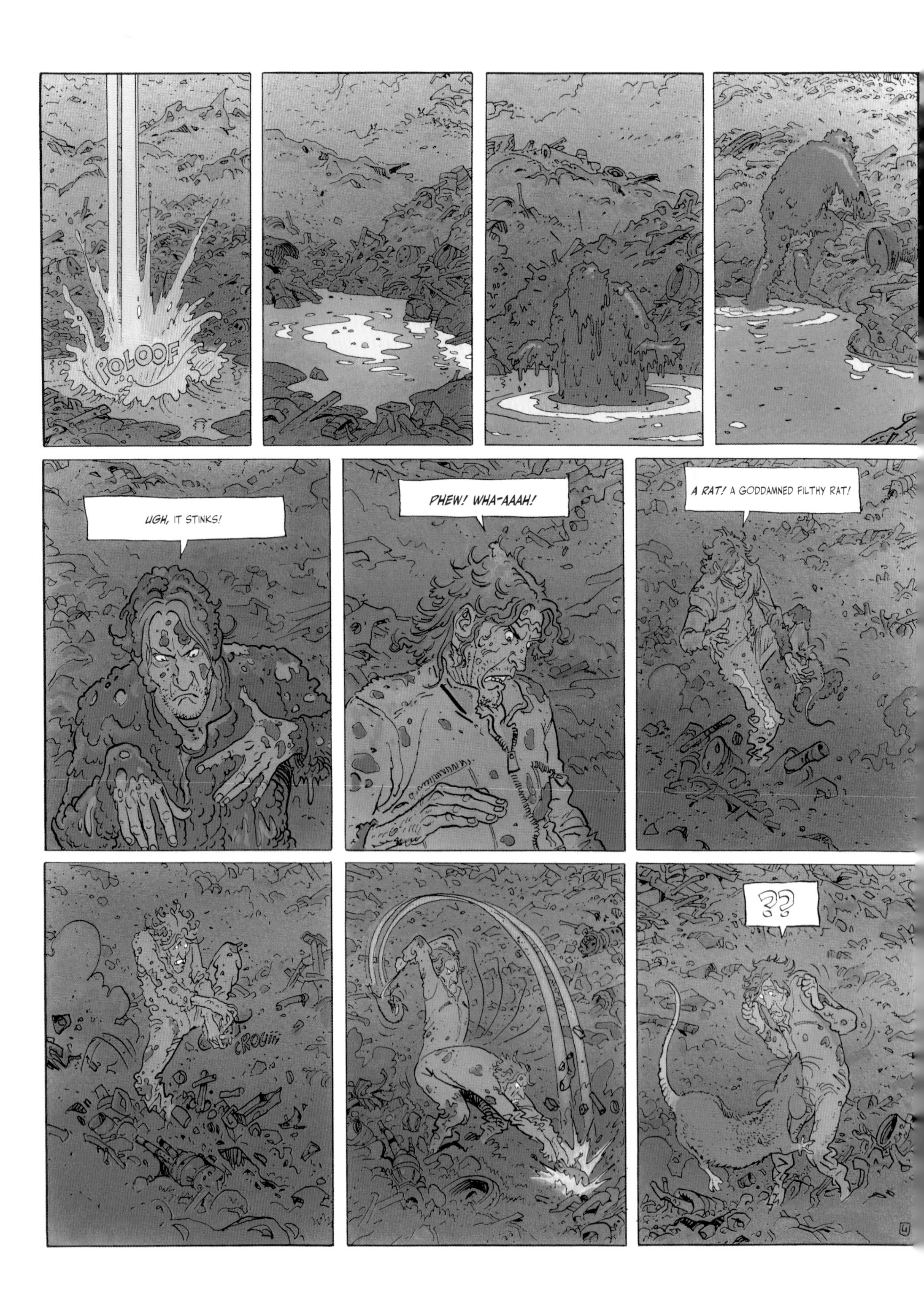
POLOOF
UGH, IT STINKS!
PHEW! WHA-AAAH!
A RAT! A GODDAMNED FILTHY RAT!
CROUIII
??

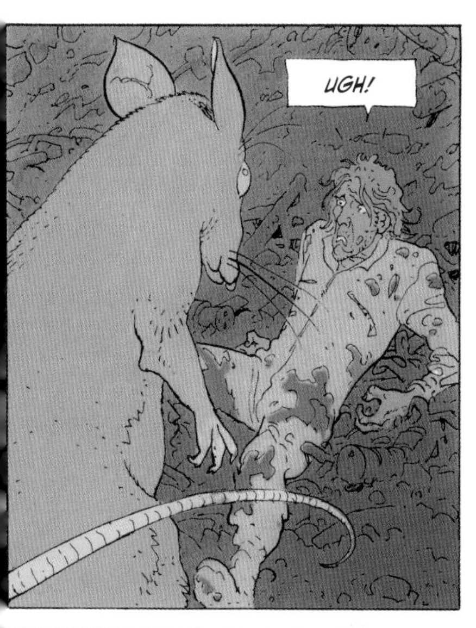
UGH!

OOH NOOOO!
HOLY SHIT!

WHERE CAN I HIDE? THERE'S GARBAGE EVERYWHERE!

COME ON, YOU BASTARDS!
NO, JOHN! USE THE INCAL! IT'S OUR ONLY CHANCE!

INCAL!
INCAL!
INCAL!
INCAL!

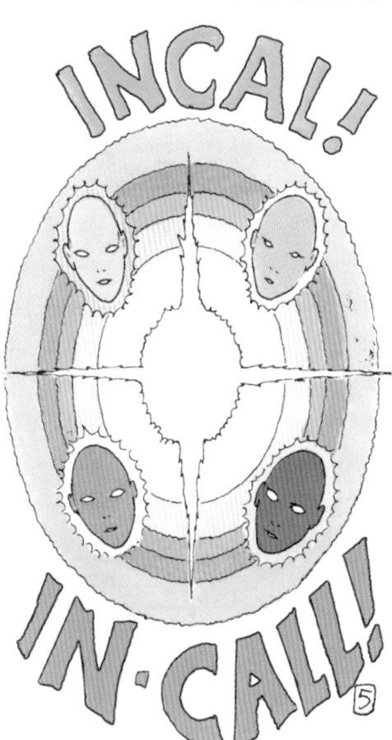
INCAL!
IN-CALL!
5

INCAL!
6

I THINK THEY'VE STOPPED GROWING!
THERE ARE MILLIONS OF THEM! WHAT ARE THEY WAITING FOR?
GRRR!
THEY WON'T TOUCH A HAIR ON HER HEAD!

THEY'RE PARTING!?

LET ME PASS, MY SUBJECTS!
I AM ANIMAH! QUEEN OF THE RATS!

THEY... THEY'RE RETREATING!
ANIMAH, HERE?! WELL, IF YOU CAN CONTROL THESE MONSTERS, THEN CALL THEM OFF!
WAKE UP! OPEN YOUR EYES!

THESE ARE PSYCHORATS! THE MORE YOU FEAR THEM, THE MORE THEY GROW AND MULTIPLY.

EMPTY YOUR MINDS! LET GO OF YOUR FEAR AND VIOLENCE!
IT'S HER! THE MOTHER I NEVER KNEW!
AN EMPTY MIND! OF COURSE!

....
STOP GROWLING, WOLFHEAD!
GRR...CATS AND RATS CALL TO MY WILD SIDE!

MAKE YOUR MIND AS EMPTY AS THAT HOLE IN YOUR EAR!

THAT'S JOHN DIFOOL'S WORK. I SHOULD KILL HIM WITH MY BARE HANDS.

HOLY CONCRETE! JOHN WILL *NEVER* GET OUT OF THIS ONE!

UNLESS...THERE! THAT'S HIM!

JOHN DIFOOL!
DEEPO! THE INCAL TOLD ME THE SECRET OF THE PSYCHORATS!

ANIMAH! I'VE FOUND YOU! AT LAST!
HURRY! WE'RE IN DANGER! CLIMB ON BEHIND ME!
JOHN DIFOOL, ALIVE!

I'VE STABILIZED THESE THREE PSYCHORATS! THEY'LL CARRY US ACROSS THE GARBAGE PLAINS.
SHE NEVER EVEN LOOKED AT ME.
HOLY MOTHER! HOLY MOTHER! WAKE UP!
WHAT A SIGHT!
GARBAGE, AS FAR AS THE EYE CAN SEE!
YES, BUT IT'S THE ONLY WAY TO GET TO THE TRUE HEART OF THE PLANET!
DETECTION CONFIRMED. THEY'RE DOWN THERE! AT THE BOTTOM OF THAT ACID WHIRLPOOL!
HA HA HA! THEY WON'T GET AWAY FROM ME!
9

THROUGH THE FILTH

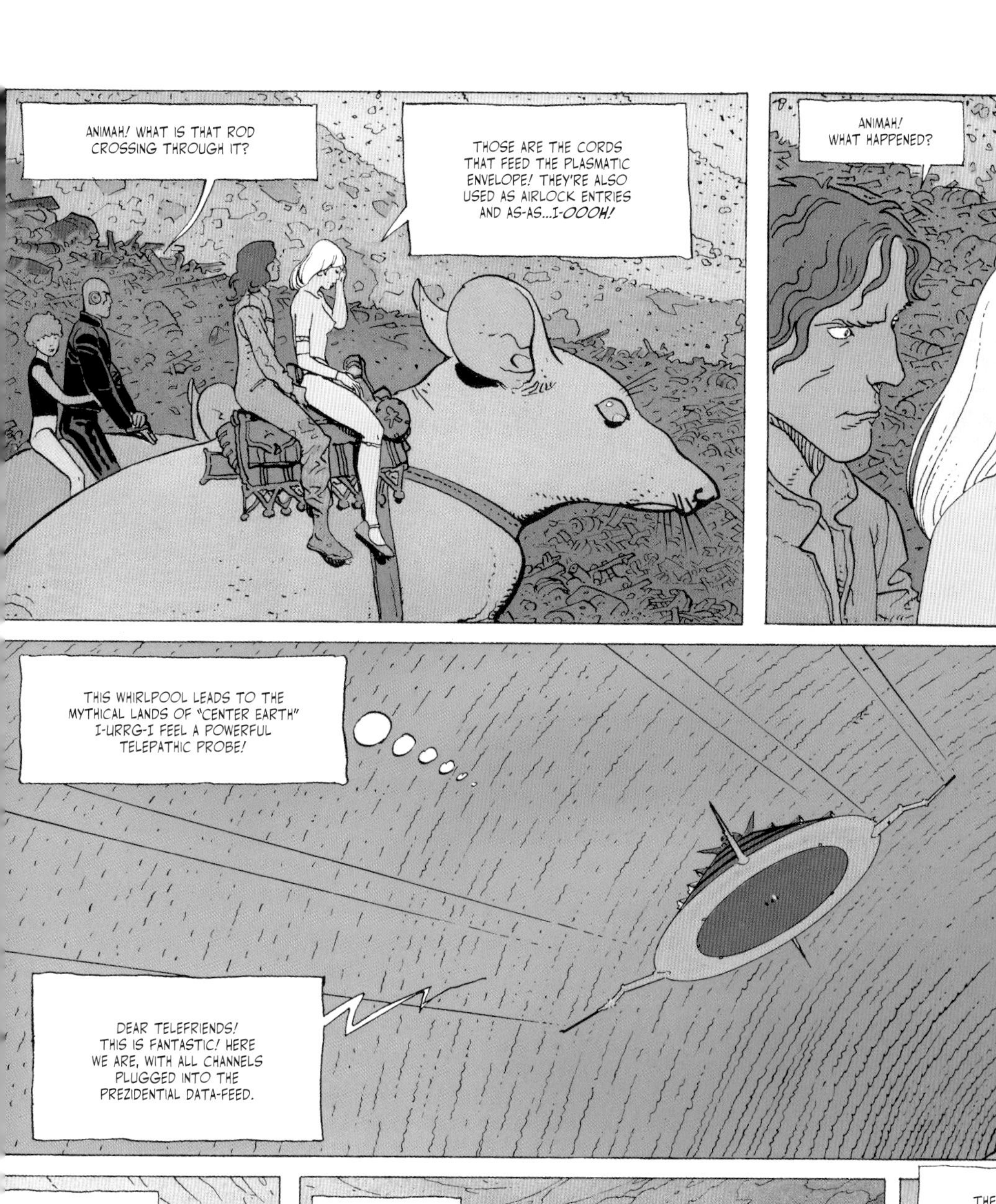
ANIMAH! WHAT IS THAT ROD CROSSING THROUGH IT?
THOSE ARE THE CORDS THAT FEED THE PLASMATIC ENVELOPE! THEY'RE ALSO USED AS AIRLOCK ENTRIES AND AS-AS...I-*OOOH!*
ANIMAH! WHAT HAPPENED?
THE...THE SIGNAL!
THIS WHIRLPOOL LEADS TO THE MYTHICAL LANDS OF "CENTER EARTH" I-URRG-I FEEL A POWERFUL TELEPATHIC PROBE!
DEAR TELEFRIENDS! THIS IS FANTASTIC! HERE WE ARE, WITH ALL CHANNELS PLUGGED INTO THE PREZIDENTIAL DATA-FEED.

THE NECRODROID. ENTERED THE WHIRLPOOL.
THE HOLY MOTHER IS STILL UNCONSCIOUS! WE HAVE TO *HELP* HER!
LATER, WOLFHEAD. RIGHT NOW WE'RE ALL IN DANGER FROM THE NECRODROID! THOSE TWO WILL NEED TO FOCUS TO TAKE CARE OF IT.

THE UNITED POWER OF OUR TWO INCALS WILL CLOSE THE ACID WHIRLPOOL ON THE NECRODROID, DESPITE ITS PSYCHIC RESISTANCE.
ALL RIGHT! LET'S CONCENTRATE ON CALLING THE INCAL!

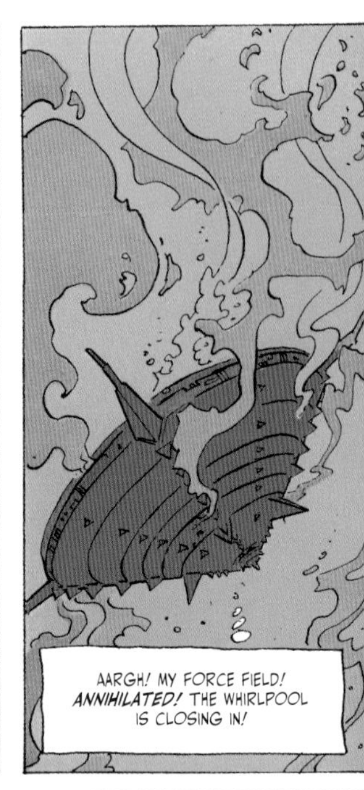
AARGH! MY FORCE FIELD! ANNIHILATED! THE WHIRLPOOL IS CLOSING IN!

THE ACID IS EATING AWAY AT MY SHIELD! I CAN'T GO BACK! THE ONLY WAY OUT IS AT THE BOTTOM!

ANIMAH!

WHAT.... WHAT'S HAPPENING?
IT LOOKS LIKE A STORM IS BREWING!
WE DESTROYED THE NECRODROID!

NO, JOHN! NOT DESTROYED! JUST DELAYED! BUT HURRY! THE METABARON IS RIGHT, THE ENERGY WE RAISED CAUSED THIS GARBAGE STORM. COME QUICKLY! WE CAN FIND SHELTER THIS WAY!
I SENT THE BIRD TO LOOK FOR SHELTER!
THERE'S DEEPO! HE MUST HAVE FOUND SOMETHING.

THERE'S SHELTER IN AN OLD STORAGE CONTAINER RIGHT OVER THIS HILL!

THAT SHOULD DO THE TRICK!

OUCH! THE WIND IS PICKING UP PIECES OF METAL!
IT'S NO FIVE NOVA HOTEL, BUT AT LEAST IT'S SHELTER!
LEAVE THE PSYCHORATS! THEY LOVE GARBAGE STORMS.

TIME PASSES... THE STORM RAGES AND CLOUDS OF TRASH BEAT FURIOUSLY AGAINST THE METAL WALLS.
WHAT A SMELL!
AND WHAT A RACKET!
WE'D SUFFOCATE IF WE WERE OUTSIDE!
WE'D BE TORN TO BITS!

SO WE HAVE TO GO INSIDE THE SUN?!? BUT...
IT IS THE SOUL OF THIS WORLD... THE SECRET VESSEL THAT...
COME LOOK! HURRY!

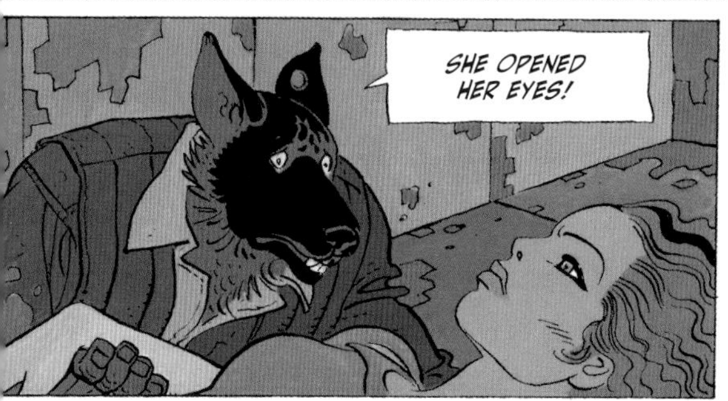
SHE OPENED HER EYES!

SHE'S TRYING TO SPEAK! BUT SHE CAN'T!
IS THERE ANYTHING WE CAN DO TO SAVE THE HOLY MOTHER?

PLEASE USE YOUR POWERS!
I AM...WAIT! THE LIFE FORCE IS BLOCKED RIGHT HERE IN HER NECK...

A BROKEN VERTEBRA!
ANIMAH! LET'S UNITE THE POWER OF OUR TWO INCALS...WE CAN'T LEAVE HER LIKE THIS.

I'LL TAKE HER RIGHT SIDE AND DRAIN THE PAIN. YOU TAKE THE LEFT SIDE AND GIVE HER THE STRENGTH TO REBUILD HERSELF!
13

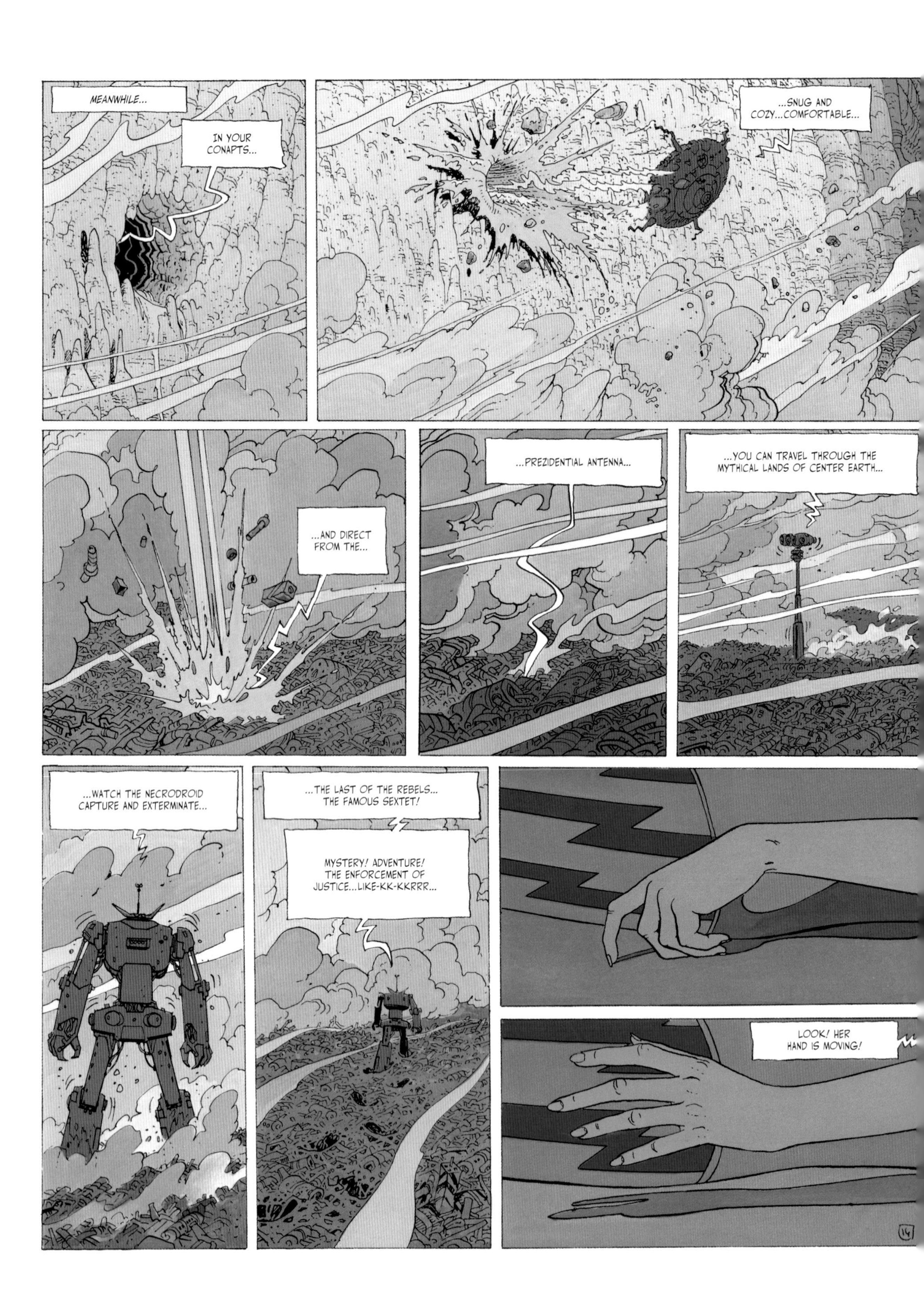
MEANWHILE...
IN YOUR CONAPTS...
...SNUG AND COZY...COMFORTABLE...
...AND DIRECT FROM THE...
...PREZIDENTIAL ANTENNA...
...YOU CAN TRAVEL THROUGH THE MYTHICAL LANDS OF CENTER EARTH...
...WATCH THE NECRODROID CAPTURE AND EXTERMINATE...
...THE LAST OF THE REBELS... THE FAMOUS SEXTET!
MYSTERY! ADVENTURE! THE ENFORCEMENT OF JUSTICE...LIKE-KK-KKRRR...
LOOK! HER HAND IS MOVING!
14

I DIDN'T ASK YOU TO HEAL ME.
LEAVE ME ALONE!
UNGRATEFUL!
ANIMAH! I'M NOT A GUARDIAN OF THE INCAL ANYMORE! YOU KNOW THERE'S NOTHING YOU CAN DO FOR ME!
LET'S GET SOME SLEEP! WE'RE IN GORGO THE FOUL'S TERRITORY AND WE'RE GOING TO NEED ALL OF OUR STRENGTH SOON.
TIME IS WASTING AND THE STORM IS CHURNING UP IMMENSE CLOUDS OF FILTH!
NOTHING WILL STOP ME!
DEAR TELEFRIENDS! LET'S LEAVE THE GARBAGE STORM BRIEFLY AND GO TO OUR GAMESHOW, "WHO WANTS TO EXECUTE A REBEL?!"
WE'RE THE BEST AT MAKING GARBAGE!
3D
AND THE MYTHICAL LANDS OF CENTER EARTH. WHO WOULD HAVE BELIEVED IT?
HOW LONG WAS I ASLEEP?
THE STORM HAS DIED DOWN! SOLUNE! WHERE IS SOLUNE?!
SOLUNE! WHERE ARE YOU?
OVER HERE, FATHER!
THIS IS THE FIRST TIME I'VE EVER SEEN YOU CRY, MY SON.
AND I THINK I KNOW WHY...IT'S HER, ISN'T IT?
SHE DIDN'T EVEN LOOK AT ME!
SHE'S MY MOTHER! YOU'RE MY FATHER... AND NOTHING!!! WHY DID SHE ABANDON US?
SHE WATCHES OVER US, SOLUNE! SHE'S THE ONE WHO OPENED THE WHIRLPOOL IN THE ACID LAKE!
SHE DOESN'T LOVE US!
SOLUNE, WE'RE IN GREAT DANGER! SHE HAS TO ACT LIKE A WARRIOR!
15

BUT I WANT TO KNOW THE TRUTH!
WHAT DO YOU MEAN?
I'M NOT AFRAID TO DIE!
FATHER! I AM YOUR SPIRITUAL SON AND... I...FATHER! I SENSE SOMETHING! DANGER!
I KNOW...THEIR BOWS ARE TAUT! THEIR ARROWS READY TO FLY! GET READY TO JUMP!
THE GARBAGE EATERS ARE ATTACKING!
HURRY! WE HAVE TO WARN THE OTHERS!
ATTACK!
16

EVIL PINK-SKINNED WITCH! YOU'RE TRAPPED, ANIMAH! LIKE ONE OF YOUR STINKING RATS!

THROW THE SLIME ROPES!
THE CONTAINER! IT'S MOVING!
DAMMIT! SHE'S TRYING TO USE HER WITCHCRAFT TO ESCAPE!

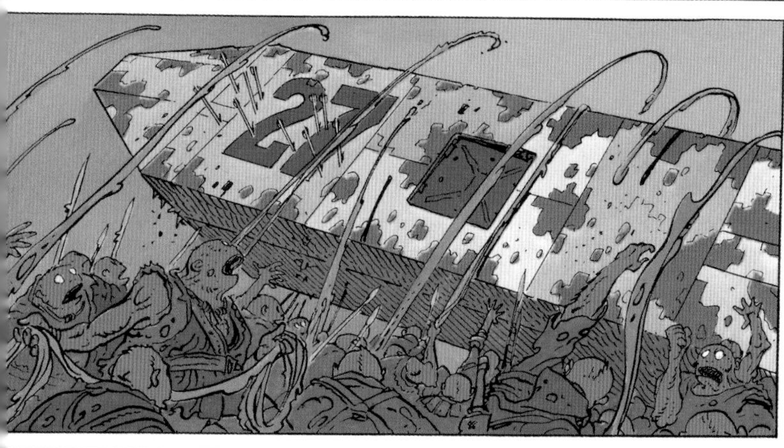

WE'VE GOT THEM!
NO! IT'S STILL MOVING!

HANG ON! BRING IN SOME ANCHOR STAKES!

THE SLIME IS GIVING!
TOO LATE!
SHOOT THEM, YOU LOSERS!

LATER...
IT'S QUIET! I THINK THEY FINALLY GAVE UP!
OPEN THE HATCH SO WE CAN SEE WHERE WE ARE!
18

SO, NOW WHAT DO WE DO?
QUIET, WOLFHEAD! YOU KNOW THOSE TWO HAVE TO CONCENTRATE TO KEEP US LEVITATED!
OOH, LOOK AT THAT!
ERG, I FEEL SEASICK!

THERE'S A TOWER AT THE BASE OF THE BEAM!

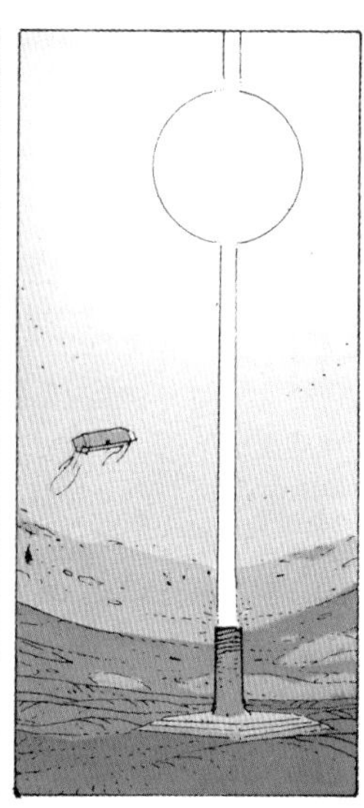

THE...THE INTERIOR SUN, IT'S TRUE...I CAN FEEL IT BEATING!

WE'RE HEADING STRAIGHT FOR THE BASE OF THE TOWER!
DIE!

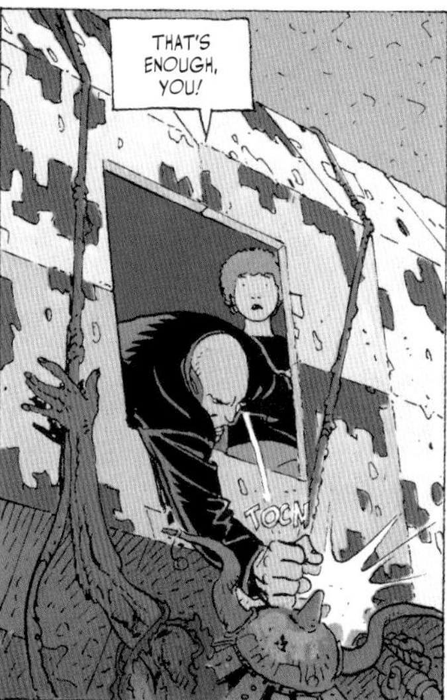
THAT'S ENOUGH, YOU!

YOU DIRTY PINK-SKINNED BASTARDS!

DEAR TELEFRIENDS. WHAT A SIGHT! THIS TOWER! THIS STRANGE SUN!
?!?!

THESE MYTHICAL LANDS OF...
I'VE GOT THEM NOW!

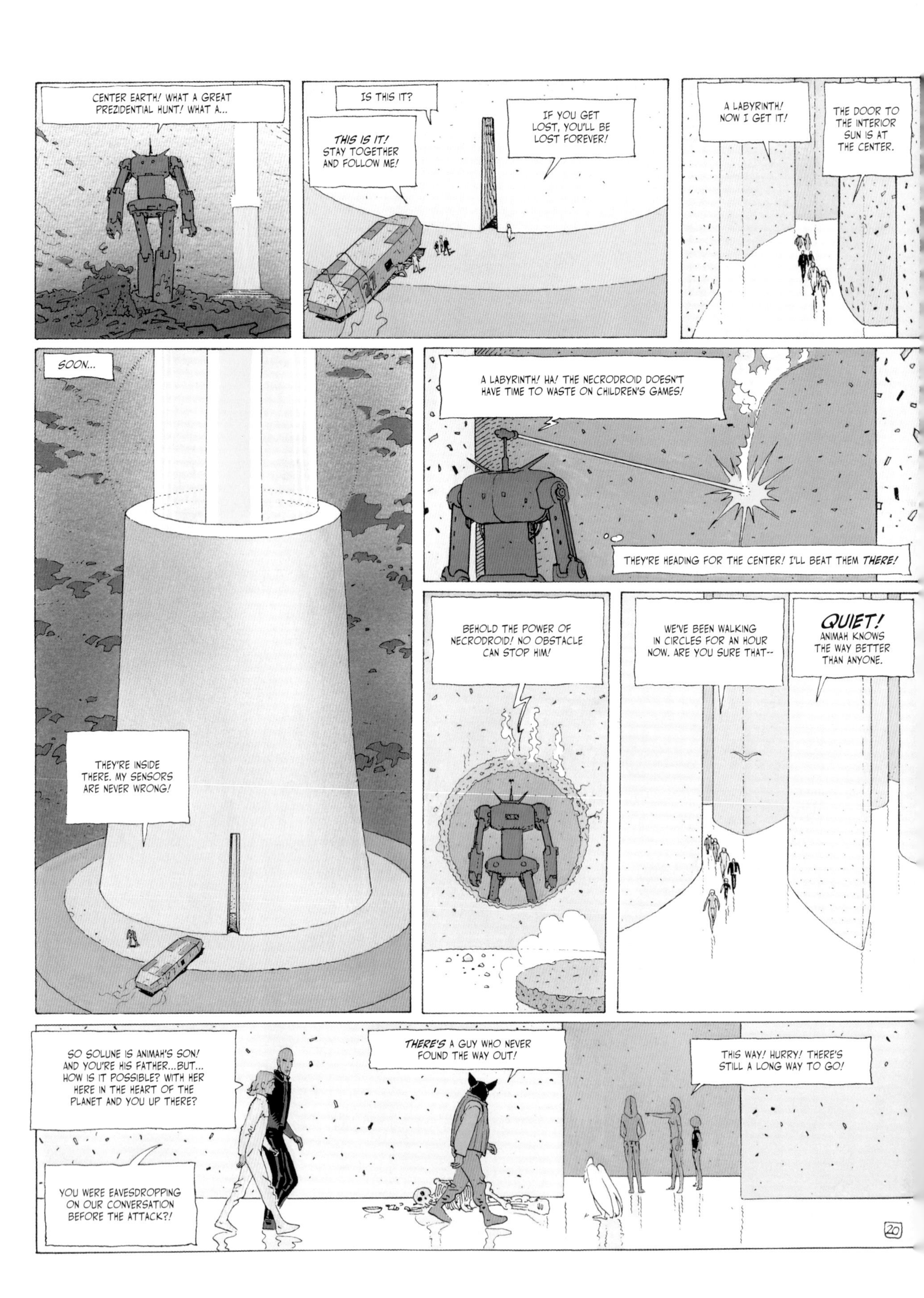
CENTER EARTH! WHAT A GREAT PREZIDENTIAL HUNT! WHAT A...
IS THIS IT?
THIS IS IT! STAY TOGETHER AND FOLLOW ME!
IF YOU GET LOST, YOU'LL BE LOST FOREVER!
A LABYRINTH! NOW I GET IT!
THE DOOR TO THE INTERIOR SUN IS AT THE CENTER.
SOON...
THEY'RE INSIDE THERE. MY SENSORS ARE NEVER WRONG!
A LABYRINTH! HA! THE NECRODROID DOESN'T HAVE TIME TO WASTE ON CHILDREN'S GAMES!
THEY'RE HEADING FOR THE CENTER! I'LL BEAT THEM THERE!
BEHOLD THE POWER OF NECRODROID! NO OBSTACLE CAN STOP HIM!
WE'VE BEEN WALKING IN CIRCLES FOR AN HOUR NOW. ARE YOU SURE THAT--
QUIET! ANIMAH KNOWS THE WAY BETTER THAN ANYONE.
SO SOLUNE IS ANIMAH'S SON! AND YOU'RE HIS FATHER...BUT... HOW IS IT POSSIBLE? WITH HER HERE IN THE HEART OF THE PLANET AND YOU UP THERE?
YOU WERE EAVESDROPPING ON OUR CONVERSATION BEFORE THE ATTACK?!
THERE'S A GUY WHO NEVER FOUND THE WAY OUT!
THIS WAY! HURRY! THERE'S STILL A LONG WAY TO GO!
20

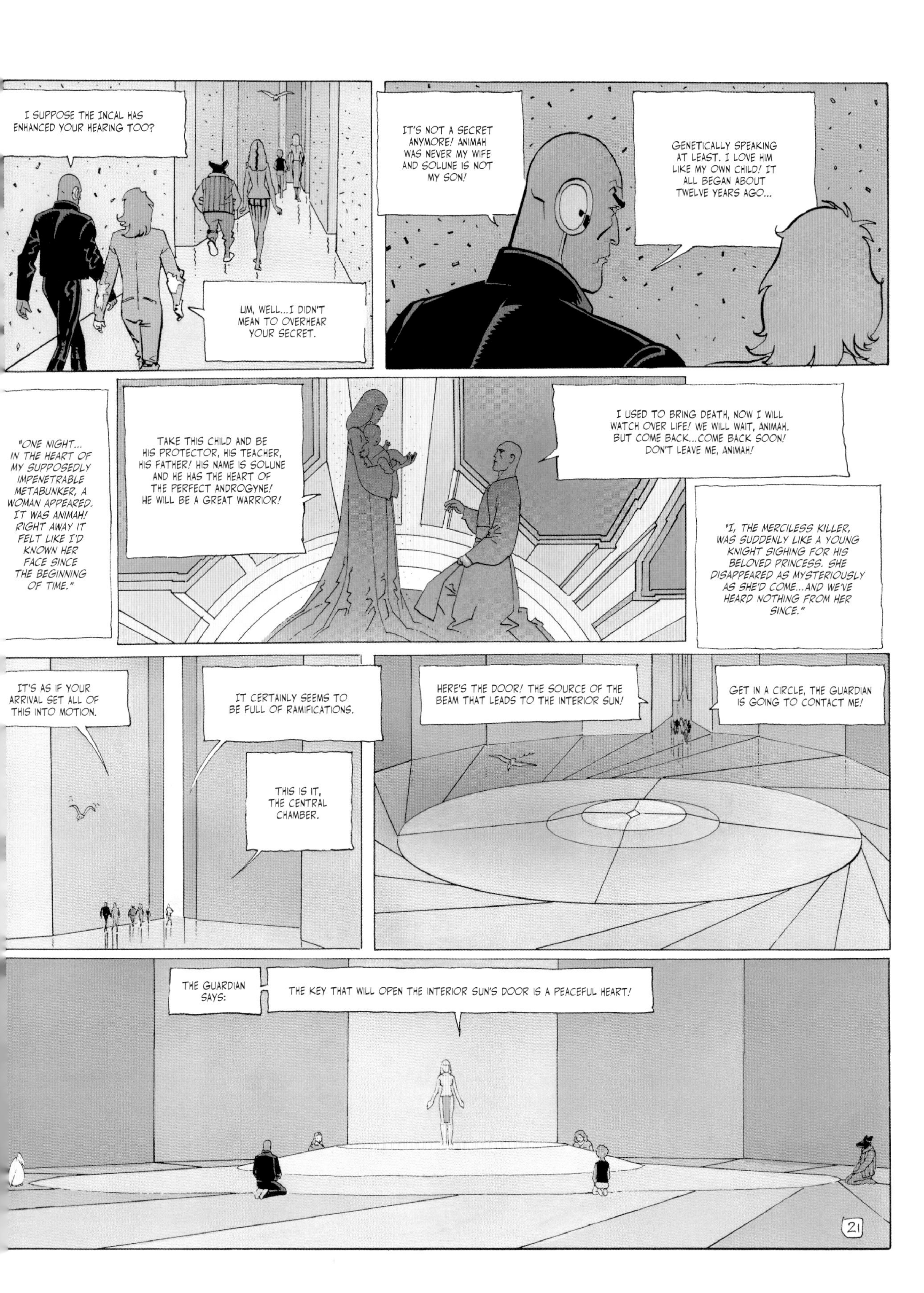
I SUPPOSE THE INCAL HAS ENHANCED YOUR HEARING TOO?
UM, WELL...I DIDN'T MEAN TO OVERHEAR YOUR SECRET.
IT'S NOT A SECRET ANYMORE! ANIMAH WAS NEVER MY WIFE AND SOLUNE IS NOT MY SON!
GENETICALLY SPEAKING AT LEAST. I LOVE HIM LIKE MY OWN CHILD! IT ALL BEGAN ABOUT TWELVE YEARS AGO...
"ONE NIGHT... IN THE HEART OF MY SUPPOSEDLY IMPENETRABLE METABUNKER, A WOMAN APPEARED. IT WAS ANIMAH! RIGHT AWAY IT FELT LIKE I'D KNOWN HER FACE SINCE THE BEGINNING OF TIME."
TAKE THIS CHILD AND BE HIS PROTECTOR, HIS TEACHER, HIS FATHER! HIS NAME IS SOLUNE AND HE HAS THE HEART OF THE PERFECT ANDROGYNE! HE WILL BE A GREAT WARRIOR!
I USED TO BRING DEATH, NOW I WILL WATCH OVER LIFE! WE WILL WAIT, ANIMAH. BUT COME BACK...COME BACK SOON! DON'T LEAVE ME, ANIMAH!
"I, THE MERCILESS KILLER, WAS SUDDENLY LIKE A YOUNG KNIGHT SIGHING FOR HIS BELOVED PRINCESS. SHE DISAPPEARED AS MYSTERIOUSLY AS SHE'D COME...AND WE'VE HEARD NOTHING FROM HER SINCE."
IT'S AS IF YOUR ARRIVAL SET ALL OF THIS INTO MOTION.
IT CERTAINLY SEEMS TO BE FULL OF RAMIFICATIONS.
THIS IS IT, THE CENTRAL CHAMBER.
HERE'S THE DOOR! THE SOURCE OF THE BEAM THAT LEADS TO THE INTERIOR SUN!
GET IN A CIRCLE, THE GUARDIAN IS GOING TO CONTACT ME!
THE GUARDIAN SAYS:
THE KEY THAT WILL OPEN THE INTERIOR SUN'S DOOR IS A PEACEFUL HEART!
21

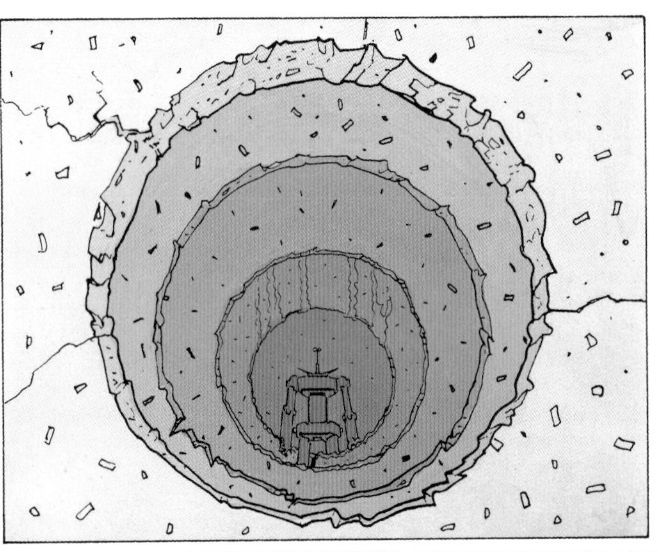

THE GUARDIAN SAYS... TRANSIT INTERRUPTED. THE KEY IS NOT UNIFIED!

DOOMMM
WHAT... WHAT'S THAT NOISE?
THE NECRODROID IS COMING *CLOSER.* HURRY.
DROMM
WE HAVE TO BE AT PEACE LIKE ANIMAH SAYS! QUICKLY!

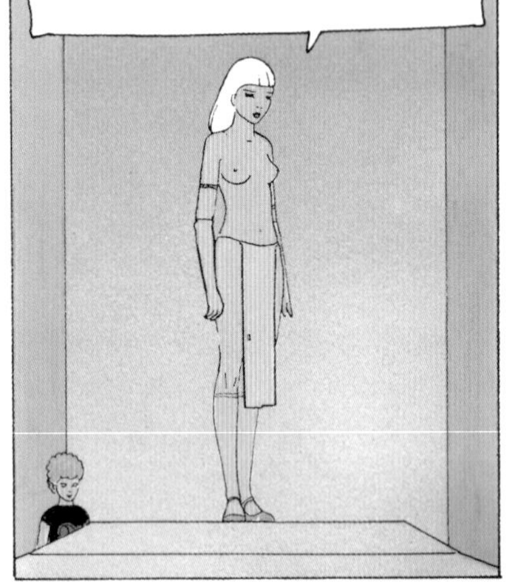
THE GUARDIAN SAYS SOLUNE MUST MAKE PEACE WITH ANIMAH! TANATAH MUST MAKE PEACE WITH ANIMAH. WOLFHEAD MUST MAKE PEACE WITH JOHN DIFOOL.

MY INSANE QUEST FOR POWER BROUGHT ONLY STRIFE TO THE SURFACE. NOW I HAVE TO CHOOSE BETWEEN MAKING A FINAL ALLIANCE WITH DARKNESS AND MAKING PEACE. I CHOOSE PEACE, ANIMAH!

MOTHER...MY HEART WAS FILLED WITH BITTERNESS. I WEPT...I-I...
SOLUNE, MY BELOVED SON, DO NOT BE UNHAPPY. I READ CLEARLY IN YOUR HEART. THOUGH YOU DON'T KNOW IT, YOUR HEART BELIEVES AND FORGIVES! THERE IS NO POINT IN ASKING FOR PEACE. YOU *ARE* PEACE!

THIS IS THE LAST WALL! I FEEL IT! THEY ARE HERE...RIGHT BEHIND IT!

SO, WOLFHEAD, YOU BEAST! ARE YOU GOING TO GET US ALL MASSACRED OVER ONE LITTLE HOLE IN YOUR EAR?

GRRR!
MISERABLE CLASS R DETECTIVE! MAKE PEACE WITH THIS...THIS...

DAMMIT!
SON OF A BITCH! I'LL TEAR HIM TO BITS! I'LL--
22

NO! NO, I CAN'T!

SOB!
JOHN...JOHN... DI...FOOL! I'M SO SORRY!

SUDDENLY A BEAM OF LIGHT BURSTS FROM THE PENTACLE, LIFTING THE SEVEN COMPANIONS TOWARDS THE TINY STAR, THE INTERIOR SUN OF THE MYTHICAL LANDS OF CENTER EARTH.
TOO LATE! DEAR TELEFRIENDS, THE REBELS HAVE ONCE AGAIN ESCAPED THE UNSTOPPABLE FORCE OF PREZIDENTIAL JUSTICE.
DAMMIT!
23
MOEBIUS

THE GOLDEN PLANET

I AM A ROBOTIC CONTROL UNIT. PLEASE IDENTIFY YOURSELVES.
THE GOLDEN PLANET!
THE PALACE IS AT THE CENTER OF THE PLANET!

HEAR YE, ALL MEMBERS OF THE HUMAN EMPIRE! THIS IMPERIAL COMMUNICATION HAS A B7 URGENCY RATING! VIOLENCE IS RAVAGING THE TERRAFORMED PLANET TER 21, IN SECTOR 669 OF THE EXOFRINGE. WE, THE EMPERORESS, THE PERFECT ANDROGYNE, SENSE THE EMERGENCE OF UNKNOWN POWERS. TER 21'S TECHNOCITY HAS BEEN MYSTERIOUSLY DESTROYED. THREE OF THE FOUR EQUATORIAL CITIES ARE TORN BY AN UNENDING SERIES OF CLASS 2 RIOTS.
THE PREZIDENT OF TER 21 WAS FORCED TO RESORT TO CLONING INTO THE NECRODROID. WORST OF ALL, LOCAL COVERAGE OF THE RIOTS HAS BEEN INEXPLICABLY TRANSMITTED TO THE HOLO-NETWORKS OF ALL 22,000 MAJOR PLANETS IN THE EMPIRE, PROVOKING A DISASTROUS RASH OF CLASS 5C TO CLASS 2C CITY RIOTS.
25

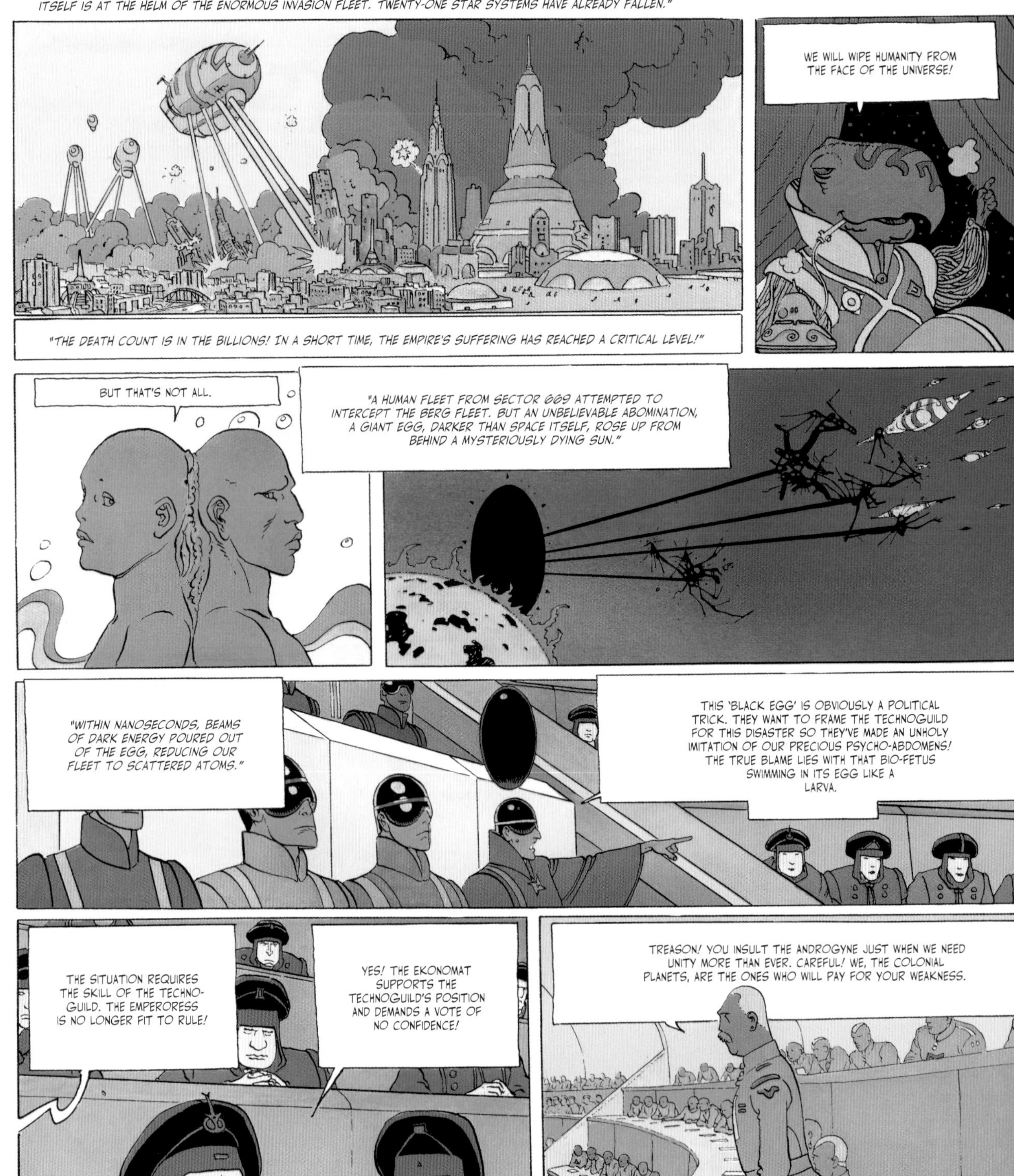
"ALSO, THE BERG EMPIRE HAS TAKEN ADVANTAGE OF THE CHAOS AND HAS ATTACKED OUR GALAXY. THE BERG ROYAL FAMILY ITSELF IS AT THE HELM OF THE ENORMOUS INVASION FLEET. TWENTY-ONE STAR SYSTEMS HAVE ALREADY FALLEN."
"THE DEATH COUNT IS IN THE BILLIONS! IN A SHORT TIME, THE EMPIRE'S SUFFERING HAS REACHED A CRITICAL LEVEL!"
WE WILL WIPE HUMANITY FROM THE FACE OF THE UNIVERSE!
BUT THAT'S NOT ALL.
"A HUMAN FLEET FROM SECTOR 669 ATTEMPTED TO INTERCEPT THE BERG FLEET. BUT AN UNBELIEVABLE ABOMINATION, A GIANT EGG, DARKER THAN SPACE ITSELF, ROSE UP FROM BEHIND A MYSTERIOUSLY DYING SUN."
"WITHIN NANOSECONDS, BEAMS OF DARK ENERGY POURED OUT OF THE EGG, REDUCING OUR FLEET TO SCATTERED ATOMS."
THIS 'BLACK EGG' IS OBVIOUSLY A POLITICAL TRICK. THEY WANT TO FRAME THE TECHNOGUILD FOR THIS DISASTER SO THEY'VE MADE AN UNHOLY IMITATION OF OUR PRECIOUS PSYCHO-ABDOMENS! THE TRUE BLAME LIES WITH THAT BIO-FETUS SWIMMING IN ITS EGG LIKE A LARVA.
THE SITUATION REQUIRES THE SKILL OF THE TECHNO-GUILD. THE EMPERORESS IS NO LONGER FIT TO RULE!
YES! THE EKONOMAT SUPPORTS THE TECHNOGUILD'S POSITION AND DEMANDS A VOTE OF NO CONFIDENCE!
TREASON! YOU INSULT THE ANDROGYNE JUST WHEN WE NEED UNITY MORE THAN EVER. CAREFUL! WE, THE COLONIAL PLANETS, ARE THE ONES WHO WILL PAY FOR YOUR WEAKNESS.
26

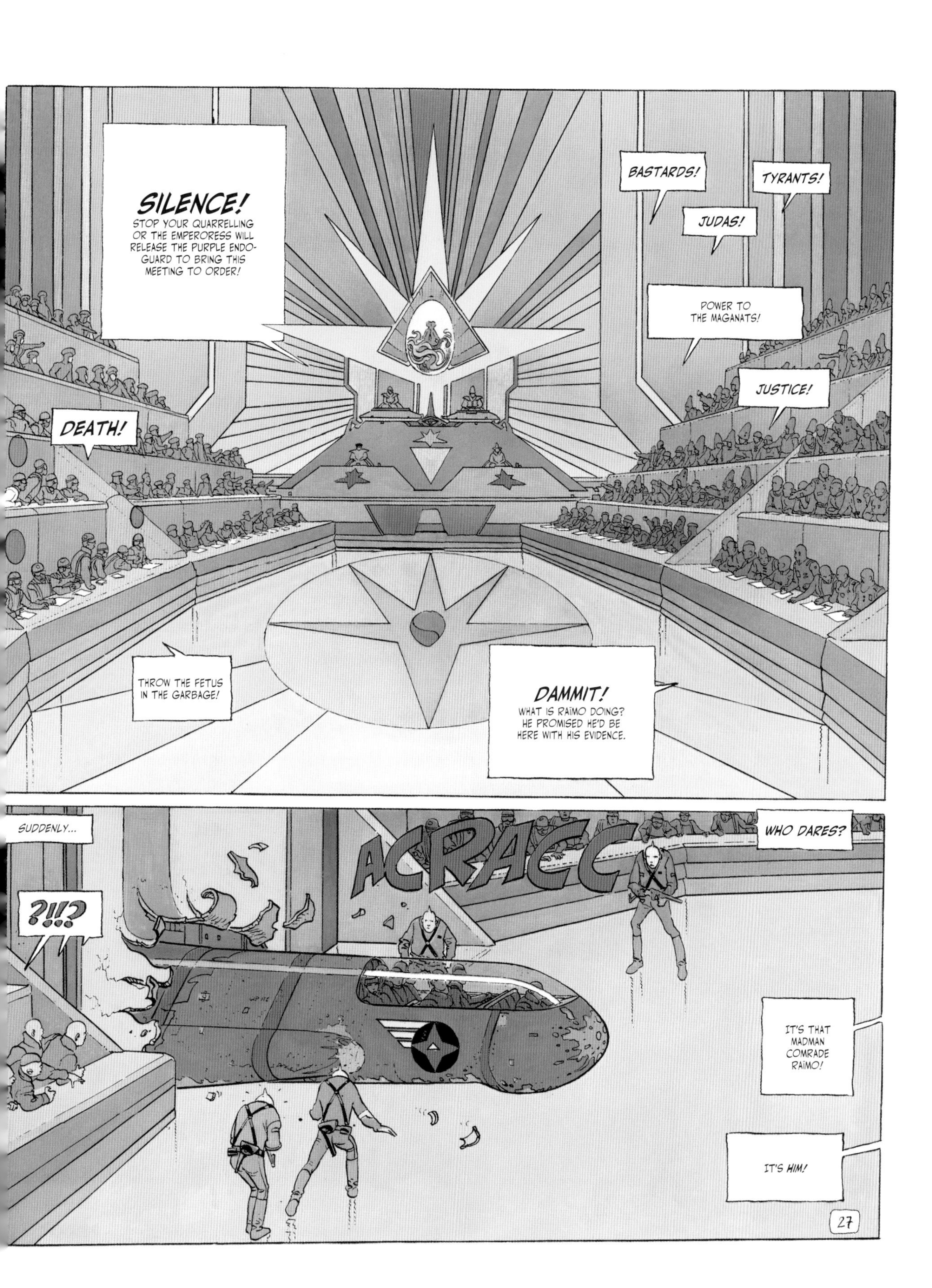
SILENCE!
STOP YOUR QUARRELLING OR THE EMPERORESS WILL RELEASE THE PURPLE ENDO-GUARD TO BRING THIS MEETING TO ORDER!
BASTARDS!
TYRANTS!
JUDAS!
POWER TO THE MAGANATS!
JUSTICE!
DEATH!
THROW THE FETUS IN THE GARBAGE!
DAMMIT!
WHAT IS RAÏMO DOING? HE PROMISED HE'D BE HERE WITH HIS EVIDENCE.
SUDDENLY...
ACRACC
WHO DARES?
?!!?
IT'S THAT MADMAN COMRADE RAÏMO!
IT'S HIM!
27

CALM DOWN AND LISTEN TO ME, ALL OF YOU!
COULD THIS BLASTED RAÏMO POSE A THREAT TO OUR PLANS, O TECHNOPOPE?!?
MM...HE IS POWERFUL, BUT WE HAVE AN ALLY WHO IS STILL MORE POWERFUL... PATIENCE...
SILENCE! HEAR THE WORDS OF COMRADE RAÏMO, WHO SPEAKS FOR ALL OF THE COLONIAL PLANETS!
A GREAT HUSH FALLS OVER THE STUNNED ASSEMBLY.
YOUR MEGAHOLINESS! SHALL I HAVE THE PURPLE ENDOGUARD REMOVE THESE INTRUDERS?
NO, GREYFIELD, RAÏMO HAS ALWAYS BEEN LOYAL. LET HIM SPEAK.
MY LORDS! COMRADES! I AM HERE TO REVEAL TO YOU THE MOST MONSTROUS PLOT EVER UNDERTAKEN AGAINST HUMANITY. AND IT HAS BEEN DONE USING THE MOST ABOMINABLE OBJECT EVER CREATED BY MAN'S FOLLY!
28

OPEN YOUR EYES AND HOLD BACK YOUR BITTER TEARS!

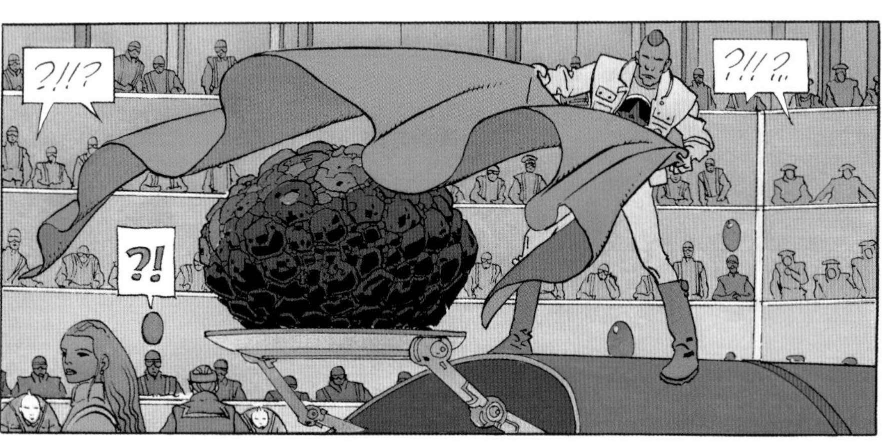
?!!?
?!!?..
?!

WHAT IS THAT THING?!
HE'S MAKING FUN OF US.
THIS HOAX FROM THE COLONIAL PLANETS AND THE TROGLOSOCIALIKS IS AN INSULT TO THE IMPERIAL ASSEMBLY!
IT LOOKS LIKE A PIECE OF COAL!

WHAT IS THE FETUS WAITING FOR? GET RID OF THIS RIDICULOUS COAL SALESMAN!
HAHAHA!..
HAHAH
HAHA!
HAHA
HAHAH
HAHA!

WHAT YOU CALL A PIECE OF COAL... LISTEN *CAREFULLY*... ALL OF YOU...
THIS IS ALL THAT REMAINS OF A SUN EATEN BY A SHADOW EGG!

THIS CARBONIZED LUMP REPRESENTS THE DEATH OF AN ENTIRE PLANETARY SYSTEM, INCLUDING TWO INHABITED WORLDS, TAEROLA AND CEERES...RIGHT NOW, THESE WORLDS ARE FLOATING LIFELESSLY IN THE FROZEN DARKNESS OF SPACE AROUND A DARK USURPER: *THE SHADOW EGG!*

MMMPFFFFF...

GRBLLL...
29

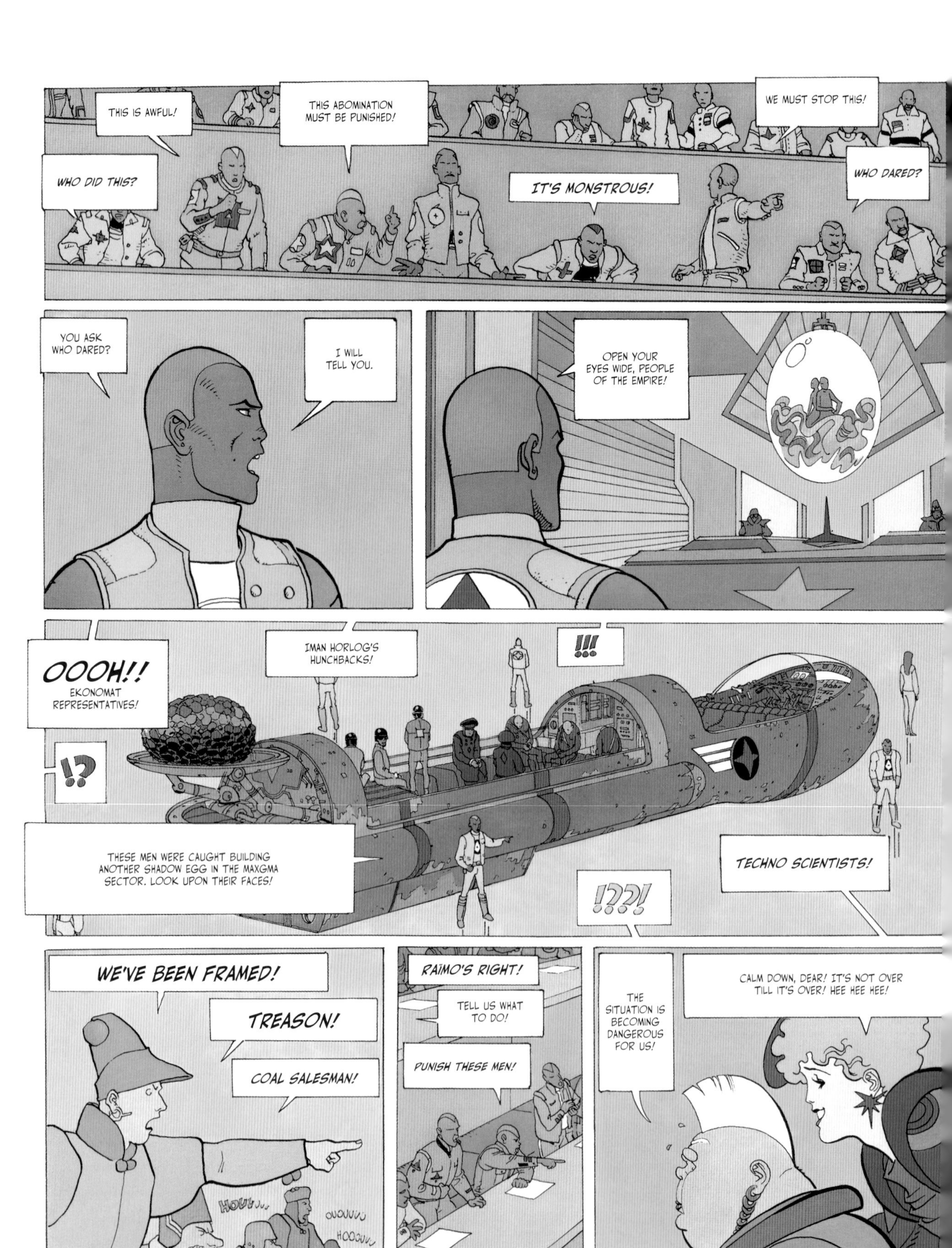
THIS IS AWFUL!
THIS ABOMINATION MUST BE PUNISHED!
WE MUST STOP THIS!
WHO DID THIS?
IT'S MONSTROUS!
WHO DARED?
YOU ASK WHO DARED?
I WILL TELL YOU.
OPEN YOUR EYES WIDE, PEOPLE OF THE EMPIRE!
OOOH!! EKONOMAT REPRESENTATIVES!
IMAN HORLOG'S HUNCHBACKS!
!!!
!?
THESE MEN WERE CAUGHT BUILDING ANOTHER SHADOW EGG IN THE MAXGMA SECTOR. LOOK UPON THEIR FACES!
!??!
TECHNO SCIENTISTS!
WE'VE BEEN FRAMED!
TREASON!
COAL SALESMAN!
HOUUUU
OUOUUUU
HOOOUUU
RAÏMO'S RIGHT!
TELL US WHAT TO DO!
PUNISH THESE MEN!
THE SITUATION IS BECOMING DANGEROUS FOR US!
CALM DOWN, DEAR! IT'S NOT OVER TILL IT'S OVER! HEE HEE HEE!
30

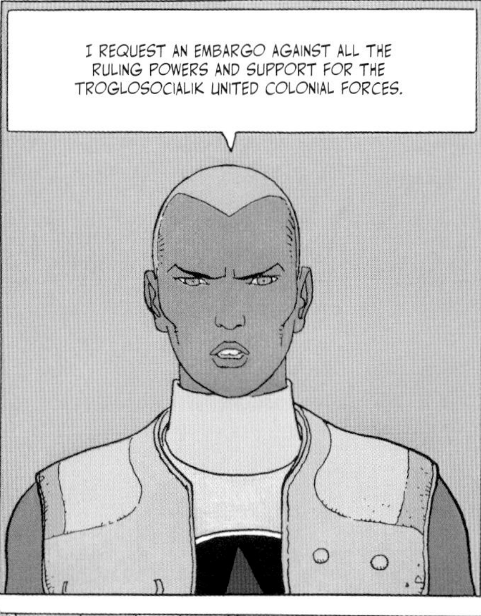
I REQUEST AN EMBARGO AGAINST ALL THE RULING POWERS AND SUPPORT FOR THE TROGLOSOCIALIK UNITED COLONIAL FORCES.

OOOH!
IT'S A COUP D'ÉTAT!
A REBELLION!

TO RETURN JUSTICE TO THE EMPIRE!
YOUR MEGAHOLINESS, HE GOES TOO FAR! SHALL I RELEASE THE ENDOGUARD?

NO! LET THIS MADNESS RUN ITS COURSE.
AND REDUCE THE PRIVILEGES OF THE TECHNOGUILD AND THE EKONOMAT WORLDS!

THEY HAVE POWER, BUT WE HAVE THE NUMBERS. AND OUR NUMBERS GIVE US THE RIGHT!!!

JUSTICE IS ON OUR SIDE. AS IS THE PROTECTION OF THE SACRED ANDROGYNE, THE EMPERORESS!

LONG LIVE THE EMPERORESS!
DEATH TO THE TECHNOS!
OUT WITH IMAN!
STOP THE EKONOMAT!

WHAT ARE YOU WAITING FOR? ACTIVATE PLAN R!
THE SITUATION IS OUT OF CONTROL!
WE HAVE 10,000 SHADOW EGGS UNDER CONSTRUCTION. WE CAN'T...
PATIENCE, THE TIME HAS NOT YET COME!
31

YOUR MEGAHOLINESS! ISN'T IT TIME TO CALL OUT THE ENDOGUARD? LET THEM ARREST THESE CRIMINALS AND EXILE THEM ON AQUAEND, THE PRISON PLANET. AFTER SUCH A HORRIBLE CRIME, THERE CAN BE NO OTHER JUSTICE!
STOP THOSE SAVAGES!
GREYFIELD...RAÏMO IS RIGHT! THE COMRADE'S EVIDENCE IS IRREFUTABLE! SUMMON THE ENDOGUARD!
CLOWNS!
SCANDALOUS!
GET BACK!
LET IT BE THEN, YOUR MEGAHOLINESS. AS ALWAYS, MADNESS BEGETS FORCE.
LONG LIVE THE EMPERORESS!
RETURN TO YOUR SEATS!
VICTORY!
LONG LIVE RAÏMO! THE FIRST GALACTIC COORDINATOR!
GET BACK!

BURSTING FROM A THOUSAND SECRET PASSAGES, A PURPLE HORDE INVADES THE GALACTIC ASSEMBLY.
TORN
TORN TORN TORN
TORN
TORN
TORN

WELL DONE, GREYFIELD! I WAS WRONG TO DOUBT YOUR LOYALTY!

YOU WERE *WRONG* IN EVERY WAY, RAÏMO. ENDOGUARDS, CARRY OUT YOUR ORDERS!
32

SUDDENLY...
HEY, WHAT ARE THEY DOING?!
TREASON!
HORRORS!
THE TRUE TRAITORS ARE REVEALED!
STOP!
ARE YOU CRAZY? WHO COULD HAVE ORDERED YOU TO...
RAÏMO!
TRAITORS!
BACK, VERMIN!
OUCH!
SHOOT! SHOOT!
STOP SHOOTING!
THE FETUS IS DONE FOR! HA HA HA!
THE EMPERORESS HAS BEEN HIT!
HOORAY! THE ROTTEN EGG IS FINALLY BROKEN!
HOW HORRIBLE! THEY'VE KILLED HIS MEGAHOLINESS!
FINALLY!
33

ALL THIS BLOOD...IT'S DISGUSTING!
BRAVO, GREYFIELD. YOU'VE DONE YOUR JOB WELL!

AS THE EMPERORESS IS NO LONGER ABLE TO PRESIDE OVER THIS MEETING. I, IMAN HORLOG, WILL TAKE ON THE RESPONSIBILITY DESPITE MY GREAT SADNESS.

ENDOGUARDS! EXECUTE ANYONE WHO DOESN'T APPLAUD LOUDLY ENOUGH!
BRAVO!
HOORAY!
BRAVO!
HURRAH!

CLAP CLAP
CLAPP CLAPP CLAP
CLAPP CLAP
CLAP CLAP
CLAP CLAP
CLAP CLAP
CLAPP CLAP
CLAP CLAPP
CLAPP CLAP CLAP CLAP
CLAP CLAP
CLAP CLAP

YOU AND I WILL BE THE NEW SACRED ANDROGYNE! HA HA HA!
YOUR EXCELLENCY, WHAT SHOULD WE DO WITH RAÏMO AND HIS PEOPLE? DEATH?

DEATH? NO, I HAVE SOMETHING BETTER IN MIND FOR THEM. THE SAME FATE THEY HAD IN MIND FOR US. SEND THEM TO AQUAEND, THE PRISON-PLANET!
34

MEANWHILE, THOUSANDS OF LIGHT YEARS AWAY...
HA HA! SEVEN! THE PERFECT NUMBER!
THAT LITTLE FURY, TANATAH, IS BACK!
OOOOOH...BUT IT LOOKS LIKE HER TIME UP THERE MIGHT HAVE CALMED HER DOWN!
ANIMAH! WELCOME BACK TO THE INTERIOR SUN! AND YOU, TANATAH, WE THOUGHT WE'D LOST YOU. AND YOU WHOSE HEARTS HAVE BEEN PURIFIED AND WHO ARE VISITING US FOR THE FIRST TIME, WE, THE ARHATS, BID YOU WELCOME!
OH! WHAT AN UNUSUAL GROUP! A WARRIOR! AND ONE WITH A DOG'S HEAD!
WELL, IT'S ABOUT TIME!
THOSE ARE THE INCALS! THEY'VE BROUGHT BACK THE INCALS!
HMMM...I FEEL SOME POWERFUL FORCES WITH THEM!
I AM HAPPY TO SEE YOU AGAIN, MY GOOD GUARDIANS.
THE ARHATS! THE ANCIENT GUARDIANS OF LEGEND!
35

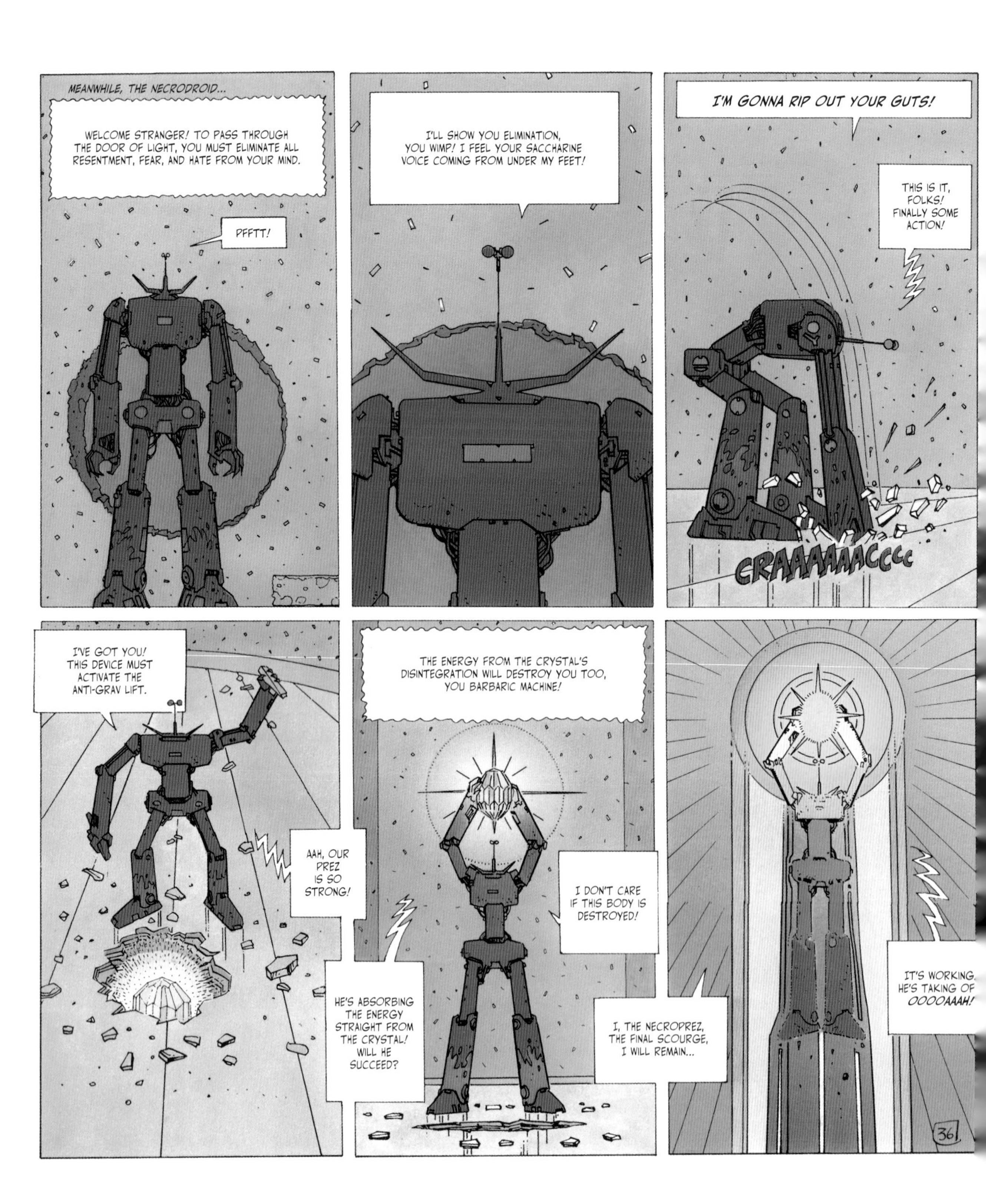
MEANWHILE, THE NECRODROID...
WELCOME STRANGER! TO PASS THROUGH THE DOOR OF LIGHT, YOU MUST ELIMINATE ALL RESENTMENT, FEAR, AND HATE FROM YOUR MIND.
PFFTT!
I'LL SHOW YOU ELIMINATION, YOU WIMP! I FEEL YOUR SACCHARINE VOICE COMING FROM UNDER MY FEET!
I'M GONNA RIP OUT YOUR GUTS!
THIS IS IT, FOLKS! FINALLY SOME ACTION!
CRAAAAAACCCC
I'VE GOT YOU! THIS DEVICE MUST ACTIVATE THE ANTI-GRAV LIFT.
AAH, OUR PREZ IS SO STRONG!
THE ENERGY FROM THE CRYSTAL'S DISINTEGRATION WILL DESTROY YOU TOO, YOU BARBARIC MACHINE!
I DON'T CARE IF THIS BODY IS DESTROYED!
HE'S ABSORBING THE ENERGY STRAIGHT FROM THE CRYSTAL! WILL HE SUCCEED?
I, THE NECROPREZ, THE FINAL SCOURGE, I WILL REMAIN...
IT'S WORKING. HE'S TAKING OF OOOOAAAH!
36

THIS MIRROR IS THE VIBRATING DOORWAY THAT OPENS ONTO THE MIRACULOUS FOREST OF SINGING CRYSTALS!
AND WHAT BEAUTIFUL SINGING IT IS!
HURRY! THE NECRODROID IS RIGHT BEHIND US! I CAN FEEL HIM!
ME TOO!
WE ARE READY TO PASS THROUGH, ANCIENT GUARDIANS!
SHHH! SILENCE!
TO GO THROUGH THE MIRROR, YOU MUST BE IN HARMONY WITH IT.
CAREFUL! IT'S NOT AS EASY AS IT LOOKS!
THE REFLECTION IS DISAPPEARING! THAT'S RIGHT! LIKE THAT!
BRAVO!
WELL DONE!
THEY'RE
BRAVE!
THEY MADE IT!
BUT IT'S NOT OVER YET!
THEY'RE IN THE FOREST NOW!
37

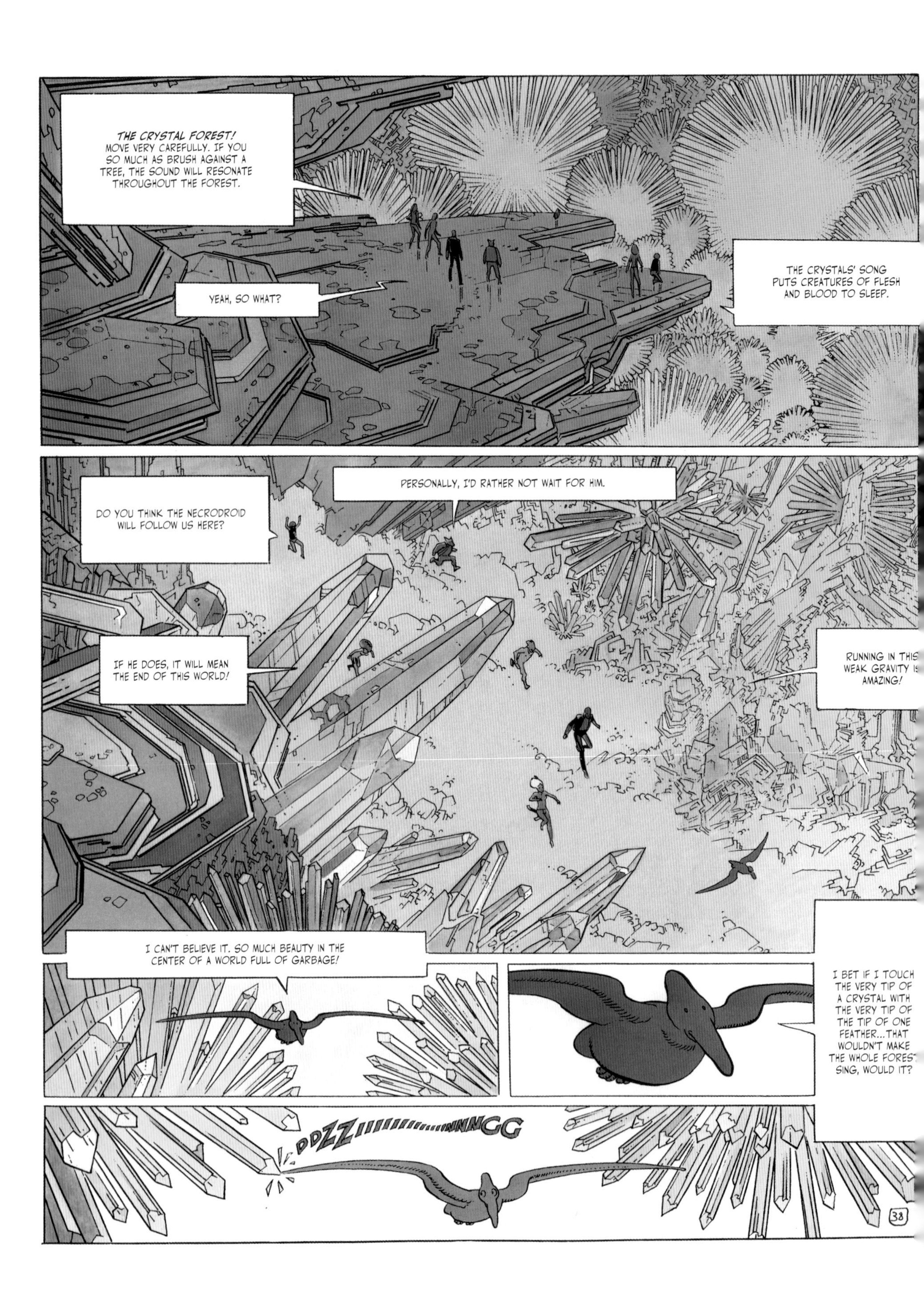
THE CRYSTAL FOREST! MOVE VERY CAREFULLY. IF YOU SO MUCH AS BRUSH AGAINST A TREE, THE SOUND WILL RESONATE THROUGHOUT THE FOREST.
YEAH, SO WHAT?
THE CRYSTALS' SONG PUTS CREATURES OF FLESH AND BLOOD TO SLEEP.
DO YOU THINK THE NECRODROID WILL FOLLOW US HERE?
PERSONALLY, I'D RATHER NOT WAIT FOR HIM.
IF HE DOES, IT WILL MEAN THE END OF THIS WORLD!
RUNNING IN THIS WEAK GRAVITY IS AMAZING!
I CAN'T BELIEVE IT. SO MUCH BEAUTY IN THE CENTER OF A WORLD FULL OF GARBAGE!
I BET IF I TOUCH THE VERY TIP OF A CRYSTAL WITH THE VERY TIP OF THE TIP OF ONE FEATHER...THAT WOULDN'T MAKE THE WHOLE FOREST SING, WOULD IT?
DDZZIIIIIIIIIIIIIIIIINNNGG
38

LISTEN!
A HYPNOTIC MELODY SUDDENLY FILLS THE TRAVELERS' EARS, FREEZING THEM WHERE THEY STAND!
WHO MADE THE FOREST SING?
TRY NOT TO FALL ASLEEP!
...
BUT SLEEP COMES, CONQUERING EVEN THE MOST WILLFUL MINDS.
ZZZZ
MEANWHILE, ELSEWHERE IN THE GALAXY, AN ENDOGUARD SHIP COMPLETES ITS SINISTER MISSION.
ENJOY YOUR STAY IN HELL, REBELS!
WHAT A HORRIBLE PLACE!
I'M COLD!
HANG ON!
39

COMRADE RAÏMO AND HIS CLAN ARE NOW PRISONERS...
...OF THE MOST DREADED PENITENTIARY PLANET IN THE EMPIRE: AQUAEND!
A WATER WORLD...A PLANET WITHOUT LAND... DROWNED IN TORRENTIAL RAIN!
FORGIVE ME FOR FAILING YOU! THIS IS MY FAULT!
BATTERED BY AN ENDLESS STREAM OF HURRICANES, CYCLONES, DOWNPOURS, AND STORMS.
BE BRAVE! WE'RE ALIVE! THAT'S THE IMPORTANT THING!
BUT FOR HOW LONG?
I'VE GOT TO GET THERE SOON! MY ROBOTIC SHELL IS DETERIORATING.
WELCOME, STRANGER. THIS MIRROR IS THE VIBRATING DOORWAY THAT OPENS ONTO THE MIRACULOUS WORLD OF THE SINGING CRYSTALS.
CLANG
TONNK
?
TIME TO SHIFT TO PANZER MODE!
YOU MUST BE IN UNISON WITH IT.
?
40

FOR YOUR REFLECTION...
WHO'S THAT OLD FART?

BOLOM
WHAT ARE THOSE EXPLOSIONS?
...TO DIS-APPEAR...
IT MUST BE THE BERGS BOMBING THE PLANET!

WE HAVEN'T SEEN ANY NEWS SINCE THE PREZIDENT'S NECRODROID TOOK OVER ALL 7,000 CHANNELS ON THE IMPERIAL NETWEB.

CHECK OUT THE PREZ'S NEW LOOK!
DEAR TELEFRIENDS...SNUG LITTLE BUGS...WATCH HOW YOUR PREZ MAKES HIS REFLECTION DISAPPEAR...
WAIT!
STOP!

STOP!
GET BACK! BACK! STOP!
YOU'RE INSANE!
CCCRIINGLIINC
DEAR GOD! THE END IS UPON US!
BARBARIC MACHINE!

THE NECRODROID HAS EVOLVED INTO A NEW FORM, THE NECRO-PANZER! THINGS ARE ABOUT TO GET UGLY, FOLKS!
THE PLASMA'S LEAKING!
41

WHO COULD'VE IMAGINED SOMETHING SO MARVELOUS! THE SOUND OF A MILLION DISHES BREAKING! HA! HA!
STUPID TRINKETS!
KLLLLLLNNGGG
AKLANG
WHAT'S THAT?
HUH?
IT MUST BE THE NECRODROID! HE SHATTERED THE VIBRATING DOORWAY! THE FOOL!
AT LEAST HIS MADNESS WOKE US FROM OUR HYPNOTIC SLEEP! HURRY! LET'S MOVE!
HEY! DEEPO! WAKE UP!
OOH! UH...AH...I WAS DREAMING... ABOUT A CONCRETE DOVE...
AND SOON...
HURRY! THE NECRODROID CAN'T BE FAR BEHIND!
LOOK, THE CRYSTAL TOWER! THE PORTAL OF TRANSFIGURATION IS AT THE TOP.
42

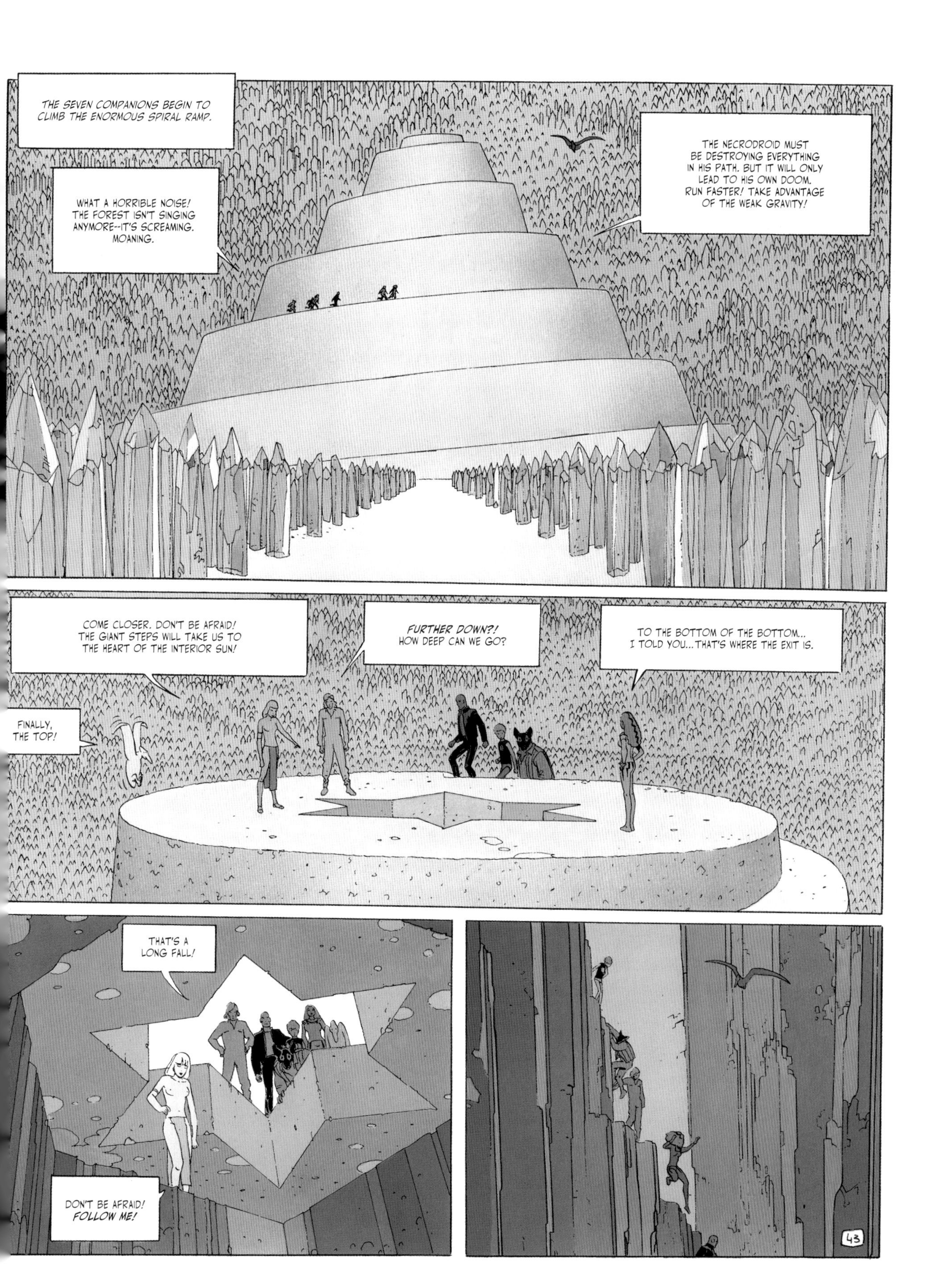
THE SEVEN COMPANIONS BEGIN TO CLIMB THE ENORMOUS SPIRAL RAMP.
WHAT A HORRIBLE NOISE! THE FOREST ISN'T SINGING ANYMORE--IT'S SCREAMING. MOANING.
THE NECRODROID MUST BE DESTROYING EVERYTHING IN HIS PATH. BUT IT WILL ONLY LEAD TO HIS OWN DOOM. RUN FASTER! TAKE ADVANTAGE OF THE WEAK GRAVITY!
COME CLOSER. DON'T BE AFRAID! THE GIANT STEPS WILL TAKE US TO THE HEART OF THE INTERIOR SUN!
FURTHER DOWN?! HOW DEEP CAN WE GO?
TO THE BOTTOM OF THE BOTTOM... I TOLD YOU...THAT'S WHERE THE EXIT IS.
FINALLY, THE TOP!
THAT'S A LONG FALL!
DON'T BE AFRAID! FOLLOW ME!
43

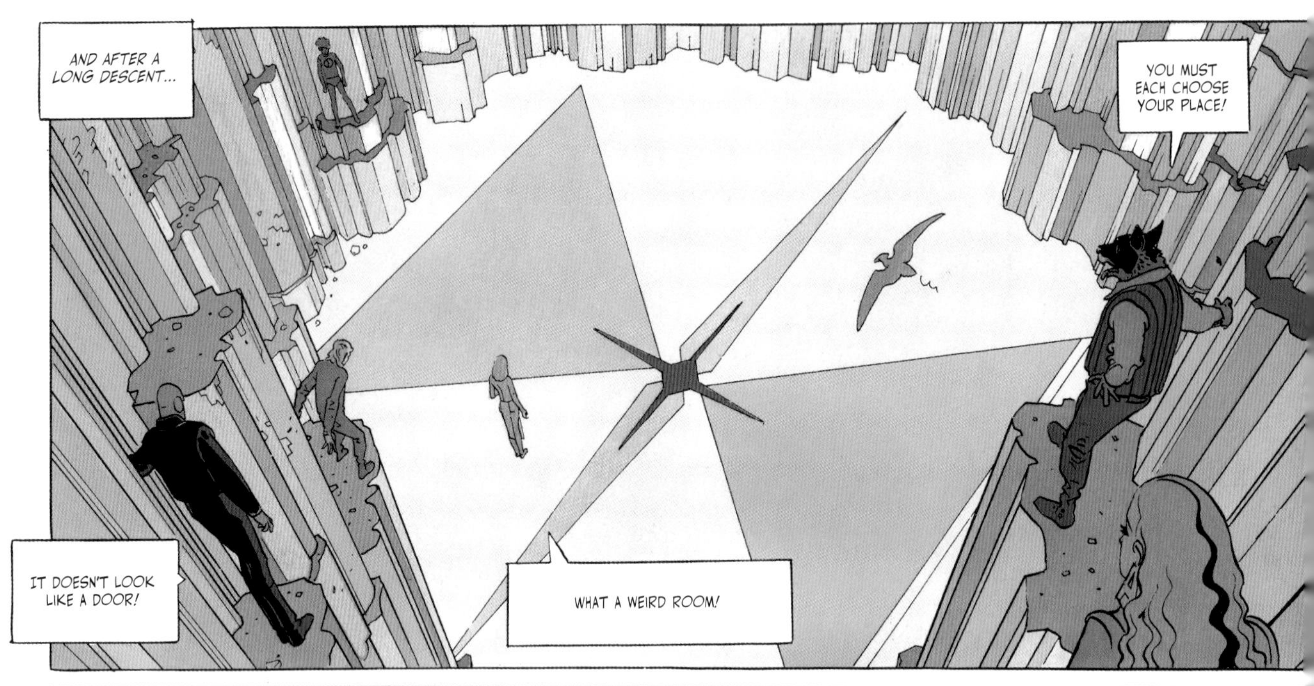
AND AFTER A LONG DESCENT...
YOU MUST EACH CHOOSE YOUR PLACE!
IT DOESN'T LOOK LIKE A DOOR!
WHAT A WEIRD ROOM!

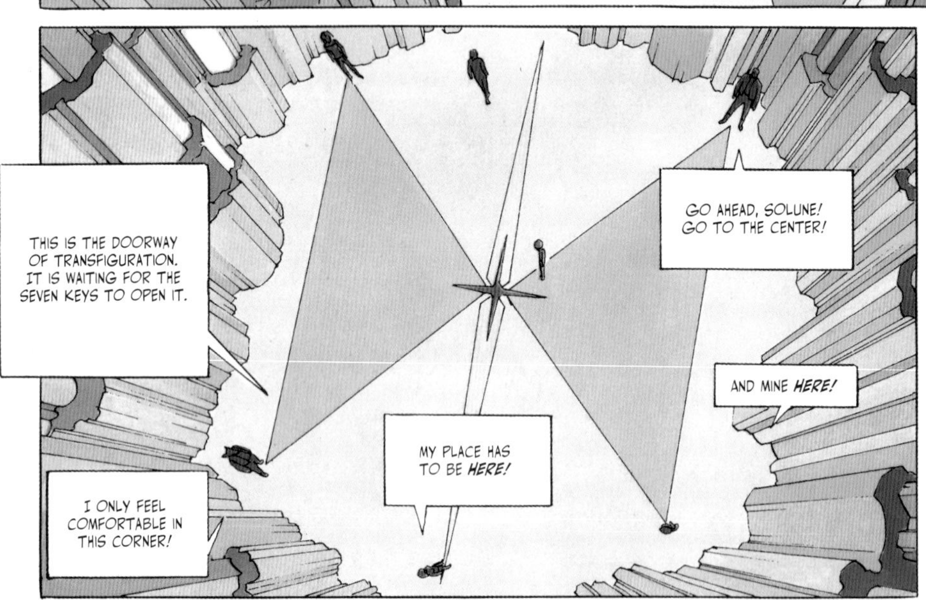
GO AHEAD, SOLUNE! GO TO THE CENTER!
THIS IS THE DOORWAY OF TRANSFIGURATION. IT IS WAITING FOR THE SEVEN KEYS TO OPEN IT.
AND MINE HERE!
MY PLACE HAS TO BE HERE!
I ONLY FEEL COMFORTABLE IN THIS CORNER!

WE ARE THE SEVEN KEYS, BUT THE ONLY WAY TO ACTIVATE THE DOOR IS TO BARE OURSELVES COMPLETELY!

OKAY, EVERYONE STRIP!

KILL! YOU IDIOT! I MEAN WE HAVE TO STRIP OUR SPIRITUAL SELF-CONCEPTS AND BARE OUR SOULS FOR TRANSFIGURATION.

MOTHER... I-I'M...SCARED! WHY DO I HAVE TO BE IN THE CENTER...I'M JUST A...
44

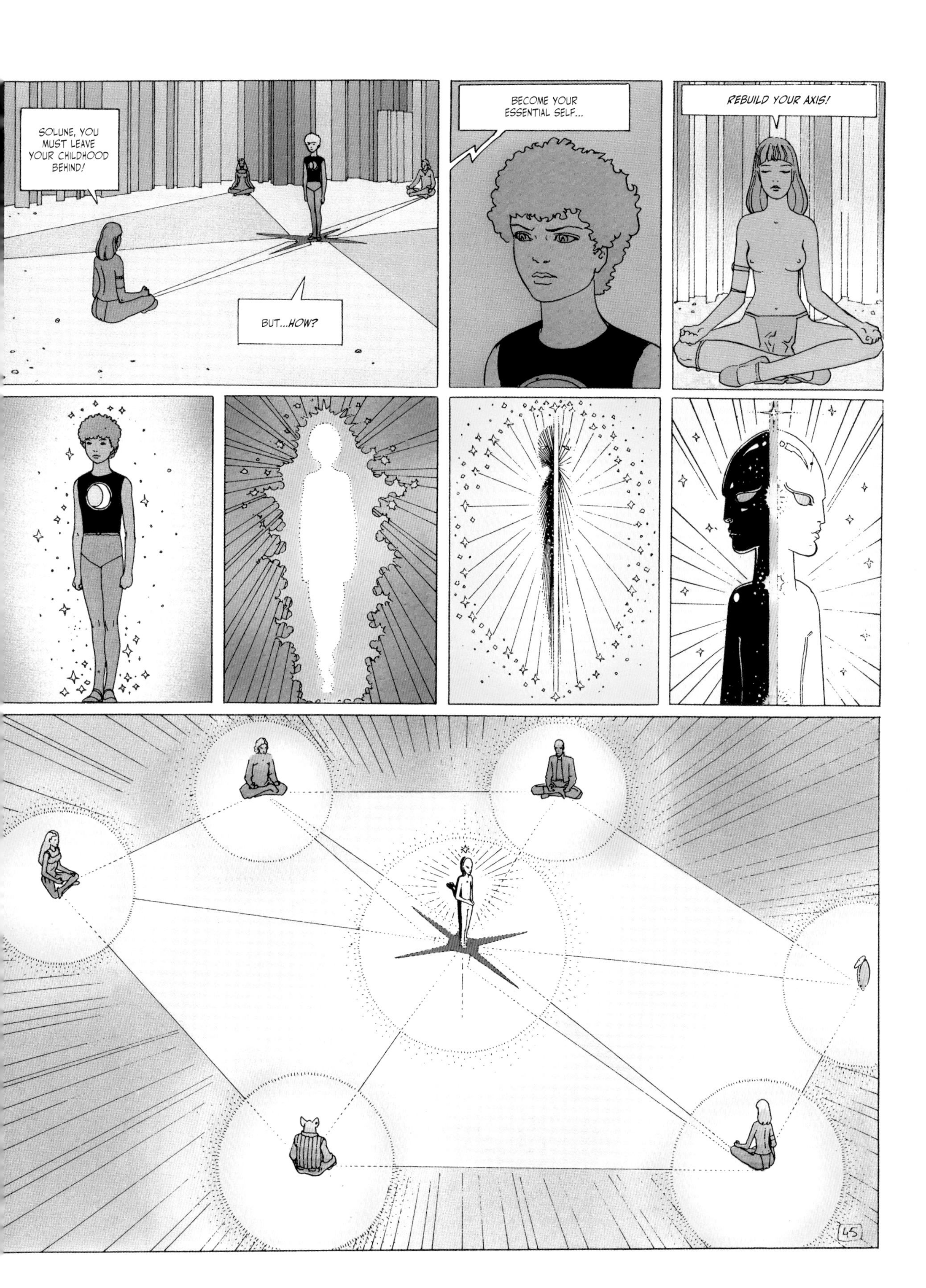
SOLUNE, YOU MUST LEAVE YOUR CHILDHOOD BEHIND!
BUT...HOW?
BECOME YOUR ESSENTIAL SELF...
REBUILD YOUR AXIS!
45

THE DOORWAY OF TRANSFIGURATION

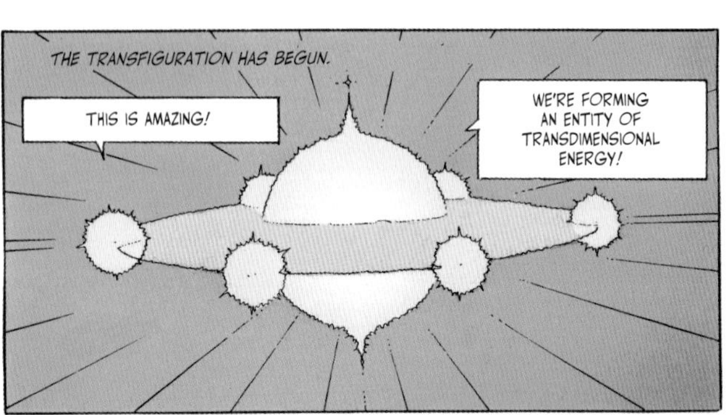

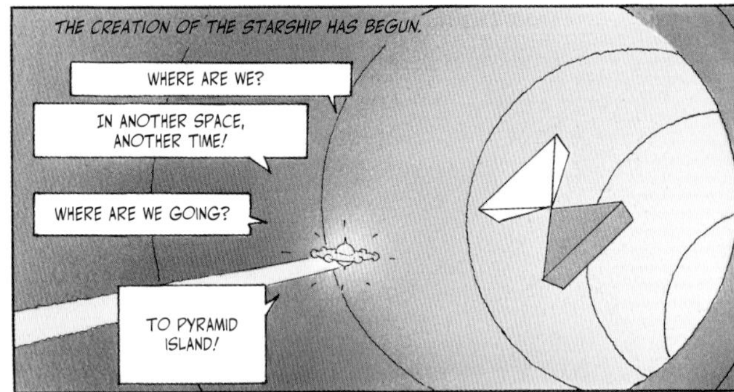

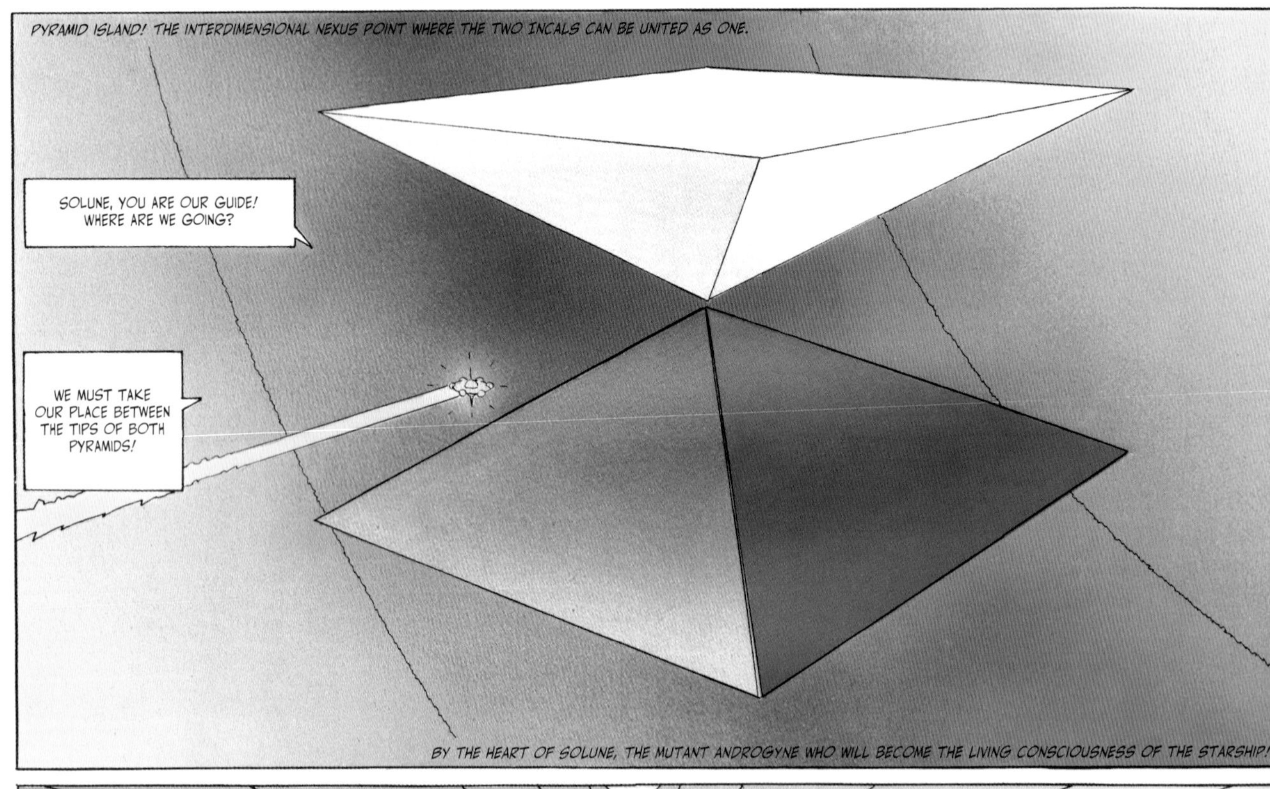

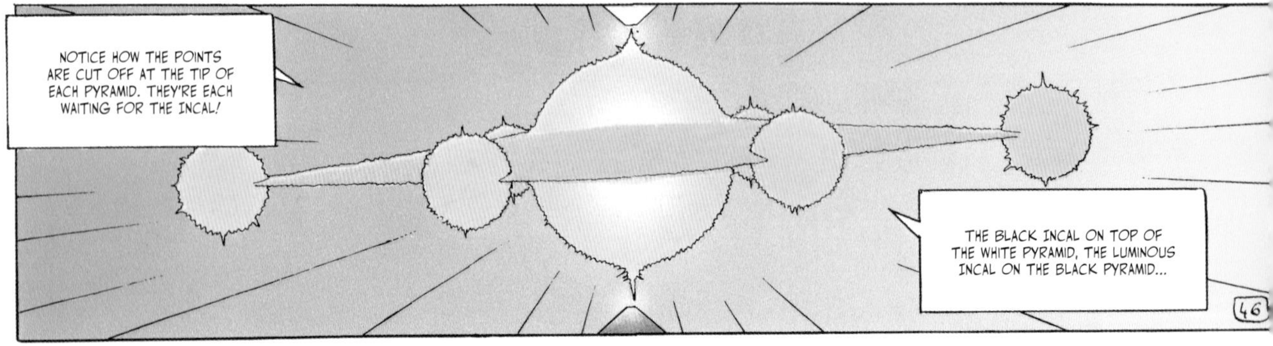

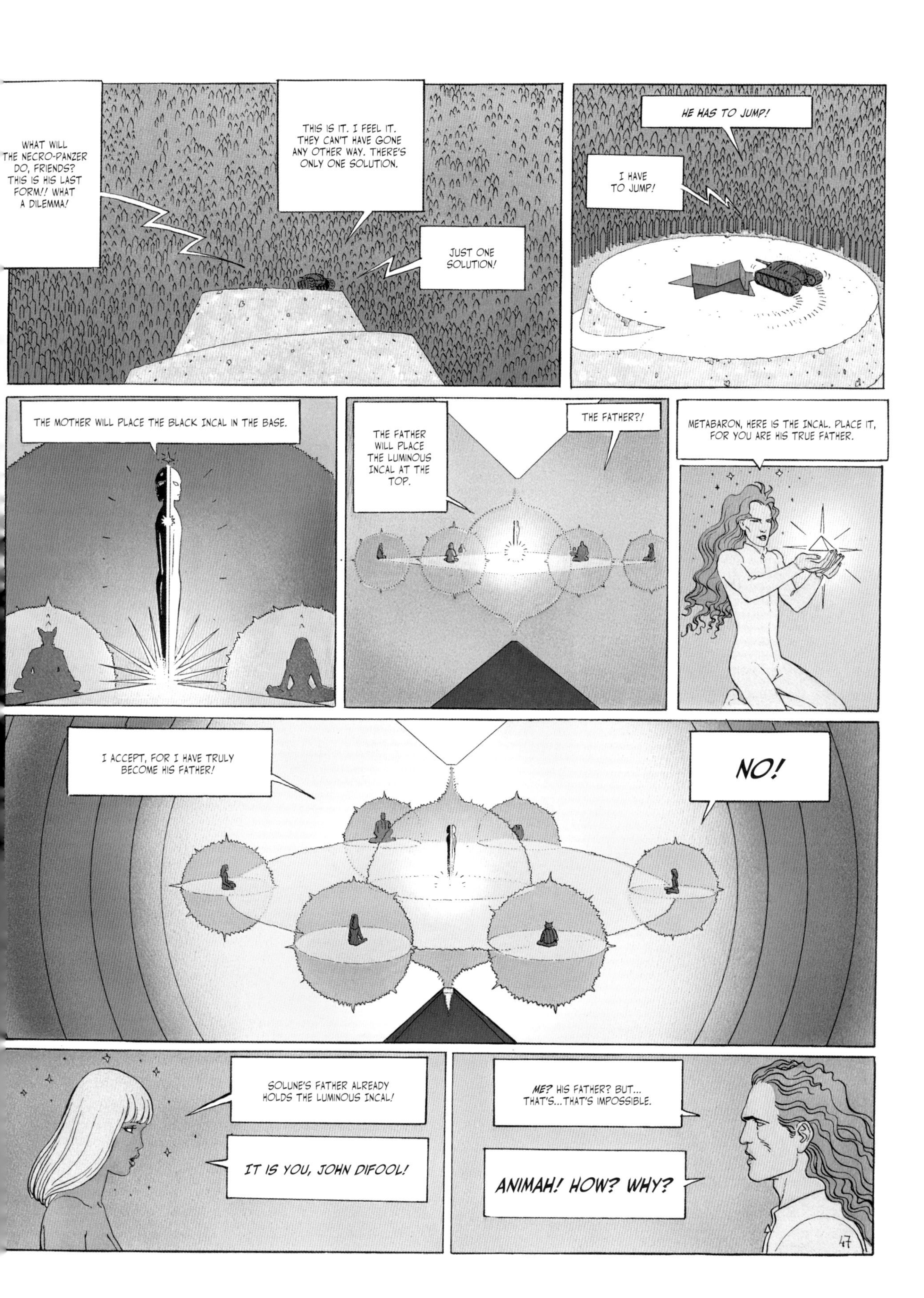
WHAT WILL THE NECRO-PANZER DO, FRIENDS? THIS IS HIS LAST FORM!! WHAT A DILEMMA!
THIS IS IT. I FEEL IT. THEY CAN'T HAVE GONE ANY OTHER WAY. THERE'S ONLY ONE SOLUTION.
JUST ONE SOLUTION!
HE HAS TO JUMP!
I HAVE TO JUMP!
THE MOTHER WILL PLACE THE BLACK INCAL IN THE BASE.
THE FATHER WILL PLACE THE LUMINOUS INCAL AT THE TOP.
THE FATHER?!
METABARON, HERE IS THE INCAL. PLACE IT, FOR YOU ARE HIS TRUE FATHER.
I ACCEPT, FOR I HAVE TRULY BECOME HIS FATHER!
NO!
SOLUNE'S FATHER ALREADY HOLDS THE LUMINOUS INCAL!
IT IS YOU, JOHN DIFOOL!
ME? HIS FATHER? BUT... THAT'S...THAT'S IMPOSSIBLE.
ANIMAH! HOW? WHY?
47

YOU HAD TO BE THE FATHER. AND FOR THAT I HAD TO TRANSFORM MYSELF INTO A HOMEO-WHORE. WHEN YOU WENT FOR ONE OF YOUR FREQUENT VISITS TO THE CRIMSON RING, I MET YOU IN THAT DEN OF INIQUITY!
IT IS TRUE...MY SISTER HAS ALWAYS OBEYED THE WILL OF THE INCAL.
BUT...WHY ME? DID YOU SENSE MY INNER STRENGTH?
DON'T BE AN IDIOT, JOHN DIFOOL! WHAT YOU HAVE BECOME IS ONLY VIRTUAL. DEEP DOWN YOU'RE STILL JUST A PATHETIC CLASS R DETECTIVE!
YOU WERE THE ONLY ONE WHOSE GENETIC CODE COULD PRODUCE SOLUNE'S MUTATION. IT WAS A ONE IN A MILLION SHOT...AND IT WORKED! DO YOU UNDERSTAND NOW?
I UNDERSTAND. I'M READY TO PLACE THE INCAL FOR THE SON WHO IS MINE BY DIVINE WILL!
MEANWHILE...
GDAMMMM
GGDEAR TELEGFREDDS...GWEE ARE GETTING CLOSEGLLD...
GDBUT...
DAMMIT!
I'M BREAKGGD APARDTT!
I FEEL NAUSEATED!
I'M GONNA PUKE!!
AND WE CAN'T CHANGE THE CHANNEL!
...GGDDOWN!...
CLANG!
...ALL THE GGDDOWN!...
THE CRYSTAL FOREST'S MICROVIBRATIONS WEAKENED MY LAST SHELL!...
48

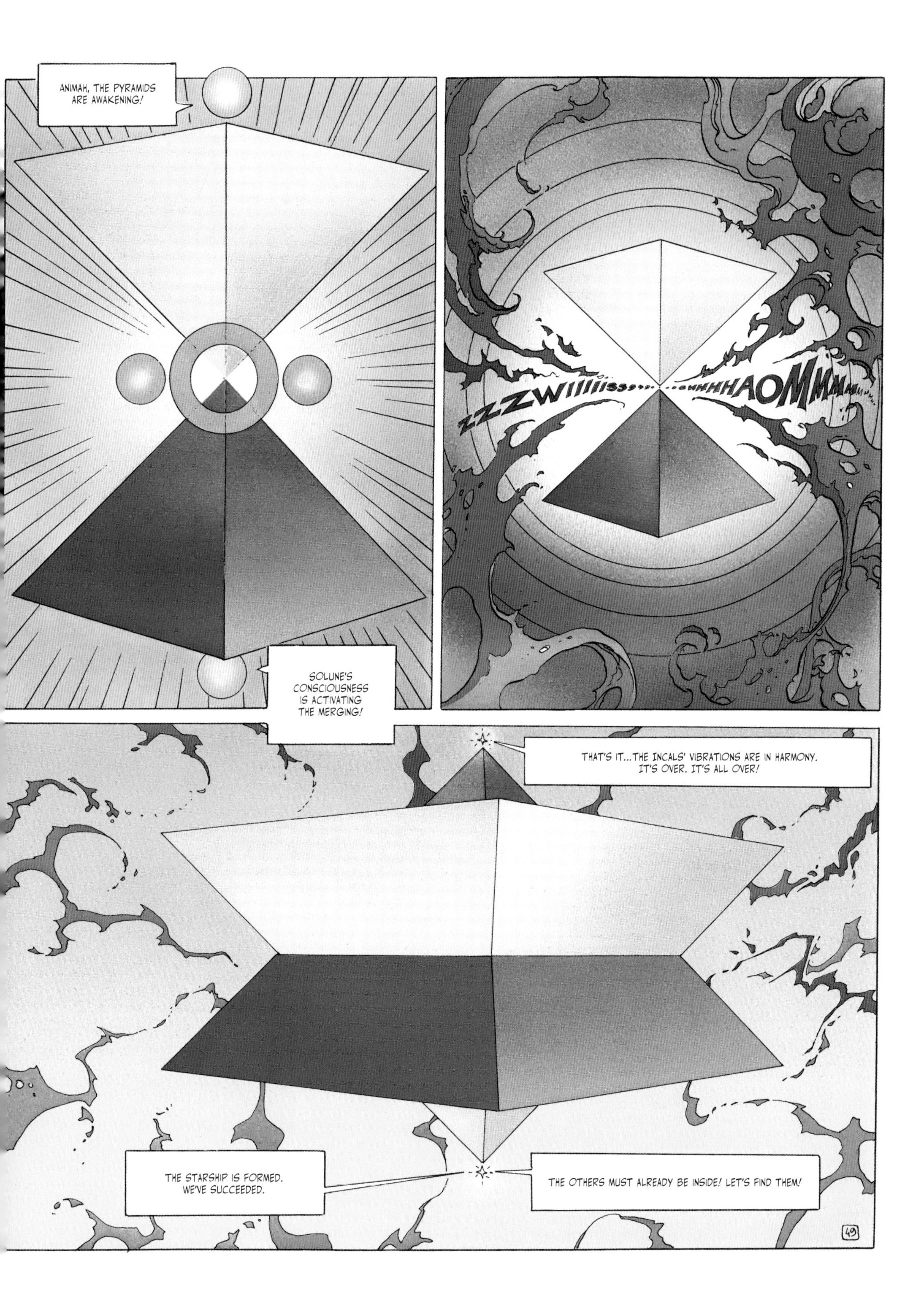
ANIMAH, THE PYRAMIDS ARE AWAKENING!
SOLUNE'S CONSCIOUSNESS IS ACTIVATING THE MERGING!
ZZZWIIIIISS... ...HHHAOMMM
THAT'S IT...THE INCALS' VIBRATIONS ARE IN HARMONY. IT'S OVER. IT'S ALL OVER!
THE STARSHIP IS FORMED. WE'VE SUCCEEDED.
THE OTHERS MUST ALREADY BE INSIDE! LET'S FIND THEM!
49

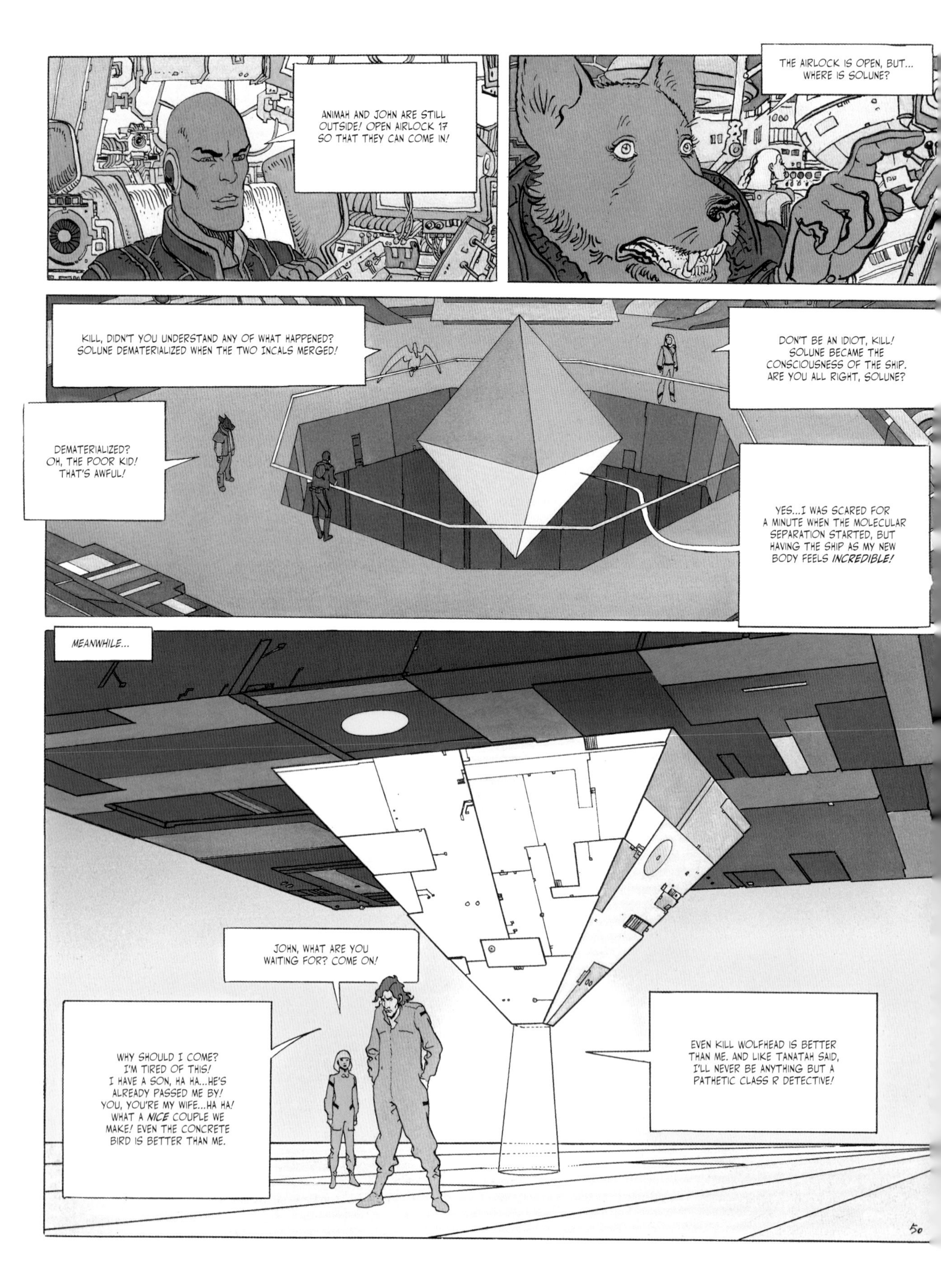
ANIMAH AND JOHN ARE STILL OUTSIDE! OPEN AIRLOCK 17 SO THAT THEY CAN COME IN!
THE AIRLOCK IS OPEN, BUT... WHERE IS SOLUNE?
KILL, DIDN'T YOU UNDERSTAND ANY OF WHAT HAPPENED? SOLUNE DEMATERIALIZED WHEN THE TWO INCALS MERGED!
DON'T BE AN IDIOT, KILL! SOLUNE BECAME THE CONSCIOUSNESS OF THE SHIP. ARE YOU ALL RIGHT, SOLUNE?
DEMATERIALIZED? OH, THE POOR KID! THAT'S AWFUL!
YES...I WAS SCARED FOR A MINUTE WHEN THE MOLECULAR SEPARATION STARTED, BUT HAVING THE SHIP AS MY NEW BODY FEELS *INCREDIBLE!*
MEANWHILE...
JOHN, WHAT ARE YOU WAITING FOR? COME ON!
WHY SHOULD I COME? I'M TIRED OF THIS! I HAVE A SON, HA HA...HE'S ALREADY PASSED ME BY! YOU, YOU'RE MY WIFE...HA HA! WHAT A *NICE* COUPLE WE MAKE! EVEN THE CONCRETE BIRD IS BETTER THAN ME.
EVEN KILL WOLFHEAD IS BETTER THAN ME. AND LIKE TANATAH SAID, I'LL NEVER BE ANYTHING BUT A PATHETIC CLASS R DETECTIVE!
50

COME ON, JOHN DIFOOL, YOU'VE MADE IT THROUGH THE HARDEST PART.
I'VE BEEN USED! THAT REALLY BUGS ME! YOU EVEN USED MY SPERM WITHOUT ASKING ME! SHIT!
AND WHERE CAN I GO NOW? EVERYTHING'S BEEN DESTROYED! NO MORE CRIMSON RING! NO MORE DETECTIVES! NO MORE DRUGS! NO MORE HOMEO-WHORES! NOTHING!
I ONLY HAD ONE ALLY... ONE ADVANTAGE... THE INCAL! AND YOU JUST TOOK THAT FROM ME TOO!
CARSHH
JOHN, COME ON! WE'LL TALK ABOUT THIS ON BOARD THE STARSHIP... I--
HUH!?
WHAT THE...?
I'VE GOT YOU NOW!
DEAR COZY TELEFRIENDS, WE ARE GGNOW AT THE BOTTOM OF THE GGBOTTOM... FACE TO FACE GWITH THE GG GGREAT REBELS! THE GBIG MOMENT HAS GGARRIVED!
THE NECRODROID! WE'RE DEAD MEAT!
I DON'T THINK SO! THERE'S NOTHING LEFT BUT A WALKING HOLO-CAMERA!
A HOLO-CAMERA? THAT'S PERFECT! I JUST HAPPEN TO HAVE SOMETHING TO SAY RIGHT NOW!
JOHN?
51

GGGDTHE CRIMINAL GDGD IS COMING-HEY!
I KNOW YOU, YOU'RE JOHN DIFOOL!! YOU'RE THE ONE WHO RUINED ME!

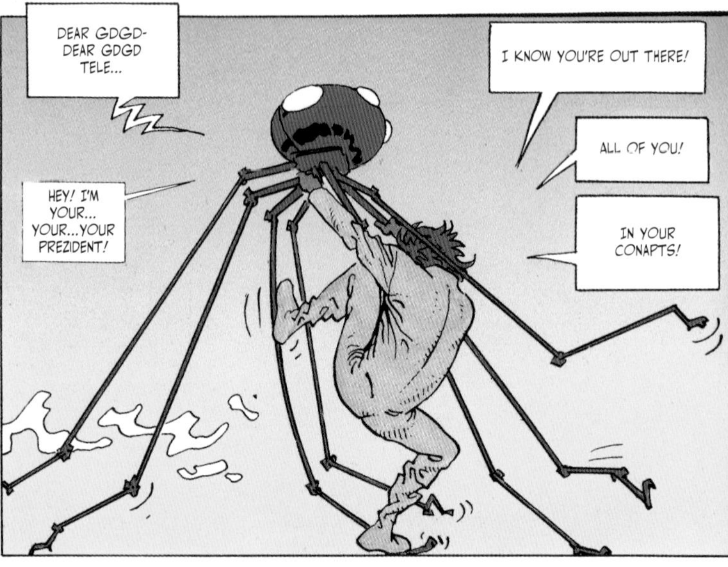
DEAR GDGD-DEAR GDGD TELE...
HEY! I'M YOUR... YOUR...YOUR PREZIDENT!
I KNOW YOU'RE OUT THERE!
ALL OF YOU!
IN YOUR CONAPTS!

THE EMPIRE IS FINISHED!
!?

DEAR TELE-FRIENDS! I GD! I GDD! GDDDD... KRIOOOO...
NO MORE HOLOVID FOR YOU!
NO MORE!

LEAVE YOUR CONAPTS! GO INTO THE WORLD! GO TOWARDS THE LIGHT! THE LIGHT!
KROUIK...

THE LIGHT!
WHAT IS THIS AD FOR?
HE'S CRAZY!
THE HOLOVID'S GONE CRAZY!
52

MAMA!
THE SCREEN'S GONE DARK!
BLANK!
OH NO! I WANNA SEE THE END!
THE HOLOVID'S DEAD!
HELP!
LEAVE YOUR CONAPTS!
I'LL TAKE WHAT'S LEFT OF YOU, YOU NECROPOD.
CRRRR ZZZZZZ
PUT ME DOWN, ASSHOLE, PUT ME DOWN!
I'M COMING, ANIMAH. WHAT OTHER CHOICE DO I HAVE?
I'M YOUR PREZ! DO YOU HEAR ME?!?
NOT MUCH, JOHN! LET'S GO. THE STARSHIP CAN TAKE US TO THE OTHER END OF THE UNIVERSE!
AND MAYBE BEYOND!
AND SOON...
READY TO ENTER SUBSPACE! WE'LL EMERGE ONE LIGHT SECOND AWAY FROM HERE.
YES, FATHER!
53

AMAZING! LOOK AT THE MOON! WHAT A VIEW!
WE CAN SEE THE WHOLE PLANET FROM HERE! SUDDENLY EVERYTHING IS SO FAR AWAY...THE ACID LAKE... THE GARBAGE...THE RIOTS...
BUT...THE...THE SUN! LOOK! SOMETHING'S HIDING THE SUN!
I RECOGNIZE IT! IT'S THE TECHNOGUILD'S SHADOW EGG! IT'S HORRIBLE! IT'S DEVOURING THE SUN!!
54

MOEBIUS

WHAT IS ABOVE

VITAVIL H²O

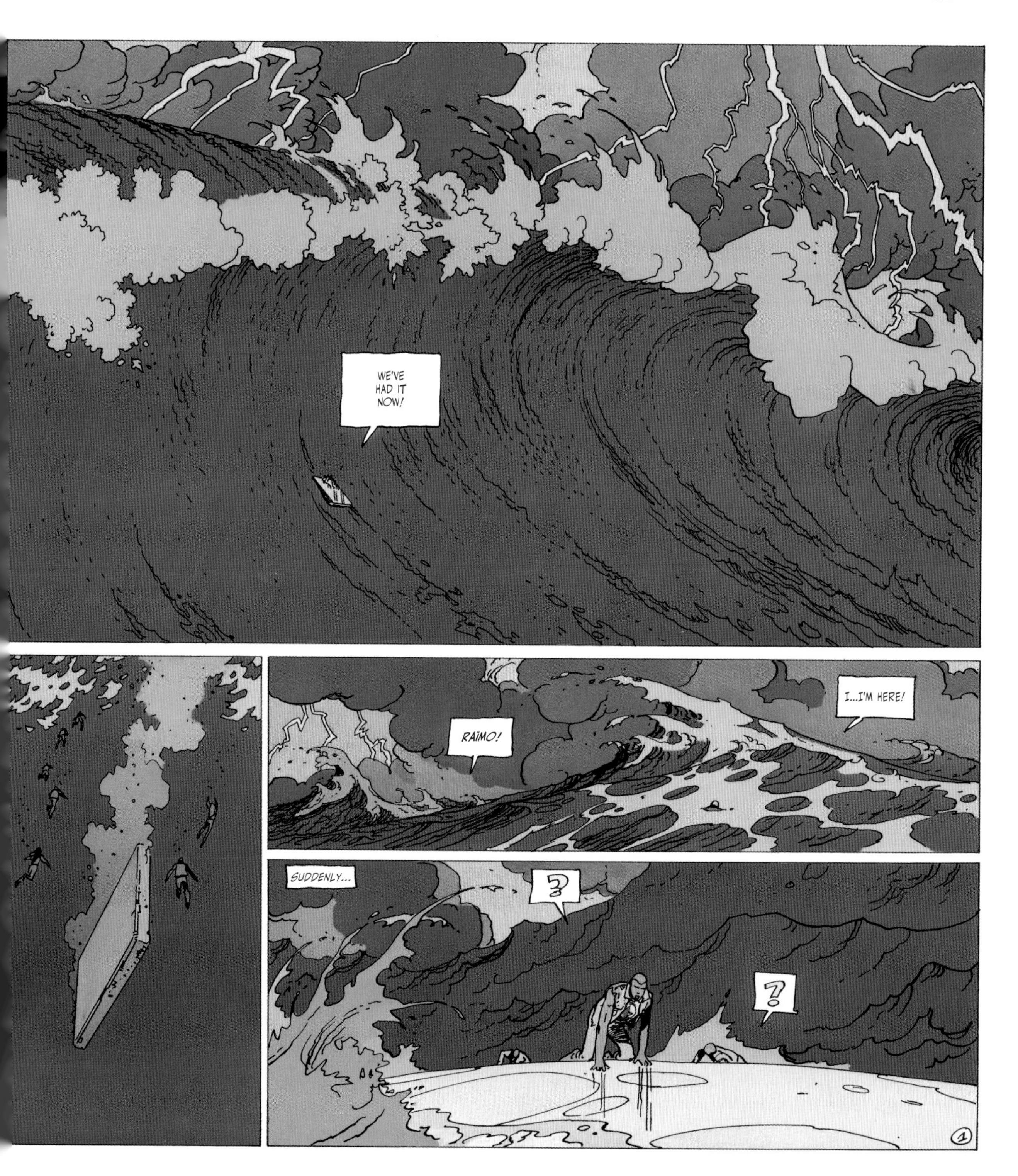

WATCH OUT! THE SURFACE STINGS!
LOOK! THERE! A MAN!
DON'T BE AFRAID, COMRADE RAÏMO! MY NAME IS EDO! I'VE BEEN SENT TO WELCOME YOU! FOLLOW MY INSTRUCTIONS AND ALL WILL BE WELL!
IT'S LIKE HE'S INSIDE THE MEDUSA!
FIRST, YOU MUST WILLINGLY ACCEPT THE MEDUSA, PHYSICALLY, MENTALLY AND PSYCHICALLY.
THEN AND ONLY THEN WILL SHE GRANT YOU HER PROTECTION!
TELL US WHAT TO DO, EDO!
2

?
RAÏMO! I FEEL A FRIENDLY MENTAL PROBE!
ON AQUAEND, THE MEDUSAE ARE OUR ALLIES! WITHOUT THEM, WE COULD NEVER HAVE SURVIVED AND BUILT A NEW CIVILIZATION! LET HER SURROUND YOU! SHE WILL BECOME YOUR SECOND SKIN, A PERFECT DIVING SUIT IN TOTAL HARMONY WITH YOUR OWN BODY.
SHE WILL ENABLE YOU TO BREATHE FREELY UNDERWATER. SHE WILL INSULATE YOU FROM THE PRESSURE OF THE DEPTHS.
BUT, WHERE ARE YOU TAKING US? EVERYONE KNOWS THAT AQUAEND IS A WATER WORLD, WITHOUT LAND OR EVEN A SOLID PLANETARY CORE! THAT'S WHY IT WAS TURNED INTO A PRISON!
AQUAEND IS FILLED WITH MANY SURPRISES! YOU'LL SEE.
FIRST, LET THE MEDUSA RECEIVE YOU INTO HER HEART!
SHE'LL TAKE US TO VITAVIL H2O, OUR CAPITAL!
AS YOU CAN SEE, IT'S PERFECTLY SAFE!
FOLLOW ME!
SOMEONE WAITS FOR YOU BELOW!
3

?
?
SOMEONE YOU MAY KNOW!

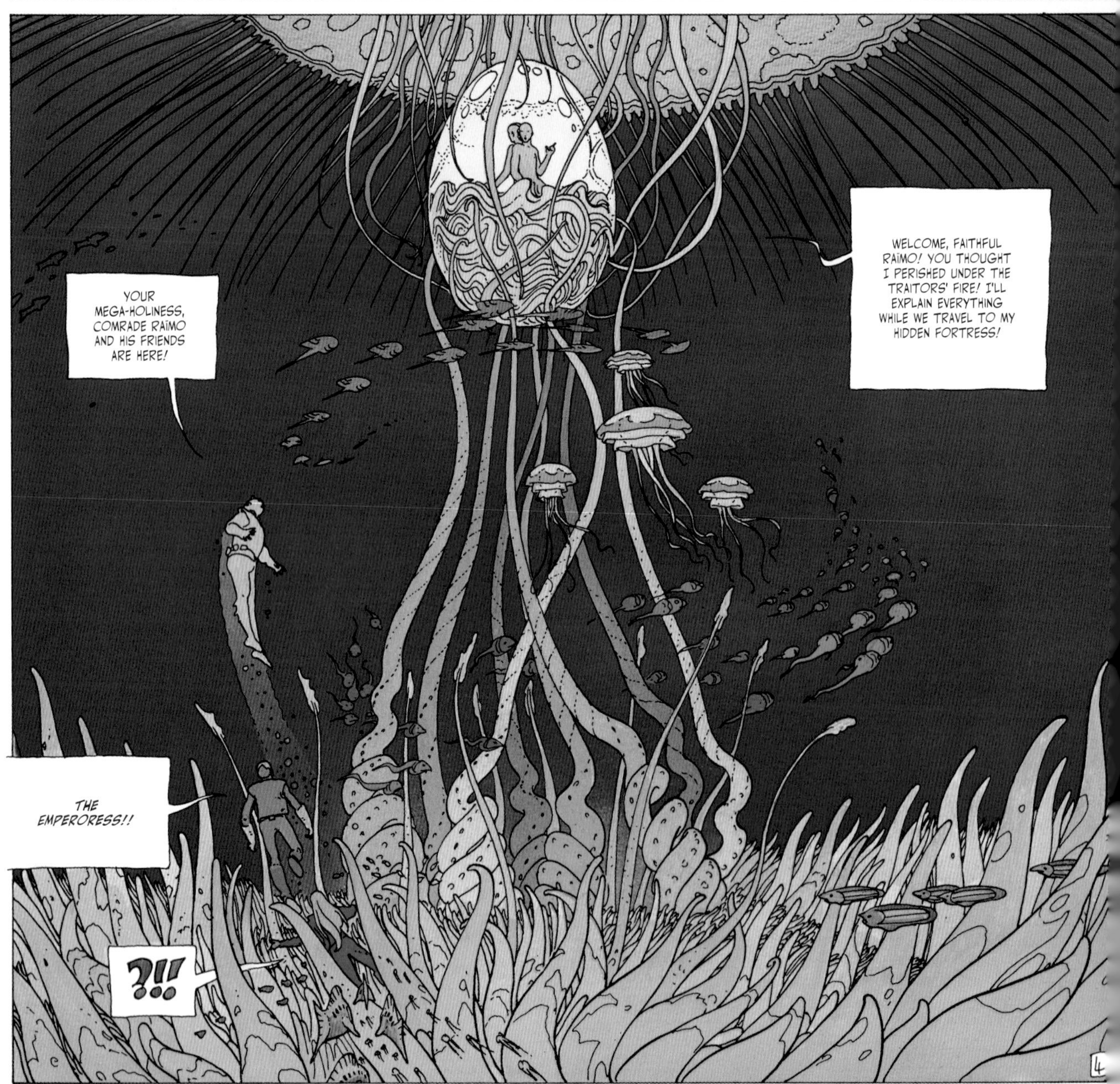
YOUR MEGA-HOLINESS, COMRADE RAÏMO AND HIS FRIENDS ARE HERE!
WELCOME, FAITHFUL RAÏMO! YOU THOUGHT I PERISHED UNDER THE TRAITORS' FIRE! I'LL EXPLAIN EVERYTHING WHILE WE TRAVEL TO MY HIDDEN FORTRESS!
THE EMPERORESS!!
?!!
4

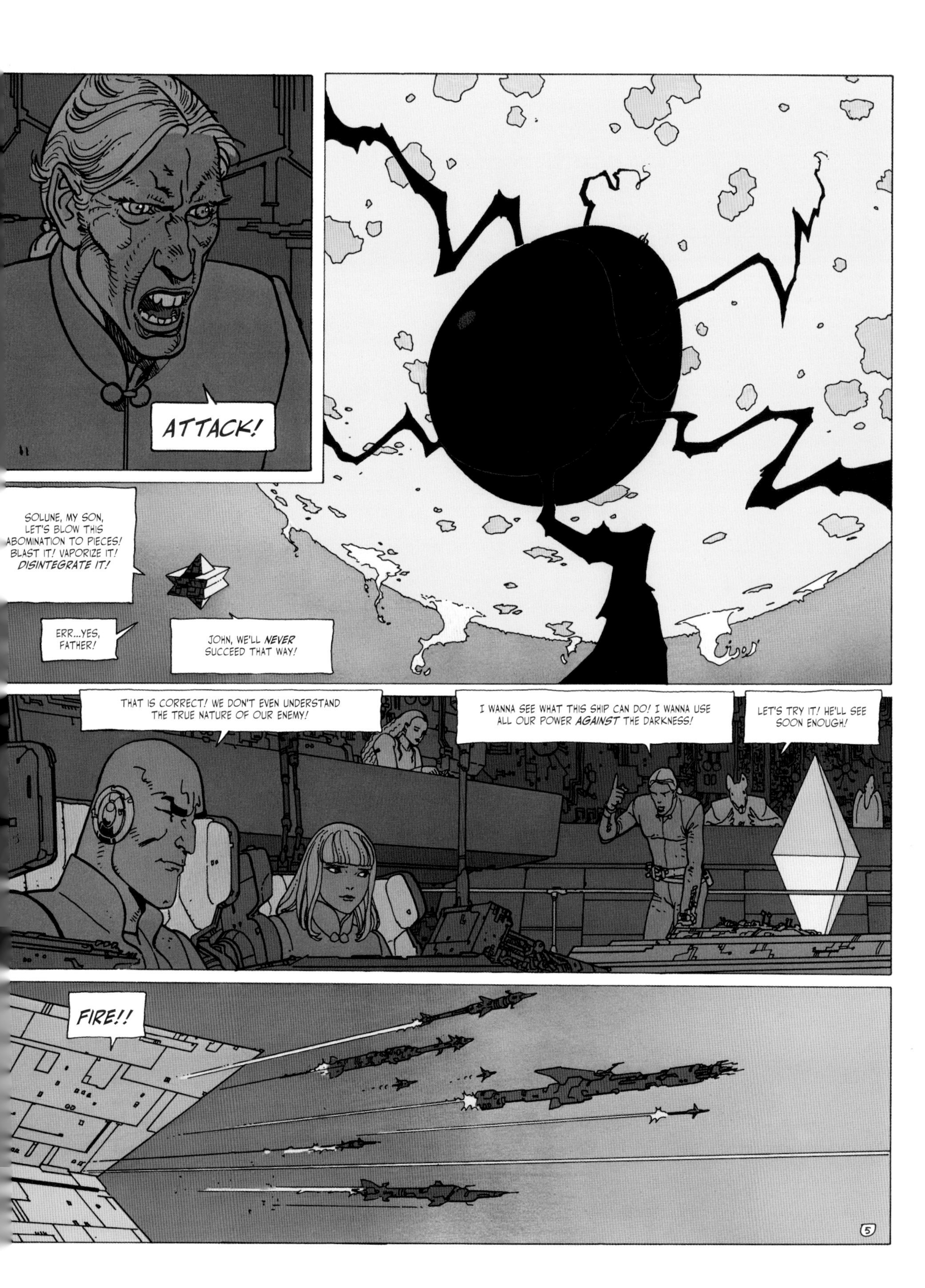
ATTACK!
SOLUNE, MY SON, LET'S BLOW THIS ABOMINATION TO PIECES! BLAST IT! VAPORIZE IT! DISINTEGRATE IT!
ERR...YES, FATHER!
JOHN, WE'LL NEVER SUCCEED THAT WAY!
THAT IS CORRECT! WE DON'T EVEN UNDERSTAND THE TRUE NATURE OF OUR ENEMY!
I WANNA SEE WHAT THIS SHIP CAN DO! I WANNA USE ALL OUR POWER AGAINST THE DARKNESS!
LET'S TRY IT! HE'LL SEE SOON ENOUGH!
FIRE!!
5

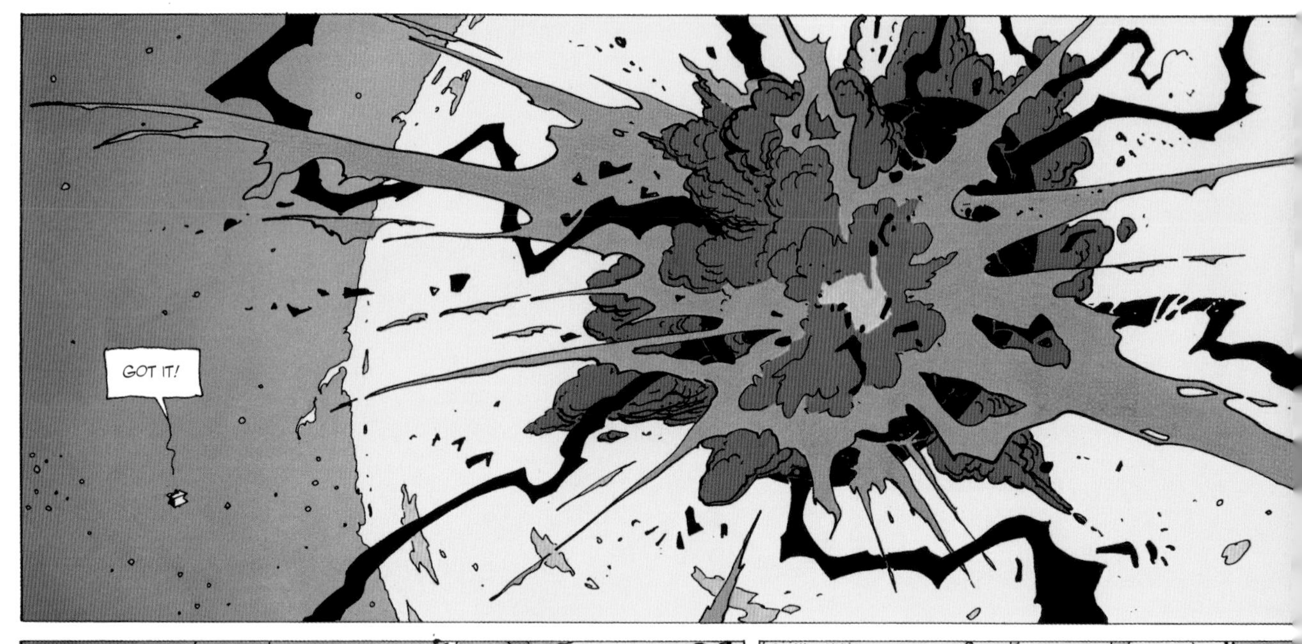
GOT IT!

?!!
THE EGG SPLIT INTO TINY BITS!
LOOK AT WHAT YOU'VE *DONE*, JOHN! NOW WE HAVE A THOUSAND SHADOW EGGS ON OUR HANDS!

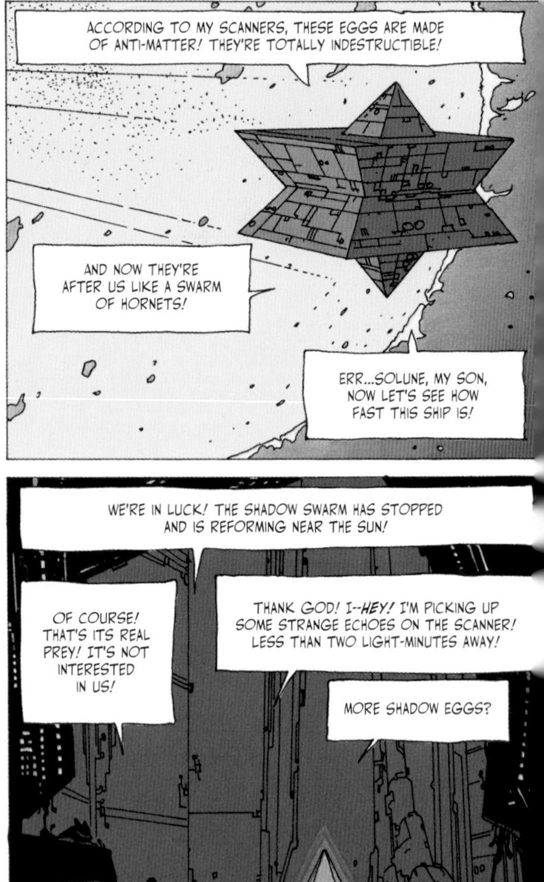
ACCORDING TO MY SCANNERS, THESE EGGS ARE MADE OF ANTI-MATTER! THEY'RE TOTALLY INDESTRUCTIBLE!
AND NOW THEY'RE AFTER US LIKE A SWARM OF HORNETS!
ERR...SOLUNE, MY SON, NOW LET'S SEE HOW FAST THIS SHIP IS!
WE'RE IN LUCK! THE SHADOW SWARM HAS STOPPED AND IS REFORMING NEAR THE SUN!
OF COURSE! THAT'S ITS REAL PREY! IT'S NOT INTERESTED IN US!
THANK GOD! I--*HEY!* I'M PICKING UP SOME STRANGE ECHOES ON THE SCANNER! LESS THAN TWO LIGHT-MINUTES AWAY!
MORE SHADOW EGGS?
6

THE BERG FLEET!
THEIR ARMADA HAS INVADED THIS GALAXY! THEY SEE US!

RIGHT! AT LEAST THOSE DAMNED PARAKEETS AREN'T MADE OF ANTI-MATTER! SOLUNE, THIS TIME WE'RE GOING TO HAVE OURSELVES SOME FUN! LET'S BLAST THE SUCKERS!

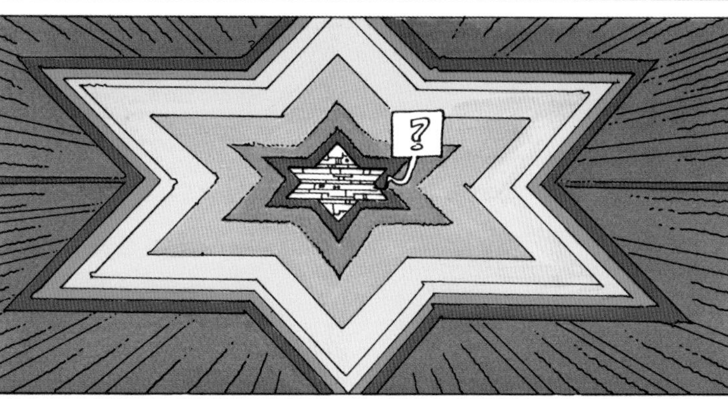
?

WHAT HAPPENED? PUT IT ON THE SCREENS. AND WHAT'S WITH THIS RED LIGHT?
WE HAD A CHANCE TO WIPE OUT THE BERGS AND INSTEAD YOU--
THE SHIPS HAVE ENTERED SUBSPACE, JOHN! THERE WON'T BE ANY FIGHT NOW!
DON'T FORGET THAT I'M THE ONE LINKED TO THE INCAL NOW, FATHER! IT TOLD ME THAT WE WOULD NEED THE BERGS SOON. SO, WHY FIGHT THEM NOW, AND TURN THEM INTO ENEMIES?
MANKIND'S REAL FOE IS THE GREAT DARKNESS, NOT THE BERGS!

BESIDES, YOU SAW HOW POWERLESS WE WERE AGAINST THE SHADOW EGGS! WHAT WE NEED TO DO IS INHIBIT THEIR FORMIDABLY INDESTRUCTIBLE DEFENSES!
INHIBIT THEIR WHAT? OKAY, GREAT, BUT, HOW? YEAH... TELL ME HOW WE DO THIS?
THE INCAL SAYS THAT THERE EXISTS SOMETHING THAT CAN CONTROL ANTI-MATTER.
7

THERE IS? AND HOW DO YOU SUGGEST WE FIND IT? SEARCH THE WHOLE GALAXY WITH A FINE-TOOTH COMB?
WE DON'T HAVE TO! THE INCAL TOLD ME WHERE TO LOOK. 120 LIGHT YEARS FROM HERE, TOWARDS THE GALACTIC CORE. WE'LL BE THERE IN 6 HOURS.
GOOD! WE ALL COULD USE A COUPLE HOURS SLEEP!

MEANWHILE...
EXCELLENCY! WE'RE APPROACHING TECHNOGEA!
WE'VE JUST ASKED FOR PERMISSION TO CROSS THE PSYCHIC BARRIER!

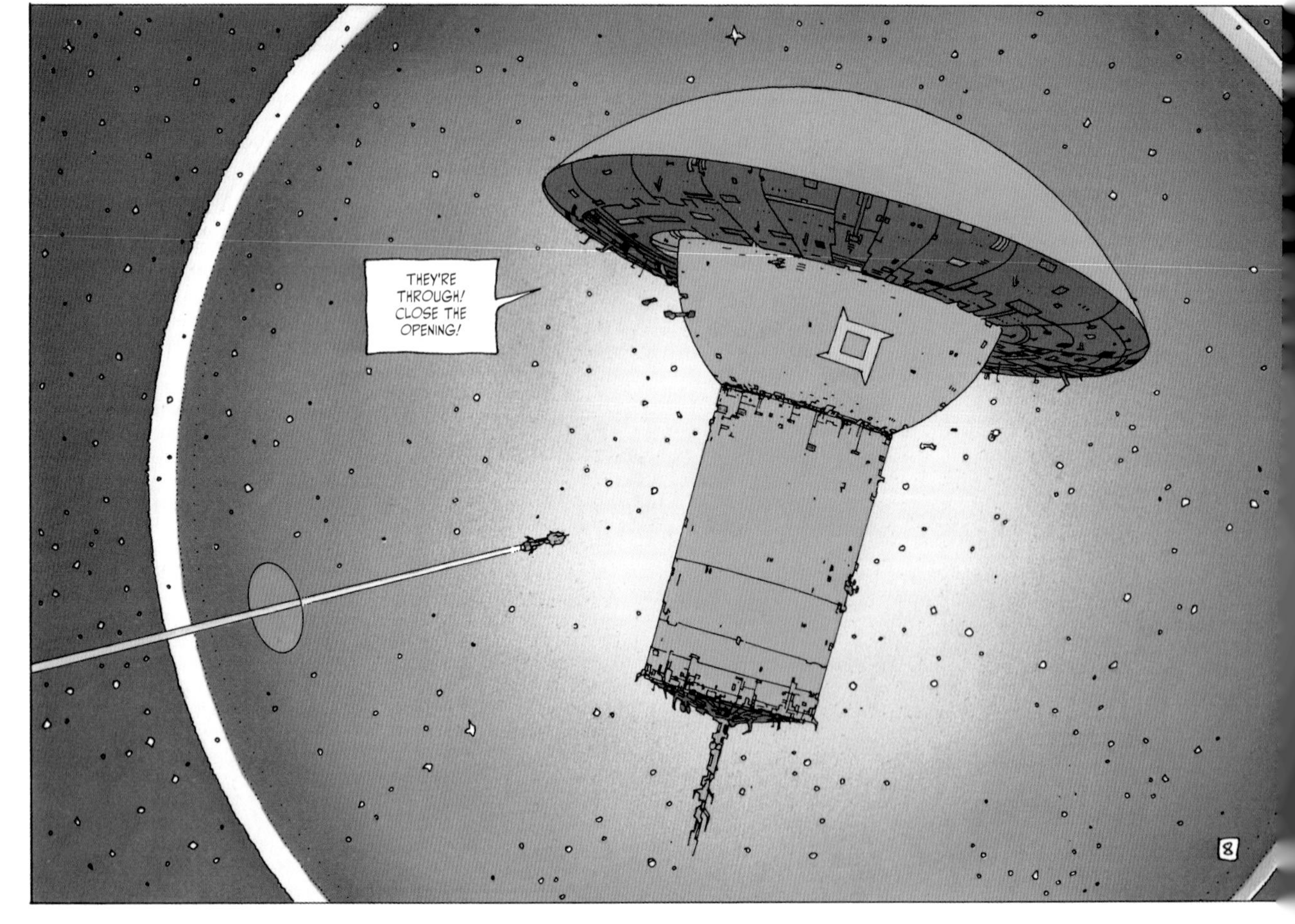
THEY'RE THROUGH! CLOSE THE OPENING!
8

THE TECHNO-CENTREUR AND THE CYCLIC COUNCIL ARE EXPECTING YOU!

I'M RECORDING, MASTER S'12! SPEAK!

ALL PROCEEDED ACCORDING TO PLAN, TECHNO-CENTREUR! THE EMPERORESS IS DEAD!
THE IMAN HORLOG'S PUPPET GOVERNMENT IS NOW IN PLACE UNDER OUR SECRET CONTROL!
CONTROL THAT PIG? I DOUBT ANYONE CAN. YOUR REPORT, MASTER TH'5. I'M RECORDING!
THE GREAT "OVE TENEBRAE" PLAN IS PROCEEDING SMOOTHLY, TECHNO-CENTREUR. 10,000 SHADOW EGGS STAND READY FOR LAUNCH THROUGHOUT THE GALAXY. SOME ARE ALREADY IN OPERATION WE--
TECHNO-CENTREUR!
EVENTS ARE OCCURRING AT THE IMAN'S PALACE. DO YOU WISH FOR A VISUAL?
BIP
I DO.

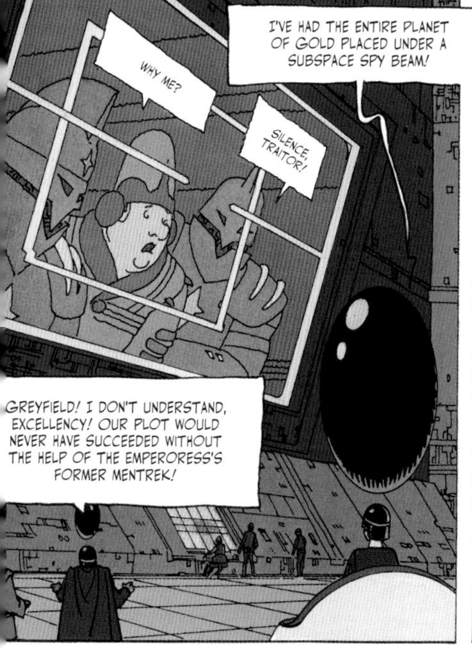
I'VE HAD THE ENTIRE PLANET OF GOLD PLACED UNDER A SUBSPACE SPY BEAM!
WHY ME?
SILENCE, TRAITOR!
GREYFIELD! I DON'T UNDERSTAND, EXCELLENCY! OUR PLOT WOULD NEVER HAVE SUCCEEDED WITHOUT THE HELP OF THE EMPERORESS'S FORMER MENTREK!

YOUR INFORMATION WAS INCOMPLETE, MASTER S'12! GREYFIELD WAS A DOUBLE AGENT FROM THE BEGINNING! THE IMAN HAS ALMOST CERTAINLY DISCOVERED THE TRUTH!

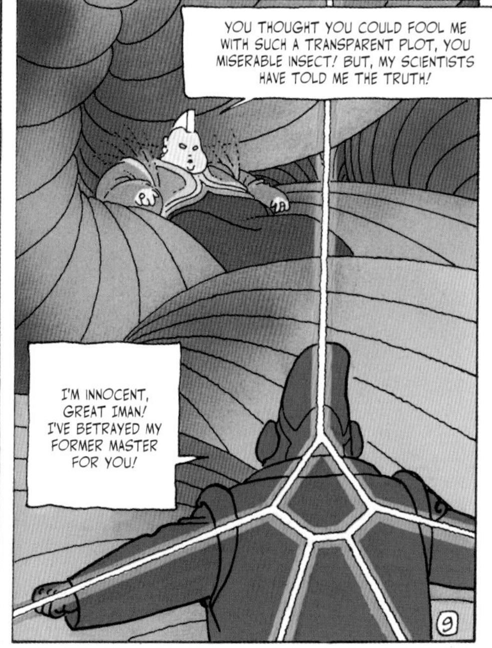
YOU THOUGHT YOU COULD FOOL ME WITH SUCH A TRANSPARENT PLOT, YOU MISERABLE INSECT! BUT, MY SCIENTISTS HAVE TOLD ME THE TRUTH!
I'M INNOCENT, GREAT IMAN! I'VE BETRAYED MY FORMER MASTER FOR YOU!
9

THAT THING KILLED IN THE PARLIAMENT WAS NOT THE REAL EMPERORESS, IT WAS A CLONE! A CLEVER TRICK, BUT DID YOU **REALLY** BELIEVE YOU COULD FOOL ME?

WHAT DO YOU ASK OF ME?

WHERE IS HE, GREYFIELD? AS LONG AS THE DAMNED, TWO-HEADED FETUS IS STILL ALIVE, MY POWER WILL NEVER BE SECURE!
YOU'RE WASTING YOUR TIME! I WON'T TALK!

THAT'S WHAT YOU THINK!
I'VE HAD INTEGRATED CONDITIONING THAT PREVENTS ME FROM TALKING! NO AMOUNT OF TORTURE CAN BREAK IT!

MAYBE NOT, BUT DO YOU THINK I'M A FOOL? A MENTREK OF YOUR CALIBER CAN OVERCOME ANY CONDITIONING! YOU JUST NEED A STRONG MOTIVATION! HA! HA!

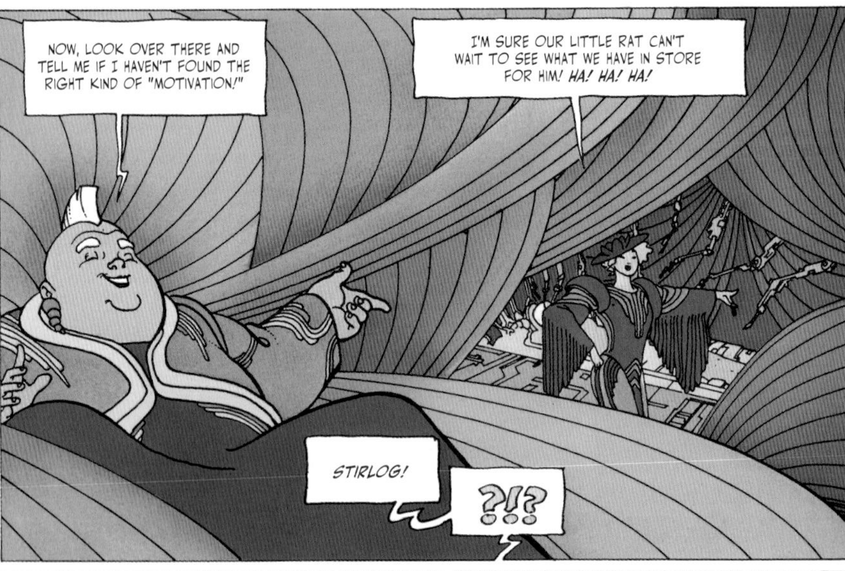

NOW, LOOK OVER THERE AND TELL ME IF I HAVEN'T FOUND THE RIGHT KIND OF "MOTIVATION!"
I'M SURE OUR LITTLE RAT CAN'T WAIT TO SEE WHAT WE HAVE IN STORE FOR HIM! HA! HA! HA!
STIRLOG!
?!?

SO? I'M WAITING FOR APPLAUSE FROM THE AUDIENCE!
AH! AT LAST!
NO!!!

CRYSTAL! MY GRANDDAUGHTER!
MONSTERS!
DON'T DARE HARM HER!
10

DO YOU RECOGNIZE THIS, GREYFIELD? IT'S A *CRYOGENOR!* YOUR DARLING CRYSTAL IS REALLY GOING TO EARN HER NAME NOW! *HA! HA! HA!*

CHOCKKKKKKKK
CLIC!

MONSTERS! HOW CAN YOU DO THIS TO AN INNOCENT CHILD?
HAHAHA!!!
COME ON, GREYFIELD! NOBODY'S *TRULY* INNOCENT!
BESIDES, SHE'S NOT ACTUALLY DEAD! SHE'S ONLY FROZEN! PROTECTED FROM THE WORLD'S UGLINESS BY AN ICY SLUMBER!

UNFORTUNATELY, THERE'S ONE LITTLE PROBLEM! THAT NEW ICE BODY IS TERRIBLY *FRAGILE!* THE LITTLEST SHOCK AND...*CRACK!* YOU CAN IMAGINE THE CATASTROPHIC RESULTS!
NO!! HAVE COMPASSION!
KACK!
TSK! TSK! AREN'T I CLUMSY? I SEEM TO HAVE BROKEN HER LITTLE FINGER! AND TO THINK THAT THE REST OF HER BODY IS JUST AS BRITTLE! IF WE'RE NOT CAREFUL, WE COULD SHATTER THAT PRETTY BODY INTO A THOUSAND PIECES!
STOP! *YOU'VE WON!* I'LL DO ANYTHING YOU WANT!
EXCELLENT! YOU SEE, STIRLOG, I WAS RIGHT! NO CONDITIONING CAN RESIST GOOD, STRONG MOTIVATION! NOW, LET'S MOVE ON TO MORE SERIOUS MATTERS: OUR DINNER PLANS!

IT'S NOT THAT SIMPLE, IMAN! I MAY BE WILLING TO DO YOUR BIDDING, BUT I'M STILL PHYSICALLY UNABLE TO REVEAL WHERE THE EMPERORESS IS!
WELL, THEN I'LL JUST HAVE TO SEND YOU STRAIGHT BACK TO YOUR MASTER, WON'T I? *HA! HA! HA!*
WITH A LITTLE PRESENT FROM US, OF COURSE!
A PRESENT? WHAT DO YOU MEAN?
MY SURGEONS WILL IMPLANT YOU WITH AN EXPLOSIVE PREPROGRAMMED TO DETONATE ONLY WHEN YOU'RE IN THE PRESENCE OF THE REAL EMPERORESS! THAT WAY, YOU'LL BE OUR LIVING BOMB, AND YET, YOU'LL DO NOTHING AGAINST YOUR VAUNTED CONDITIONING.
11

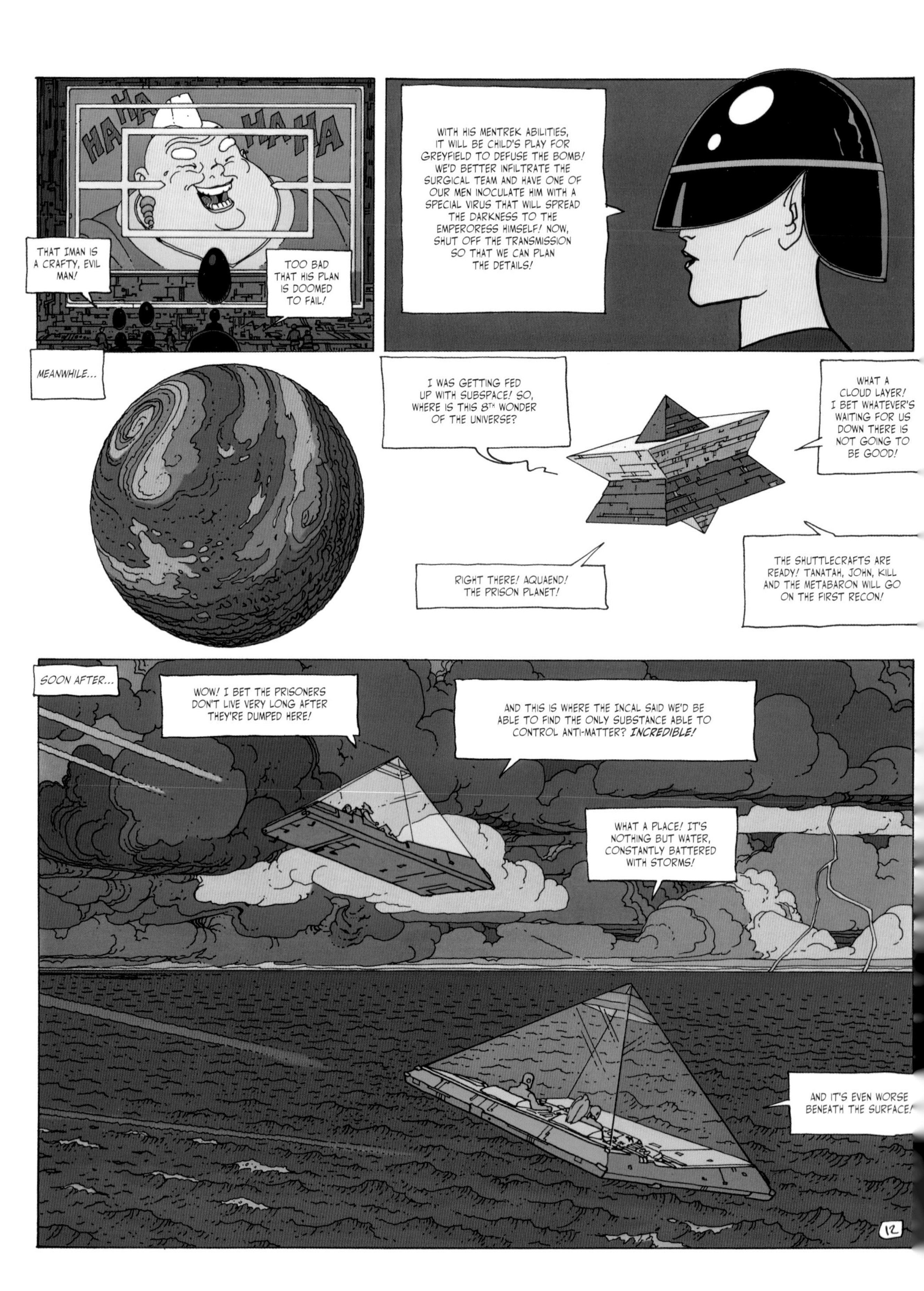
HA HA
HA HA
THAT IMAN IS A CRAFTY, EVIL MAN!
TOO BAD THAT HIS PLAN IS DOOMED TO FAIL!
WITH HIS MENTREK ABILITIES, IT WILL BE CHILD'S PLAY FOR GREYFIELD TO DEFUSE THE BOMB! WE'D BETTER INFILTRATE THE SURGICAL TEAM AND HAVE ONE OF OUR MEN INOCULATE HIM WITH A SPECIAL VIRUS THAT WILL SPREAD THE DARKNESS TO THE EMPERORESS HIMSELF! NOW, SHUT OFF THE TRANSMISSION SO THAT WE CAN PLAN THE DETAILS!
MEANWHILE...
I WAS GETTING FED UP WITH SUBSPACE! SO, WHERE IS THIS 8TH WONDER OF THE UNIVERSE?
RIGHT THERE! AQUAEND! THE PRISON PLANET!
WHAT A CLOUD LAYER! I BET WHATEVER'S WAITING FOR US DOWN THERE IS NOT GOING TO BE GOOD!
THE SHUTTLECRAFTS ARE READY! TANATAH, JOHN, KILL AND THE METABARON WILL GO ON THE FIRST RECON!
SOON AFTER...
WOW! I BET THE PRISONERS DON'T LIVE VERY LONG AFTER THEY'RE DUMPED HERE!
AND THIS IS WHERE THE INCAL SAID WE'D BE ABLE TO FIND THE ONLY SUBSTANCE ABLE TO CONTROL ANTI-MATTER? INCREDIBLE!
WHAT A PLACE! IT'S NOTHING BUT WATER, CONSTANTLY BATTERED WITH STORMS!
AND IT'S EVEN WORSE BENEATH THE SURFACE!
12

ACCORDING TO THE GALACTIC GUIDE, THE SEA IS FULL OF POISONOUS ALGAE, ACID BASED PLANKTON, CARNIVOROUS FISH, AND ALL THAT.
AND WE'RE SUPPOSED TO FIND AN ALLY AGAINST THE SHADOW EGGS IN THE MIDST OF THIS DAMN WATER JUNGLE?

IF ONLY THE INCAL TOLD US *WHAT* WE'RE LOOKING FOR--*HEY!*
WHAT ABOUT THAT? IS THAT THING IN YOUR GUIDE?

CRIPES! THAT'S HUGE!
KILL! LOOK! OVER THERE! SOMETHING WEIRD IS GOING ON!

!?
WHAT'S THAT?!
13

TELEPATHICALLY I FEEL THE CREATURE IS ALIVE AND FRIENDLY. IT'S INVITING US TO FOLLOW.
FOLLOW IT!

A MEDUSA! IT'S SOME KIND OF GIANT MEDUSA! WELL, WHY DON'T WE JUST DO WHAT IT ASKS?
WHAT? YOU'RE GOING TO TRUST A JELLYFISH?
HA! HA! HEY! IT'S DIVING BENEATH THE SURFACE! I THINK YOU'RE RIGHT, JOHN! BESIDES, I'M CONVINCED THERE'S A LINK BETWEEN THAT CREATURE AND WHAT WE'VE COME HERE FOR!

IT'S SINKING DEEPER, UNDER THOSE HUGE ALGAE COLONIES.
LET'S FOLLOW IT!

SOON AFTER...
TWENTY-THOUSAND FATHOMS!
THERE! LIGHTS!
14

AN UNDERWATER CITY!
THE GUIDE DOESN'T MENTION *THIS!*
15

THE MEDUSA STRATEGY

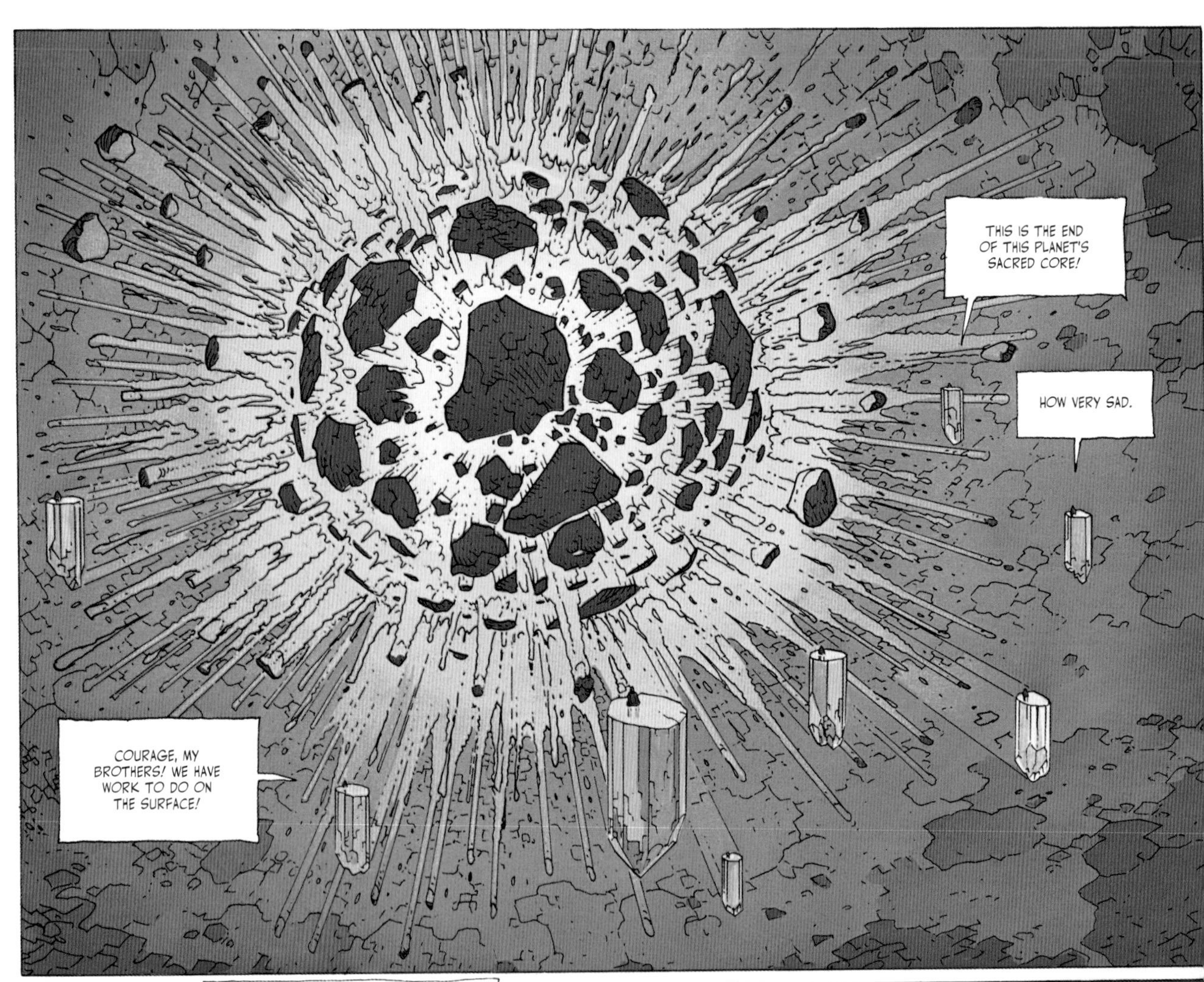

MEANWHILE, PANIC REIGNS IN THE GREAT BURIED CITY!
TO THE SURFACE! HURRY!
BUT, THE BERGS WILL KILL US WHEN WE GET UP THERE!!
DON'T PUSH!
HELP ME!
HELP!
BOOM!
NO! THEY'RE ONLY INTERESTED IN THE WAR MACHINES! BESIDES, THERE'S WORSE THAN THEM!

MUTANTS FROM BELOW ARE RIDING A TIDAL WAVE OF GARBAGE INTO THE CITY! THEY'RE KILLING EVERYONE IN THEIR PATH!
THIS IS AWFUL! WHAT'S GOING TO HAPPEN TO US?

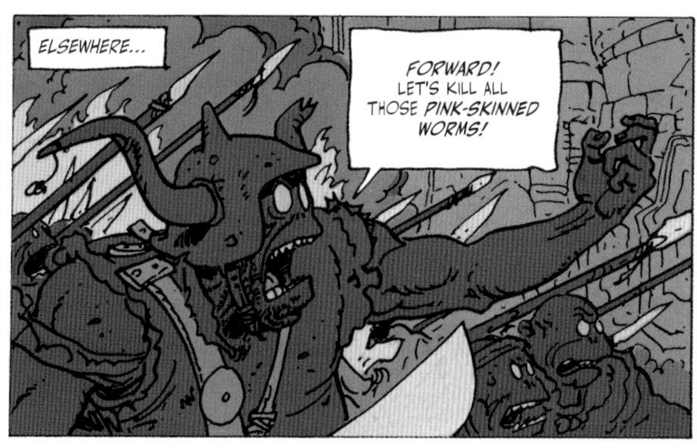
ELSEWHERE...
FORWARD! LET'S KILL ALL THOSE PINK-SKINNED WORMS!

ATTACK, MY SLIMEYS!!

THE MUTANTS!
THEY'RE COMING!
TAKE ME!
NO, ME!
HELP US!
WE CAN'T! THE ANTI-G BARGES ARE FULL!
WE'RE OVERLOADED AS IT IS!

THOSE STUPID BERGS KEEP MISTAKING THE HARVESTER ROBOTS FOR WEAPONS!
COME! DON'T STAY HERE! LET'S JOIN THE SURVIVORS!
18

ALL RESISTANCE HAS BEEN PUT DOWN! THE PLANET IS *OURS!*
GOOD! SOON, WE CAN BEGIN SELECTING THE MOST AGGRESSIVE HUMANS!

WHAT ABOUT ALL THOSE REFUGEES, CHIEF?
THEY'RE NOTHING BUT OLD MEN AND CHILDREN! THEY'LL NEVER BE ABLE TO COPE ON THE SURFACE! THEY'LL DIE SOON!

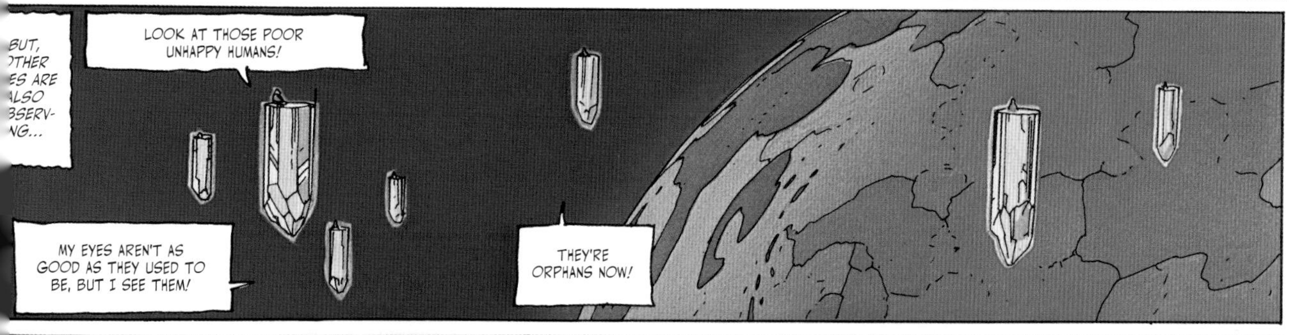
LOOK AT THOSE POOR UNHAPPY HUMANS!
MY EYES AREN'T AS GOOD AS THEY USED TO BE, BUT I SEE THEM!
THEY'RE ORPHANS NOW!

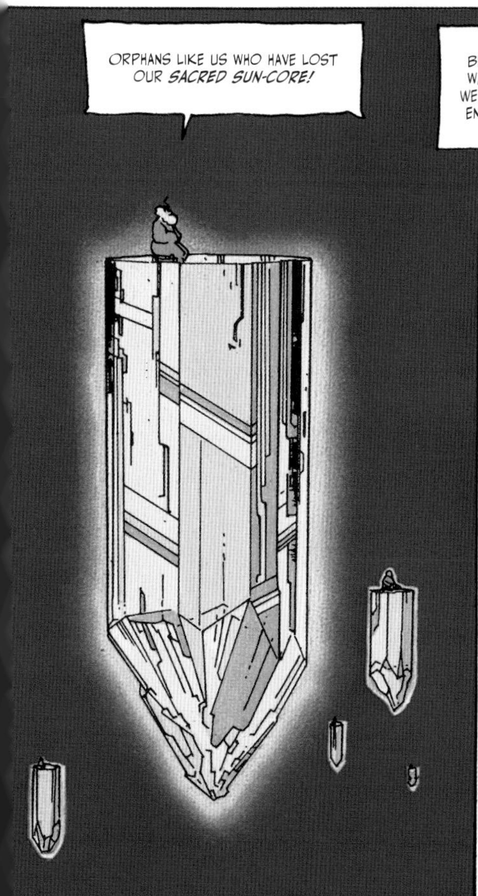
ORPHANS LIKE US WHO HAVE LOST OUR *SACRED SUN-CORE!*

BROTHERS, THE SUN-CORE WAS LIKE A RIPENED FRUIT! WE ARE ITS PRECIOUS SEEDS ENTRUSTED TO THE WINDS!
TRUE! WE SHALL TEACH THESE MEN TO CULTIVATE THE VIRTUES OF THEIR *EARTH MOTHER!*

YES! LET US SHOW THEM THE *WAY!*
FORM A NEW ALLIANCE!
SOON, THESE CHILDREN WILL LEARN HOW TO SOW, TO REAP... TO *LIVE!*
19

BOOOMM
THE PREZIDENTIAL THRONE! WE'VE WON, MY STINKY SLIMEYS!
BUT, BOSS, THERE'S SHOOTING GOING ON EVERYWHERE!
BAAAMMM
YEAH! AMOK KILLERS ARE STILL AROUND!
AND SOLDIERS ARMED TO THE TEETH!
AND OUT OF WHACK ROBOCOPS!
AND AS MANY HUNCHBACKS AS YOU COULD EVER WANT!
SHUT UP, YOU BELLYACHING SLIMEYS! FROM NOW ON, I'M THE NEW PREZIDENT! I'LL TAKE CARE OF ALL THOSE ASSHOLES, YOU'LL SEE!

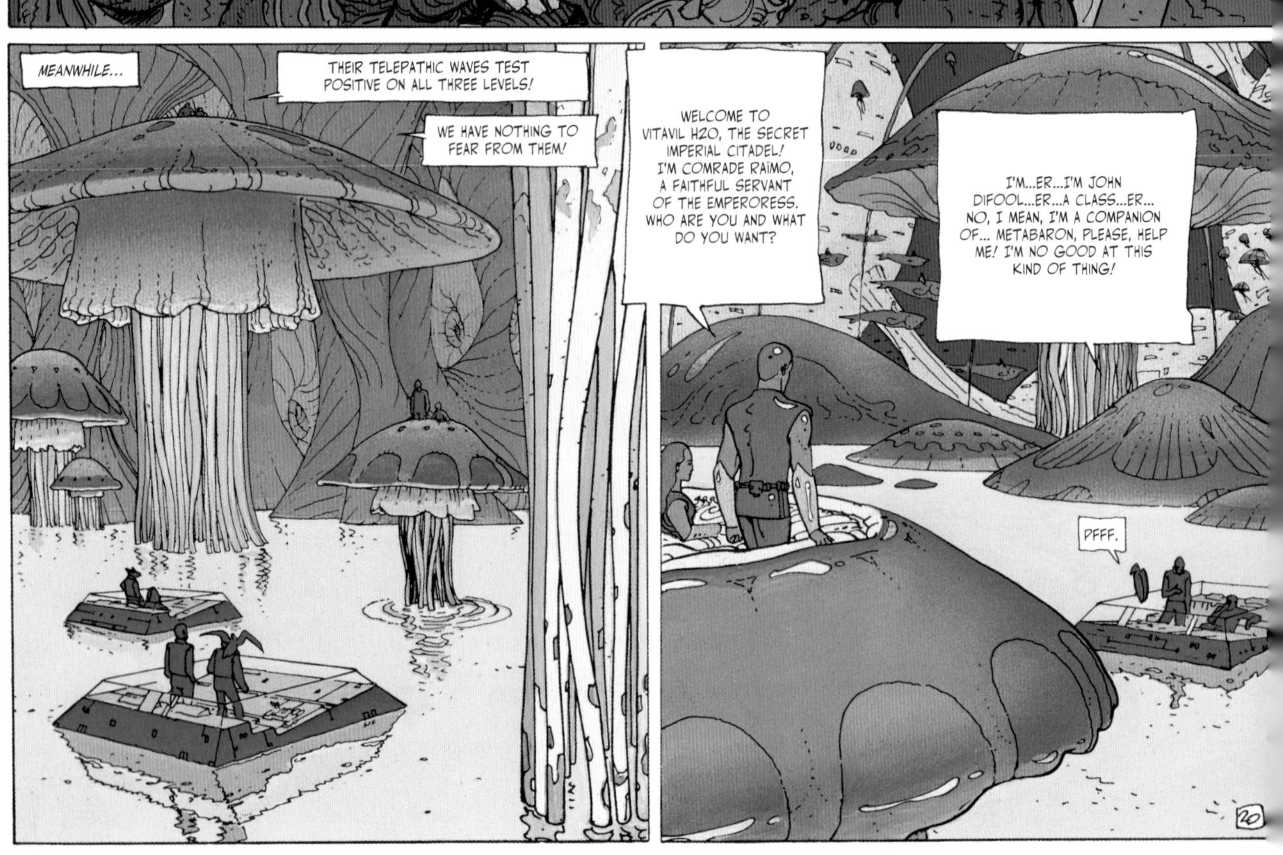
MEANWHILE...
THEIR TELEPATHIC WAVES TEST POSITIVE ON ALL THREE LEVELS!
WE HAVE NOTHING TO FEAR FROM THEM!
WELCOME TO VITAVIL H2O, THE SECRET IMPERIAL CITADEL! I'M COMRADE RAÏMO, A FAITHFUL SERVANT OF THE EMPERORESS. WHO ARE YOU AND WHAT DO YOU WANT?
I'M...ER...I'M JOHN DIFOOL...ER...A CLASS...ER... NO, I MEAN, I'M A COMPANION OF... METABARON, PLEASE, HELP ME! I'M NO GOOD AT THIS KIND OF THING!
PFFF.
20

I'VE HEARD OF YOU, COMRADE RAÏMO. WE MAY HAVE OUR *DIFFERENCES*, BUT I KNOW ABOUT YOUR FIGHT AND I APPROVE OF THE COLONIAL PLANET'S POSITION! I AM CALLED THE METABARON!

THE METABARON! I'VE HEARD OF YOU, TOO! YOU'RE ONE OF THE GREATEST WARRIORS OF LEGEND!

GOOD! WE NEED FIGHTERS LIKE YOU IN OUR BATTLE TO RESTORE THE EMPERORESS TO HIS RIGHTFUL THRONE!

THE BIGGEST THREATS RIGHT NOW ARE THE SHADOW EGGS! OUR GROUP IS SMALL, BUT OUR POWER IS GREAT.
WE HAVE A STARSHIP IN ORBIT AROUND THIS PLANET. BUT MORE IMPORTANTLY, WE BRING WITH US THE INCAL! IT REPRESENTS MANKIND'S ONLY CHANCE AGAINST THE POWER OF THE GREAT DARKNESS!

THE INCAL? WHAT IS THAT? I'VE NEVER HEARD OF IT. IS IT A MAN? A WEAPON? A CULT? WHAT ARE ITS POWERS?
IT IS NONE OF THESE THINGS! IT WAS BORN ON THE EMPIRE'S MOST INSIGNIFICANT PLANET. IT IS THE NEW LIGHT THAT WILL ONE DAY ILLUMINATE THE GALAXY. IT IS PURE CONSCIOUSNESS, A DIRECT EMANATION OF THE DIVINE WILL--THE POWER OF GOD INCARNATE!
DIVINE WILL?
GOD?

I HAVEN'T HEARD *GOD* MENTIONED IN A LONG TIME!
I DON'T MUCH BELIEVE IN ALL THOSE FAIRY TALES!
YEAH! WE WANT TO SEE SOMETHING CONCRETE!

MAYBE YOUR INCAL, OR EVEN YOUR OLD-FASHIONED *GOD* COULD PERFORM ONE OF THOSE OLD-FASHIONED MIRACLES?
A MIRACLE? *WHY NOT?*
21

I WAS ONCE HOST OF THE INCAL!* IT GRANTED ME THE POWER OF SPEECH, AS WELL AS A FEW OTHER TALENTS. I STILL HAVE SOME OF THOSE.
*SEE BOOK 1: THE BLACK INCAL

OH, INCAL! HELP ME CONVINCE THIS MIGHTY WARRIOR!
?
HOLD YOUR HAND OUT TO ME, RAÏMO!

WELL, I DON'T MIND PLAYING YOUR LITTLE GAME, BIRD, BUT...

BUT...

!!?

INCREDIBLE! IT LOOKS JUST LIKE A ROSE!
BUT, THAT'S IMPOSSIBLE!

A ROSE?!
IT'S A LEGENDARY FLOWER THAT HAS BEEN EXTINCT FOR GENERATIONS!
IT'S A MIRACLE!!

HA! HA! CONGRATULATIONS, LITTLE CONCRETE SEAGULL! YOU'VE WON!
NOW WE'LL TAKE YOU TO SEE HIS MEGA-HOLINESS, THE EMPERORESS.
WAIT! I'LL CALL THE OTHERS!

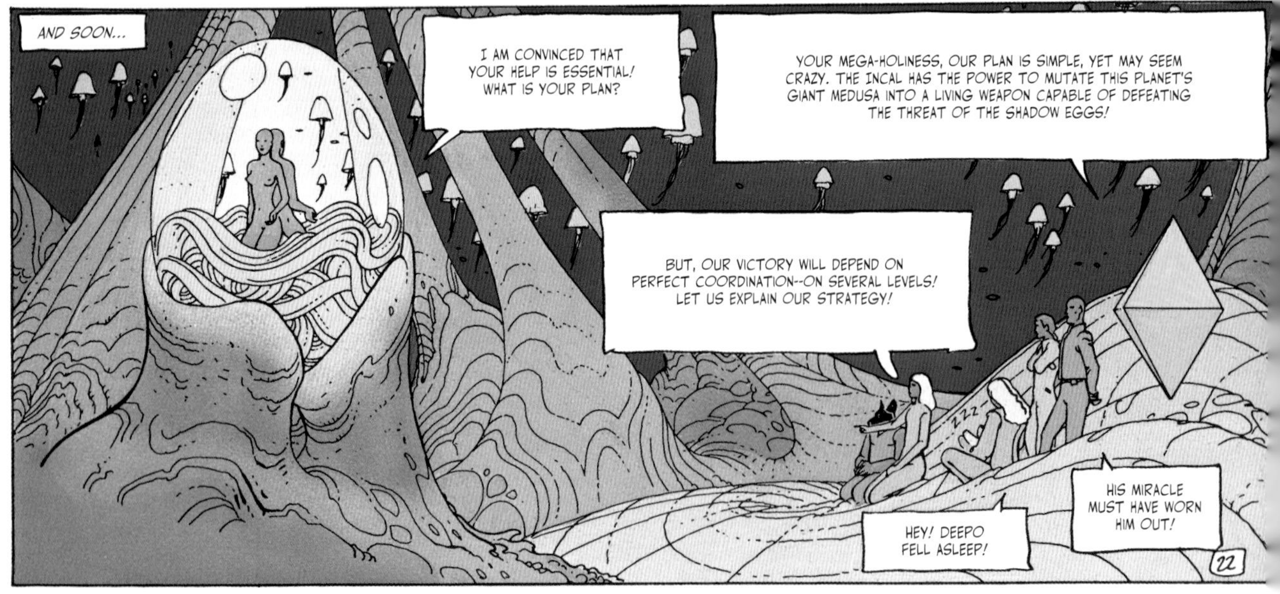
AND SOON...
I AM CONVINCED THAT YOUR HELP IS ESSENTIAL! WHAT IS YOUR PLAN?
YOUR MEGA-HOLINESS, OUR PLAN IS SIMPLE, YET MAY SEEM CRAZY. THE INCAL HAS THE POWER TO MUTATE THIS PLANET'S GIANT MEDUSA INTO A LIVING WEAPON CAPABLE OF DEFEATING THE THREAT OF THE SHADOW EGGS!
BUT, OUR VICTORY WILL DEPEND ON PERFECT COORDINATION--ON SEVERAL LEVELS! LET US EXPLAIN OUR STRATEGY!
HEY! DEEPO FELL ASLEEP!
HIS MIRACLE MUST HAVE WORN HIM OUT!
22

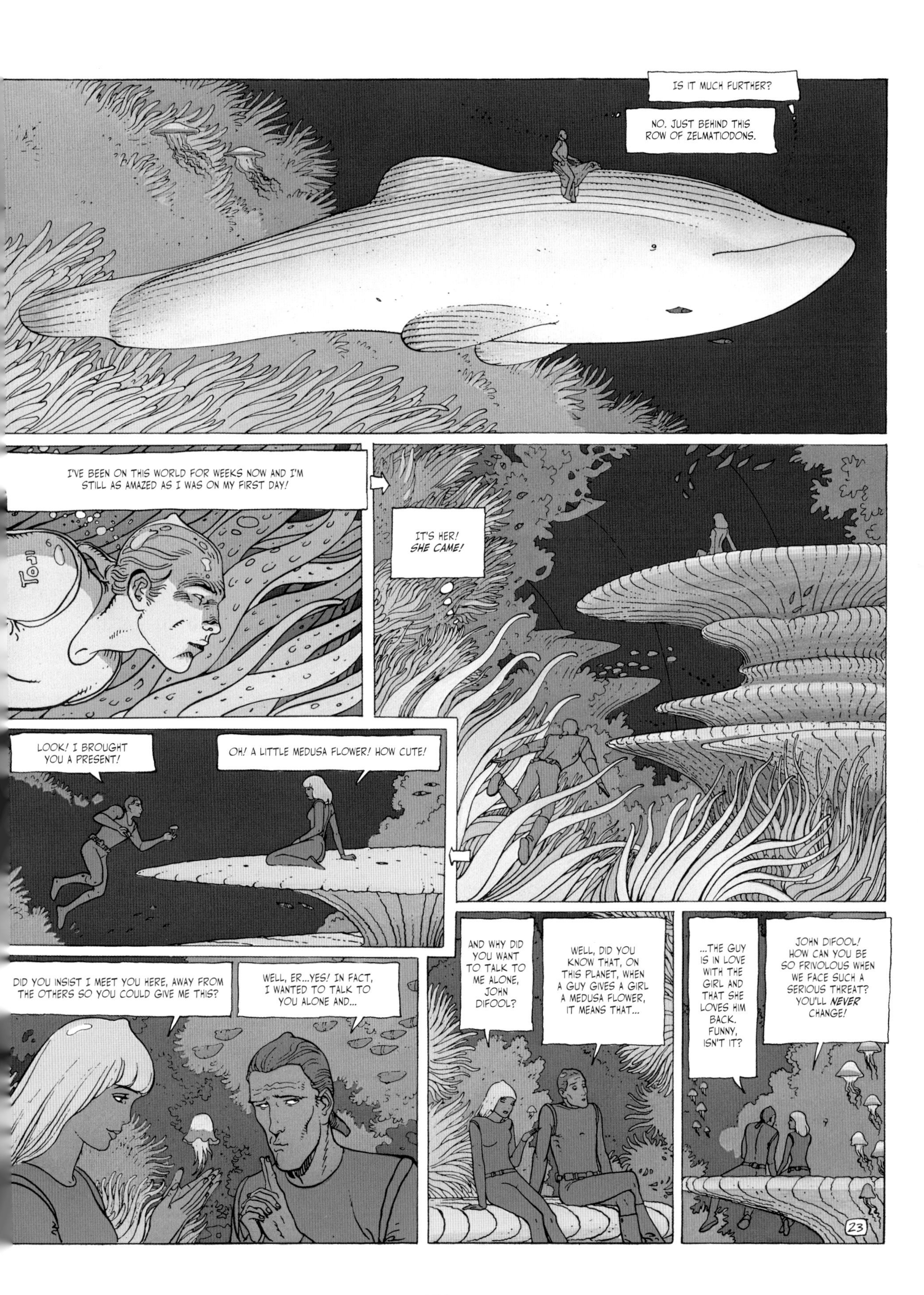
IS IT MUCH FURTHER?
NO. JUST BEHIND THIS ROW OF ZELMATIODONS.
I'VE BEEN ON THIS WORLD FOR WEEKS NOW AND I'M STILL AS AMAZED AS I WAS ON MY FIRST DAY!
IT'S HER! *SHE CAME!*
LOOK! I BROUGHT YOU A PRESENT!
OH! A LITTLE MEDUSA FLOWER! HOW CUTE!
DID YOU INSIST I MEET YOU HERE, AWAY FROM THE OTHERS SO YOU COULD GIVE ME THIS?
WELL, ER...YES! IN FACT, I WANTED TO TALK TO YOU ALONE AND...
AND WHY DID YOU WANT TO TALK TO ME ALONE, JOHN DIFOOL?
WELL, DID YOU KNOW THAT, ON THIS PLANET, WHEN A GUY GIVES A GIRL A MEDUSA FLOWER, IT MEANS THAT...
...THE GUY IS IN LOVE WITH THE GIRL AND THAT SHE LOVES HIM BACK. FUNNY, ISN'T IT?
JOHN DIFOOL! HOW CAN YOU BE SO FRIVOLOUS WHEN WE FACE SUCH A SERIOUS THREAT? YOU'LL *NEVER* CHANGE!
23

BUT, ANIMAH, MY LOVE, FOR YOU IT IS PURE AND SINCERE!
BAH! YOUR LUST IS NOTHING BUT A PROWLING BEAST! YOUR THOUGHTS ARE IMPURE AND YOUR SOUL TORMENTED!
I'VE TOLD YOU BEFORE, LEAVE ME ALONE!

ANIMAH! WAIT!
I KNOW THAT YOU LOVE ME AND WANT ME!
DO I?

OUCH!
LISTEN TO WHAT I HAVE TO SAY, JOHN DIFOOL!

INSTEAD OF PLAYING AT SEDUCTION, YOU SHOULD BE WITH RAÏMO AND THE METABARON HUNTING WILD MEDUSAE AT THE RISK OF YOUR OWN LIFE!

PFF! THE MEDUSAE ARE NOTHING COMPARED TO HER!

I HAVE A SCHOOL OF MEDUSAE ON MY SONAR!
LET'S GO!
24

THEY'RE GIANTS!

PREPARE TO CIRCLE!

LAUNCH TELEPATHIC HOOKS!
THIS CREATURE REMINDS ME OF MY GOOD OLD META-SKIFF.

WATCH OUT FOR THEIR ELECTRICAL STINGERS!
WE NEED TO PUSH THEM WEST, TOWARDS THE PEN WHERE THE TAME ONES ARE!
25

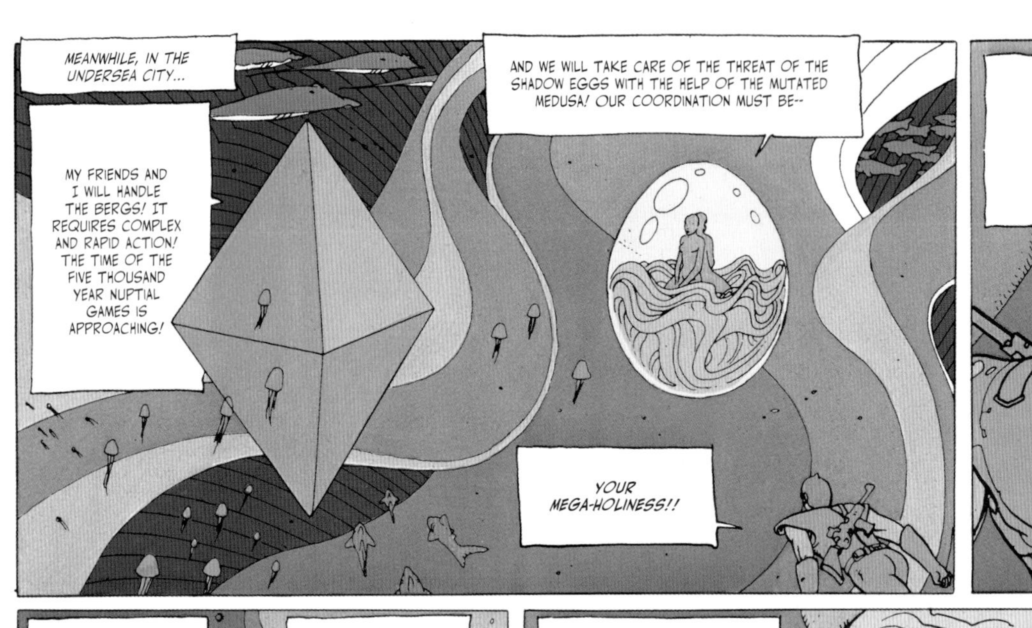
MEANWHILE, IN THE UNDERSEA CITY...
MY FRIENDS AND I WILL HANDLE THE BERGS! IT REQUIRES COMPLEX AND RAPID ACTION! THE TIME OF THE FIVE THOUSAND YEAR NUPTIAL GAMES IS APPROACHING!
AND WE WILL TAKE CARE OF THE THREAT OF THE SHADOW EGGS WITH THE HELP OF THE MUTATED MEDUSA! OUR COORDINATION MUST BE--
YOUR MEGA-HOLINESS!!

WE'VE JUST FOUND A MAN ON A SPACE WRECK! HE CLAIMS TO HOLD VITAL INFORMATION FOR YOU!

YOUR MEGA-HOLINESS!
YOUR SECRET HAS BEEN DISCOVERED!
GREYFIELD! MY FAITHFUL MENTREK!

THEY KNOW YOU'RE ALIVE! I WAS BARELY ABLE TO ESCAPE TO ALERT YOU!

THE MICRO-CAMERAS WE'VE IMPLANTED IN GREYFIELD'S EYES ARE WORKING PERFECTLY!
BY THE DARKNESS! WHAT'S THAT FLYING PYRAMID?
WE MUST MOVE QUICKLY!
IT MUST BE THE UNIFIED INCAL! THIS ISN'T A VERY GOOD DEVELOPMENT!
IT'S NOT IMPORTANT! NOTHING CAN STOP US NOW! HOWEVER, I BELIEVE WE, TOO, SHOULD ACCELERATE OUR PROGRAM!

MASTER, WON'T THE TELEPATHIC POWERS OF THE INCAL SEE RIGHT THOUGH GREYFIELD'S MENTAL SCREENS?
SO WHAT? HE WAS UNCONSCIOUS WHEN HE RECEIVED THE VIRAL IMPLANTS. HE'S UNAWARE OF WHAT HE CARRIES INSIDE HIM. HE GENUINELY BELIEVES HE ESCAPED FROM THE MAGNATE. WE--

SILENCE!
I'VE JUST RECEIVED A TELEPATHIC ORDER FROM THE GREAT DARKNESS! THE TIME HAS COME TO LAUNCH THE 10,000 SHADOW EGGS!
26

APPROACH!

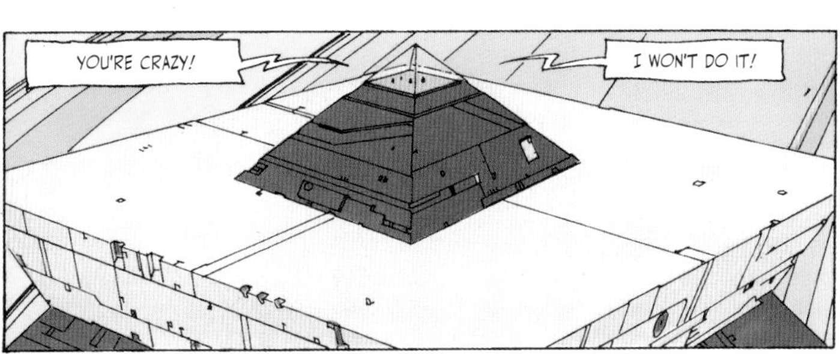

YOU'RE CRAZY!
I WON'T DO IT!

YOU WANT TO DROP ME ALONE ON THE BERGS' HOME WORLD? FACE TO...ER...BEAK WITH THOSE GODDAMN PARAKEETS! AND YOU WANT ME TO IMPREGNATE SOME KIND OF QUEEN, TOO? NO WAY! A THOUSAND TIMES NO!

WHY DON'T YOU SEND THE METABARON? HE'S THE MIGHTY WARRIOR, NOT ME! REMEMBER, I DON'T HAVE THE INCAL INSIDE ME ANYMORE! SO, WHO'S THE GENIUS THAT THOUGHT UP THIS CRAZY IDEA ANYWAY.
THE INCAL.

THE INCAL? ERR... WELL...I GUESS IT'S OKAY THEN! WHAT'S THAT PYRAMID THERE?
IT'S YOUR ROBOTRAINER. I'VE PROGRAMMED IT ESPECIALLY FOR YOU. IT'LL MAKE YOU INTO A CHAMPION!
ME? A CHAMPION? HA!

FIRST, IT WILL EVALUATE, THEN DEVELOP YOUR STRENGTH, SPEED, ENDURANCE AND SKILL.
I HATE IT ALREADY!

WE'LL START ON THE SLOWEST SPEED.
WHY? DO YOU THINK I'M AFRAID OF THAT HUNK O' JUNK?
CRRRRR

"JUNK," YOU SAY? HA! HA! HA! I TOLD YOU, JOHN, I PROGRAMMED IT MYSELF!
BIG DEAL! I'VE WORKED WITH ROBOTS BEFORE IN DETECTIVE SCHOOL!
MAYBE YOU DID, BUT THIS ONE IS A LITTLE MORE ADVANCED. THERE ARE TEN LEVELS. I'LL START YOU ON LEVEL ONE.
27

LEVEL ONE? YOU THINK I'M A *CRIPPLE* OR WHAT?
IT'S ONLY FOR THE EVALUATION MODE. WE'LL SEE HOW IT GOES.

FINE WITH ME! *LET'S GO!*

I'M READY FOR YOU, *TIN CAN!*
BEGIN RECORDING! KLIK!

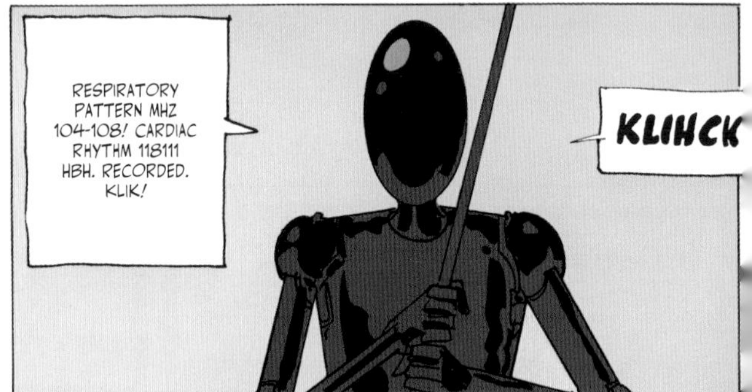
RESPIRATORY PATTERN MHZ 104-108! CARDIAC RHYTHM 118111 HBH. RECORDED. KLIK!
KLIHCK

VITAL FLUX LEVEL A:12! FLUX LEVEL B:17! FLUX LEVEL C...
KLIK!
BARON, CAN'T YOU GET THAT DAMNED THING TO *SHUT UP?*
WHATEVER YOU WANT, JOHN!

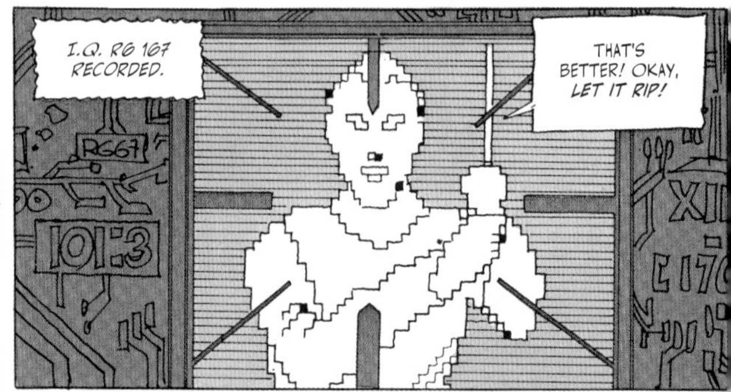
I.Q. RG 167 RECORDED.
THAT'S BETTER! OKAY, *LET IT RIP!*
RG67
101:3

AAHRHH!...

CKLIIIIKK!!

THERE! I TOLD YOU! WHAT ABOUT SOME *REAL* ACTION NOW?
TAKE IT EASY, JOHN! I'LL RESET IT TO LEVEL TWO!
KL-IIK!

NEED A BODY JOB, TIN CAN?
KLIK!
28

CLICK

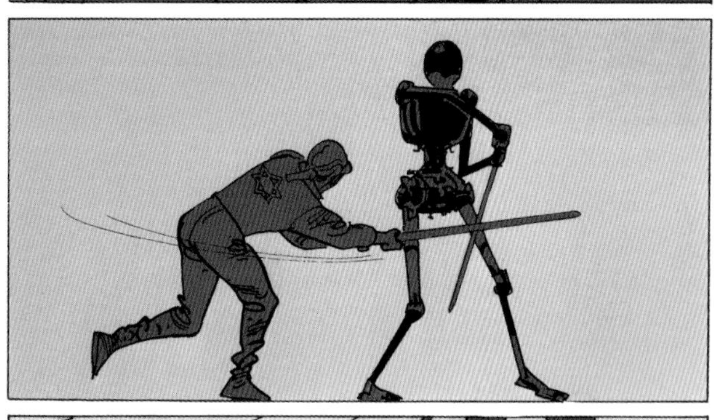

MAYBE WE COULD GO STRAIGHT TO FOUR?
HMM... YOU'RE DOING BETTER THAN I THOUGHT. OKAY, LET'S GIVE IT A TRY!

HEY!

OUCH!

STOP THE DAMN ROBOT!
I TURNED IT OFF! BUT, TOMORROW YOU'LL HAVE TO DO SIX HOURS OF BASIC TRAINING!
29

I'VE HAD IT WITH YOUR STUPID ROBOT, METABARON! IT'S TRYING TO *KILL* ME!
YOU'RE MAKING PROGRESS, JOHN! TODAY YOU WERE ON FIVE, AND YOU DID OKAY! NOW, WE'VE GOT TO WORK ON YOUR SPEED!
HE'S TERRIBLE! WHY WOULD THE INCAL CHOOSE HIM OVER THE METABARON? I'LL NEVER...
NO WAY HE'LL BE READY IN TIME!
YOU MAY BE RIGHT, KILL! I'LL ASK THE INCAL IF I CAN GO ALONG AND HELP HIM.
HEY, *WAIT A MINUTE!* IF ANYONE'S GOING TO HELP JOHN, IT SHOULD BE ME!
ISN'T FIVE ENOUGH?
NO! YOU HAVE TO GO TO EIGHT! LET'S TRY AGAIN!
MEANWHILE, ON AQUAEND, THE DAY HAS ARRIVED.
WHAT A SIGHT! MORE THAN 100,000 MUTATED MEDUSAE LAUNCHED AGAINST THE SHADOW EGGS!
LET'S HOPE THE METABARON AND HIS TEAM ARE READY, TOO!
THE FIVE THOUSAND YEAR GAMES BEGIN IN TWELVE HOURS.
I'M GLAD I'M NOT JOHN DIFOOL RIGHT NOW!
30

I'VE COME TO SEE HOW YOU'RE DOING. POOR JOHN, YOU SEEM TO SPEND MOST OF YOUR TIME WITH THE AUTO-MEDIC THESE DAYS.
BUT, I UNDERSTAND YOU WERE UP TO SIX YESTERDAY.
WHAT? WHO? OH, HI, TANATAH! YEAH, SIX. DAMN ROBOT!
LET ME GO YOU MANGY MUTT!
I KNOW THAT VOICE!
I'M YOUR PREZ! I DEMAND RESPECT!
IT'S THE PREZ'S HEAD FROM THE NECROPOD.* KILL'S TRYING TO FIX IT.
* SEE BOOK 3: WHAT LIES BENEATH
THAT'S IT! I'VE REPLACED ALL THE BURNED OUT CIRCUITRY! THE UGLY LUMP IS BACK ON LINE AND ON THE HOLOVID NET!
AH-HA!
I'LL KILL YOU, YOU BASTARD!
CAN'T YOU SHUT THE DAMNED THING UP? I'VE HAD ENOUGH ROBOTS TO LAST ME A LIFETIME!
I CAN'T SHUT HIM UP, BUT I CAN PUT IT AWAY IF YOU WANT!
TEAR
YOUR
YES!
NO, WAIT! IF I UNDERSTOOD, YOU SAY IT'S STILL PLUGGED INTO THE IMPERIAL BROADCAST NET?
YEAH, SOMETHING MUST HAVE HAPPENED WHEN THEY SWITCHED ON THE NECRO-PROGRAM!*
GREAT! THEN I KNOW JUST THE MESSAGE I WANT TO DELIVER!
* SEE BOOK 2: THE LUMINOUS INCAL
LISTEN TO ME, ALL YOU CHICKENS, SNUGLY SEQUESTERED IN YOUR COZY CONAPTS! I BRING YOU NEWS– ENOUGH NEWS TO GET THAT BIG FAT PIG, THE IMAN HORLOG, TO SHAKE IN HIS BOOTS!
JOHN, WHAT ARE YOU DOING?
HEY!
'S THAT
K AGAIN!
FIRST, THE EMPERORESS STILL LIVES!
BUT HE'S A DANGEROUS JERK! HE'S BROADCASTING ON A PRIORITY CHANNEL THAT WE CAN'T SCRAMBLE! THERE'S NOTHING WE CAN DO!
ON TECHNOGEA...
WITH THE HELP OF COMRADE RAÏMO, SHE'S/HE'S PREPARING HIS/HER RETURN AND THE DESTRUCTION OF ALL TRAITORS AND TECHNOS!
ON DEMOS, A COLONIAL PLANET IN THE PHYDAR SYSTEM...
LONG LIVE RAÏMO!
HURRAH!
BACK TO THE FIGHT!
31

ON ALYX III...
BUT, THE WORST IS THAT BECAUSE OF THE TRAITORS, 10,000 SHADOW EGGS ARE GOING TO ATTACK AND DEVOUR OUR SUNS!
WHAT!?
HUH!?
CURSES!

ON BADMEK...
YOUR MAJESTY, THE REBELS NOW CONTROL THE HIGH TERMITARIUM! THE SITUATION IS BECOMING MORE CRITICAL!
DAMN! IT'S BECAUSE OF THAT MADMAN ON THE HOLOVID!

AND ON THE PLANET OF GOLD...
WHAT?! THIS IS INTOLERABLE! 300 RIM WORLDS HAVE JOINED THE REBELLION! A THOUSAND MORE ARE RIOTING! EVEN THIS PLANET IS BEING TORN APART! I'LL USE THE PURPLE ENDOGUARD TO BRING THE REBELS TO THEIR KNEES! I'LL ORDER A BLOODBATH!
PREPARE A SHIP FOR TECHNOGEA! I WANT TO HAVE A WORD OR TWO WITH THAT TECHNO-CENTREUR!
RIGHT-O, BIG BOY! CAN'T LET THOSE PEASANTS WALK ALL OVER US!

MEANWHILE...
WE'VE FOLLOWED ALL YOUR INSTRUCTIONS, GOOD ARAHT!
WE'VE SOWN AND PLANTED AS YOU ADVISED!
WE'VE RECLAIMED AND FERTILIZED THE GROUND, AS YOU SAID!
WE'VE BUILT THE VILLAGES AND THE ROADS, AS YOU PLANNED!
VERY GOOD, MY CHILDREN!
BUT, GOOD ARAHT, THE SUN GETS A LITTLE DARKER EVERY DAY! IT'S AS IF IT WERE DYING!

IT IS NOTHING! DO NOT CONCERN YOURSELVES! CONCENTRATE ON MAKING PROGRESS IN YOUR TASKS!
32

SEE HOW THE CRYSTAL HAS GROWN? IT IS LINKED TO THE PLANTS AND THE WORKS THAT YOU HAVE BUILT! IT RESONATES WITH ITS ELEVEN BROTHERS SCATTERED ALL ACROSS THE PLANET!
GOOD ARAHT! ANOTHER SURVIVOR FROM THE BURIED CITY HAS JUST ARRIVED IN THE VILLAGE! IT'S A GROWN-UP!
A GROWN-UP? AFTER THE LAST BERG OFFENSIVE, I DIDN'T THINK THERE WERE ANY LEFT!
LET'S GO AND GREET HIM!
WHAT'S HE LOOK LIKE?
WEIRD! HE SAYS HE BRINGS NEWS FROM THE REST OF THE EMPIRE!
DEAR VIDFANS! THE EMPIRE IS IN FLAMES! EVERYWHERE, DEATH, RIOTS...
HE'S DELIRIOUS!
I RECOGNIZE HIM! IT'S DIAVALOO, THE HOLO-ANCHOR!
SANYA, WHAT'S THAT ON HIS WRIST?
A MINI HOLOVID!
THE EGGS! THE SHADOW EGGS!
HEY! MY HOLOVID JUST EXPLODED!
HA! HA! IT'S THE GOOD ARAHT! HE LOVES MAKING HOLOVIDS EXPLODE WHENEVER HE CAN!
WELL, THAT'S NICE, BUT WE'VE GOT TO MOW THE WATERFALL FIELD!
AND BAKE THE BREAD TOO!
LET'S GO!
LET'S GO!
THE HOLOVID! THIS IS TERRIBLE! NOW I HAVE NOTHING LEFT! NO MORE NEWS TO BROADCAST! NO MORE VIDFANS! I'M CUT OFF FROM THE UNIVERSE!
NO, NO! YOU WON'T BE BORED! THERE'S PLENTY OF WORK TO DO! YOU DON'T LOOK VERY STRONG, BUT WE'LL TAKE CARE OF THAT!
HERE, DRINK THIS!
YES, I'M GOING TO TECHNOGEA! I WANT TO MEET WITH THAT TECHNO-CENTREUR OF YOURS! YOU MUST DO SOMETHING TO STOP THE INSIDIOUS PROPAGANDA THAT'S TEARING MY EMPIRE APART!
BUT, IMAN HORLONG, OUR 10,000 SHADOW EGGS WILL SOON HERALD THE NEW REIGN OF DARKNESS! YOU WILL THEN RULE WITHOUT OPPOSITION!
33

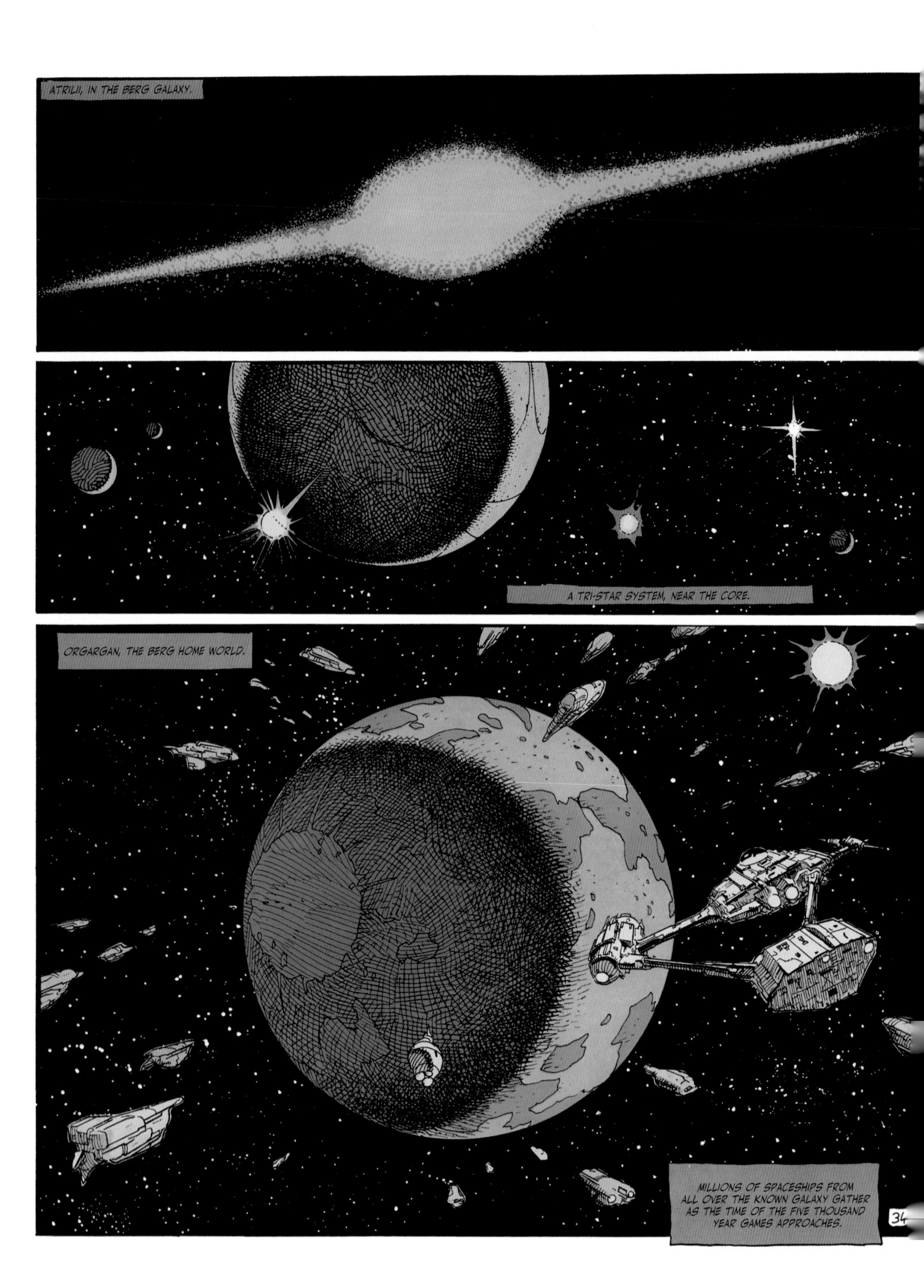
ATRILII, IN THE BERG GALAXY.
A TRI-STAR SYSTEM, NEAR THE CORE.
ORGARGAN, THE BERG HOME WORLD.
MILLIONS OF SPACESHIPS FROM ALL OVER THE KNOWN GALAXY GATHER AS THE TIME OF THE FIVE THOUSAND YEAR GAMES APPROACHES.
34

AT THE CENTER OF THE DESERT OF THE THREE COMMANDMENTS STANDS THE HUGE MASS OF OOROR, THE ORIGINAL MOTHERHILL. ONE HUNDRED TWENTY THOUSAND YEARS OLD, SEAT OF THE PRIMORDIAL OVULATION AND HOME OF THE BELOVED PROTOQUEEN.
INSIDE THE HUGE CRATER, A VAST CROWD AWAITS THE INAUGURAL CEREMONIES OF THE GREAT FIVE THOUSAND YEAR NUPTIAL GAMES!
I HEREBY SOLEMNLY DECLARE THE GREAT AND SACRED FIVE THOUSAND YEAR GAMES OPEN! I ASSUME THAT ALL THE CONTESTANTS KNOW THE RULES?
I HAVE A FEELING THIS IS GOING TO BE A BEAUTIFUL IMPREGNATION!
LOOK HOW FIERCE THEY ARE!
THEY'RE FROM GALAXY XIAM 45.
THEY'VE BEEN SELECTED FROM THE POPULATION OF TWENTY-SEVEN PLANETS OF THE HUMAN EMPIRE!
35

THE BERG RELIGION MAKES IT CLEAR... EVERY FIVE BERG YEARS (ROUGHLY 5,000 TERRESTRIAL DAYS) THE MOST CAPABLE MEMBER OF A CAREFULLY SELECTED ALIEN RACE MUST IMPREGNATE THEIR BELOVED PROTOQUEEN. AFTER 24,000 SUCH IMPREGNATIONS, THE LEGEND STATES THAT THE BERGS WILL ENTER THE GOLDEN AGE OF ETERNAL PROSPERITY.
THE RULES ARE SIMPLE. ENERGY OR BALLISTIC WEAPONS ARE FORBIDDEN. PHYSICAL STRENGTH, SKILL, ENDURANCE AND KNOWLEDGE OF COMBAT MAY BE YOUR ONLY TOOLS!
THEY DON'T LOOK VERY IMPRESSIVE TO ME!
DON'T LET IT FOOL YOU! THESE HUMANS CAN BE DECEPTIVELY SAVAGE!
THEY LOOK FUNNY WITH THEIR BEAKLESS FACES!
THERE WILL BE ONLY ONE WINNER! ONLY ONE SURVIVOR! THE FIRST TO REACH THE NUPTIAL CONE ALIVE! THE OTHERS...
PHEW! THAT ONE STINKS TO HIGH HEAVEN!
YEAH! HE'S ALREADY TRYING TO KILL US WITH HIS STENCH! THERE SHOULD BE RULES AGAINST THAT!
GRRR...
...WILL BE SERVED AT THE GREAT NUPTIAL BANQUET...
THEY EAT ALL THE LOSERS? THAT'S COMPLETELY CRAZY! I WANT TO GET OUTTA HERE! FAST!
DON'T PANIC, JOHN! YOU'VE BEEN WELL TRAINED AND WE'RE HERE TO HELP YOU!
...WHICH IS A UNIQUE AND SUBLIME PRIVILEGE, ESPECIALLY SINCE THIS IMPREGNATION IS IMPORTANT AND SACRED IN THE LONG HISTORY OF OUR RACE...
THE RIGHT TIME IS NOW, BEFORE THE MASSACRE STARTS! I DON'T WANT TO END UP THE MAIN COURSE ON ONE OF THESE PARAKEETS' PLATES.
COURAGE! THE INCAL IS WATCHING YOU!
QUIET!
HUSH!
36

IF HE'S WATCHING OVER ME, WHY DOESN'T HE GET ME OUTTA--
SHUT UP, YOU GODDAMN FOOL!
DONG!
...FOR THIS IS THE TWENTY-FOUR THOUSANDTH IMPREGNATION. THE ONLY ONE, WHICH, AFTER ONE HUNDRED TWENTY MILLION YEARS, WILL HERALD THE BEGINNING OF OUR GOLDEN AGE! HUMAN CONTESTANTS, THE HONOR THAT HAS BEEN GRANTED TO YOU AND YOUR GALAXY IS INDEED SUBLIME. I ALREADY SALUTE THE BRAVE MAN WHO ALONE AMONG YOU WILL ENTER THE NUPTIAL CONE AND TASTE THE SWEET BROTH OF ETERNAL BLISS!
NICE TURN OF PHRASE!
NOW, BE PREPARED FOR THE ASCENSION TO THE SACRED CONE!
THREE...
TWO...
37

ONE!

JOHN! DO SOMETHING! BITE 'EM! CLAW 'EM!
UP THERE!
BACK OFF, ROMEO!
SHE'S CALLING ME!
NO, ME!
SHE'S WAITING FOR ME!
I-I CAN'T TAKE IT ANYMORE!

I'M RECORDING A LEVEL 5 TELEPATHIC MATING CALL EMANATING FROM THE TOP OF THAT CONE!
WHERE'S JOHN?
WAY BEHIND!

HE'S TOO WELL CONDITIONED! HIS MIND IS RESISTING THE CALL!
HE'LL ACT EVENTUALLY! I DIDN'T TRAIN HIM FOR NOTHING!
HE WON'T LAST ANOTHER TEN SECONDS!
GOOD LORD! WE'RE DOOMED!

MAYBE NOT. BUT, ALL THESE MEN ARE LEVEL 8 FIGHTERS AND JOHN NEVER MADE IT TO LEVEL 6!
THE INCAL SUGGESTS THAT WE BOOST HIS METABOLISM!
I'LL PROGRAM IT AT ONCE!

LOOK! IT'S WORKING! NOW WE'RE GOING TO SEE SOME ACTION!
OKAY, THAT'S IT! I'M TIRED OF BEING TRAMPLED!
?
WOW!
AIIE!
38

MOVE IT!!
LOOK OUT!
TAKE THIS! AND THAT!
UP THERE!
I'M COMING, MY DEAR!
AARGH!
LEMME THROUGH! OUT OF MY WAY!
I'VE SEEN YOUR KIND BEFORE AND I'M GONNA TAKE CARE OF YOU RIGHT AWAY!
WHAT? TAKE CARE OF ME?!
AHH...BRAVO!
THAT'S WHAT I CALL A SHOW!
WHAT A FIGHT!
LOOK AT THAT FAT ONE THAT JUST FELL! I WANT TO EAT THAT ONE!
THESE HUMANS ARE REALLY FUNNY!
YEAH! THEY LOVE LIFE SO MUCH THEY FALL LIKE FLIES!
OUCH! OUCH! OUCH! OUCH! OUCH! OUCH!
HEY, WAIT FOR ME!!
HOURS GO BY WITH THE DIN OF CLASHING WEAPONS, BONES BREAKING, THE CRIES OF VICTORY AND AGONY. AND THE INCREASINGLY LOUD CHEER OF THE BERGS AS THEY EGG ON THE CONTESTANTS.
MY BELOVED! I'M THE ONE FOR YO--ARRGH!
HA! GOTCHA!
A FEW HUNDRED SURVIVORS, STILL FIGHTING, FINALLY REACH THE MUCH COVETED CONE, LEAVING BEHIND A RIVER OF BLOOD.
THE CONE! SHE'S THERE WAITING FOR ME!
NO... ME!!
39

HE'S FIGHTING LIKE A LION, BUT HE BEGAN TOO LATE!
I SUGGEST WE MOVE THE SHIP CLOSER TO THE CORTEX. THE INCAL SAYS THAT BY STIMULATING CERTAIN NEURONS, WE CAN GET HIM TO LEVITATE FOR A FEW SECONDS.
THAT SHOULD DO THE TRICK. LET'S TRY IT!

THE WAY TO THE TOP IS COMPLETELY BLOCKED! HEY GUYS, CAN'T YOU FIND...

...A WAY TO HELP MEEEEE!?
WE JUST DID! TO DIRECT YOUR FLIGHT, CONCENTRAT ON WHERE YOU WANT TO GO AND THEN PULL!
?!
GOT-GOTCHA!

HEY, LOOK AT THAT ONE! ISN'T HE JUMPING A BIT HIGH FOR A HUMAN?
I'D SAY IT'S MORE LIKE HE'S FLYING!
BUT, MY MONEY'S STILL ON THE FAT UGLY ONE WITH THE RED EYES!

HE'S ALMOST REACHED THE NUPTIAL CHAMBER!
BACK OFF, YOU BASTARDS! GORGO THE FOUL IS THE BEST!

THOSE DAMN BIRDS GRABBED ME FROM MY THRONE, BUT I'LL BE THE ONE IMPREGNATING THEIR WHORE!

AND I-- WHAT?
?
!?

OH...NOOOOOOOOOOO!!!
40

HE'S CHEATING!
NO! THERE'S NOTHING IN THE RULES AGAINST PSYCHIC-POWERS!
THANKS FOR THE HELP, GUYS!
BRAVO! WHAT A FEAT!
THE 24,000TH IMPREGNATION REALLY DELIVERED!
THE GOLDEN AGE WILL COME!
LIKE THE PROPHECY PREDICTED!
STOP HIM!
IT'S MAGIC!
TOO LATE!
BY ALL THE RATS! I RECOGNIZE HIM! IT'S THAT HUMAN WIMP WHO WAS WITH THAT PINK-SKINNED WITCH! DAMNATION!!!
IT'S NOT FAIR!
WHAT ROTTEN LUCK!
IT'S ALL OVER FOR US!
NO WAY IN!
BOY, ARE WE UP A CREEK!
I WAS HERE FIRST!
NO, I WAS!
WHO CARES NOW?
ME, THEY'RE GONNA EAT US NOW!
THE FIRST PHASE OF THE SACRED IMPREGNATION IS NOW OVER! THE DEAD WILL BE COLLECTED FOR THE RITUALISTIC BANQUET! THE SURVIVORS FOUGHT SO WELL I PROPOSE WE LET THEM LIVE!
HURRAH!!
GOOD IDEA! THEIR FLESH MIGHT BE TOO CHEWY ANYWAY!
ANYONE THERE?
APPROACH!
41

THE ROYAL WEDDING

IT'S... IT'S A NIGHTMARE!
SOB!
FORGIVE ME! I SHOULD HAVE REMEMBERED!

YOU SHORT-LIVED MORTALS NEED AN IMAGE TO LOVE!
RELAX! I MUST FIND YOUR IDEAL IMAGE INSIDE YOUR MIND! THE ONE THAT WILL MAXIMIZE YOUR SEX DRIVE!
STAY CALM... VERY CALM... I'M RELAXED.
OPEN YOUR MIND! LET ME PROBE YOU!

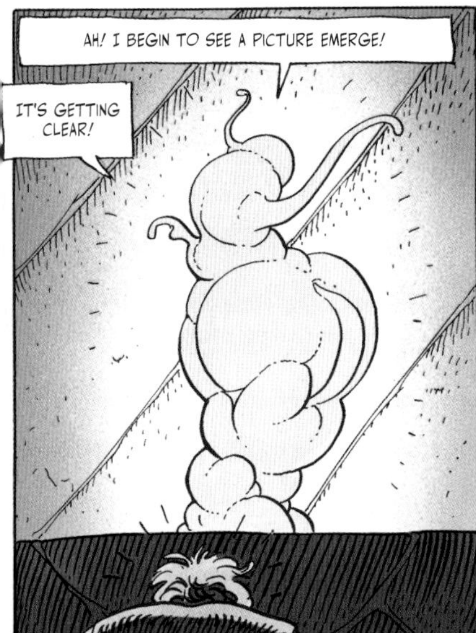
AH! I BEGIN TO SEE A PICTURE EMERGE!
IT'S GETTING CLEAR!

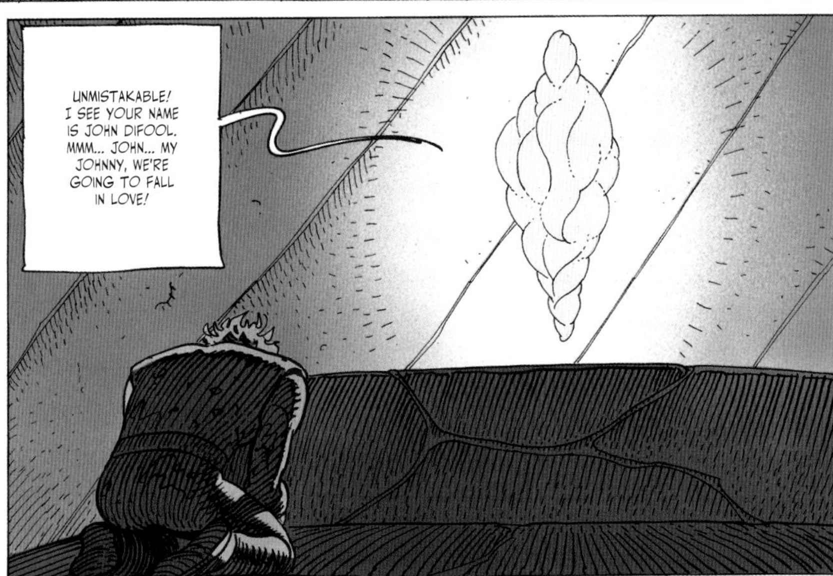
UNMISTAKABLE! I SEE YOUR NAME IS JOHN DIFOOL. MMM... JOHN... MY JOHNNY, WE'RE GOING TO FALL IN LOVE!

MADLY IN LOVE!
I CAN'T, I WON'T!

JOHN DIFOOL, YOU SPINELESS WIMP! WHERE'S YOUR VAUNTED AGGRESSIVENESS? GO FOR IT! DO IT!
?

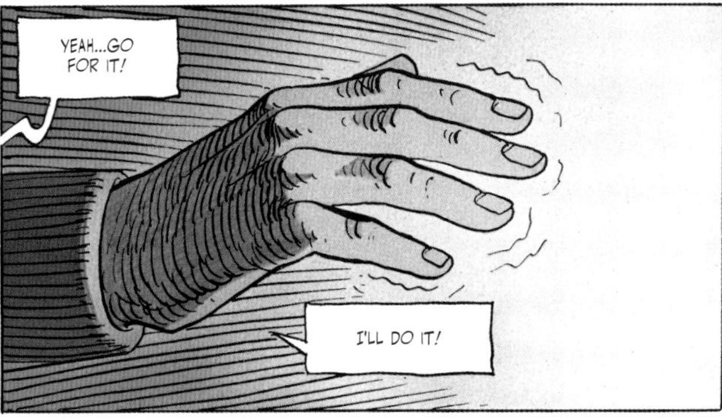
YEAH...GO FOR IT!
I'LL DO IT!

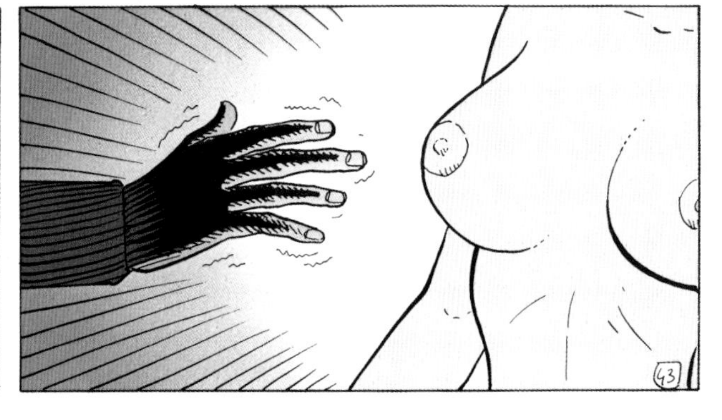
43

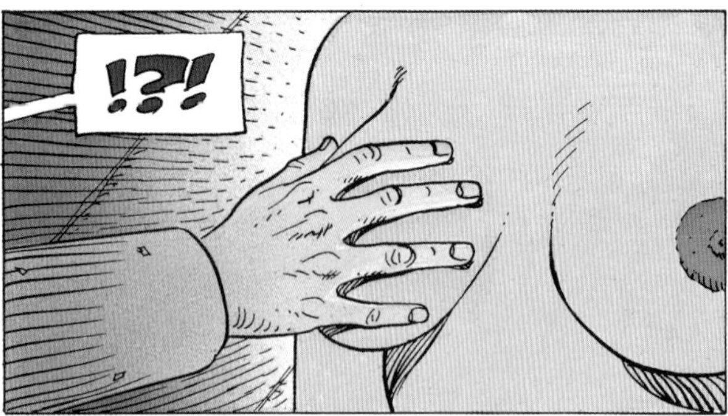
!?!

WHAT'S WRONG, JOHN? AM I NOT THE ONE YOU'VE BEEN WAITING FOR SINCE THE BEGINNING OF TIME?
AM I NOT--
ANIMAH!

NOT...EXACTLY. I'VE ONLY ASSUMED HER FORM. I'M STILL THE PROTOQUEEN, BUT YOU CAN CALL ME BARBARIAH!

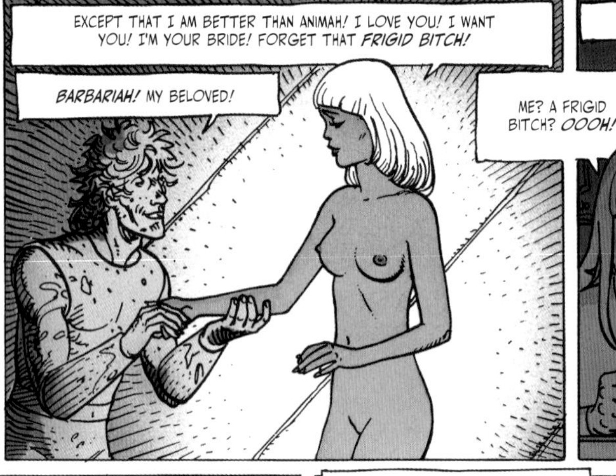
EXCEPT THAT I AM BETTER THAN ANIMAH! I LOVE YOU! I WANT YOU! I'M YOUR BRIDE! FORGET THAT *FRIGID BITCH!*
BARBARIAH! MY BELOVED!
ME? A FRIGID BITCH? *OOOH!*

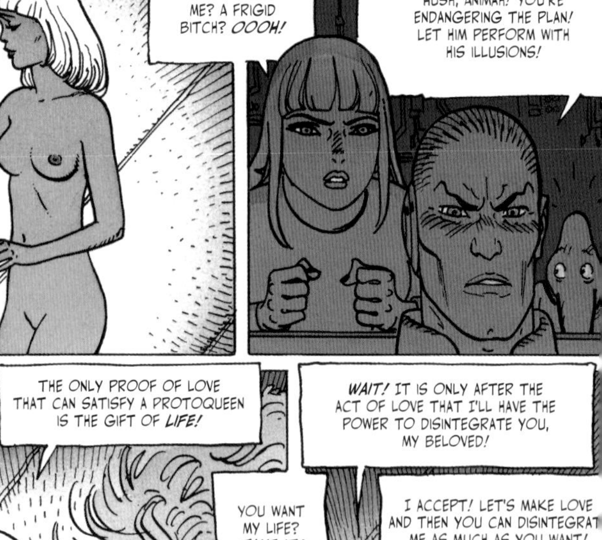
IT'S A TRAP, JOHN! *WATCH OUT!*
HUSH, ANIMAH! YOU'RE ENDANGERING THE PLAN! LET HIM PERFORM WITH HIS ILLUSIONS!

BUT, TO BE IMPREGNATED, I MUST BE TRULY LOVED!
BUT, BARBARIAH, I TRULY LOVE YOU!

IF YOU DO, PROVE IT TO ME!
AT ONCE! TELL ME HOW?
I'LL DO WHATEVER YOU WISH!

THE ONLY PROOF OF LOVE THAT CAN SATISFY A PROTOQUEEN IS THE GIFT OF *LIFE!*
YOU WANT MY LIFE? *TAKE IT!*

WAIT! IT IS ONLY AFTER THE ACT OF LOVE THAT I'LL HAVE THE POWER TO DISINTEGRATE YOU, MY BELOVED!
I ACCEPT! LET'S MAKE LOVE AND THEN YOU CAN DISINTEGRAT ME AS MUCH AS YOU WANT!
44

THEN COME CLOSE, MY LOVE! COME JOIN YOUR BRIDE ON HER NUPTIAL BED!
MY GOD! ANIMAH! WHAT HAVE I DONE? I'VE BETRAYED YOU WITH YOUR OWN IMAGE!
JOHN...NOW THAT WE'VE MADE LOVE...
...AND I'VE BEEN IMPREGNATED, READY TO BIRTH BILLIONS OF NEW SUBJECTS. THE TRULY SACRED TIME OF YOUR DISINTEGRATION HAS COME! WHEN YOUR BELOVED ATOMS WILL MERGE WITH THE HEART OF THE GREAT COSMIC MOTHER!
THE *DISINTEGRATION!*
45

NO, WAIT!
THE GREAT COSMIC MOTHER AWAITS YOU, JOHN DIFOOL!

STOP!
I'VE GOT A BETTER OFFER FOR YOU, BETTER THAN MY LIFE!
BETTER THAN YOUR LIFE?

DO SOMETHING! THAT HORRIBLE CREATURE IS TRYING TO DISINTEGRATE JOHN!
STOP WORRYING, ANIMAH! THE INCAL PLANNED FOR ALL THIS!

GET READY! THE TIME TO EMERGE HAS ARRIVED! WE MUST PREPARE TO LEAVE JOHN'S BODY!
WE'LL BE EMERGING FROM HIS LEFT PALM IN NINE SECONDS!
GREAT! I'VE HAD IT WITH BEING MINIATURIZED TO VIRAL SIZE!
HURRY! SHE'S BEGUN THE DISINTEGRATION PROCESS!
THEN, IMMEDIATE DE-MINIATURIZATION TO 4779.

WHAT DARE YOU OFFER IN EXCHANGE FOR YOUR LIFE?
I HAVE SOMETHING IN MY HAND THAT THE ENTIRE BERG EMPIRE COVETS!... THE INCAL!

THE INCAL RIGHTFULLY BELONGS TO THE BERGS! THE HIDDEN PART OF THE PROPHECY REVEALS THAT IT IS THE KEY TO OUR GOLDEN AGE!
THEN, WATCH THIS!

THE INCAL!
THE INCAL!
66

THE INCAL! GIVE IT TO ME! NOW!
OKAY, BUT...

...YOU WON'T EVEN BE ABLE TO TOUCH IT UNLESS YOU GIVE ME WHAT I WANT FIRST!
A GIFT THAT I WILL CHOOSE FOR MYSELF!
OOOH!

ASK FOR WHAT YOU WANT AND YOU SHALL HAVE IT!
WELL...ER...I WANT...I WANT...
JOHN...

I WANT A SMALL PLANET OF PARADISE WITH LOTSA FLOWERS AND BANANAS, BEACHES AND HOMEO-WHORES OF ALL COLORS...
HE'S GONE MAD!

WHAT AN ASSHOLE! WHAT A JERK!
JOHN, STOP YOUR STUPID JOKE!

YOU KNOW WHAT YOU HAVE TO ASK FOR?
I...ER...OKAY...I WANT TECHNOGEA!
THAT NASTY SPACE MUSHROOM? WHAT AN ODD REQUEST! IT'S NOT EVEN A NICE PLACE!

THAT'S RIGHT, I WANT TO DESTROY IT!
YOU HAVE FUNNY IDEAS, BUT IF THAT'S WHAT IT TAKES TO GET THE INCAL, YOU'VE GOT YOURSELF A DEAL!
WE'VE WON. PREPARE TO EXPAND! WE'LL HAVE TO LEAD THE BERG FLEET TO TECHNOGEA!
BUT FIRST MY HUMAN FORM NEEDS MORE LOVE! COME, MY JOHNNY, LOVE ME WITH ALL YOUR PASSION!
47

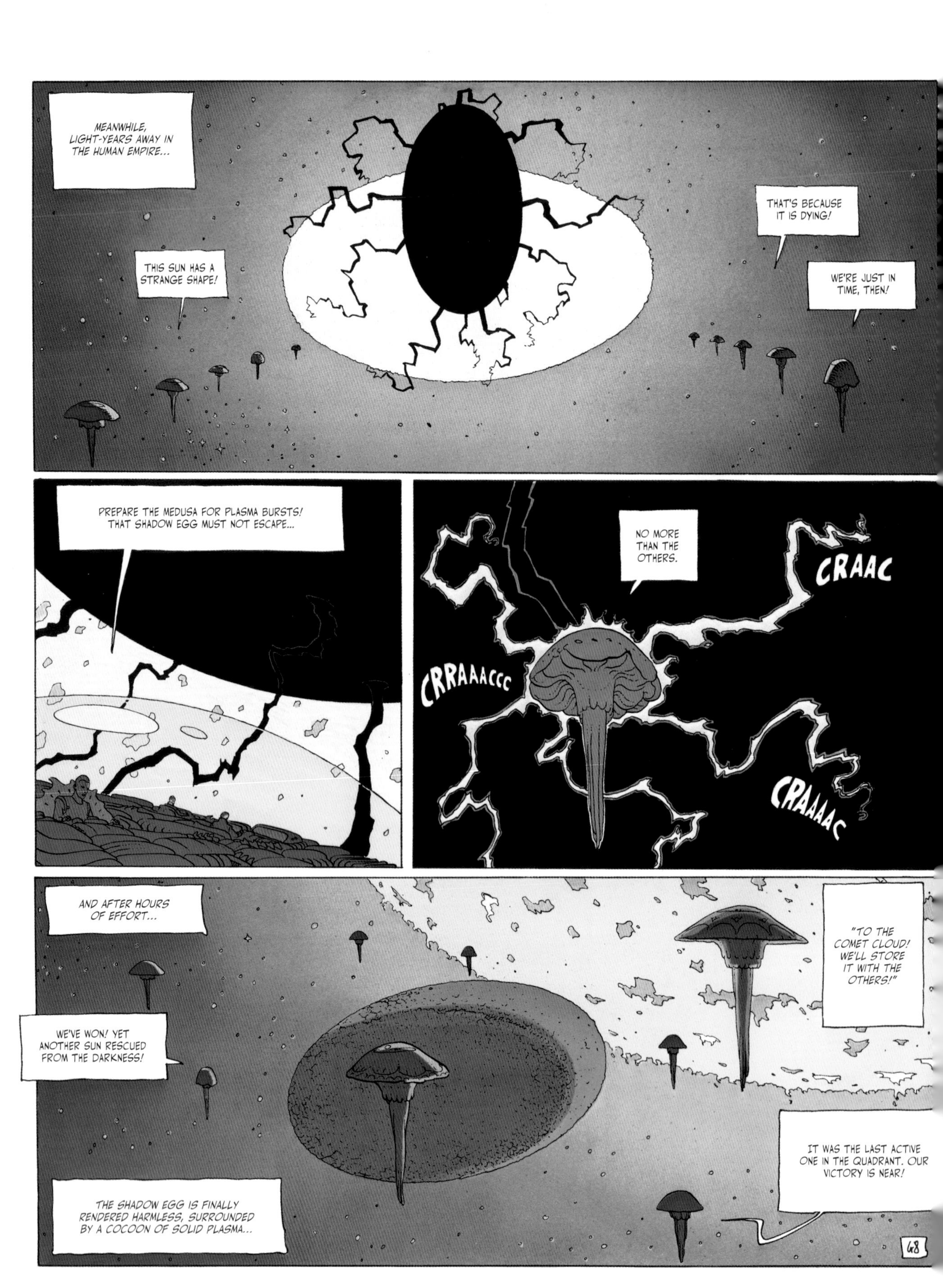
MEANWHILE, LIGHT-YEARS AWAY IN THE HUMAN EMPIRE...
THIS SUN HAS A STRANGE SHAPE!
THAT'S BECAUSE IT IS DYING!
WE'RE JUST IN TIME, THEN!
PREPARE THE MEDUSA FOR PLASMA BURSTS! THAT SHADOW EGG MUST NOT ESCAPE...
NO MORE THAN THE OTHERS.
CRAAC
CRRAAACCC
CRAAAAC
AND AFTER HOURS OF EFFORT...
"TO THE COMET CLOUD! WE'LL STORE IT WITH THE OTHERS!"
WE'VE WON! YET ANOTHER SUN RESCUED FROM THE DARKNESS!
IT WAS THE LAST ACTIVE ONE IN THE QUADRANT. OUR VICTORY IS NEAR!
THE SHADOW EGG IS FINALLY RENDERED HARMLESS, SURROUNDED BY A COCOON OF SOLID PLASMA...
48

GREAT TECHNO-CENTREUR! IT'S A REAL CATASTROPHE! 310 NEW DISAPPEARANCES OF SHADOW EGGS IN SECTOR 707-7A IN THE LAST 48 HOURS!
ZONE F86 OPERATION COMPLETELY STOPPED! ALL THE SHADOW EGGS HAVE BEEN ELIMINATED!
OUR SHADOW EGGS ARE MADE OF ANTI-MATTER! THEY'RE INVULNERABLE!
ZONE A30, SAME THING TECHNO-CENTREUR. NO EXPLANATION AT ALL!
WHAT DOES THIS MEAN?
IT MEANS THAT JERK ON THE HOLOVID WAS RIGHT!
BUT, THE DARKNESS PROMISED!
IF I UNDERSTAND CORRECTLY, ALL YOUR "PROMISES OF TRIUMPH" WERE NOTHING BUT A LOT OF HOT AIR!
WHAT DOES THE DARKNESS SAY? IS THERE STILL HOPE?
THE DARKNESS ALWAYS FINDS A WAY! REMAIN ASSERTIVE!

SUDDENLY...
NORMAL SPACE AT LAST!
HAVE THE BERGS FOLLOWED US?
THEY SHOULD EMERGE AT THE SAME TIME AS US AND ENCIRCLE TECHNOGEA!

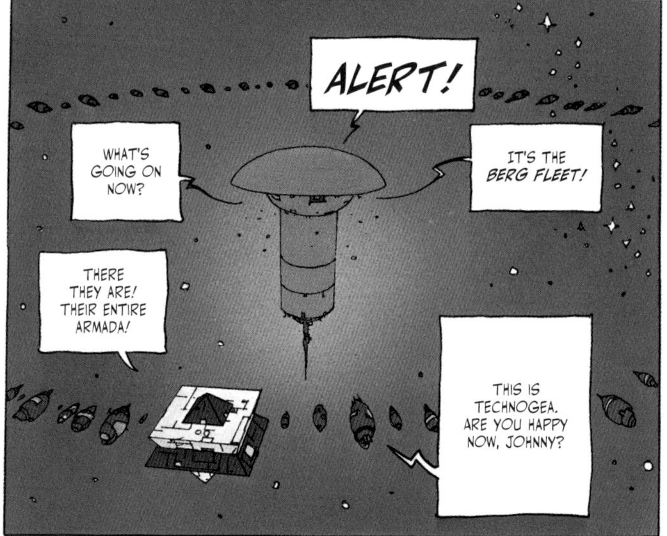
ALERT!
WHAT'S GOING ON NOW?
IT'S THE BERG FLEET!
THERE THEY ARE! THEIR ENTIRE ARMADA!
THIS IS TECHNOGEA. ARE YOU HAPPY NOW, JOHNNY?

YES, BARBARIAH DEAR. WHEN IT'S ALL OVER THE BERGS WILL HAVE THEIR INCAL AT LAST!!
BEGIN THE ATTACK! TOTAL DESTRUCTION!
BY YOUR COMMAND, PROTOQUEEN!

DON'T WORRY, OUR PSYCHIC BARRIER MAKES US TOTALLY INVULNERABLE!
BUT, THAT'S NOT TRUE! LOOK AT THE SCREENS!! THEY'RE THROUGH!!
IT'S TRUE!
HMM... THAT'S VERY STRANGE!

I ONLY SEE ONE POSSIBLE EXPLANATION: THE BARRIER IS PROGRAMMED TO STOP ANY MATTER OR ENERGY FROM OUR OWN GALAXY. THE BERGS' MOLECULAR STRUCTURE MUST BE SUBTLY DIFFERENT FROM OURS. THAT'S WHY OUR SHIELD IS INOPERATIVE. IT WILL BE NECESSARY TO FIGHT!
STIRLOG, LISTEN TO THAT IDIOT! IT'S HOPELESS!
C'MON, BIG BOY, SUCK IT UP! WE MUST RETURN TO OUR SHIP AND LEAVE THIS STINKING RATS NEST BEHIND!
49

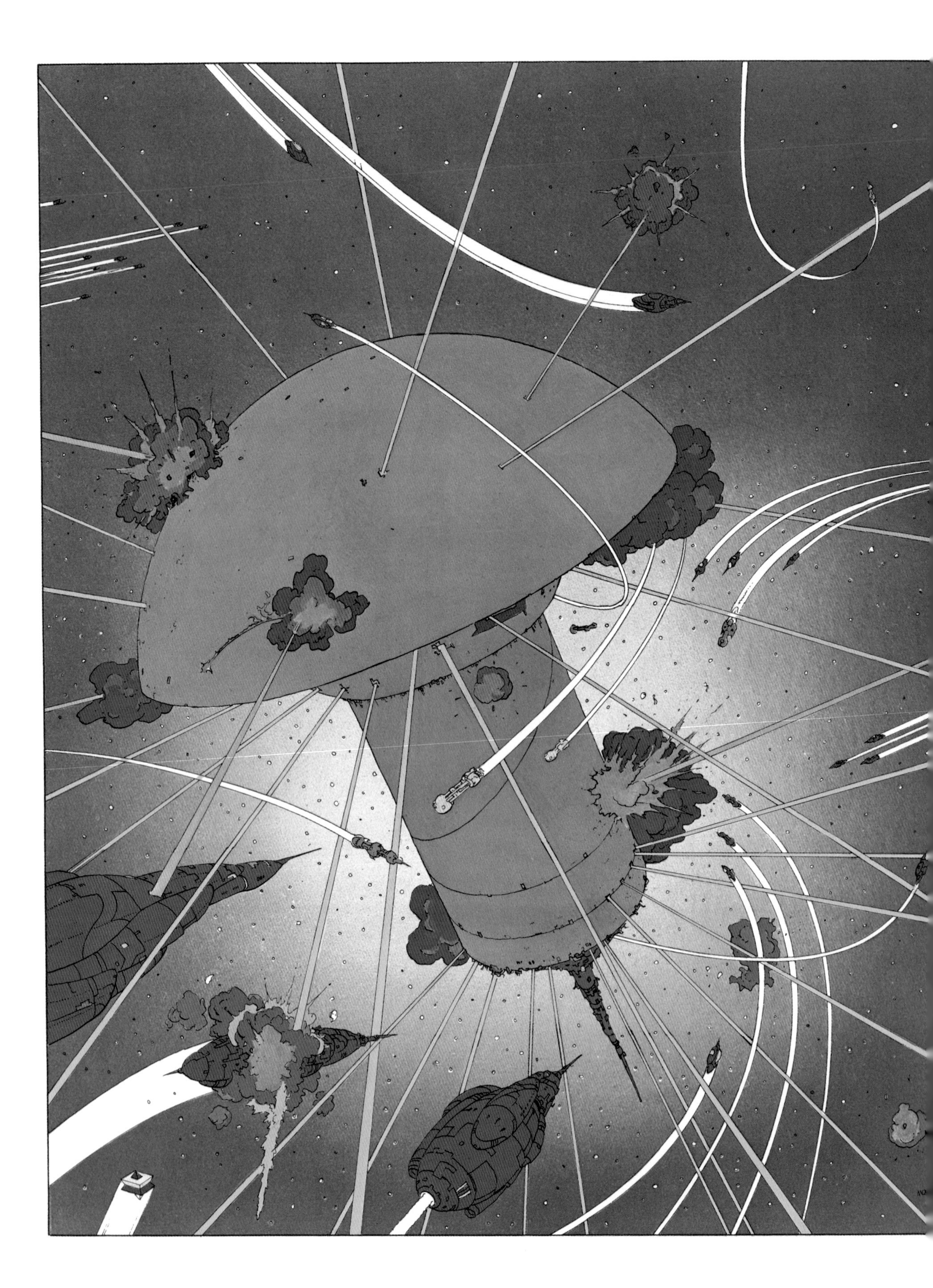

PSYCHO VIRUS

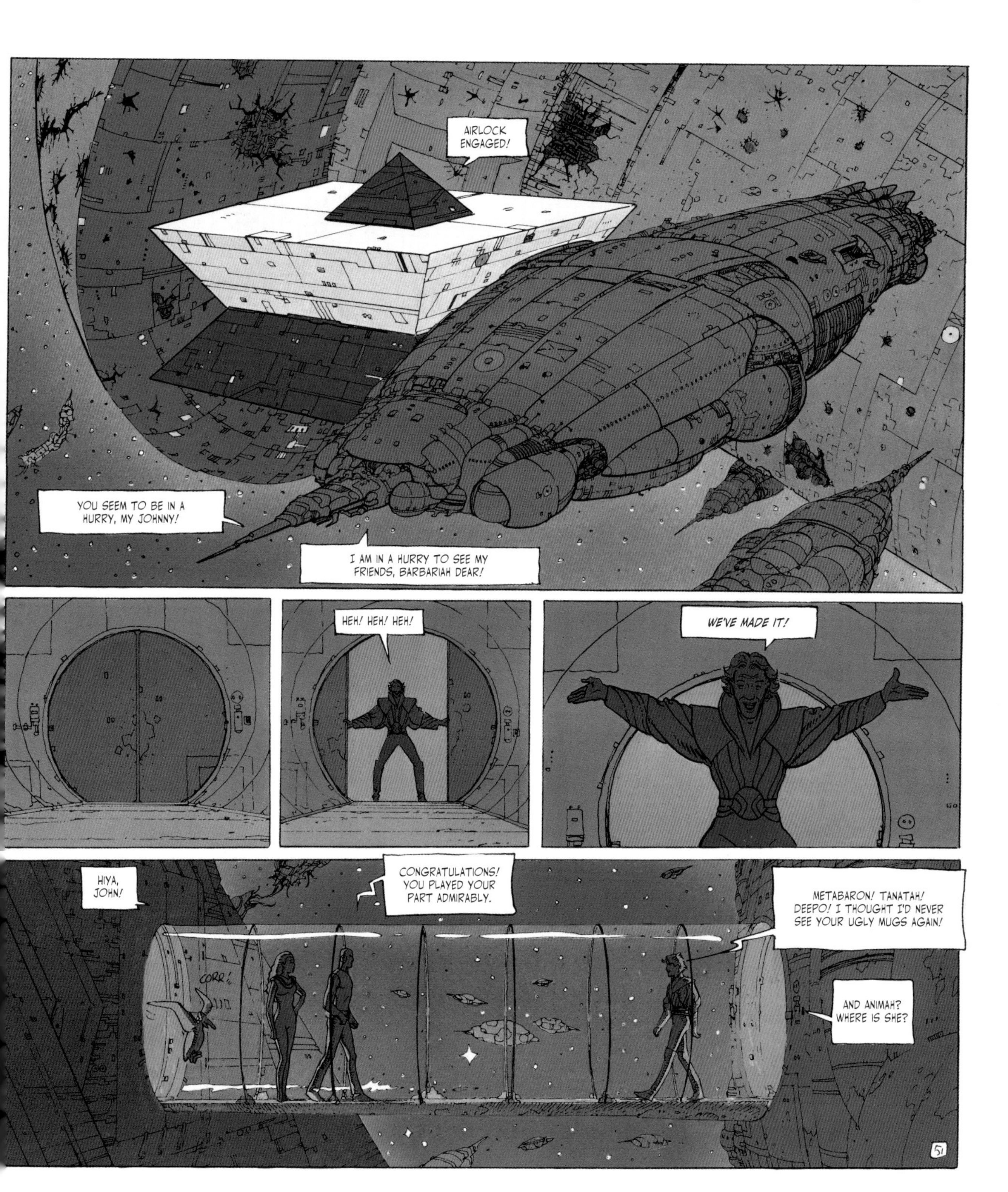

JOHN?

JOHN!
ANIMAH!

JOHNNY!!
MY JOHNNY!

SO, SHE'S THE ONE WHOSE IMAGE FILLS YOUR MIND.

AND YOU DARE PREFER THAT MORTAL TO ME, THE PROTOQUEEN?

YOU CAN KEEP YOUR INCAL! I'LL TAKE YOUR LIFE INSTEAD! MAY YOUR ATOMS WANDER ENDLESSLY IN THE VOID!
JOHN!
NO! I--
OOOOOK!

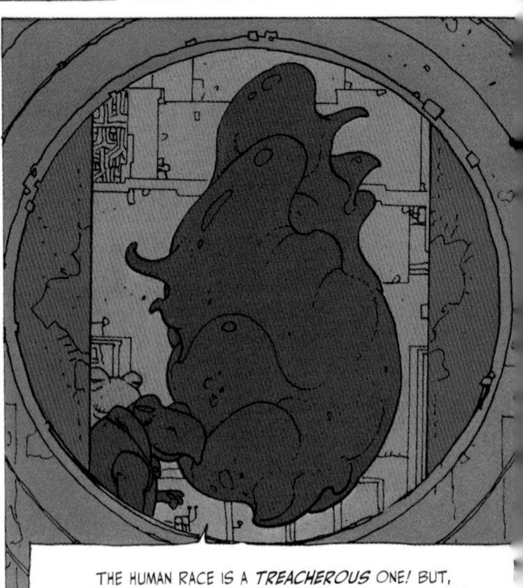
THE HUMAN RACE IS A TREACHEROUS ONE! BUT, NO MATTER, I'VE BEEN IMPREGNATED! WE NO LONGER NEED ANY OTHER RACE! COME, MY SUBJECTS, LET US RETURN TO OUR HOME WORLD AND WAIT FOR THE GOLDEN AGE OF THE BERG EMPIRE!
52

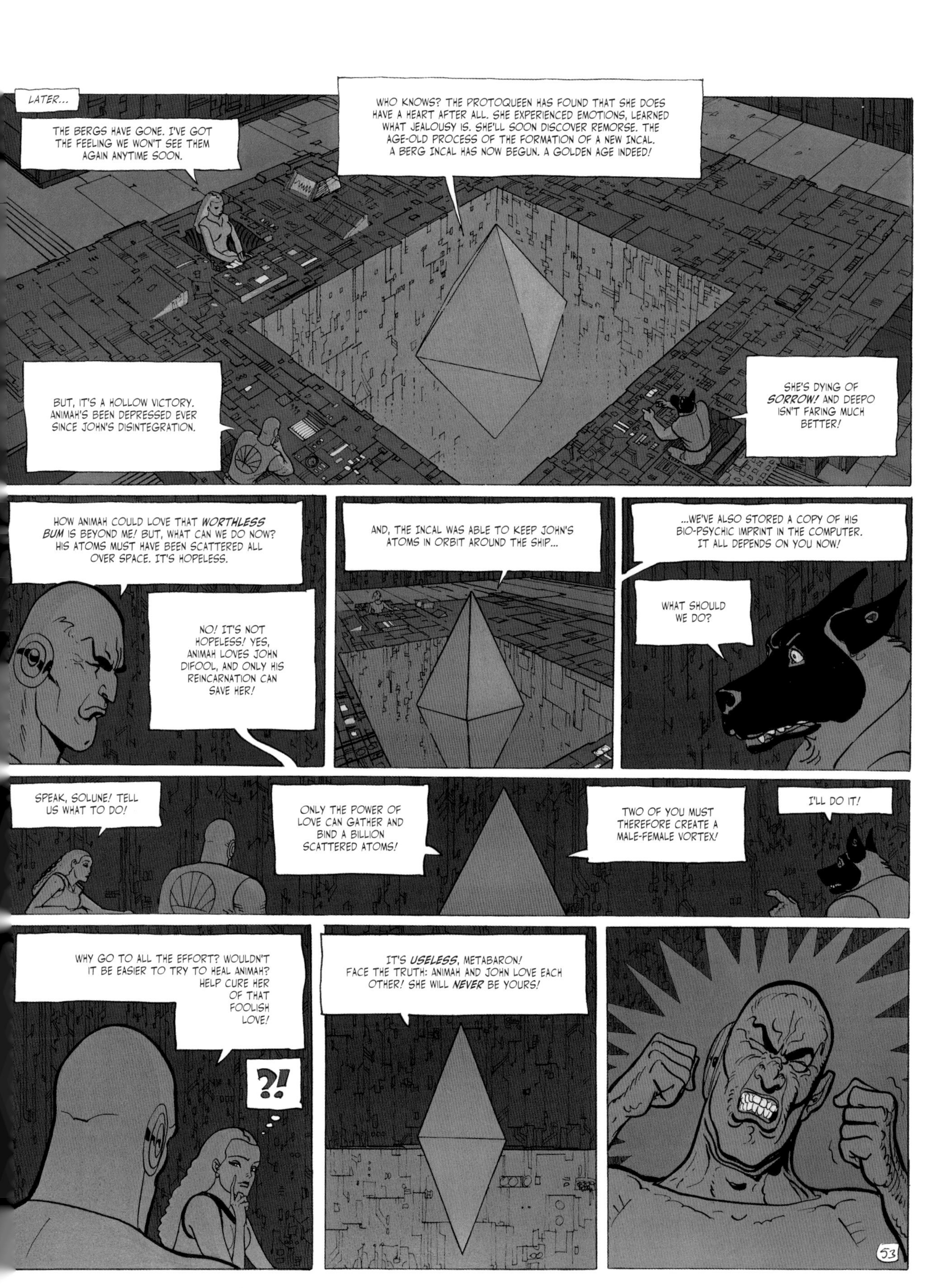
LATER...
THE BERGS HAVE GONE. I'VE GOT THE FEELING WE WON'T SEE THEM AGAIN ANYTIME SOON.
WHO KNOWS? THE PROTOQUEEN HAS FOUND THAT SHE DOES HAVE A HEART AFTER ALL. SHE EXPERIENCED EMOTIONS, LEARNED WHAT JEALOUSY IS. SHE'LL SOON DISCOVER REMORSE. THE AGE-OLD PROCESS OF THE FORMATION OF A NEW INCAL. A BERG INCAL HAS NOW BEGUN. A GOLDEN AGE INDEED!
BUT, IT'S A HOLLOW VICTORY. ANIMAH'S BEEN DEPRESSED EVER SINCE JOHN'S DISINTEGRATION.
SHE'S DYING OF SORROW! AND DEEPO ISN'T FARING MUCH BETTER!
HOW ANIMAH COULD LOVE THAT WORTHLESS BUM IS BEYOND ME! BUT, WHAT CAN WE DO NOW? HIS ATOMS MUST HAVE BEEN SCATTERED ALL OVER SPACE. IT'S HOPELESS.
NO! IT'S NOT HOPELESS! YES, ANIMAH LOVES JOHN DIFOOL, AND ONLY HIS REINCARNATION CAN SAVE HER!
AND, THE INCAL WAS ABLE TO KEEP JOHN'S ATOMS IN ORBIT AROUND THE SHIP...
...WE'VE ALSO STORED A COPY OF HIS BIO-PSYCHIC IMPRINT IN THE COMPUTER. IT ALL DEPENDS ON YOU NOW!
WHAT SHOULD WE DO?
SPEAK, SOLUNE! TELL US WHAT TO DO!
ONLY THE POWER OF LOVE CAN GATHER AND BIND A BILLION SCATTERED ATOMS!
TWO OF YOU MUST THEREFORE CREATE A MALE-FEMALE VORTEX!
I'LL DO IT!
WHY GO TO ALL THE EFFORT? WOULDN'T IT BE EASIER TO TRY TO HEAL ANIMAH? HELP CURE HER OF THAT FOOLISH LOVE!
?!
IT'S USELESS, METABARON! FACE THE TRUTH: ANIMAH AND JOHN LOVE EACH OTHER! SHE WILL NEVER BE YOURS!
53

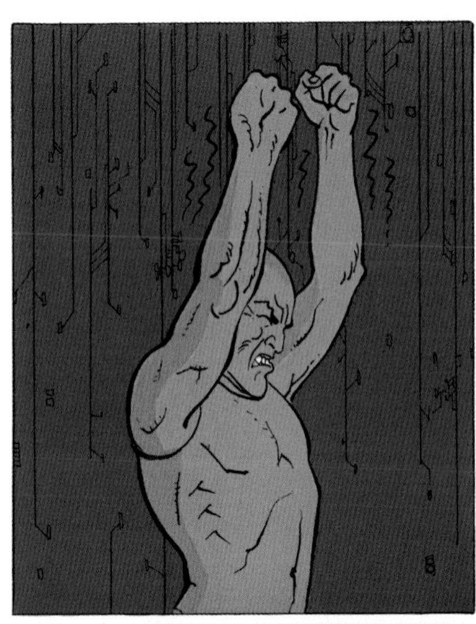

STOP!
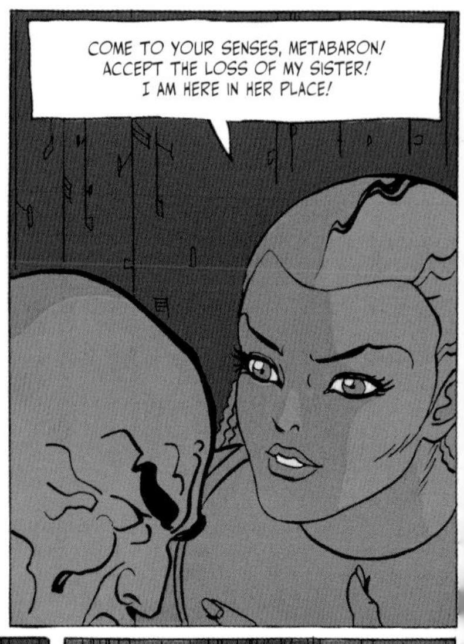
COME TO YOUR SENSES, METABARON! ACCEPT THE LOSS OF MY SISTER! I AM HERE IN HER PLACE!

YOU?...
YES, ME! LET'S JOIN OUR ENERGIES AND BRING BACK THAT IDIOT, JOHN DIFOOL.

EH...I'LL GO SEE HOW DEEPO'S DOING! THE POOR THING WAS FEELING PRETTY LOW!
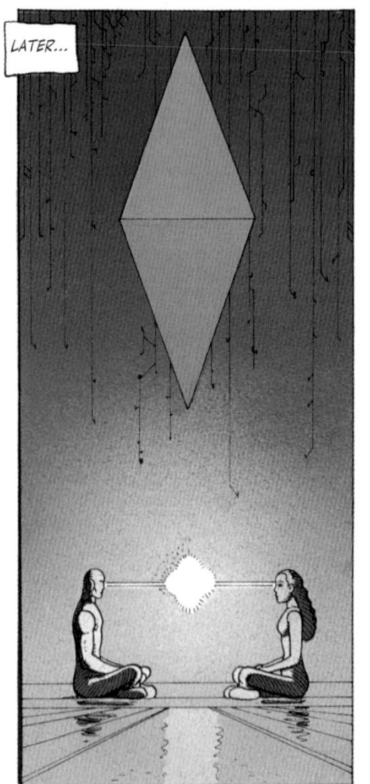
LATER...
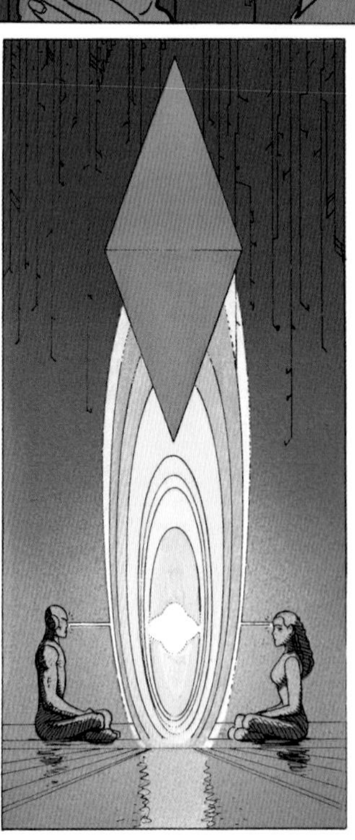
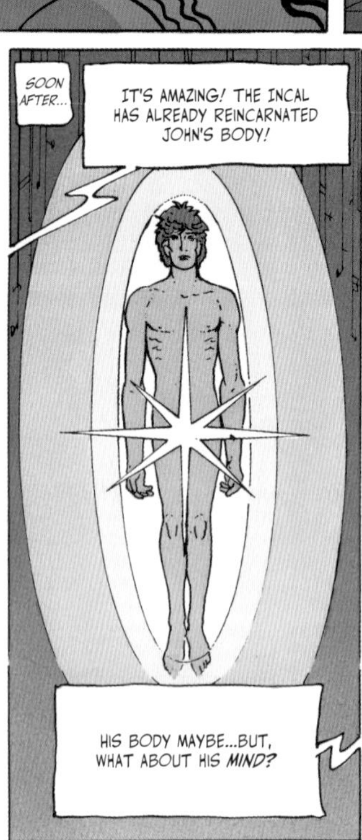
SOON AFTER...
IT'S AMAZING! THE INCAL HAS ALREADY REINCARNATED JOHN'S BODY!
HIS BODY MAYBE...BUT, WHAT ABOUT HIS MIND?

ANIMAH! WHERE ARE YOU, ANIMAH?
IN MY OPINION HIS MIND IS FINE! WELCOME BACK, JOHN DIFOOL!
54

LATER, ON AQUAEND...
COMPLETE SUCCESS! ALL THE SHADOW EGGS HAVE BEEN NEUTRALIZED!
THE TECHNOS HAVE BEEN DISBANDED AND THE MAGNATES BANISHED!
THERE'S STILL A MYSTERY, THOUGH! WHAT COULD INDUCE THEM TO BETRAY MANKIND TO THE POWER OF THE DARKNESS?
THE INCAL BELIEVES IT'S SOME KIND OF PSYCHO VIRUS!
WHAT IS THIS ENTITY THAT CALLS ITSELF THE DARKNESS ANYWAY? WHERE DOES IT COME FROM AND WHAT DOES IT WANT?
INDEED, MANY MYSTERIES STILL REMAIN! BUT, WE HAVE A MORE PRESSING CONCERN: THE *EMPERORESS!*
?
?

HE/SHE WAS SUPPOSED TO RETURN TO THE PLANET OF GOLD TO RECEIVE A TRIUMPHANT HONOR FROM THE COLONIAL PLANETS WHEN HE/SHE WAS OVERCOME BY A STRANGE SICKNESS!
LET'S SEE HIM/HER! THE INCAL CAN PERFORM MIRACLES!
IT WON'T BE EASY! HIS MEGA-HOLINESS TOLERATES NO ONE BUT GREYFIELD AT HIS SIDE!
LET'S TRY IT ANYWAY!

NOW THAT IT'S ALL OVER, WHAT WOULD YOU LIKE TO DO, JOHN?
WHO CARES, AS LONG AS WE'RE TOGETHER.
I SUSPECT IT'S A TRICK OF THE DARKNESS.
THIS SICKNESS IS STRANGE. IN THEORY, THE ENERGY EGGS THAT SURROUND THE EMPERORESS ARE IMPERVIOUS TO ANY KIND OF VIRUS.
BUT, A PSYCHO VIRUS IS DIFFERENT.

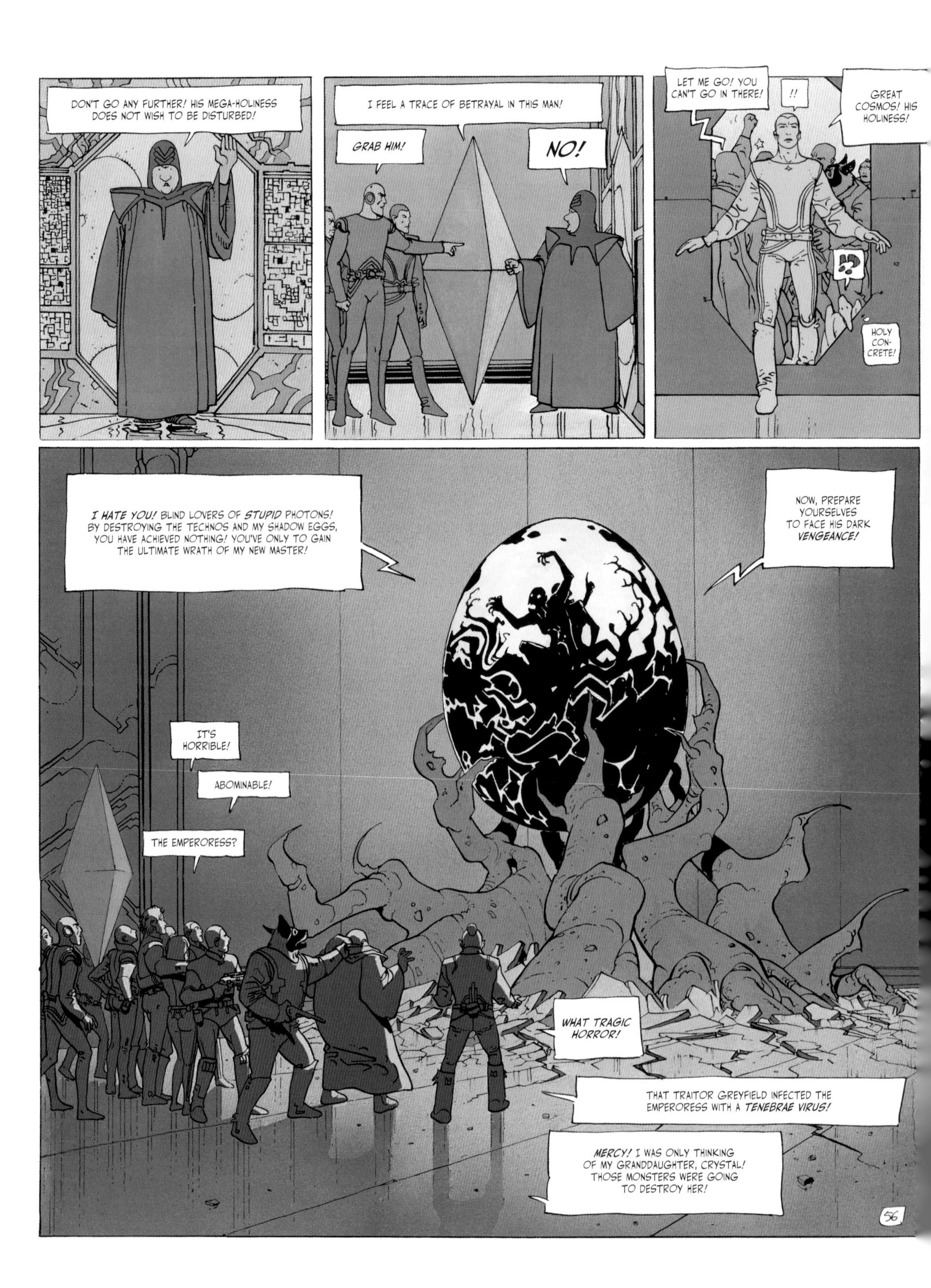
DON'T GO ANY FURTHER! HIS MEGA-HOLINESS DOES NOT WISH TO BE DISTURBED!
I FEEL A TRACE OF BETRAYAL IN THIS MAN!
GRAB HIM!
NO!
LET ME GO! YOU CAN'T GO IN THERE!
!!
GREAT COSMOS! HIS HOLINESS!
HOLY CONCRETE!
I HATE YOU! BLIND LOVERS OF STUPID PHOTONS! BY DESTROYING THE TECHNOS AND MY SHADOW EGGS, YOU HAVE ACHIEVED NOTHING! YOU'VE ONLY TO GAIN THE ULTIMATE WRATH OF MY NEW MASTER!
NOW, PREPARE YOURSELVES TO FACE HIS DARK VENGEANCE!
IT'S HORRIBLE!
ABOMINABLE!
THE EMPERORESS?
WHAT TRAGIC HORROR!
THAT TRAITOR GREYFIELD INFECTED THE EMPERORESS WITH A TENEBRAE VIRUS!
MERCY! I WAS ONLY THINKING OF MY GRANDDAUGHTER, CRYSTAL! THOSE MONSTERS WERE GOING TO DESTROY HER!
56

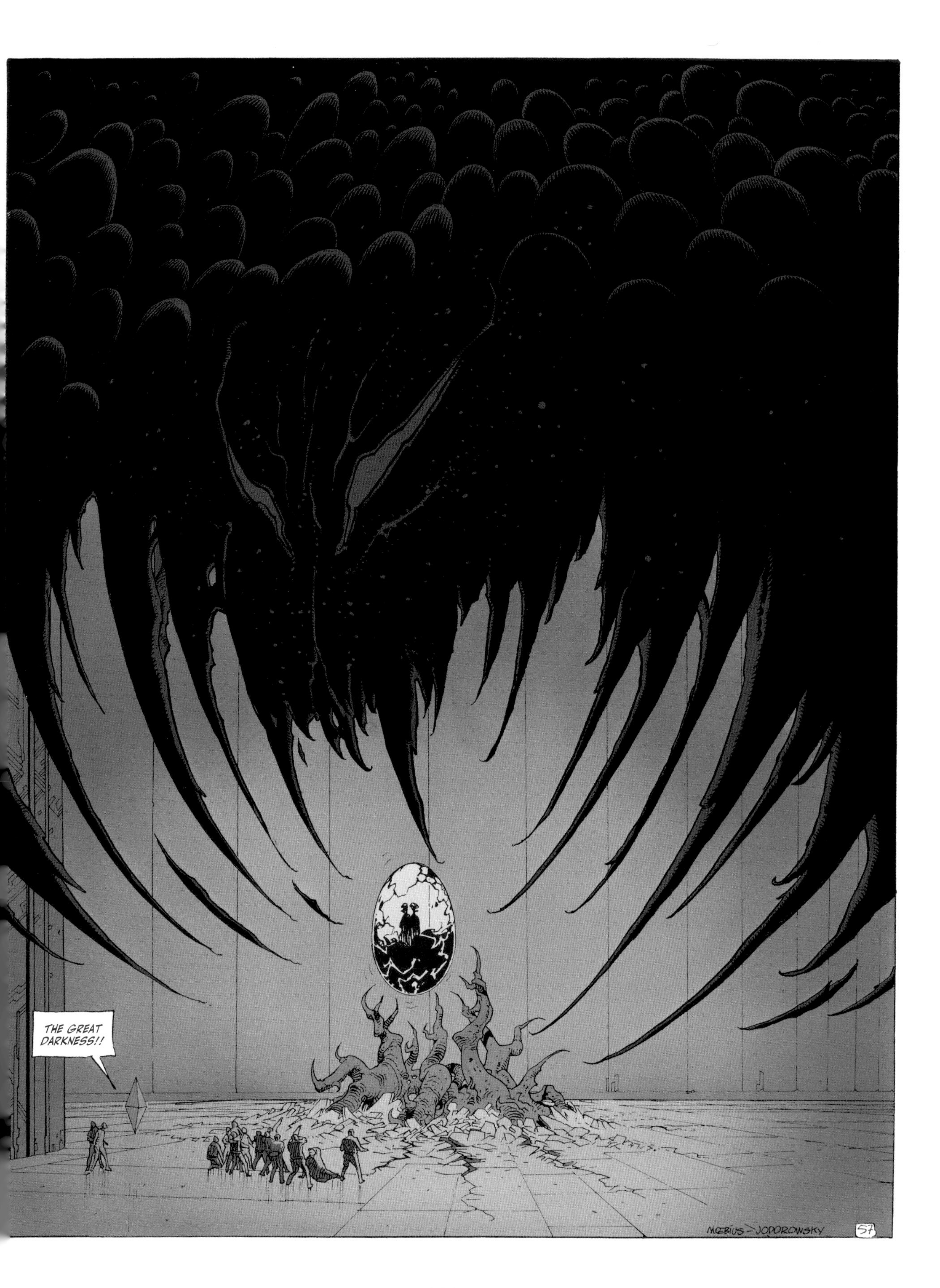
THE GREAT DARKNESS!!
MŒBIUS - JODOROWSKY
57

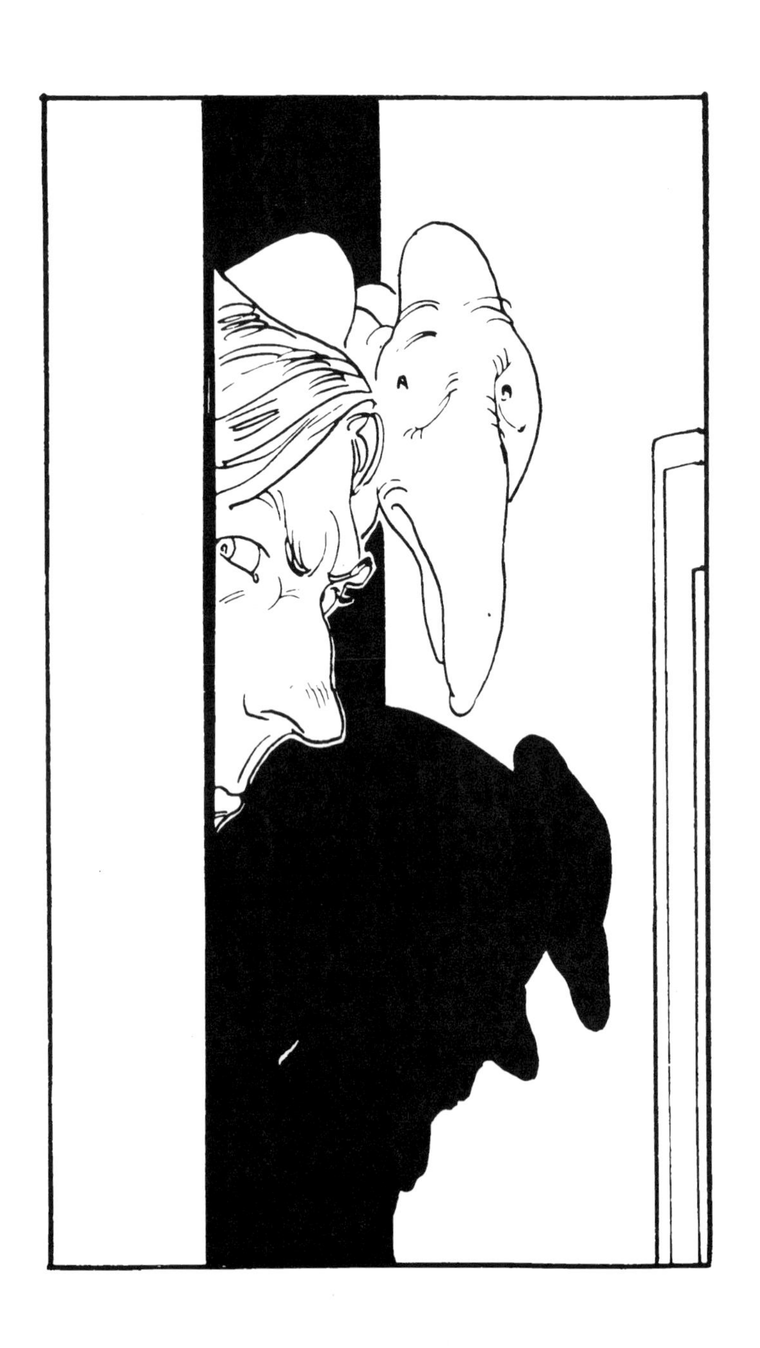

MŒBIUS 87

THE FIFTH ESSENCE
part one: the dreaming galaxy

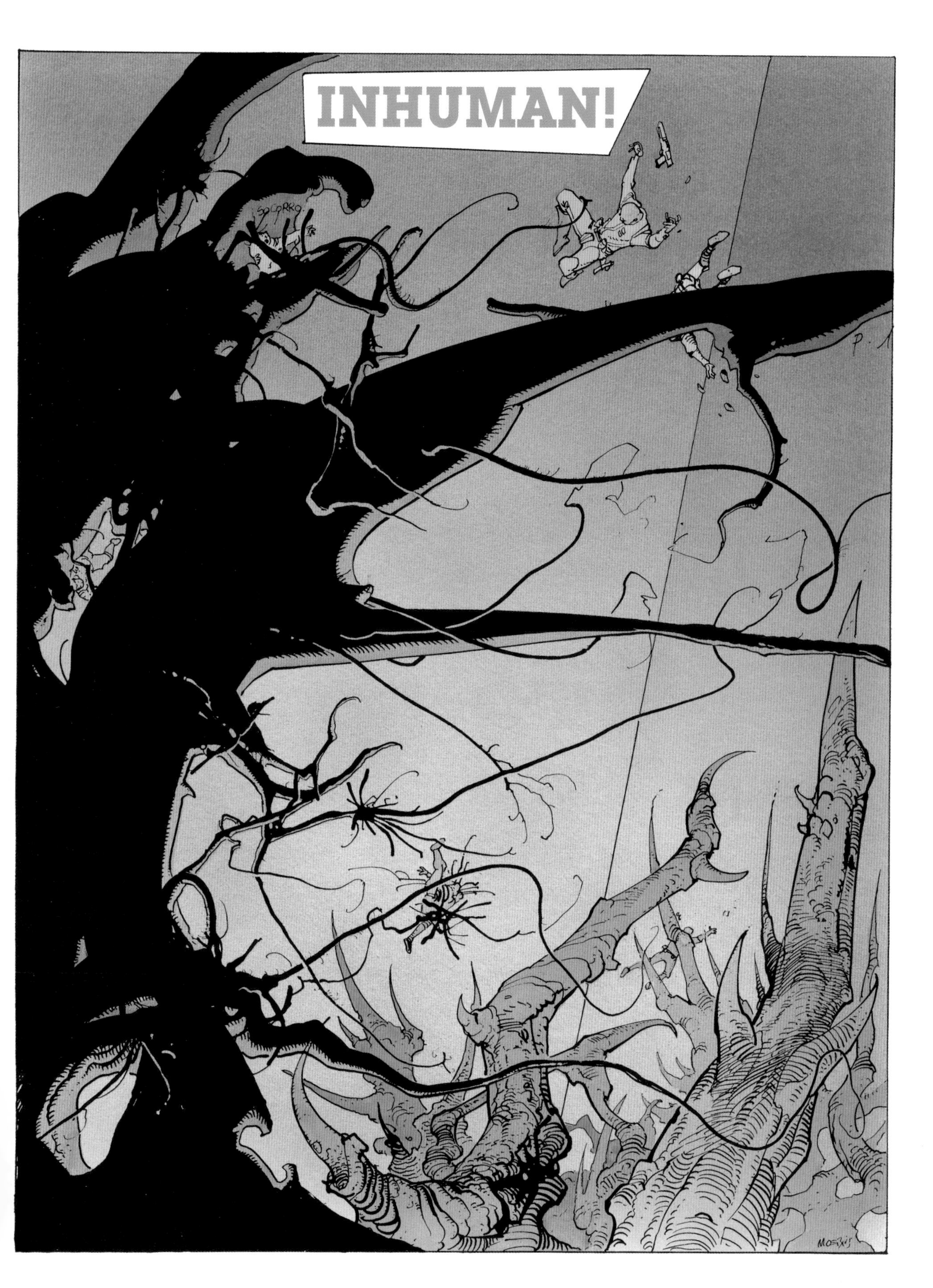
INHUMAN!
SOCORRO.
MOEBIUS

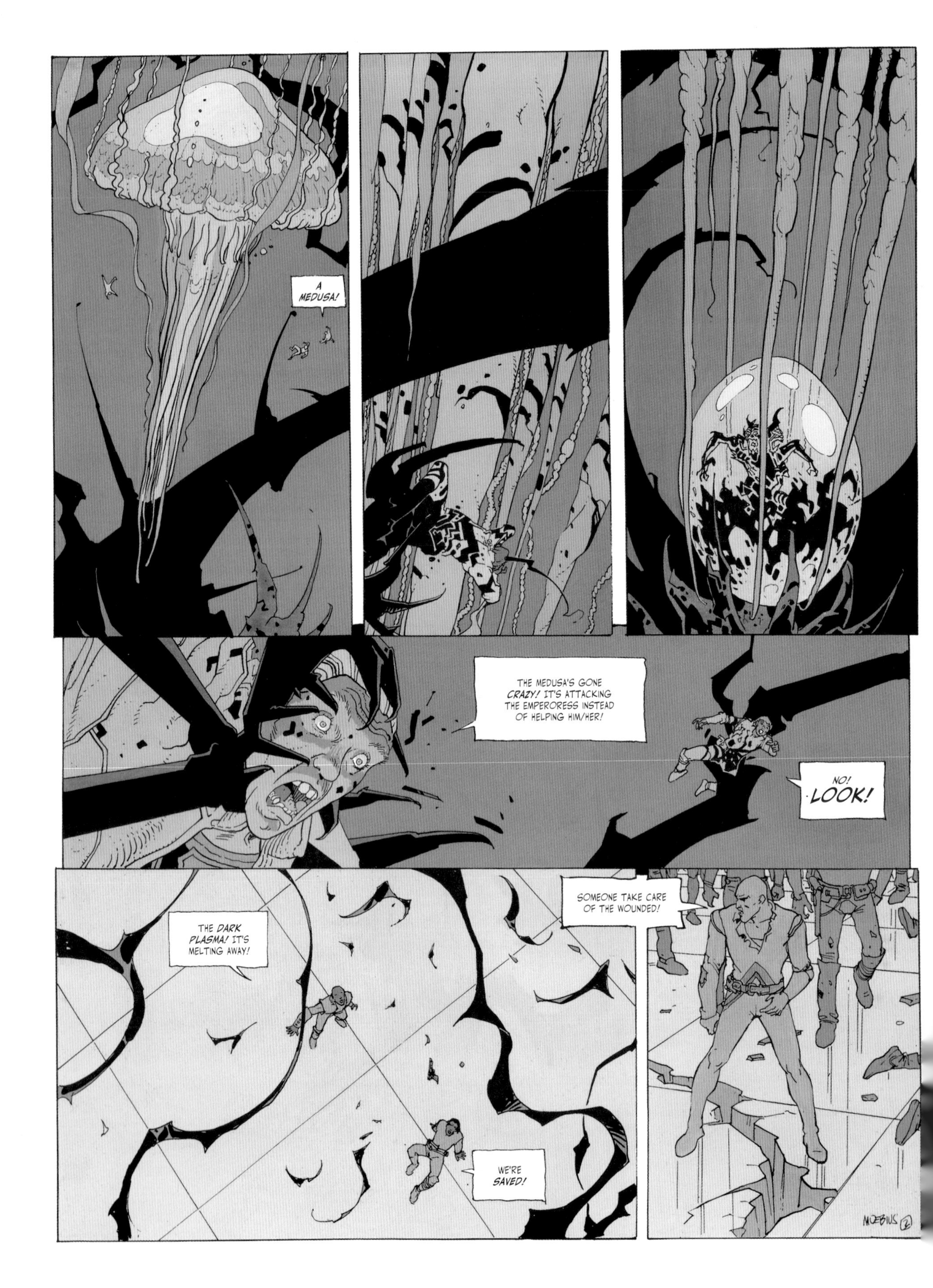
A MEDUSA!
THE MEDUSA'S GONE CRAZY! IT'S ATTACKING THE EMPERORESS INSTEAD OF HELPING HIM/HER!
NO! LOOK!
THE DARK PLASMA! IT'S MELTING AWAY!
WE'RE SAVED!
SOMEONE TAKE CARE OF THE WOUNDED!
MŒBIUS

IT'S HOPELESS! OUR REAL ENEMY IS THE GREAT DARKNESS, BUT IT APPEARS INVINCIBLE!
DEFEAT IT?
BUT, DIDN'T WE JUST DEFEAT IT?
WE'VE BARELY STALLED IT! THE EMPERORESS IS ONLY A MEDIUM! THE DARKNESS CAN STRIKE ANYWHERE! AT ANY TIME!
THE INCAL SENT THAT MEDUSA JUST IN TIME!
BUT, HOW MANY WILL IT TAKE TO--
ENOUGH!
I'VE HAD IT WITH ALL OF THIS! WE AGREED I'D BE OFF THE HOOK AFTER THE BERG CAPER! NOW, I WANT A WELL DESERVED VACATION ON SOME PLANET OF PARADISE WITH ANIMAH!
A "VACATION?" WHAT'S THAT?
I'VE HATED THIS THING SINCE THE VERY BEGINNING, AND IT'S GETTING WORSE! SO, I'M TELLING YOU NOW... I'VE HAD IT UP TO HERE! HAD IT!
KEEP ON SAVING THE GALAXY, THE UNIVERSE IF YOU WANT, BUT DO IT WITHOUT ME!
COME ON, JOHN! YOU'RE A DETECTIVE! YOU CAN'T QUIT NOW!
WHAT'S GOTTEN INTO HIM?
I'M HURT, REALLY...
I'M DONE!
BUT, JOHN--
STUPID BIRD! LEAVE ME ALONE!
STUPID BIRD???
IT MUST BE THE SHOCK!
MOEBIUS 3

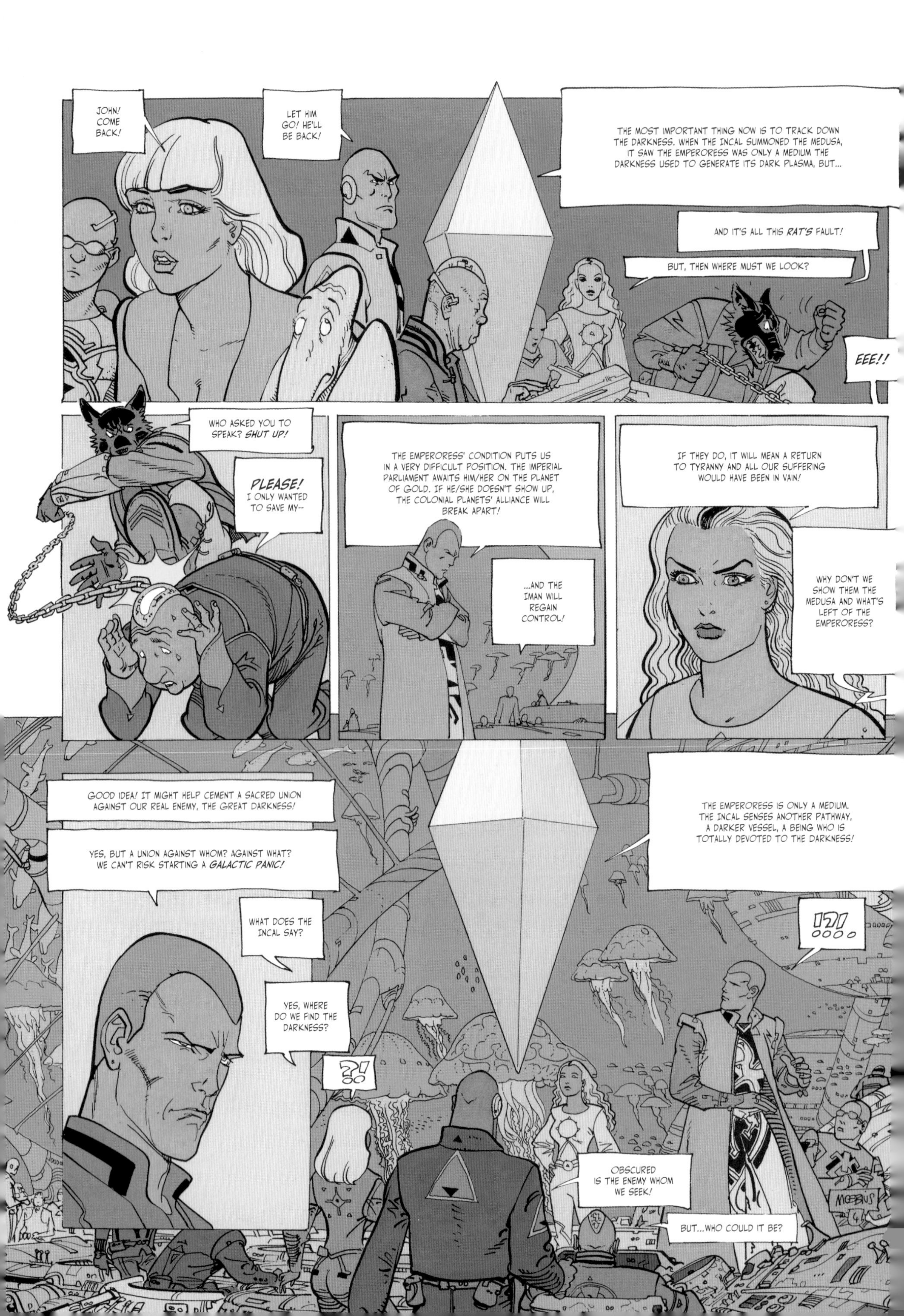
JOHN! COME BACK!
LET HIM GO! HE'LL BE BACK!
THE MOST IMPORTANT THING NOW IS TO TRACK DOWN THE DARKNESS. WHEN THE INCAL SUMMONED THE MEDUSA, IT SAW THE EMPERORESS WAS ONLY A MEDIUM THE DARKNESS USED TO GENERATE ITS DARK PLASMA, BUT...
AND IT'S ALL THIS RAT'S FAULT!
BUT, THEN WHERE MUST WE LOOK?
EEE!!
WHO ASKED YOU TO SPEAK? SHUT UP!
PLEASE! I ONLY WANTED TO SAVE MY--
THE EMPERORESS' CONDITION PUTS US IN A VERY DIFFICULT POSITION. THE IMPERIAL PARLIAMENT AWAITS HIM/HER ON THE PLANET OF GOLD. IF HE/SHE DOESN'T SHOW UP, THE COLONIAL PLANETS' ALLIANCE WILL BREAK APART!
...AND THE IMAN WILL REGAIN CONTROL!
IF THEY DO, IT WILL MEAN A RETURN TO TYRANNY AND ALL OUR SUFFERING WOULD HAVE BEEN IN VAIN!
WHY DON'T WE SHOW THEM THE MEDUSA AND WHAT'S LEFT OF THE EMPERORESS?
GOOD IDEA! IT MIGHT HELP CEMENT A SACRED UNION AGAINST OUR REAL ENEMY, THE GREAT DARKNESS!
YES, BUT A UNION AGAINST WHOM? AGAINST WHAT? WE CAN'T RISK STARTING A GALACTIC PANIC!
THE EMPERORESS IS ONLY A MEDIUM. THE INCAL SENSES ANOTHER PATHWAY, A DARKER VESSEL, A BEING WHO IS TOTALLY DEVOTED TO THE DARKNESS!
WHAT DOES THE INCAL SAY?
!?!
YES, WHERE DO WE FIND THE DARKNESS?
?!
OBSCURED IS THE ENEMY WHOM WE SEEK!
BUT...WHO COULD IT BE?
MOEBIUS

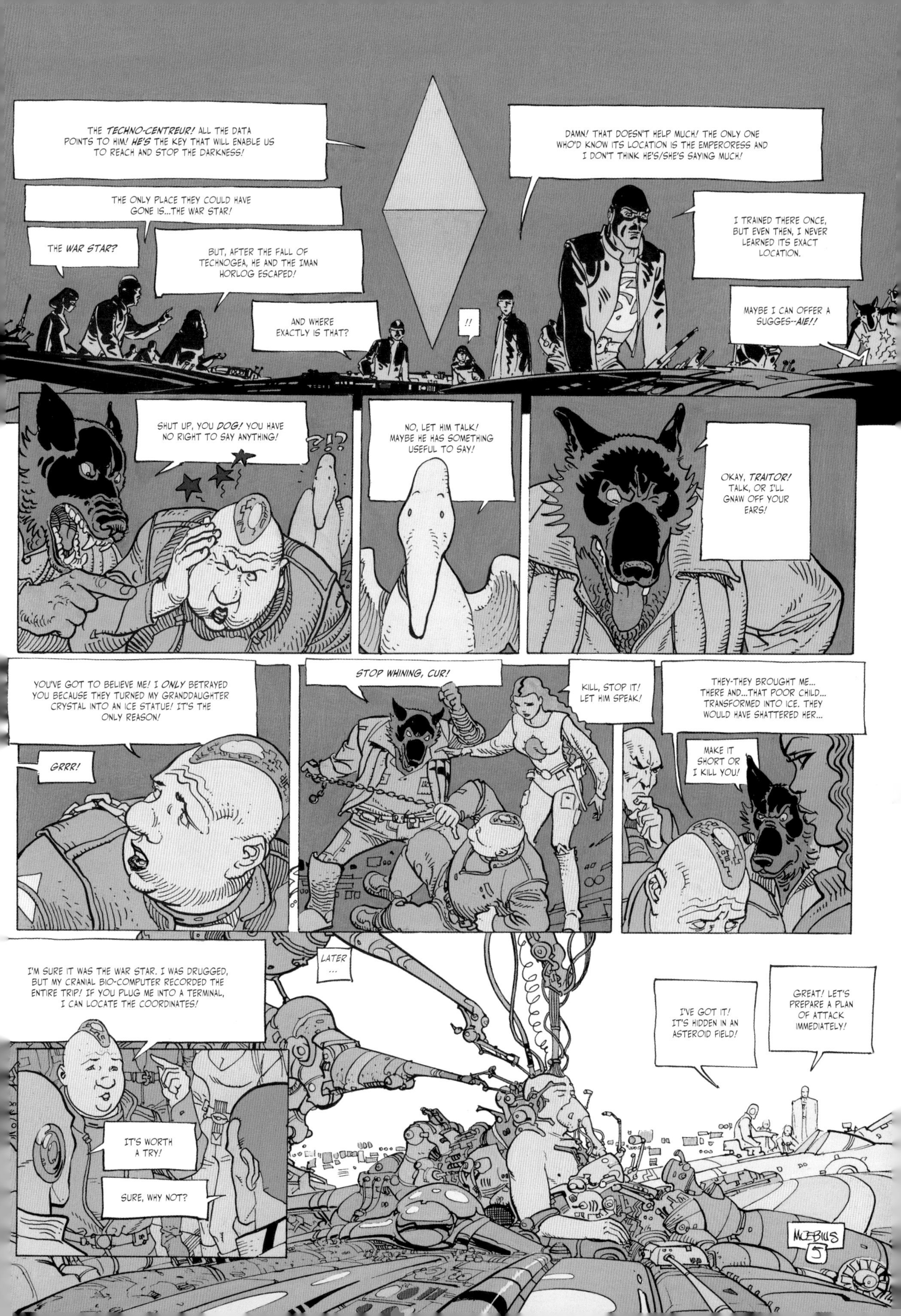
THE TECHNO-CENTREUR! ALL THE DATA POINTS TO HIM! HE'S THE KEY THAT WILL ENABLE US TO REACH AND STOP THE DARKNESS!
THE ONLY PLACE THEY COULD HAVE GONE IS...THE WAR STAR!
THE WAR STAR?
BUT, AFTER THE FALL OF TECHNOGEA, HE AND THE IMAN HORLOG ESCAPED!
AND WHERE EXACTLY IS THAT?
!!
DAMN! THAT DOESN'T HELP MUCH! THE ONLY ONE WHO'D KNOW ITS LOCATION IS THE EMPERORESS AND I DON'T THINK HE'S/SHE'S SAYING MUCH!
I TRAINED THERE ONCE, BUT EVEN THEN, I NEVER LEARNED ITS EXACT LOCATION.
MAYBE I CAN OFFER A SUGGES--AIE!!
SHUT UP, YOU DOG! YOU HAVE NO RIGHT TO SAY ANYTHING!
?!?
NO, LET HIM TALK! MAYBE HE HAS SOMETHING USEFUL TO SAY!
OKAY, TRAITOR! TALK, OR I'LL GNAW OFF YOUR EARS!
YOU'VE GOT TO BELIEVE ME! I ONLY BETRAYED YOU BECAUSE THEY TURNED MY GRANDDAUGHTER CRYSTAL INTO AN ICE STATUE! IT'S THE ONLY REASON!
GRRR!
STOP WHINING, CUR!
KILL, STOP IT! LET HIM SPEAK!
THEY-THEY BROUGHT ME... THERE AND...THAT POOR CHILD... TRANSFORMED INTO ICE. THEY WOULD HAVE SHATTERED HER...
MAKE IT SHORT OR I KILL YOU!
I'M SURE IT WAS THE WAR STAR. I WAS DRUGGED, BUT MY CRANIAL BIO-COMPUTER RECORDED THE ENTIRE TRIP! IF YOU PLUG ME INTO A TERMINAL, I CAN LOCATE THE COORDINATES!
LATER ...
IT'S WORTH A TRY!
SURE, WHY NOT?
I'VE GOT IT! IT'S HIDDEN IN AN ASTEROID FIELD!
GREAT! LET'S PREPARE A PLAN OF ATTACK IMMEDIATELY!
MŒBIUS
5

JOHN?
I KNOW...
I ACTED LIKE A JERK AGAIN!
DON'T SAY THAT. WE WERE ALL PRETTY SHAKEN UP!
IT IS WITH YOU THAT I FIND THE COURAGE TO--OH, ANIMAH, LET'S LEAVE! FAR FROM ALL THIS. FIND A QUIET PLANET SOMEWHERE WHERE WE WOULD BE HAPPY TOGETHER.
JOHN, THAT IS MY DEAREST DESIRE!
IT REALLY IS? YOU MEAN IT? YOU'D GO WITH ME? RIGHT NOW?
OF COURSE! WHY NOT?
OOOH, ANIMAH!
BUT, THERE'S ONE TINY THING YOU'VE GOT TO DO FOR ME BEFORE WE CAN GO--
SURE! ANYTHING YOU WANT! I'M SO HAPPY! WHAT DO YOU WANT ME TO DO?
INFILTRATE THE WAR STAR.
INFILTRATE THE WAR STAR?
THERE'S NOTHING TO BE AFRAID OF! THE METABARON PLANNED IT ALL VERY CAREFULLY!
MOEBIUS
6

...
THERE IS NO WAY IT CAN FAIL, DON'T YOU AGREE?
WHY AREN'T YOU SAYING ANYTHING?
WHAT THE HELL DID YOU THINK I WOULD SAY?!
THE WAR STAR? THE MASSIVE MILITARY COMPLEX THAT'S HIDDEN *SOMEWHERE* OUT IN SPACE?
YES. AT LEAST I THINK THAT'S WHAT RAÏMO SAID!
DID RAÏMO ALSO SAY THAT IS THE PLACE WHERE THE EMPIRE KEEPS ALL ITS WAR TOYS AND ITS PURPLE ENDOGUARD? THERE ARE THOUSANDS OF SOLDIERS THERE. EACH ONE AS POWERFUL AS THE METABARON!
I KNOW, BUT--
NO, YOU *DON'T* KNOW! THAT DAMN FORTRESS CAN ATOMIZE AN ENTIRE SOLAR SYSTEM IN A MATTER OF SECONDS! IT'S FILLED TO THE BRIM WITH MURDEROUS SUPER-SOLDIERS!
IT'S THE MOST DANGEROUS PLACE IN THE WHOLE GALAXY, AND I'M BEING CONSERVATIVE, AND YOU WANT ME TO--
BUT, JOHN, WE'LL HAVE THE INCAL WITH US!
GREAT! JUST *GREAT!* IF YOU HAVE THE HOLY WONDER OF THE UNIVERSE, WHAT DO YOU NEED *ME* FOR? *WHAT?*
BUT, JOHN...
I *DON'T* WANT TO DISCUSS IT ANYMORE! I DON'T WANT TO! I CANNOT! I *WON'T!* NO, NO AND
NO!
NEVER!
NO!
NEVER!
JOHN...
7
MŒBIUS

SO, THAT IS THE "WAR STAR?"
YES.
SEEMS DESERTED...
HEY! *WHAT THE--?!*
MY NAME IS GREYFIELD! TAKE ME TO THE TECHNO-CENTREUR.
DON'T SHOOT!
TAKE CARE OF THESE TWO JERKS! THEY'RE NOT ARMED!
HERE WE GO AGAIN!
MOEBIUS 84
8

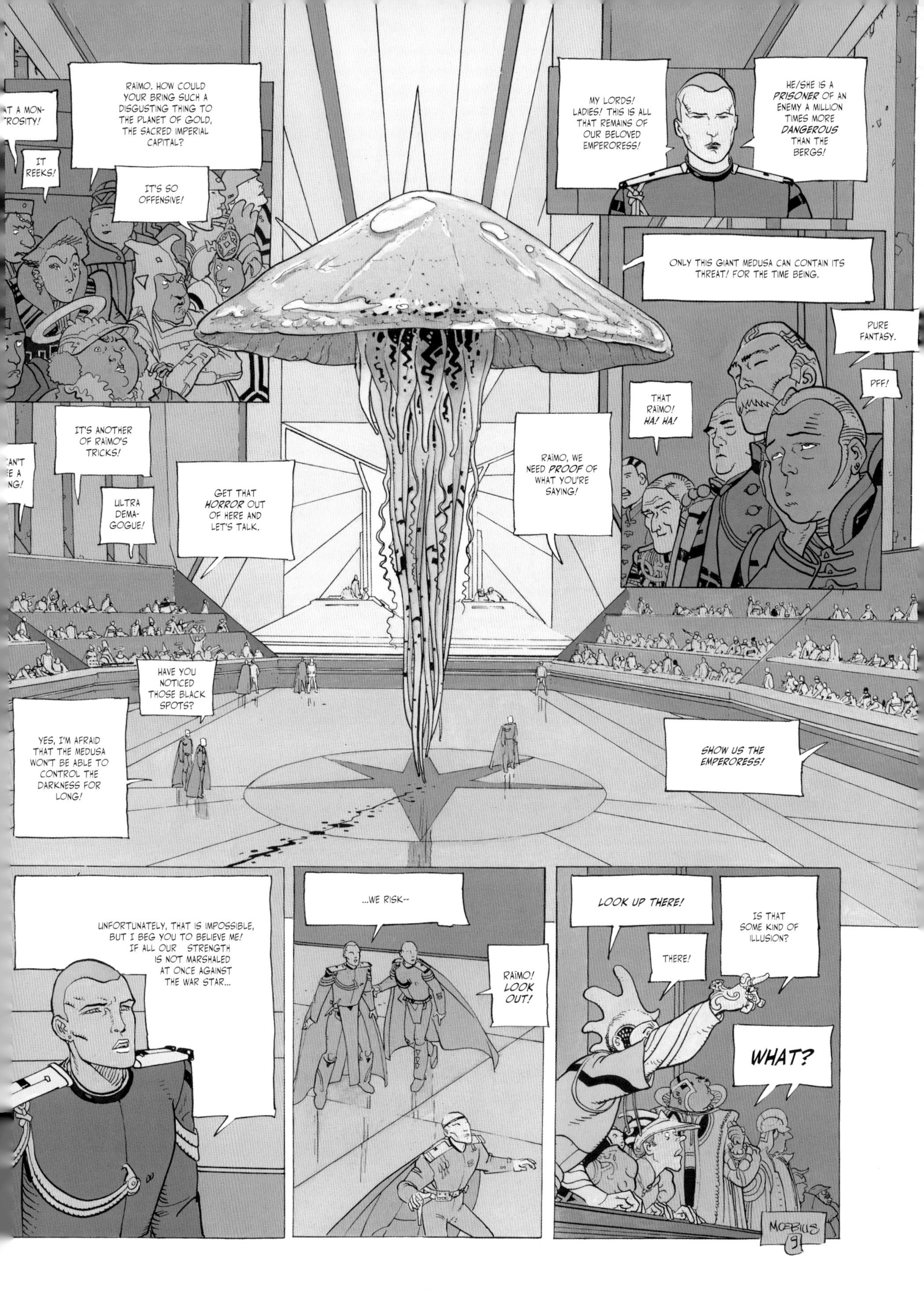

...AT A MONSTROSITY!
RAÏMO. HOW COULD YOUR BRING SUCH A DISGUSTING THING TO THE PLANET OF GOLD, THE SACRED IMPERIAL CAPITAL?
IT REEKS!
IT'S SO OFFENSIVE!
MY LORDS! LADIES! THIS IS ALL THAT REMAINS OF OUR BELOVED EMPERORESS!
HE/SHE IS A PRISONER OF AN ENEMY A MILLION TIMES MORE DANGEROUS THAN THE BERGS!
ONLY THIS GIANT MEDUSA CAN CONTAIN ITS THREAT! FOR THE TIME BEING.
PURE FANTASY.
PFF!
THAT RAÏMO! HA! HA!
IT'S ANOTHER OF RAÏMO'S TRICKS!
ULTRA DEMAGOGUE!
GET THAT HORROR OUT OF HERE AND LET'S TALK.
RAÏMO, WE NEED PROOF OF WHAT YOU'RE SAYING!
HAVE YOU NOTICED THOSE BLACK SPOTS?
YES, I'M AFRAID THAT THE MEDUSA WON'T BE ABLE TO CONTROL THE DARKNESS FOR LONG!
SHOW US THE EMPERORESS!
UNFORTUNATELY, THAT IS IMPOSSIBLE, BUT I BEG YOU TO BELIEVE ME! IF ALL OUR STRENGTH IS NOT MARSHALED AT ONCE AGAINST THE WAR STAR...
...WE RISK--
RAÏMO! LOOK OUT!
LOOK UP THERE!
THERE!
IS THAT SOME KIND OF ILLUSION?
WHAT?
MOEBIUS
9

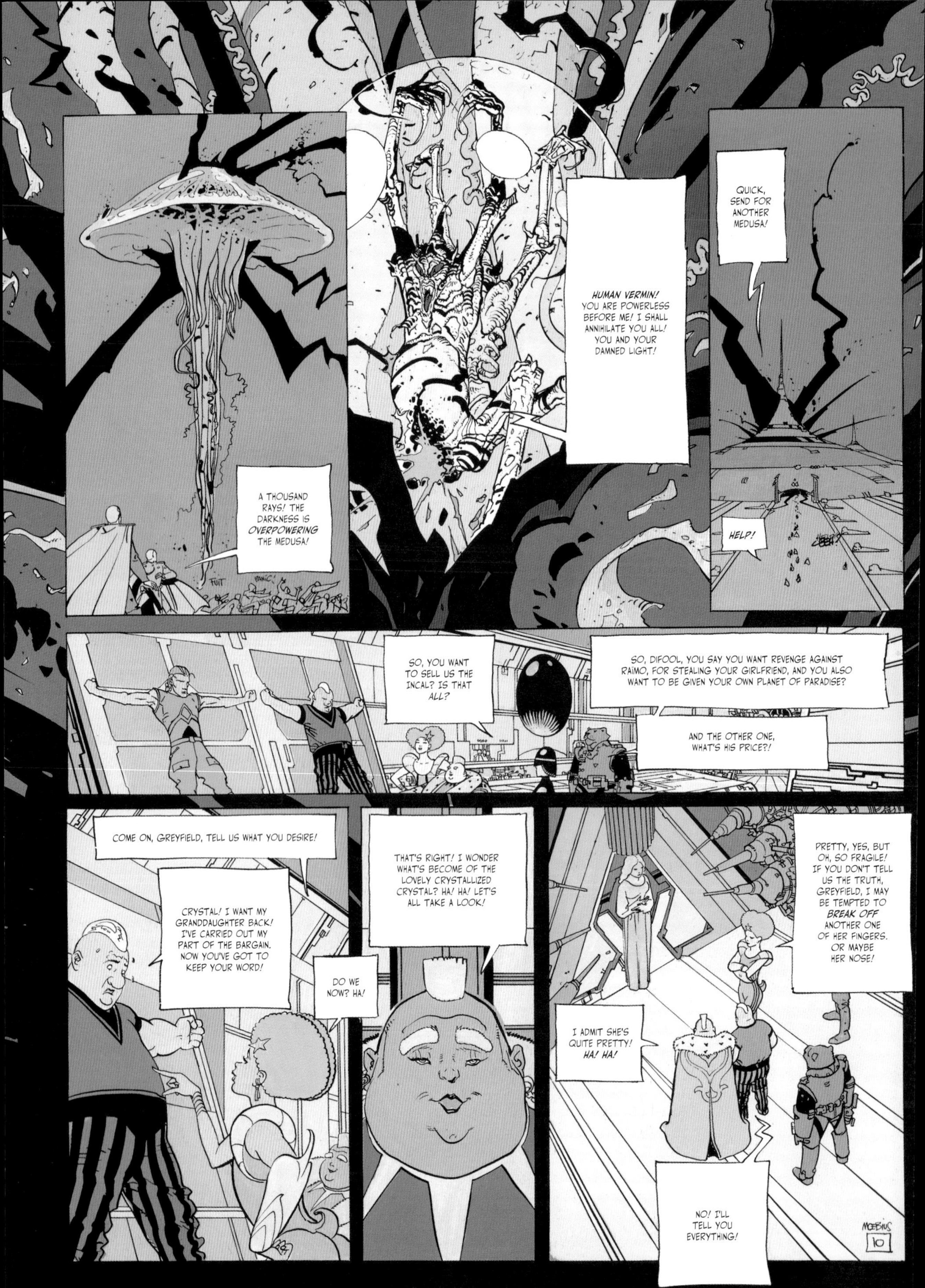
A THOUSAND RAYS! THE DARKNESS IS *OVERPOWERING* THE MEDUSA!
HUMAN VERMIN! YOU ARE POWERLESS BEFORE ME! I SHALL ANNIHILATE YOU ALL! YOU AND YOUR DAMNED LIGHT!
QUICK, SEND FOR ANOTHER MEDUSA!
HELP!
SO, YOU WANT TO SELL US THE INCAL? IS THAT *ALL?*
SO, DIFOOL, YOU SAY YOU WANT REVENGE AGAINST RAÏMO, FOR STEALING YOUR GIRLFRIEND, AND YOU ALSO WANT TO BE GIVEN YOUR OWN PLANET OF PARADISE?
AND THE OTHER ONE, WHAT'S HIS PRICE?!
COME ON, GREYFIELD, TELL US WHAT YOU DESIRE!
CRYSTAL! I WANT MY GRANDDAUGHTER BACK! I'VE CARRIED OUT MY PART OF THE BARGAIN. NOW YOU'VE GOT TO KEEP YOUR WORD!
DO WE NOW? HA!
THAT'S RIGHT! I WONDER WHAT'S BECOME OF THE LOVELY CRYSTALLIZED CRYSTAL? HA! HA! LET'S ALL TAKE A LOOK!
I ADMIT SHE'S QUITE PRETTY! ***HA! HA!***
PRETTY, YES, BUT OH, SO FRAGILE! IF YOU DON'T TELL US THE TRUTH, GREYFIELD, I MAY BE TEMPTED TO ***BREAK OFF*** ANOTHER ONE OF HER FINGERS. OR MAYBE HER NOSE!
NO! I'LL TELL YOU EVERYTHING!
MOEBIUS
10

GODDAMN TRAITOR! DON'T SAY A WORD OR I'LL--
KEEP THAT MADMAN AWAY FROM ME! I'LL TALK!
RAÏMO AND THE METABARON PLANNED IT ALL! THE INCAL IS MINIATURIZED INSIDE JOHN DIFOOL! AND THE COLONIALS ARE GOING TO LAUNCH A MASSIVE ASSAULT ON THE WAR STAR! I SWEAR IT'S THE TRUTH!
OUCH! HEY!
AGAIN?
THE COLONIALS! AN ASSAULT? THIS IS TERRIBLE!
OH, NO!
ALERT!!
SILENCE! ALL OF YOU!
THE COLONIALS ARE IRRELEVANT SCUM! THE INCAL IS THE REAL THREAT!
WE HAVE BEEN DISCOVERED!
BUT, WE CAN'T DO ANYTHING UNTIL THE IMPERIAL FLEET GETS HERE!
WHAT DOES THE INCAL SAY?
LEMME GO! NOOOO!
BEUARK! I'LL NEVER GET USED TO THOSE SLIMY THINGS!
MOVE ASIDE! THE DARKNESS WILL CLAIM ITS PREY!
DIFOOL!
MOEBIUS
11

WE'VE GOT TO GO OUT THERE, OR JOHN IS FINISHED!
THE INCAL SAYS IT'S NOT TIME!
WHERE'S THE FLEET? THEY'RE LATE! IF THEY DON'T ARRIVE SOON, WE'LL BE FINISHED, TOO!
THE INCAL! ALWAYS THE INCAL! WHAT ABOUT JOHN?!?
¡¡¡INCAL!!!
HEEELP!
ARGH!
STIRLOG! LET CRYSTAL GO! PLEASE! I'VE DONE EVERYTHING YOU'VE ASKED OF ME!
STOP YOUR INSOLENT WHINING, GREYFIELD, OR I'LL TURN YOU INTO A CHANDELIER!
TECHNO-CENTREUR! WE'VE GOT TO DO SOMETHING!
IT'S UNNECESSARY, HORLOG! THE WAR STAR IS INVULNERABLE! 10 IMPERIAL FLEETS ARE NO MATCH FOR ITS SUPREME POWER!
WE'LL NEVER MAKE IT ON TIME!
SENDING FOR ANOTHER MEDUSA DELAYED US!
I HAVE AN IDEA, BUT IT'S KIND OF RISKY...
LET'S GO SUBSPACE!
THAT'S CRAZY!
WE DON'T HAVE THE EXACT COORDINATES! REMATERIALIZATION WOULD BE EXTREMELY DANGEROUS!
WE DON'T HAVE ANY OTHER CHOICE!
THEY'LL NEVER MAKE IT! IF WE WAIT ANY LONGER, JOHN DIFOOL IS GOING TO DIE!
YOU'RE RIGHT! LET'S ATTACK! I'D RATHER DIE FIGHTING ANYWAY!
MŒBIUS
12

NO! WE MUST WAIT UNTIL THE VERY LAST MINUTE!
EVEN IF IT MEANS THE DEATH OF JOHN DIFOOL!
!
NO!
INHUMAN!
INHUMAN MONSTER! I AM YOUR MOTHER AND JOHN DIFOOL IS YOUR FATHER! YOU MUST OBEY ME!
NO!
HA! HA! HA! YOU'RE MINE NOW, INCAL! YOU AND YOUR HUMAN HOST NOW BELONG TO THE GREAT DARKNESS!!
METABARON! DO SOMETHING!
I CAN'T, ANIMAH! YOU KNOW WE MUST OBEY THE WILL OF THE INCAL!
BUT, IT...IT'S...
THIS IS DISGUSTING! THAT STUFF REALLY SMELLS LIKE SHIT!
QUICK! GIVE ME SOME PERFUME! I THINK I'M GOING TO FAINT!
MOEBIUS 13

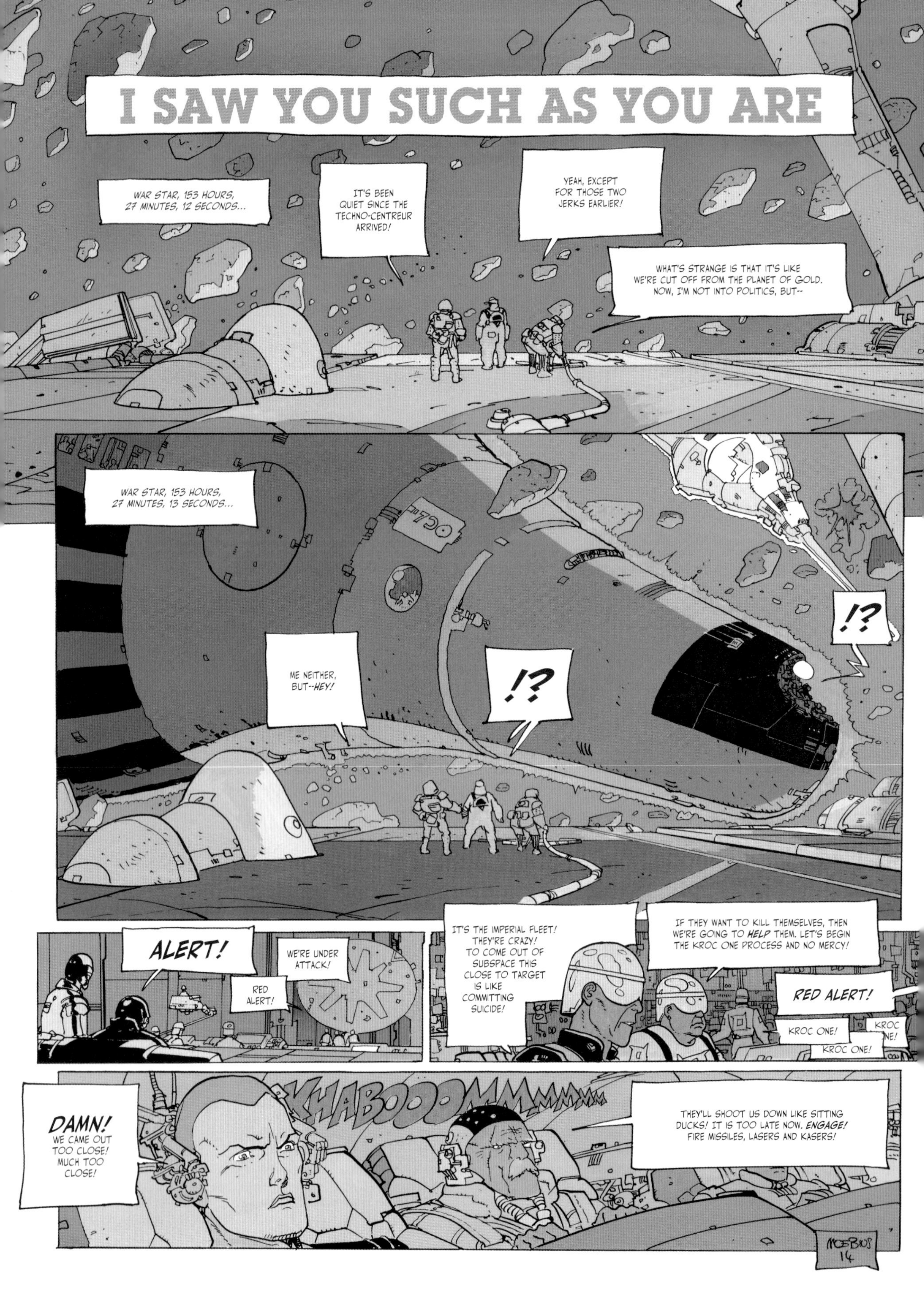
I SAW YOU SUCH AS YOU ARE
WAR STAR, 153 HOURS, 27 MINUTES, 12 SECONDS...
IT'S BEEN QUIET SINCE THE TECHNO-CENTREUR ARRIVED!
YEAH, EXCEPT FOR THOSE TWO JERKS EARLIER!
WHAT'S STRANGE IS THAT IT'S LIKE WE'RE CUT OFF FROM THE PLANET OF GOLD. NOW, I'M NOT INTO POLITICS, BUT--
WAR STAR, 153 HOURS, 27 MINUTES, 13 SECONDS...
ME NEITHER, BUT--HEY!
!?
!?
ALERT!
WE'RE UNDER ATTACK!
RED ALERT!
IT'S THE IMPERIAL FLEET! THEY'RE CRAZY! TO COME OUT OF SUBSPACE THIS CLOSE TO TARGET IS LIKE COMMITTING SUICIDE!
IF THEY WANT TO KILL THEMSELVES, THEN WE'RE GOING TO HELP THEM. LET'S BEGIN THE KROC ONE PROCESS AND NO MERCY!
RED ALERT!
KROC ONE!
KROC ONE!
KROC ONE!
DAMN! WE CAME OUT TOO CLOSE! MUCH TOO CLOSE!
KHABOOOMMMMM
THEY'LL SHOOT US DOWN LIKE SITTING DUCKS! IT IS TOO LATE NOW. ENGAGE! FIRE MISSILES, LASERS AND KASERS!
MOEBIUS 14

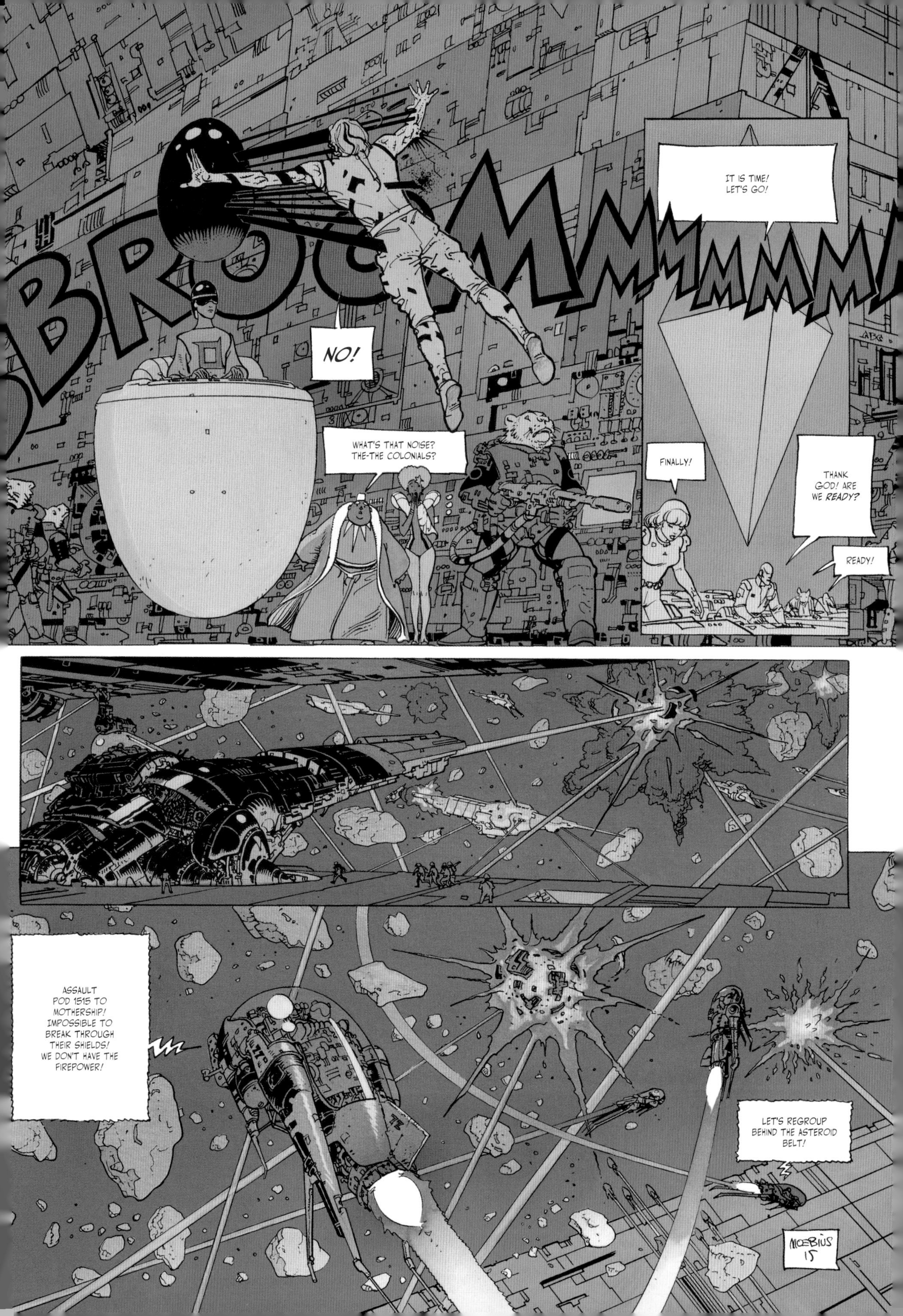
BRROOMMMMMMMM
IT IS TIME!
LET'S GO!
NO!
WHAT'S THAT NOISE?
THE-THE COLONIALS?
FINALLY!
THANK GOD! ARE WE *READY?*
READY!
ASSAULT POD 1515 TO MOTHERSHIP! IMPOSSIBLE TO BREAK THROUGH THEIR SHIELDS! WE DON'T HAVE THE FIREPOWER!
LET'S REGROUP BEHIND THE ASTEROID BELT!
MOEBIUS 15

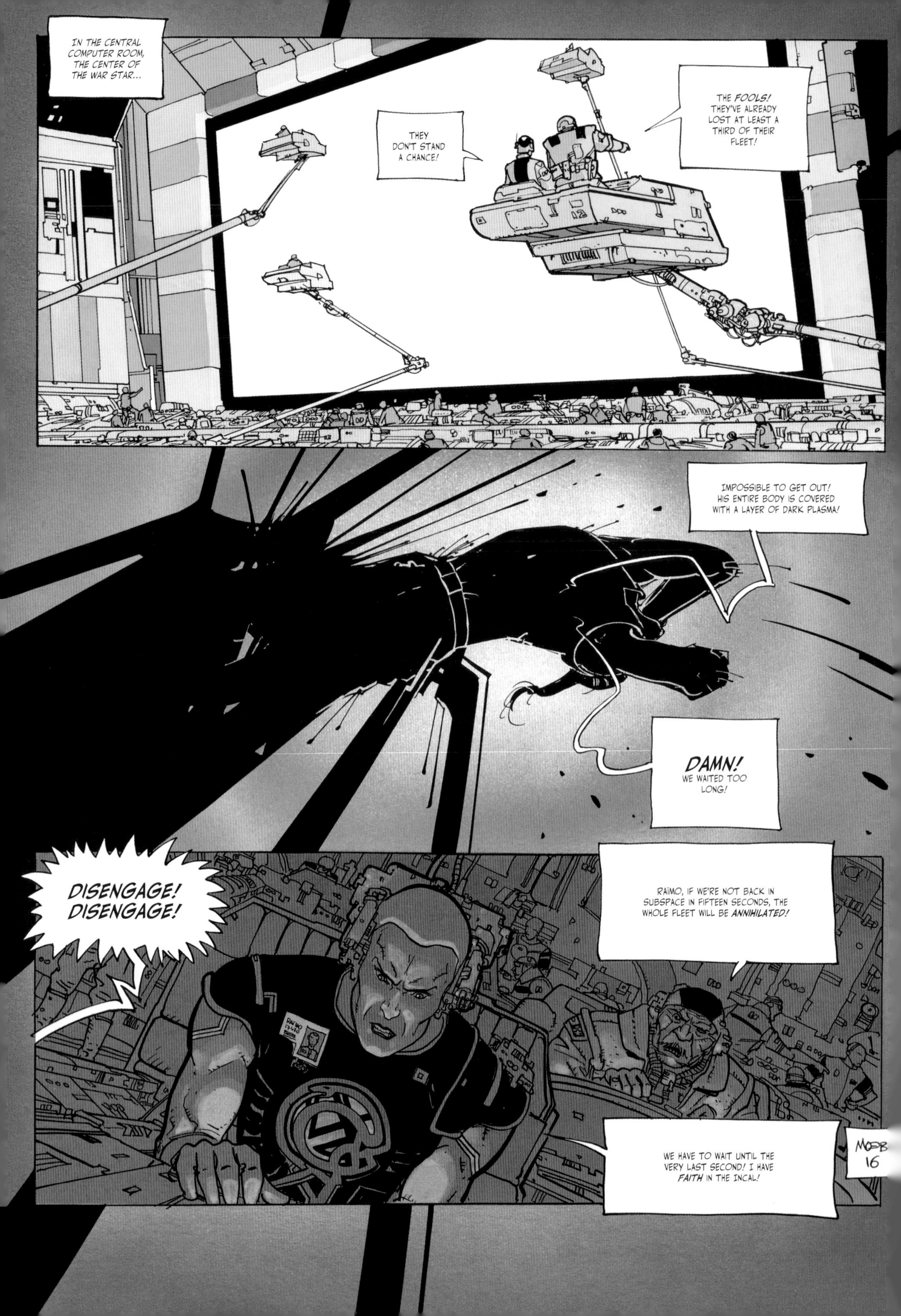
IN THE CENTRAL COMPUTER ROOM, THE CENTER OF THE WAR STAR...
THEY DON'T STAND A CHANCE!
THE FOOLS! THEY'VE ALREADY LOST AT LEAST A THIRD OF THEIR FLEET!
IMPOSSIBLE TO GET OUT! HIS ENTIRE BODY IS COVERED WITH A LAYER OF DARK PLASMA!
DAMN! WE WAITED TOO LONG!
DISENGAGE! DISENGAGE!
RAÏMO, IF WE'RE NOT BACK IN SUBSPACE IN FIFTEEN SECONDS, THE WHOLE FLEET WILL BE ANNIHILATED!
WE HAVE TO WAIT UNTIL THE VERY LAST SECOND! I HAVE FAITH IN THE INCAL!
MOEB 16

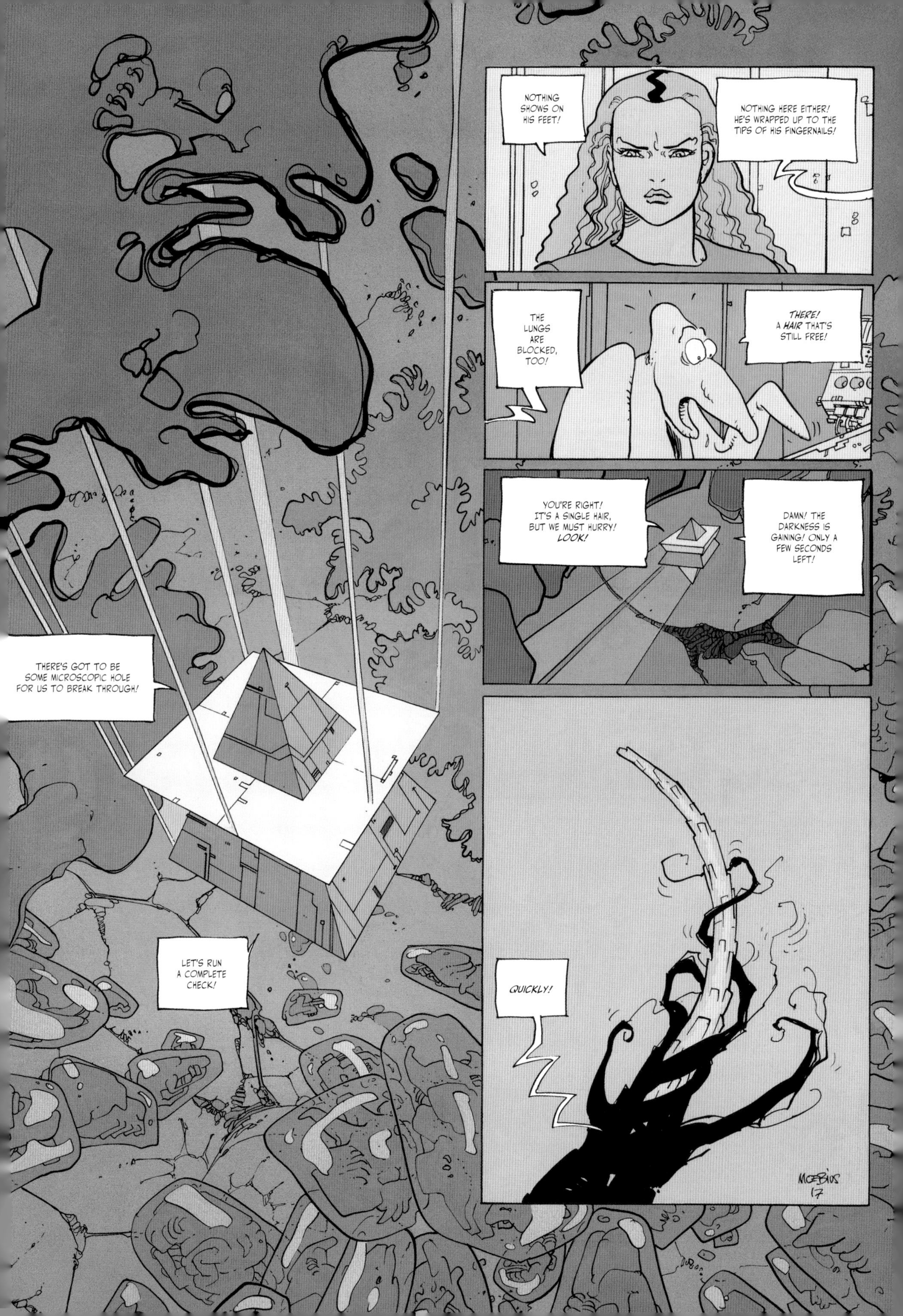
NOTHING SHOWS ON HIS FEET!
NOTHING HERE EITHER! HE'S WRAPPED UP TO THE TIPS OF HIS FINGERNAILS!
THE LUNGS ARE BLOCKED, TOO!
THERE! A HAIR THAT'S STILL FREE!
YOU'RE RIGHT! IT'S A SINGLE HAIR, BUT WE MUST HURRY! LOOK!
DAMN! THE DARKNESS IS GAINING! ONLY A FEW SECONDS LEFT!
QUICKLY!
THERE'S GOT TO BE SOME MICROSCOPIC HOLE FOR US TO BREAK THROUGH!
LET'S RUN A COMPLETE CHECK!
MOEBIUS
17

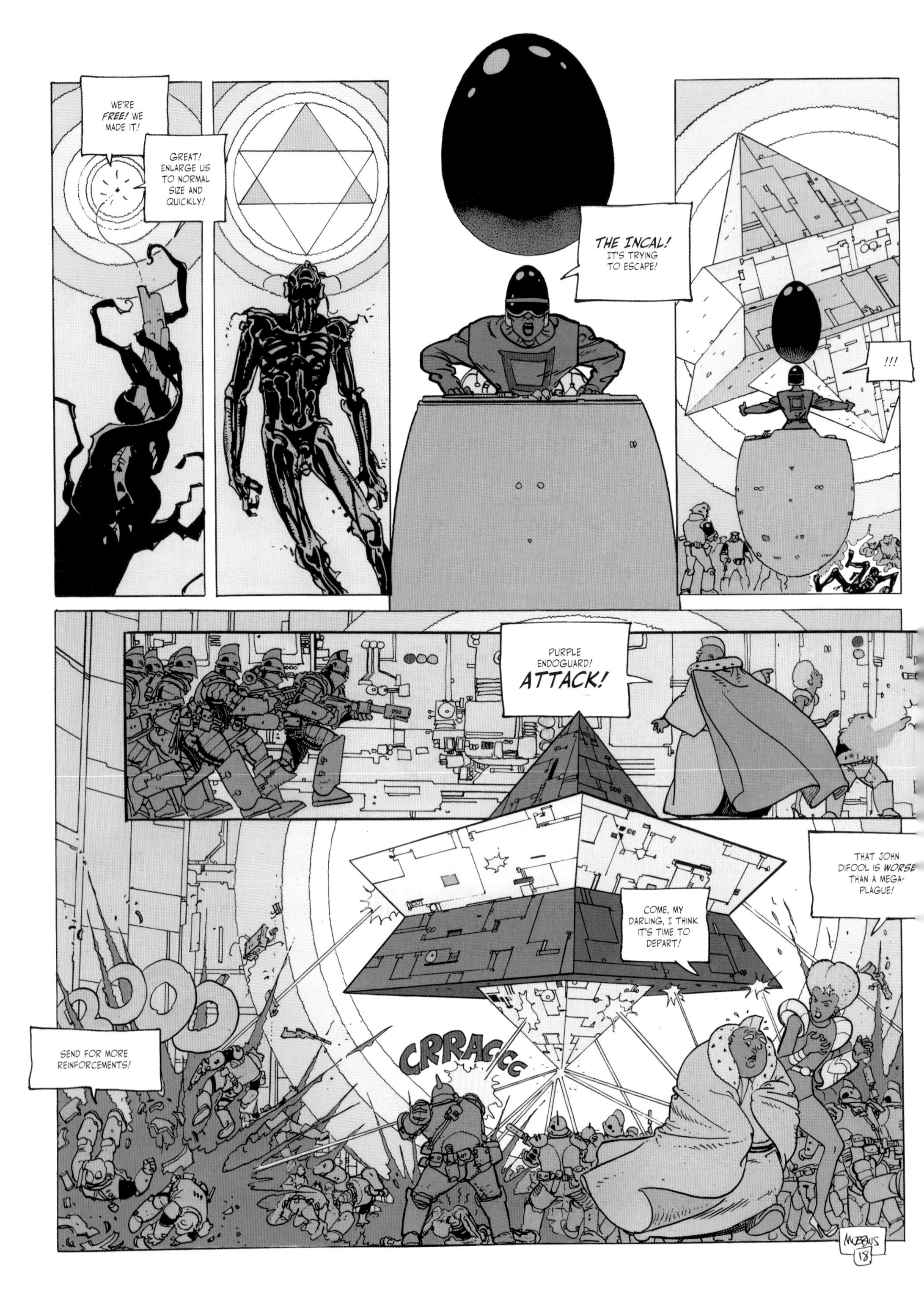
WE'RE FREE! WE MADE IT!
GREAT! ENLARGE US TO NORMAL SIZE AND QUICKLY!
THE INCAL! IT'S TRYING TO ESCAPE!
!!!
PURPLE ENDOGUARD! ATTACK!
THAT JOHN DIFOOL IS WORSE THAN A MEGA-PLAGUE!
COME, MY DARLING, I THINK IT'S TIME TO DEPART!
SEND FOR MORE REINFORCEMENTS!
CRRACCC
MOEBIUS 18

EVERYONE TO THE CENTRAL COMPUTER!
FUSHHH
SHCRAC
STOP!
OH, NO! NOT HIM AGAIN!
BOOOM
MOEBIUS

STIRLOG, YOU *PROMISED* ME YOU'D UNFREEZE MY CRYSTAL!
BY A THOUSAND BLACK HOLES, *LET ME GO!*
HURRY!
BITCH!
ARGH!
TOUCC
OUCH
HOW *DARE* YOU!
PAF
MY PUSSY! *HURRY!*
AIEEE! HE *BROKE* MY NOSE!
?!
NOO! WATCH OUT!!
BY THE GRAND UNIVERSE! WHAT HAVE I DONE?!
CRYSTAL!
NO! NOT MY NOSE!
MY LOVELY NOSE!
ARE YOU WOUNDED, PUSSY?
THEY'RE DROPPING LIKE FLIES!
BOOOMMM
QUICKLY!
DON'T DELAY! OUR FIRST PRIORITY IS TO REACH THE CENTRAL COMPUTER!
ZWFFFFFFF
TOUFM TOUFM TOUFM
WE CAN'T BREAK THROUGH THEIR SHIELDS!
SSSAARHKK
MŒBIUS

ONLY THE MEGASER CAN STOP THEM!
RETREAT!
RUN!
THAT ONE!
!!?
KKRK
GOTCHA!
DAMN!
ZZZZNG
KILL'S BEEN HIT!
MY SHIELD IS DOWN!
SWITCH
YOU MAY BE A VILE MUTT, BUT WHO AM I TO JUDGE?
TAKE THAT, YOU *DIRTY SCARAB!*
DROOOM
DEEPO, YOU ARE MY *BROTHER!*
MŒBIUS

JOHN!
THE MONSTERS! LOOK WHAT THEY'VE DONE TO YOU!
MY POOR DARLING!
IT'S AWFUL! I'M BLEEDING!
COME, MY SWEET! WE'VE GOT TO GET OUT OF THIS HORRIBLE PLACE!
OUR ONLY CHANCE IS TO REACH THE TRANSMIT STATION!
AOUEK!
CHOFFF
FOFFch
I BET THE TECHNO-CENTREUR'S ALREADY THERE-- HEY!!
HA! HA! HA! I AM AVENGED!
OOOH! MY STIRLOG! NO!
TRANSFORMED INTO ICE! NO!
AND BROKEN INTO A THOUSAND PIECES!
OOH!
TIGLINGGG
MOEBIUS 22

CRYSTAL, YOU'VE BEEN AVENGED!
NOW YOU KNOW...
MY SUGAR LUMP...
...NOW YOU UNDERSTAND *REAL PAIN*, HORLOG!
IT'S IMPOSSIBLE!
OH, NO!
AAARGGG
FACHH
TWELVE SECONDS! WE'VE GOT TO GET OUT, RAÏMO!
NO! GIVE IT TWO MORE SECONDS!
MOEBIUS

THE CENTRAL COMPUTER! THE MAIN PROCESSOR IS BEHIND THAT BRIGHT RED LIGHT.
HEY, NICE TARGET!
?!
WHERE'S ANIMAH?! I DON'T SEE HER ANYWHERE!
ZIIIFFTTT!..
DOM
SHE'S TAKING CARE OF DIFOOL!
ZOOWUKA
HEY, THAT'S A GREAT SHOT!
MOEBIUS 24

HEY! MY GUN JUST WENT DEAD!
MOTHERSHIP! THEY'VE STOPPED FIRING!
?
THE CONTROLS RE FROZEN!
WHAT...WHAT'S HAPPENING!
THAT'S IT! THEY'VE DONE IT!
TO ALL ASSAULT PODS! IMMEDIATE ATTACK!
YOUR INCAL WAS RIGHT, RAÏMO!
THAT BLACK GUNK IS STICKING TO HIS SKIN!
JOHN? THANK GOD HE ISN'T DEAD--ONLY UNCONSCIOUS!
...
WHAT HE NEEDS IS OXYGEN... I'LL...HEY!
!?
VICTORY IS OURS! WE'VE WON! THE WAR STAR HAS OFFICIALLY SURRENDERED!
MMM...ANIMAH! YOUR KISSES!
JOHN!
DIFOOL! THIS REALLY ISN'T THE RIGHT TIME!
MOEBIUS

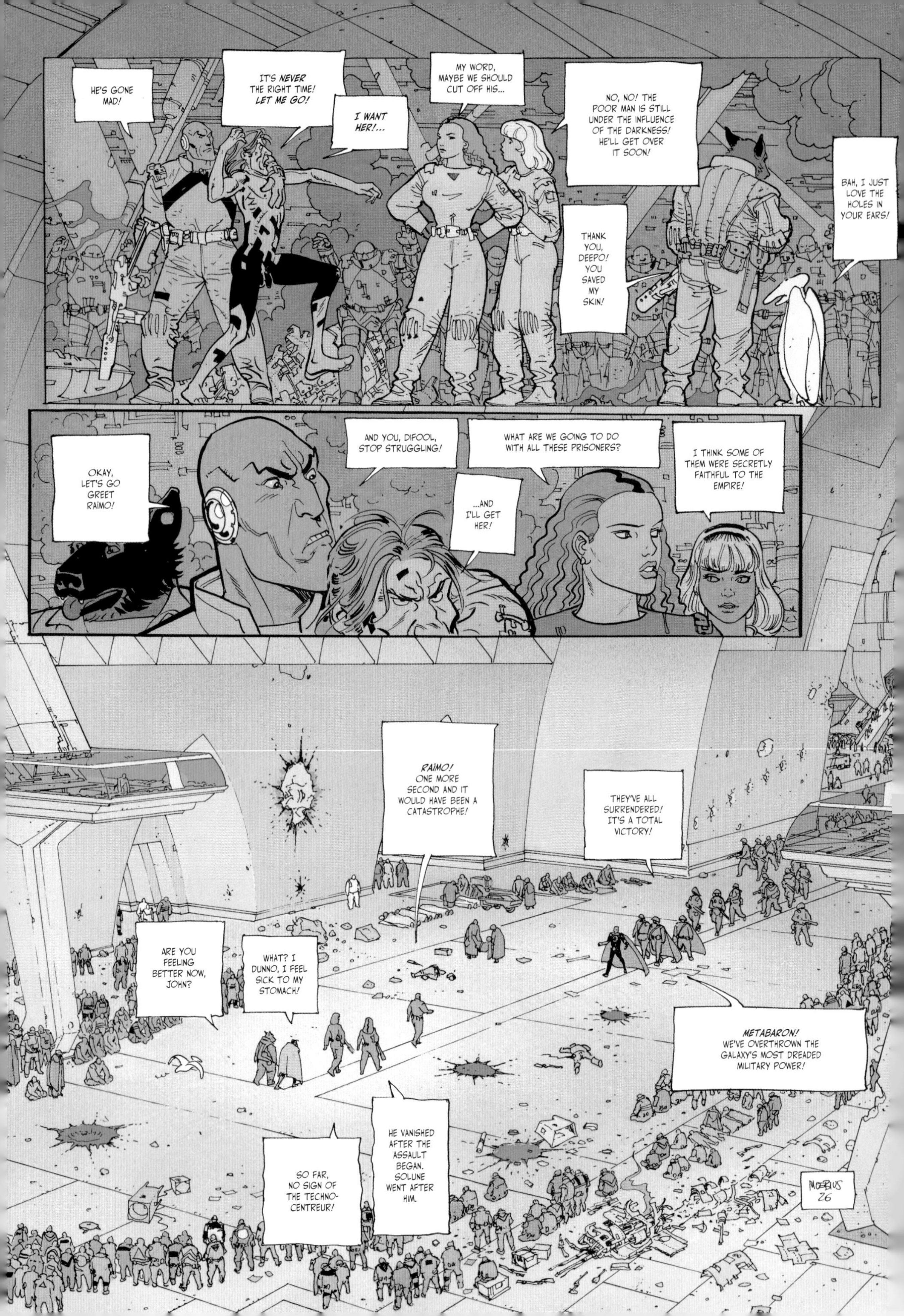
HE'S GONE MAD!
IT'S NEVER THE RIGHT TIME! LET ME GO!
I WANT HER!...
MY WORD, MAYBE WE SHOULD CUT OFF HIS...
NO, NO! THE POOR MAN IS STILL UNDER THE INFLUENCE OF THE DARKNESS! HE'LL GET OVER IT SOON!
THANK YOU, DEEPO! YOU SAVED MY SKIN!
BAH, I JUST LOVE THE HOLES IN YOUR EARS!
OKAY, LET'S GO GREET RAÏMO!
AND YOU, DIFOOL, STOP STRUGGLING!
...AND I'LL GET HER!
WHAT ARE WE GOING TO DO WITH ALL THESE PRISONERS?
I THINK SOME OF THEM WERE SECRETLY FAITHFUL TO THE EMPIRE!
RAÏMO! ONE MORE SECOND AND IT WOULD HAVE BEEN A CATASTROPHE!
THEY'VE ALL SURRENDERED! IT'S A TOTAL VICTORY!
ARE YOU FEELING BETTER NOW, JOHN?
WHAT? I DUNNO, I FEEL SICK TO MY STOMACH!
METABARON! WE'VE OVERTHROWN THE GALAXY'S MOST DREADED MILITARY POWER!
SO FAR, NO SIGN OF THE TECHNO-CENTREUR!
HE VANISHED AFTER THE ASSAULT BEGAN. SOLUNE WENT AFTER HIM.
MOEBIUS 26

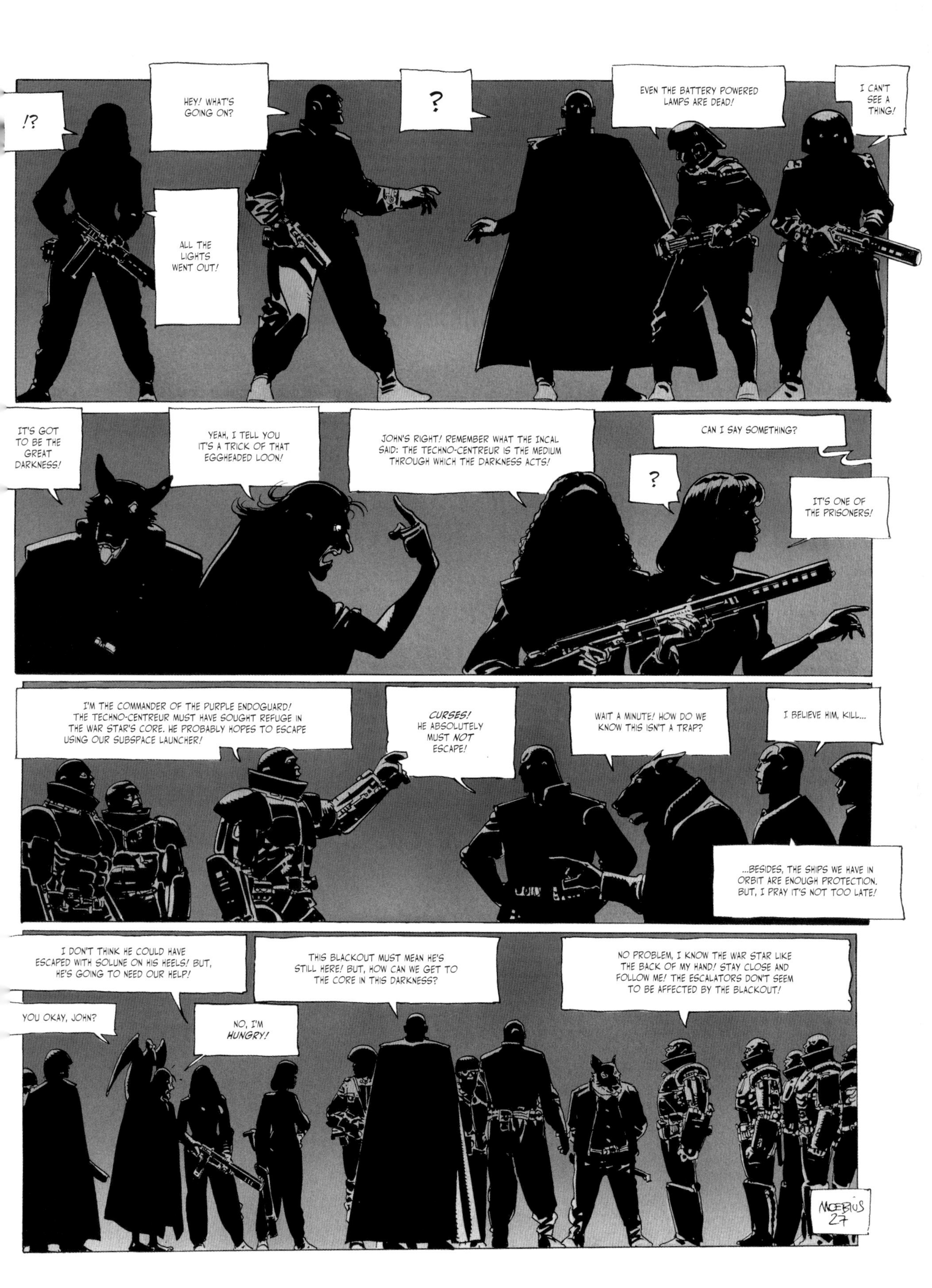
!?
HEY! WHAT'S GOING ON?
ALL THE LIGHTS WENT OUT!
?
EVEN THE BATTERY POWERED LAMPS ARE DEAD!
I CAN'T SEE A THING!
IT'S GOT TO BE THE GREAT DARKNESS!
YEAH, I TELL YOU IT'S A TRICK OF THAT EGGHEADED LOON!
JOHN'S RIGHT! REMEMBER WHAT THE INCAL SAID: THE TECHNO-CENTREUR IS THE MEDIUM THROUGH WHICH THE DARKNESS ACTS!
?
CAN I SAY SOMETHING?
IT'S ONE OF THE PRISONERS!
I'M THE COMMANDER OF THE PURPLE ENDOGUARD! THE TECHNO-CENTREUR MUST HAVE SOUGHT REFUGE IN THE WAR STAR'S CORE. HE PROBABLY HOPES TO ESCAPE USING OUR SUBSPACE LAUNCHER!
CURSES! HE ABSOLUTELY MUST *NOT* ESCAPE!
WAIT A MINUTE! HOW DO WE KNOW THIS ISN'T A TRAP?
I BELIEVE HIM, KILL...
...BESIDES, THE SHIPS WE HAVE IN ORBIT ARE ENOUGH PROTECTION. BUT, I PRAY IT'S NOT TOO LATE!
I DON'T THINK HE COULD HAVE ESCAPED WITH SOLUNE ON HIS HEELS! BUT, HE'S GOING TO NEED OUR HELP!
YOU OKAY, JOHN?
NO, I'M *HUNGRY!*
THIS BLACKOUT MUST MEAN HE'S STILL HERE! BUT, HOW CAN WE GET TO THE CORE IN THIS DARKNESS?
NO PROBLEM, I KNOW THE WAR STAR LIKE THE BACK OF MY HAND! STAY CLOSE AND FOLLOW ME! THE ESCALATORS DON'T SEEM TO BE AFFECTED BY THE BLACKOUT!
MOEBIUS 27

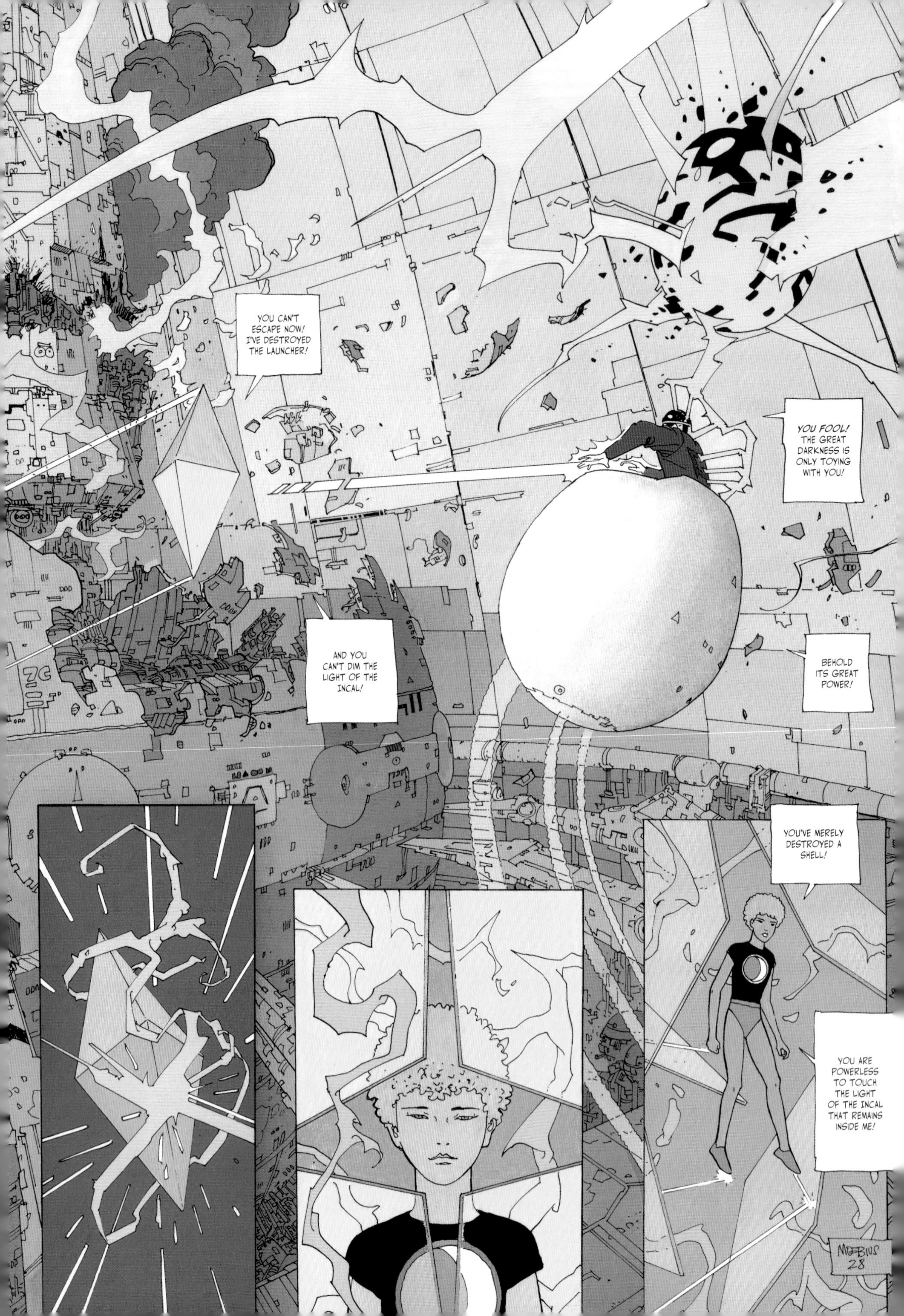
YOU CAN'T ESCAPE NOW! I'VE DESTROYED THE LAUNCHER!
YOU FOOL! THE GREAT DARKNESS IS ONLY TOYING WITH YOU!
AND YOU CAN'T DIM THE LIGHT OF THE INCAL!
BEHOLD ITS GREAT POWER!
YOU'VE MERELY DESTROYED A SHELL!
YOU ARE POWERLESS TO TOUCH THE LIGHT OF THE INCAL THAT REMAINS INSIDE ME!
MOEBIUS 28

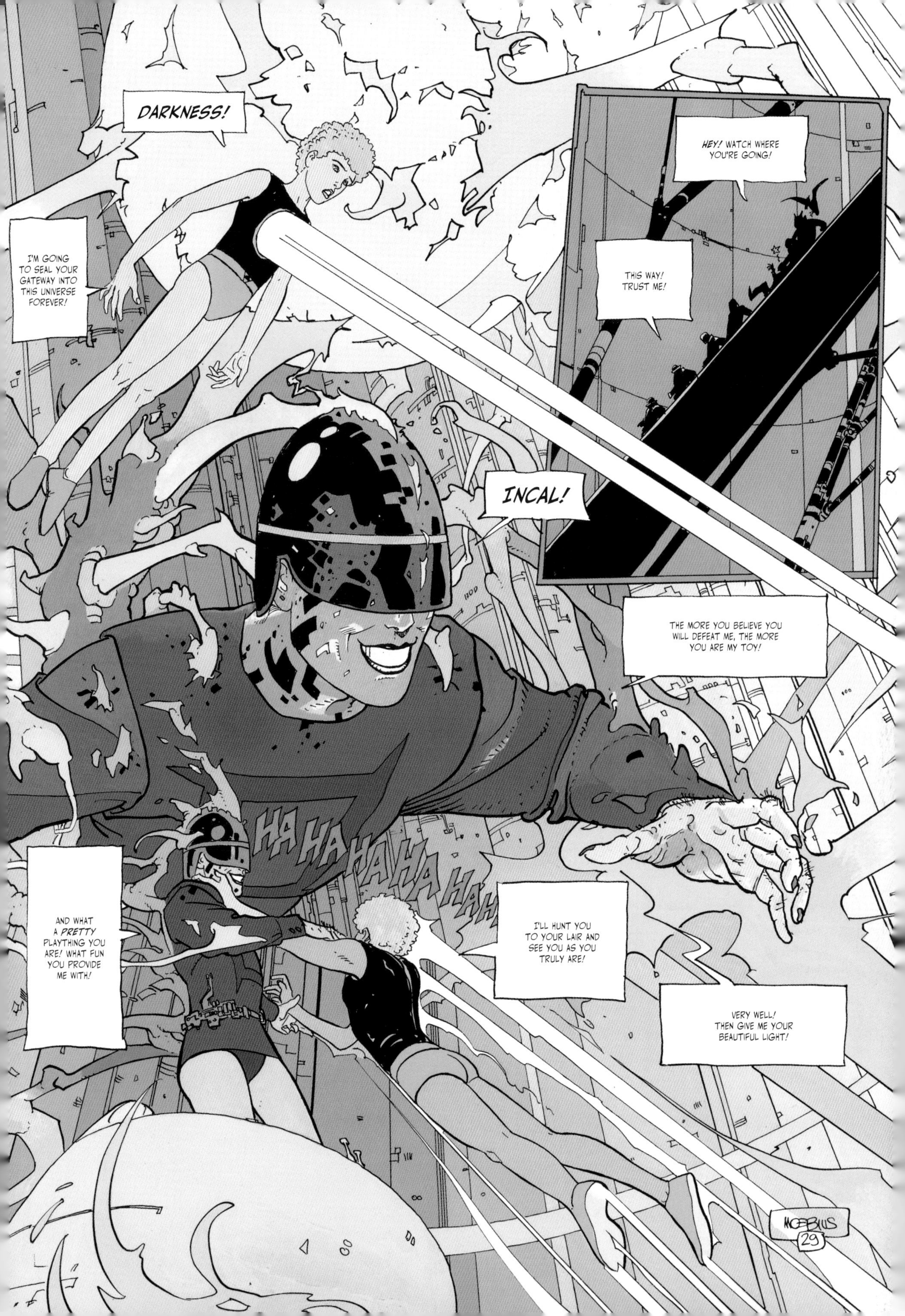
DARKNESS!
I'M GOING TO SEAL YOUR GATEWAY INTO THIS UNIVERSE FOREVER!
HEY! WATCH WHERE YOU'RE GOING!
THIS WAY! TRUST ME!
INCAL!
THE MORE YOU BELIEVE YOU WILL DEFEAT ME, THE MORE YOU ARE MY TOY!
HAHAHAHAHAHAH
AND WHAT A PRETTY PLAYTHING YOU ARE! WHAT FUN YOU PROVIDE ME WITH!
I'LL HUNT YOU TO YOUR LAIR AND SEE YOU AS YOU TRULY ARE!
VERY WELL! THEN GIVE ME YOUR BEAUTIFUL LIGHT!
MOEBIUS

MADMAN! I'LL DESTROY YOU AND...
HA HA HA HA HA HA!!! HA
...AND YOUR LAUGH?
HAHA HA
IT'S HERE!
BUT, IT'S LOCKED!
ANYONE HAVE A KEY?
HAHAHAHAH
MOEBIUS

?
INCAL!
INCAL!
ANSWER ME! WHAT'S HAPPENING?! IS THIS FALL NOTHING BUT A DREAM?
IS IT REAL?
INCAL!!
INCAL!
IT'S NOT OPENING! THE FORCES FIGHTING BEHIND IT MUST BE POWERFUL BEYOND BELIEF!

THE GREAT DARKNESS!
INCAL! MY FAVORITE SON! APPROACH!

I AWAITED YOU WITH SUCH EAGERNESS!
INCAL, WHAT IS HAPPENING?
HAVE YOU ABANDONED ME? AM I LOST?
MOEBIUS 82

INCAL!
BY DESCENDING HERE, YOU'VE BROKEN THE BARRIER! YOU'VE GIVEN ME FREEDOM! EVERY ATOM OF MATTER CAN NOW BECOME A NEW PATHWAY FOR THE GREAT DARKNESS!
YOUR LIGHT CAN NO LONGER INTIMIDATE ME!
INCAL! YOU'RE HERE!
FINALLY!
ACCURSED LIGHT!
EXTINGUISH!

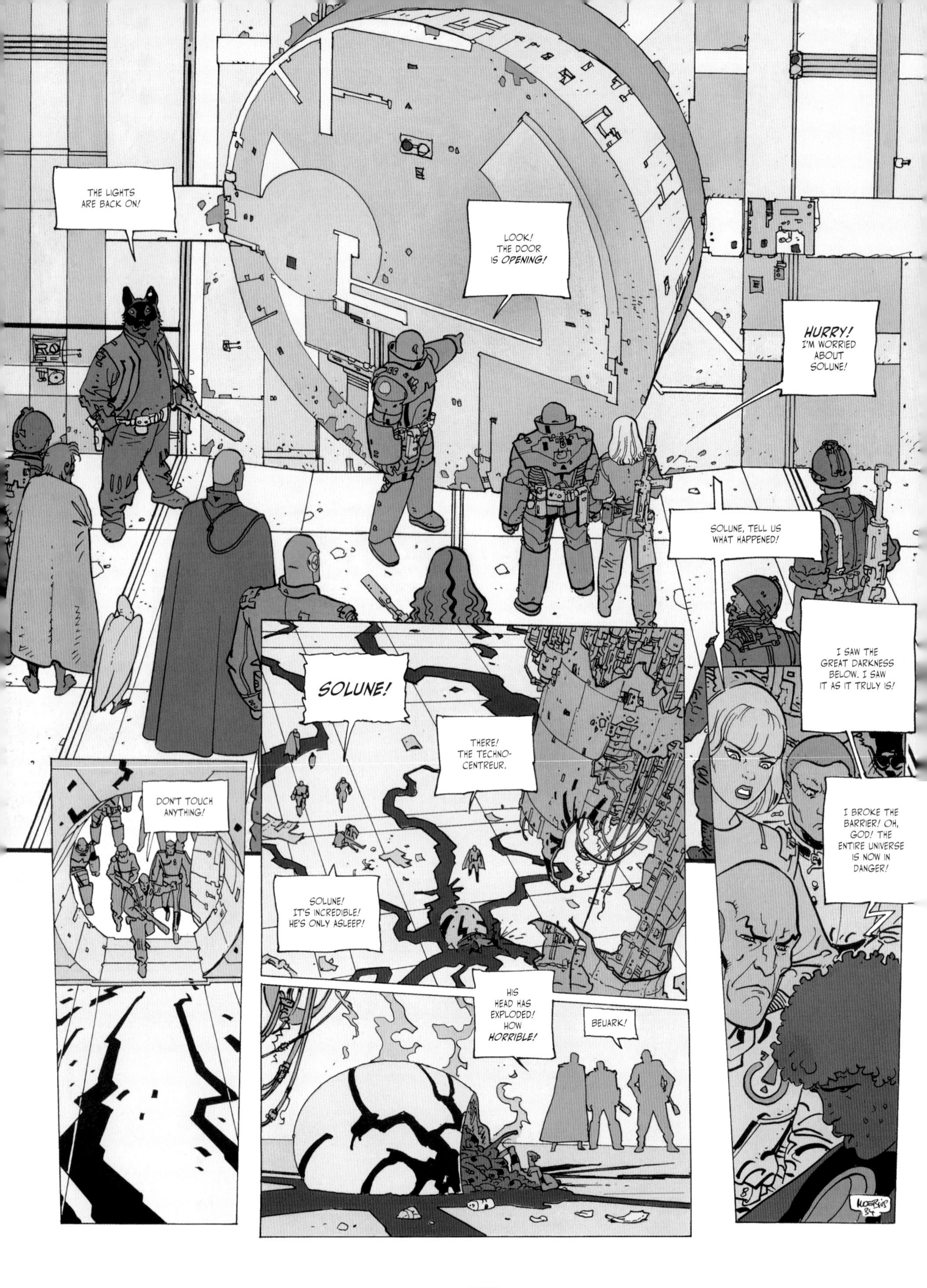
THE LIGHTS ARE BACK ON!
LOOK! THE DOOR IS OPENING!
HURRY! I'M WORRIED ABOUT SOLUNE!
SOLUNE, TELL US WHAT HAPPENED!
I SAW THE GREAT DARKNESS BELOW. I SAW IT AS IT TRULY IS!
I BROKE THE BARRIER! OH, GOD! THE ENTIRE UNIVERSE IS NOW IN DANGER!
DON'T TOUCH ANYTHING!
SOLUNE!
THERE! THE TECHNO-CENTREUR.
SOLUNE! IT'S INCREDIBLE! HE'S ONLY ASLEEP!
HIS HEAD HAS EXPLODED! HOW HORRIBLE!
BEUARK!

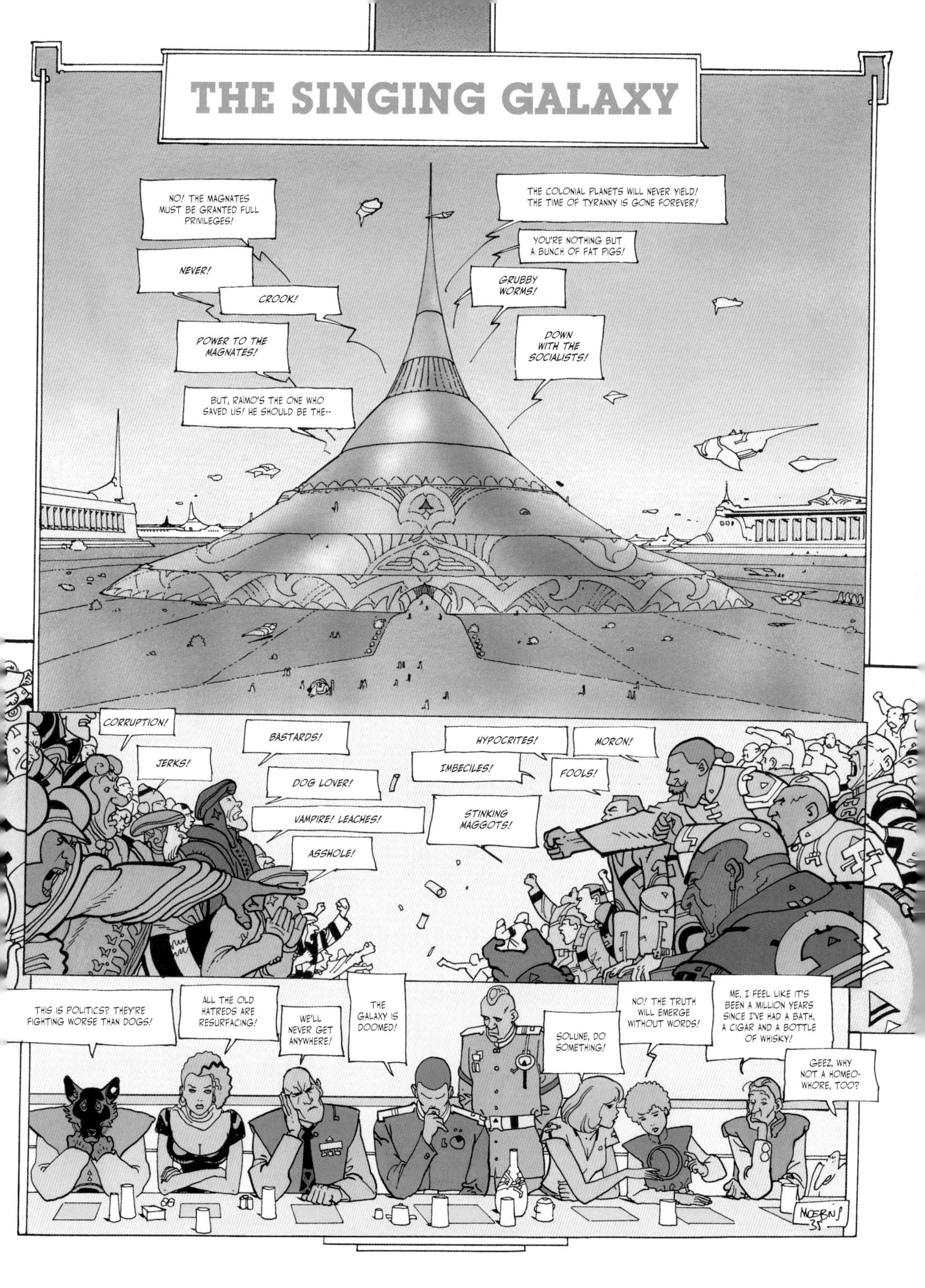
THE SINGING GALAXY
NO! THE MAGNATES MUST BE GRANTED FULL PRIVILEGES!
NEVER!
CROOK!
POWER TO THE MAGNATES!
BUT, RAÏMO'S THE ONE WHO SAVED US! HE SHOULD BE THE--
THE COLONIAL PLANETS WILL NEVER YIELD! THE TIME OF TYRANNY IS GONE FOREVER!
YOU'RE NOTHING BUT A BUNCH OF FAT PIGS!
GRUBBY WORMS!
DOWN WITH THE SOCIALISTS!
CORRUPTION!
JERKS!
BASTARDS!
DOG LOVER!
VAMPIRE! LEACHES!
ASSHOLE!
HYPOCRITES!
MORON!
IMBECILES!
FOOLS!
STINKING MAGGOTS!
THIS IS POLITICS? THEY'RE FIGHTING WORSE THAN DOGS!
ALL THE OLD HATREDS ARE RESURFACING!
WE'LL NEVER GET ANYWHERE!
THE GALAXY IS DOOMED!
SOLUNE, DO SOMETHING!
NO! THE TRUTH WILL EMERGE WITHOUT WORDS!
ME, I FEEL LIKE IT'S BEEN A MILLION YEARS SINCE I'VE HAD A BATH, A CIGAR AND A BOTTLE OF WHISKY!
GEEZ, WHY NOT A HOMEO-WHORE, TOO?
MOEBIUS

ALERT!
THE EMPERORESS HAS KILLED THE LAST MEDUSA! NOTHING IS STOPPING HIM/HER!
THE DARKNESS IS ATTACKING THE PALA--HEY!
WHO CAN SAVE US?!
WHO WILL?!
WORMS OF LIGHT! I SHALL CRUSH YOU ALL!
SOLUNE! COME BACK!
THIS IS INSANE!
WHAT'S THE EMPERORESS DOING?
LOOK! THE BLACK PLASMA IS SLOWING.
MOEBIUS

BY THE INCAL, I WILL DESTROY YOU!
BY THE GREAT DARKNESS, I WILL CURSE YOU! HA! HA!
THE DEMON IS ATTACKING!
OOH! SOLUNE IS GENERATING AN ENERGY EGG!
LOOK AT HIM!
HE'S MUTATED BEFORE OUR VERY EYES!
IT'S INCREDIBLE!
HE IS TWO BEINGS!
MALE AND FEMALE!
THIS IS NEVER GOING TO END!
BE CAREFUL, SOLUNE!
DO NOT FEAR FOR HIM! IT'S HIS ANDROGYNOUS WAY OF COMBATING THE DARKNESS!
MŒBIUS

YOU ARE TOO LATE, INCAL! THE GATEWAY IS NOW OPEN! HA! HA! HARRR. IN 22 DAYS, DARKNESS WILL FALL ACROSS THE HEART OF THE GALAXY! HA! HA! H--RRRAAHH...A!
!?!
THE DARKNESS HAS BEEN ROUTED!!
MOEBIUS

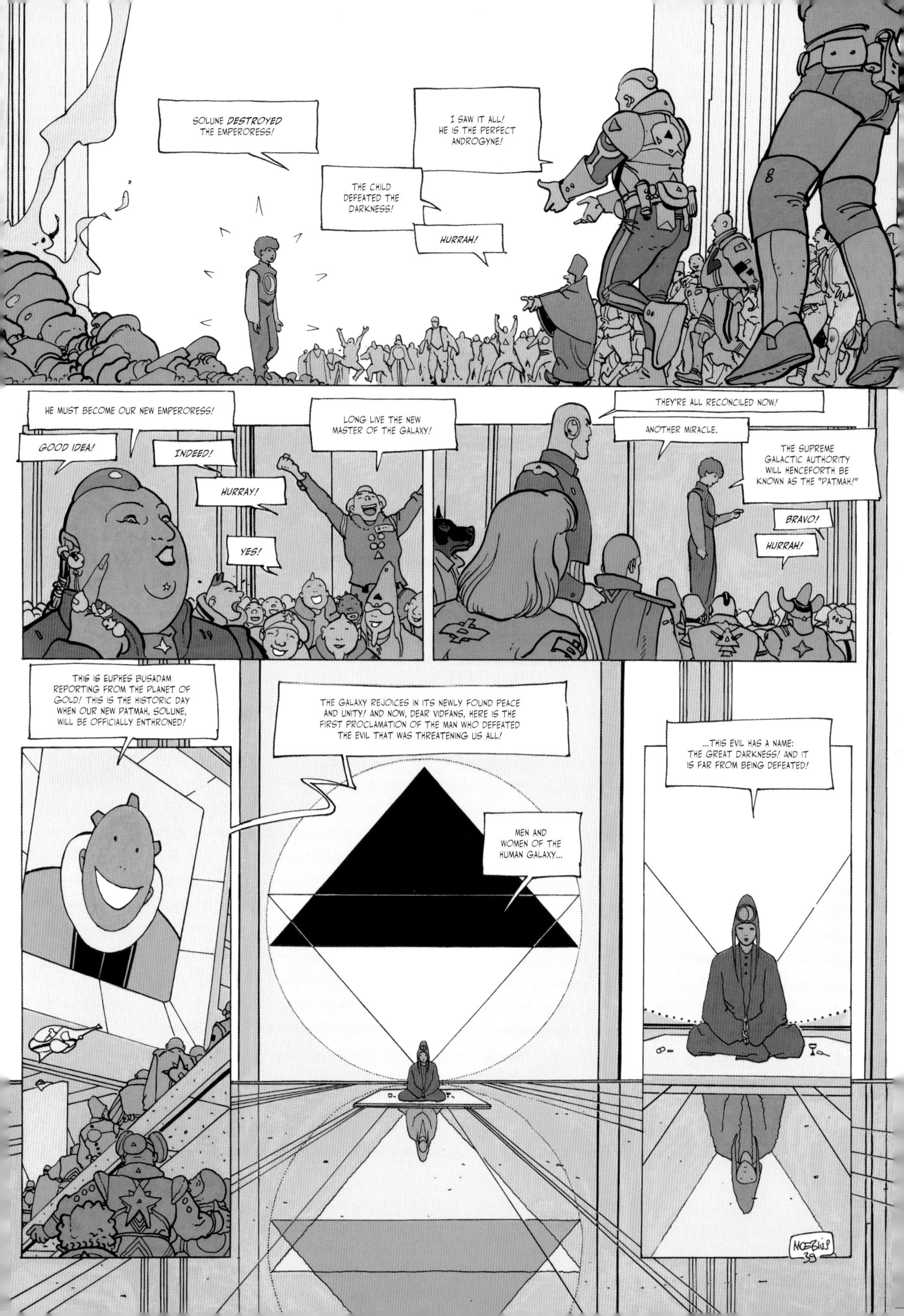
SOLUNE DESTROYED THE EMPERORESS!
THE CHILD DEFEATED THE DARKNESS!
I SAW IT ALL! HE IS THE PERFECT ANDROGYNE!
HURRAH!
HE MUST BECOME OUR NEW EMPERORESS!
GOOD IDEA!
INDEED!
HURRAY!
YES!
LONG LIVE THE NEW MASTER OF THE GALAXY!
THEY'RE ALL RECONCILED NOW!
ANOTHER MIRACLE.
THE SUPREME GALACTIC AUTHORITY WILL HENCEFORTH BE KNOWN AS THE "PATMAH!"
BRAVO!
HURRAH!
THIS IS EUPHES BUSADAM REPORTING FROM THE PLANET OF GOLD! THIS IS THE HISTORIC DAY WHEN OUR NEW PATMAH, SOLUNE, WILL BE OFFICIALLY ENTHRONED!
THE GALAXY REJOICES IN ITS NEWLY FOUND PEACE AND UNITY! AND NOW, DEAR VIDFANS, HERE IS THE FIRST PROCLAMATION OF THE MAN WHO DEFEATED THE EVIL THAT WAS THREATENING US ALL!
MEN AND WOMEN OF THE HUMAN GALAXY...
...THIS EVIL HAS A NAME: THE GREAT DARKNESS! AND IT IS FAR FROM BEING DEFEATED!
MOEBIUS

WE ARE NOW LIVING IN A MOST CRITICAL TIME IN MANKIND'S HISTORY. WE FACE TOTAL EXTERMINATION OF ALL LIFE! THE INCAL SPEAKS THROUGH ME! HE SAYS THAT ALL THE PLANETS MUST UNITE AND FACE THIS THREAT AS ONE, WITHOUT EXCEPTION!
IF EVEN ONE OF US REFUSES TO JOIN THE OTHERS, THEN WE ALL DIE!
IN 22 DAYS, DARKNESS WILL FALL. ALREADY, THE UNIVERSAL LIGHT INDEX HAS FALLEN TO 0.18 SYNTEX.
IT'S HORRIBLE!
WHAT CAN WE DO?
THE PATMAH IS NOTHING BUT A DOOMSAYER!
GOSH! WE'VE HAD IT!
YOU MUST NOW ASK YOURSELF THE QUESTION: WHAT CAN WE DO TO FIGHT SUCH AN ENEMY?!
HERE IS THE INCAL'S ANSWER: ALL BEINGS MUST ENTER A STATE OF DEEP SLUMBER THAT IS CALLED...
...THE THETA DREAM!
THE WHAT?
HE'S LOONY!
METABARON, I DON'T UNDERSTAND!
WE'LL FIND OUT SOON ENOUGH!
THIS WILL NEVER WORK! 70% OF THE EMPIRE'S POPULATION ONLY CARES ABOUT THEIR DAILY DOSE OF S.P.V.'S AND WHAT'S ON THE HOLOVID! I'M SORRY TO HAVE TO SAY THIS, BUT I STRONGLY DOUBT THAT PATMAH CAN GET THOSE PEOPLE TO JOIN HIM IN THAT THETA DREAM OF HIS!
THE GREAT MAGNATE IS RIGHT!
AND SO, DEAR VIDFANS, THIS ENDS PATMAH SOLUNE'S FIRST GALACTIC ADDRESS FROM THE PLANET OF GOLD, THE NEW PATMAHNIC CAPITAL!
FOR ONCE, THE COLONIAL PLANETS AGREE WITH THE MAGNATES. IF WE HAD TO RAISE AN ARMY TO FIGHT SOME INTANGIBLE FOE, WE'D DO SO AT ONCE! BUT, THIS "THETA DREAM" SEEMS...WELL...RATHER VAGUE!
COMRADE RAÏMO ASKS TO BE RECOGNIZED.
LET HIM SPEAK!
FRIENDS!
I UNDERSTAND YOUR RESERVATIONS, BUT THE TIME FOR FRUITLESS BICKERING IS OVER. WE MUST NOW FOCUS ON A POSITIVE COURSE OF ACTION! TO ACHIEVE THE INCAL'S GOAL, WE ONLY NEED TO CONVINCE ONE WORLD TO ENTER THE THETA DREAM. THEN THE REST OF THE GALAXY WILL FOLLOW. BUT, WE WILL NEED ALL THE IMPERIAL HOLOVID NET'S RESOURCES AND A MEDIA STAR OF SUCH MAGNITUDE THAT HE WILL SWAY THE MASSES TO OUR SIDE!
ARE YOU DREAMING ALREADY?
IMPOSSIBLE!
THE MAN IS CRAZY!
NO! LET HIM SPEAK!
MOEBIUS
40.

RAÏMO, YOU KNOW THAT THE SUCCESS OF EVEN ONE PLANET REQUIRES MORE THAN THE 22 DAYS WE HAVE LEFT!
BESIDES, THE HOLOVID NET IS OFF LINE! WE DON'T EVEN KNOW WHAT'S WRONG WITH IT! HOW CAN WE BE SURE THAT IT WILL BE FIXED IN TIME?
AS FOR A MEDIA STAR? YOU MIGHT AS WELL FORGET IT! WHY WOULD ANY OF THEM WANT TO HELP US? THEY ONLY CARE ABOUT WHAT'S IN THEIR CONTRACTS!
WHAT YOU SAY IS TRUE...
...BUT, THERE IS STILL HOPE!
LISTEN TO YOUR HEARTS! SEARCH FOR THE DIVINE SPARK THAT STILL LIVES WITHIN YOU! PRAY TO GOD, OUR CREATOR! I'VE HAD PROOF THAT MIRACLES CAN STILL HAPPEN!
?!?
?
?!!
WHAT?
HUH?
PRAY?
PRAY? WHAT'S THAT?
I'LL TRY.
IT'S ANOTHER OF RAÏMO'S FANTASIES!
PFFF!
WHY NOT? WHAT DO WE HAVE TO LOSE?
MOEBIUS - JODOROWSKY
HI, JOHN, WHAT ARE YOU DOING?
EVERYTHING ON THIS GODDAMN PLANET IS MADE OF GOLD!
ARE YOU GOING SOMEWHERE?
YOU BET! I'M FED UP WILL ALL THIS SHIT! I'M CUTTING OUT!
BUT, JOHN...
WHAT ABOUT WHAT THE PATMAH SAID?
HE SAID WE HAD 22 DAYS LEFT! WELL, FOR ME IT'LL BE 22 DAYS OF PURE JOY ON A PLANET OF PARADISE WITH A HOMEO-WHORE ON EACH ARM!
UNLESS, OF COURSE, ANIMAH COMES WITH ME!
BUT...
I KNOW, WHAT ABOUT THE THETA DREAM? DON'T WORRY! WHEN THE TIME COMES, I'LL KICK BACK A BOTTLE OF FAKE BOURBON WITH SOME S.P.V.'S!
BUT...
CAN'T BEAT THAT FOR NICE DREAMS!
WHAT?! THE PREZIDENT'S HEAD?
I FORGOT ABOUT IT!
SORRY, BUT YOU'RE OUT! YOU TAKE UP TOO MUCH SPACE AND WHERE WE'RE GOING, I'LL NEED PLENTY OF GOLD!
PARADISE COSTS A LOT!
YOU'RE WRONG, DIFOOL!
YOU CAN'T CHOOSE ILLUSION OVER REALITY!
FORGET ALL THAT MORALISTIC CRAP, DEEPO, AND COME WITH ME INSTEAD! I'M SURE I CAN FIND A NICELY STACKED CONCRETE CHICK!
CRRR.. CLIC!
PONG
BUT, YOU DO WHAT YOU WANT! MY SHIP LEAVES IN FIFTEEN MINUTES AND I...
AND I...
?
HAA! FINALLY!
MOEBIUS 41

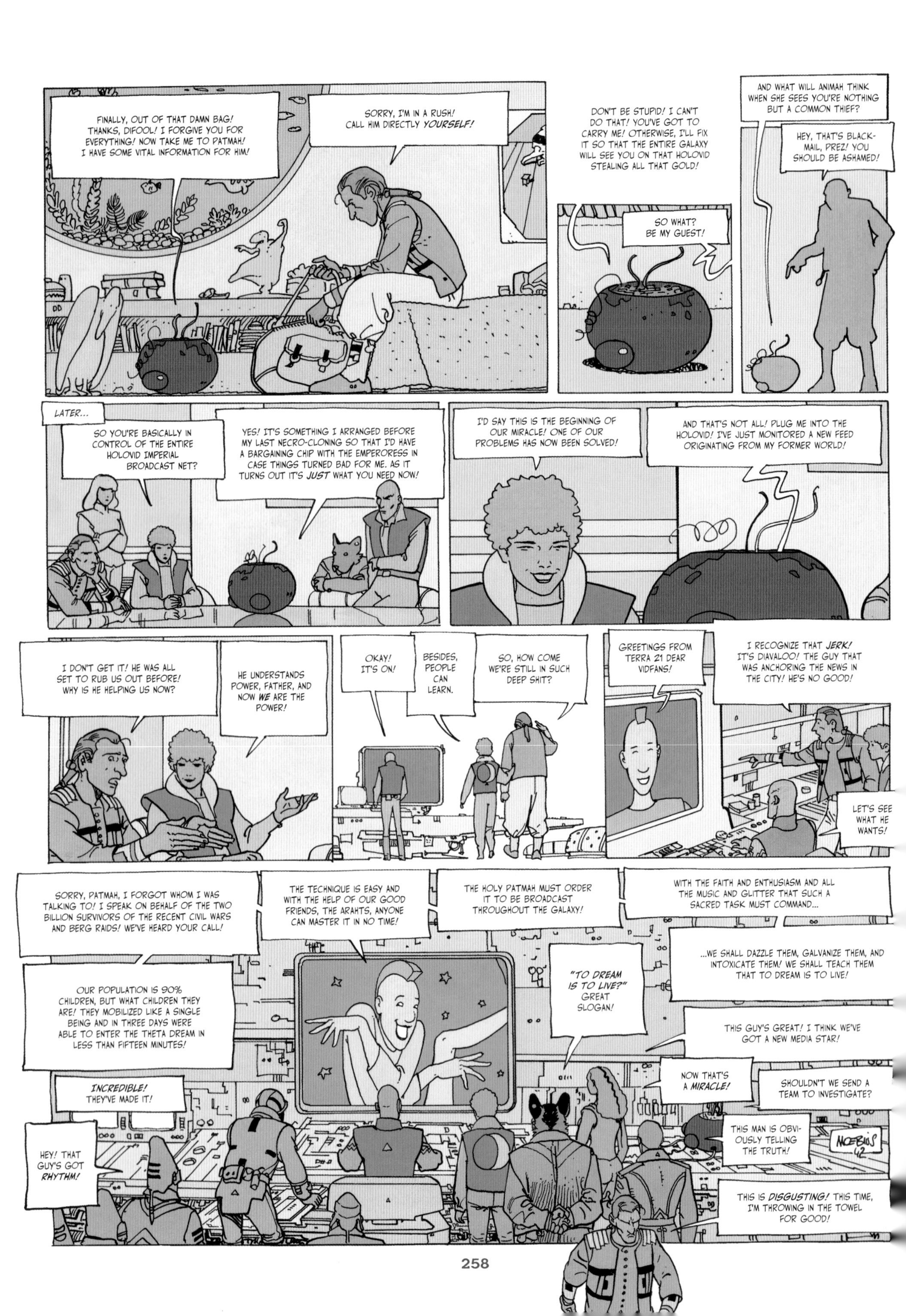
FINALLY, OUT OF THAT DAMN BAG! THANKS, DIFOOL! I FORGIVE YOU FOR EVERYTHING! NOW TAKE ME TO PATMAH! I HAVE SOME VITAL INFORMATION FOR HIM!
SORRY, I'M IN A RUSH! CALL HIM DIRECTLY *YOURSELF!*
DON'T BE STUPID! I CAN'T DO THAT! YOU'VE GOT TO CARRY ME! OTHERWISE, I'LL FIX IT SO THAT THE ENTIRE GALAXY WILL SEE YOU ON THAT HOLOVID STEALING ALL THAT GOLD!
SO WHAT? BE MY GUEST!
AND WHAT WILL ANIMAH THINK WHEN SHE SEES YOU'RE NOTHING BUT A COMMON THIEF?
HEY, THAT'S BLACK-MAIL, PREZ! YOU SHOULD BE ASHAMED!
LATER...
SO YOU'RE BASICALLY IN CONTROL OF THE ENTIRE HOLOVID IMPERIAL BROADCAST NET?
YES! IT'S SOMETHING I ARRANGED BEFORE MY LAST NECRO-CLONING SO THAT I'D HAVE A BARGAINING CHIP WITH THE EMPEROROESS IN CASE THINGS TURNED BAD FOR ME. AS IT TURNS OUT IT'S *JUST* WHAT YOU NEED NOW!
I'D SAY THIS IS THE BEGINNING OF OUR MIRACLE! ONE OF OUR PROBLEMS HAS NOW BEEN SOLVED!
AND THAT'S NOT ALL! PLUG ME INTO THE HOLOVID! I'VE JUST MONITORED A NEW FEED ORIGINATING FROM MY FORMER WORLD!
I DON'T GET IT! HE WAS ALL SET TO RUB US OUT BEFORE! WHY IS HE HELPING US NOW?
HE UNDERSTANDS POWER, FATHER, AND NOW *WE* ARE THE POWER!
OKAY! IT'S ON!
BESIDES, PEOPLE CAN LEARN.
SO, HOW COME WE'RE STILL IN SUCH DEEP SHIT?
GREETINGS FROM TERRA 21 DEAR VIDFANS!
I RECOGNIZE THAT *JERK!* IT'S DIAVALOO! THE GUY THAT WAS ANCHORING THE NEWS IN THE CITY! HE'S NO GOOD!
LET'S SEE WHAT HE WANTS!
SORRY, PATMAH, I FORGOT WHOM I WAS TALKING TO! I SPEAK ON BEHALF OF THE TWO BILLION SURVIVORS OF THE RECENT CIVIL WARS AND BERG RAIDS! WE'VE HEARD YOUR CALL!
OUR POPULATION IS 90% CHILDREN, BUT WHAT CHILDREN THEY ARE! THEY MOBILIZED LIKE A SINGLE BEING AND IN THREE DAYS WERE ABLE TO ENTER THE THETA DREAM IN LESS THAN FIFTEEN MINUTES!
THE TECHNIQUE IS EASY AND WITH THE HELP OF OUR GOOD FRIENDS, THE ARAHTS, ANYONE CAN MASTER IT IN NO TIME!
THE HOLY PATMAH MUST ORDER IT TO BE BROADCAST THROUGHOUT THE GALAXY!
WITH THE FAITH AND ENTHUSIASM AND ALL THE MUSIC AND GLITTER THAT SUCH A SACRED TASK MUST COMMAND...
...WE SHALL DAZZLE THEM, GALVANIZE THEM, AND INTOXICATE THEM! WE SHALL TEACH THEM THAT TO DREAM IS TO LIVE!
"TO DREAM IS TO LIVE?" GREAT SLOGAN!
THIS GUY'S GREAT! I THINK WE'VE GOT A NEW MEDIA STAR!
INCREDIBLE! THEY'VE MADE IT!
NOW THAT'S A *MIRACLE!*
SHOULDN'T WE SEND A TEAM TO INVESTIGATE?
HEY! THAT GUY'S GOT *RHYTHM!*
THIS MAN IS OBVIOUSLY TELLING THE TRUTH!
MOEBIUS 42
THIS IS *DISGUSTING!* THIS TIME, I'M THROWING IN THE TOWEL FOR GOOD!

IT'S WORKING! IN FOUR DAYS WE'VE GONE UP FOURTEEN POINTS IN THE RATINGS!
SURE! WE'RE ON ALL THE CHANNELS!
4TH DAY ON NOVA CYGNAE...
HEY, IT'S THE SAME SHOW ON ALL THE CHANNELS!
THAT JERK MAKES ME SICK WITH HIS BETA SONG!
THAT'S NOT BETA!
STILL, IT'S GOT A NICE SOUND!
HEY, LOOK, MOMO FELL ASLEEP!
ZZ
I KNOW HOW IT GOES! THEY'LL WIN AGAIN BUT, ONLY TO LAND THEMSELVES INTO AN EVEN BIGGER MESS, SO I'D RATHER SKIP OUT RIGHT NOW!
BUT, TO GO WHERE? DARKNESS IS EVERYWHERE!
BY ANALYZING THE ARAHT'S TECHNIQUE, WE'VE DEVELOPED A THETA PROCESSOR THAT WILL ACCELERATE THE PROCESS BY 90%!
WELL DONE, DOCTOR CHOBB!
TO DREAM IS TO LIVE!
8TH DAY ON BARNAB...
I'VE HEARD THESE NEW THETA PROCESSORS ARE A REAL TRIP!
LOOK! THEY'RE ALL ASLEEP!
ZZZ!
ZZZ!
ZZZ!
ZZZ!
IT'S CRAZY, BUT THE MORE I SEE IT THE MORE I'M TEMPTED TO TRY IT!
WOW! NO DEPARTURES ON ANY OF THE REGULAR FLIGHTS? WHAT HAPPENED TO THE SHIPS?
THEY'VE ALL BEEN REQUISITIONED FOR THE TRANSPORT OF THETA PROCESSORS. WHY? ARE YOU GOING SOMEPLACE?
I'M AFRAID HE'S LOST HIS VOICE AND HE'LL NEED A FEW DAYS' REST TO REGAIN HIS STRENGTH.
THEY CAN SHOW TAPES OF HIM FOR A WHILE!
THE ATTACK WAS PLANNED FOR TODAY AND NOW ALL THOSE ASSHOLES ARE ALL ASLEEP! MY REVOLUTION IS ALL WASHED UP!
13TH DAY ON DEL RAY III...
HEY, CHIEF, MAYBE THIS TIME IT IS DREAMING THAT'S REVOLUTIONARY!
LET'S SEE...IF I GET RID OF THESE OLD SHOES I CAN PACK ONE MORE BAR OF GOLD! I'VE TO THINK OF THE FUTURE!
IF THERE IS ONE!
WE'RE GETTING CLOSE TO MAXIMUM SATURATION, BUT THE ENCROACHING DARKNESS IS MAKING THINGS DIFFICULT!
WE HAVE TO CONTINUE! REDOUBLE OUR EFFORTS!
17TH DAY, ON LAYLIN...
MY DEAR YOBOCHA, HOW CAN YOU STAND THAT AWFUL HOST?
BUT, YABOCHO DARLING, IT'S THE CHILDREN ON HIS PLANET THAT ARE JUST WONDERFUL! IT'LL BE EXQUISITE TO FOLLOW THEIR EXAMPLE!
SAY, JOHN, WE NEVER SEE YOU AT THE THETA TRAINING CLASSES!
I DO MY OWN KIND OF EXERCISE. IT MOSTLY INVOLVES GOLD AND SUITCASES!
100% SATURATION REACHED! WE'VE MADE IT! WE'RE TWO DAYS AHEAD OF SCHEDULE AND READY FOR ZERO HOUR!
GREAT! LET'S GO INFORM THE PATMAH!
PLANET OF GOLD, 20TH DAY...
BREATHE DEEPER! RELAX YOUR CHEST MUSCLES...
CONCENTRATE ON YOUR THETA PROCESSORS!
EVEN THE FUSION TORCHES BARELY GIVE ANY LIGHT!
HUSH! WE MUST NOT DISTURB THEIR EXERCISE!
FINALLY, A ROBOSHIP IS ON THE SCHEDULE! THAT'S IT! I'M LEAVING! GOODBYE, DEEPO, HAVE A NICE DREAM! I'M GOING TO A PLANET OF PARADISE!
CAREFUL NOT TO GET SUNBURNED!
MOEBIUS
43

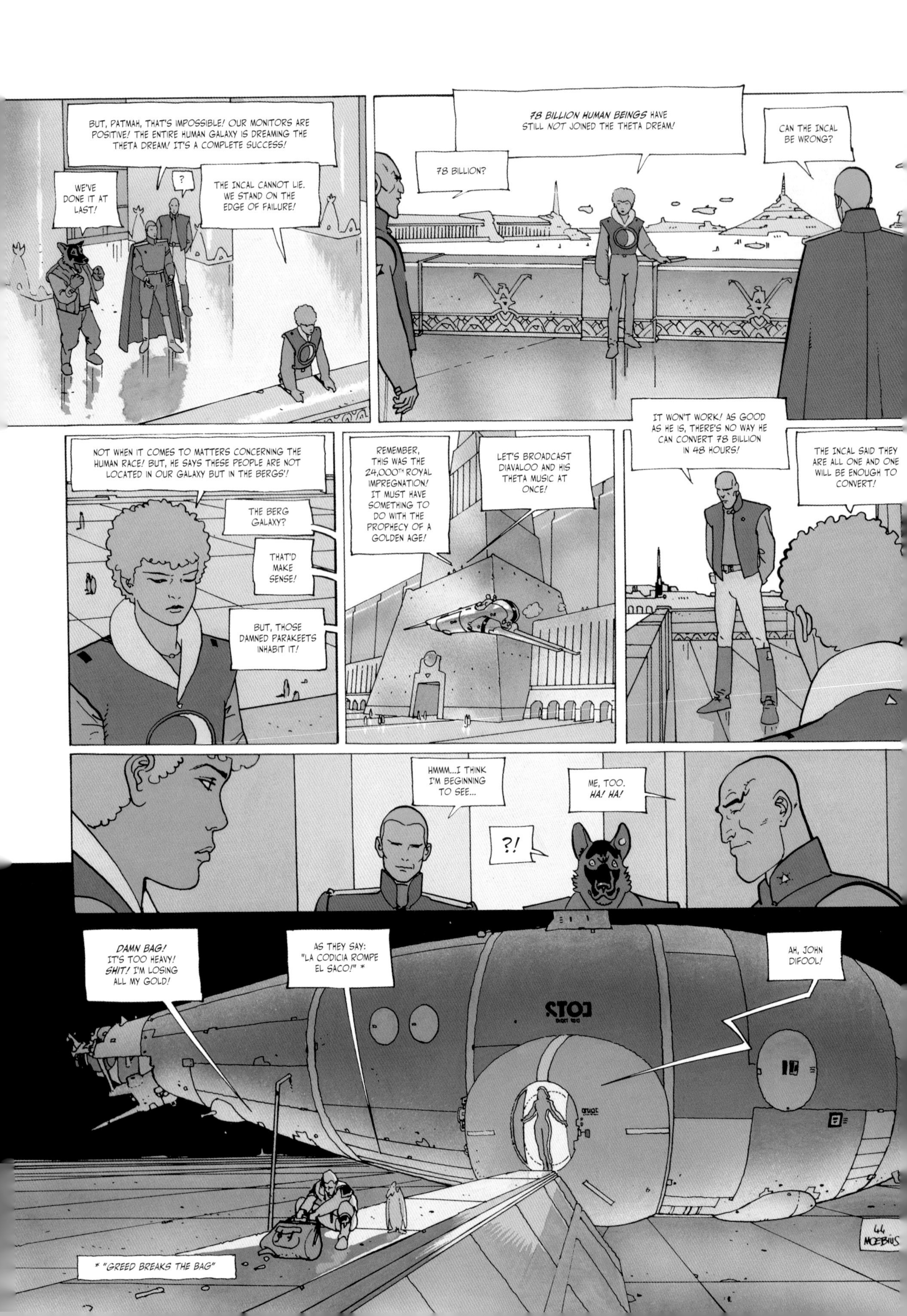
BUT, PATMAH, THAT'S IMPOSSIBLE! OUR MONITORS ARE POSITIVE! THE ENTIRE HUMAN GALAXY IS DREAMING THE THETA DREAM! IT'S A COMPLETE SUCCESS!
WE'VE DONE IT AT LAST!
?
THE INCAL CANNOT LIE. WE STAND ON THE EDGE OF FAILURE!
78 BILLION HUMAN BEINGS HAVE STILL NOT JOINED THE THETA DREAM!
78 BILLION?
CAN THE INCAL BE WRONG?
NOT WHEN IT COMES TO MATTERS CONCERNING THE HUMAN RACE! BUT, HE SAYS THESE PEOPLE ARE NOT LOCATED IN OUR GALAXY BUT IN THE BERGS'!
THE BERG GALAXY?
THAT'D MAKE SENSE!
BUT, THOSE DAMNED PARAKEETS INHABIT IT!
REMEMBER, THIS WAS THE 24,000TH ROYAL IMPREGNATION! IT MUST HAVE SOMETHING TO DO WITH THE PROPHECY OF A GOLDEN AGE!
LET'S BROADCAST DIAVALOO AND HIS THETA MUSIC AT ONCE!
IT WON'T WORK! AS GOOD AS HE IS, THERE'S NO WAY HE CAN CONVERT 78 BILLION IN 48 HOURS!
THE INCAL SAID THEY ARE ALL ONE AND ONE WILL BE ENOUGH TO CONVERT!
HMMM...I THINK I'M BEGINNING TO SEE...
?!
ME, TOO. HA! HA!
DAMN BAG! IT'S TOO HEAVY! SHIT! I'M LOSING ALL MY GOLD!
AS THEY SAY: "LA CODICIA ROMPE EL SACO!" *
AH, JOHN DIFOOL!
* "GREED BREAKS THE BAG"
44
MOEBIUS

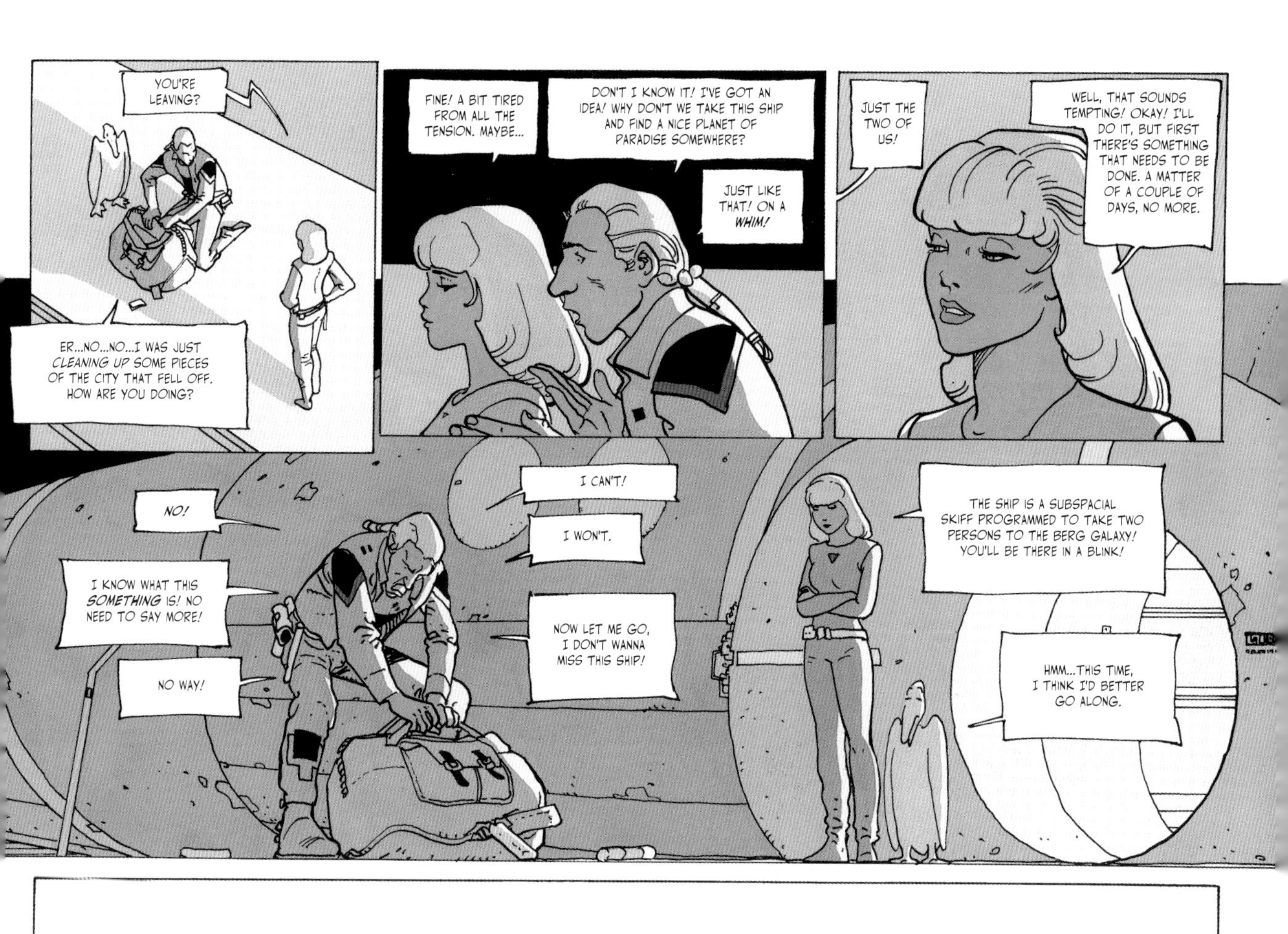
YOU'RE LEAVING?
ER...NO...NO...I WAS JUST CLEANING UP SOME PIECES OF THE CITY THAT FELL OFF. HOW ARE YOU DOING?
FINE! A BIT TIRED FROM ALL THE TENSION. MAYBE...
DON'T I KNOW IT! I'VE GOT AN IDEA! WHY DON'T WE TAKE THIS SHIP AND FIND A NICE PLANET OF PARADISE SOMEWHERE?
JUST LIKE THAT! ON A WHIM!
JUST THE TWO OF US!
WELL, THAT SOUNDS TEMPTING! OKAY! I'LL DO IT, BUT FIRST THERE'S SOMETHING THAT NEEDS TO BE DONE. A MATTER OF A COUPLE OF DAYS, NO MORE.
NO!
I KNOW WHAT THIS SOMETHING IS! NO NEED TO SAY MORE!
NO WAY!
I CAN'T!
I WON'T.
NOW LET ME GO, I DON'T WANNA MISS THIS SHIP!
THE SHIP IS A SUBSPACIAL SKIFF PROGRAMMED TO TAKE TWO PERSONS TO THE BERG GALAXY! YOU'LL BE THERE IN A BLINK!
HMM...THIS TIME, I THINK I'D BETTER GO ALONG.

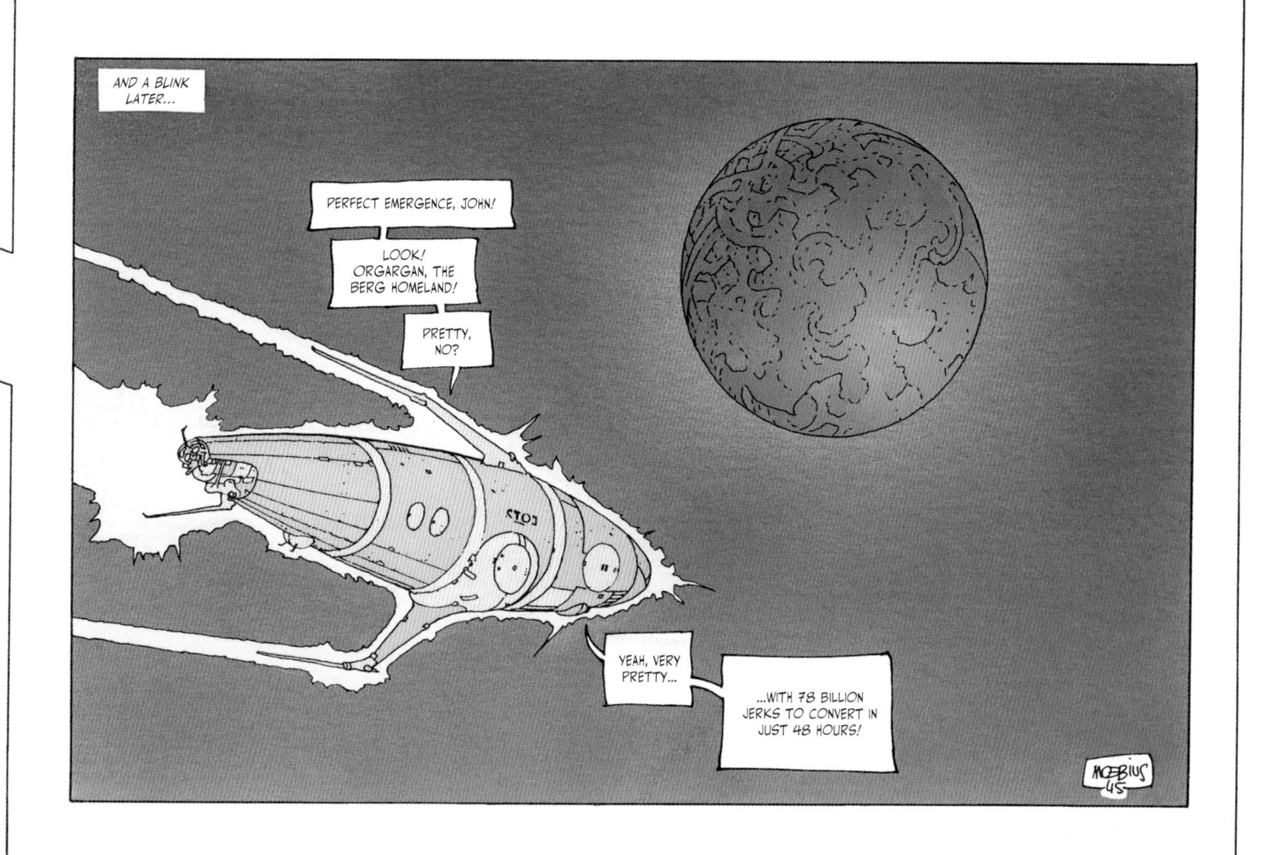
AND A BLINK LATER...
PERFECT EMERGENCE, JOHN!
LOOK! ORGARGAN, THE BERG HOMELAND!
PRETTY, NO?
YEAH, VERY PRETTY...
...WITH 78 BILLION JERKS TO CONVERT IN JUST 48 HOURS!
MOEBIUS 45

THE FIFTH ESSENCE
part two: planet difool

78 BILLION IN 1

DO YOU HAVE THE TIME TO STUDY THE THETA DREAM TECHNIQUE?

YES! YOU EXPECT ME TO BELIEVE IT'S GOING TO PUT 78 BILLION PEOPLE TO SLEEP IN LESS THAN TWO DAYS? YOU MUST BE CRAZY!

WHERE ARE WE GOING TO LAND? IT'S A BIG PLANET!

THE METABARON SUGGESTED THE SAME PLACE AS LAST TIME, SO WE'LL BE CLOSE TO THE PROTOQUEEN'S CONE!

THE SUBSPACIAL SKIFF CARRYING JOHN DIFOOL AND HIS FAITHFUL PAL DEEPO HAS NOW REACHED ORGARGAN, THE HOME WORLD OF THE BERG GALAXY.

REQUEST IMMEDIATE IDENTIFICATION. WHO ARE YOU? WHAT DO YOU WANT? RESPOND OR YOU WILL BE DISINTEGRATED!

THAT'S IT! WE'VE BEEN SPOTTED!

THEY SOUND KIND OF MAD!

LET'S SHOOT HIM DOWN!

NO, WAIT! ***LET HIM TALK!***

ERR...I BRING IMPORTANT INFORMATION!

IMPORTANT INFORMATION? WHAT DO YOU MEAN?

I COME FROM THE HUMAN GALAXY!

MOEBIUS

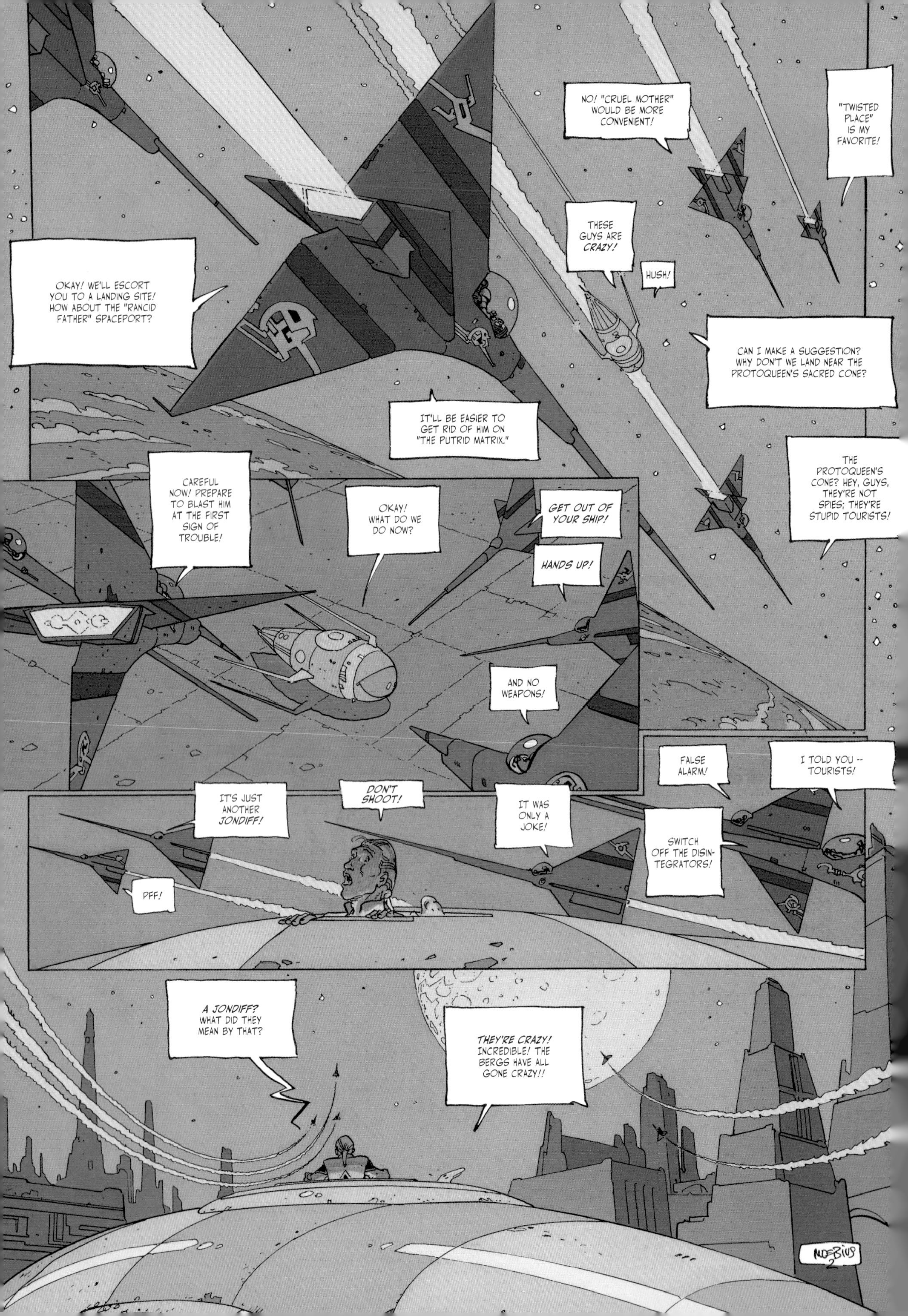
OKAY! WE'LL ESCORT YOU TO A LANDING SITE! HOW ABOUT THE "RANCID FATHER" SPACEPORT?
NO! "CRUEL MOTHER" WOULD BE MORE CONVENIENT!
"TWISTED PLACE" IS MY FAVORITE!
THESE GUYS ARE CRAZY!
HUSH!
CAN I MAKE A SUGGESTION? WHY DON'T WE LAND NEAR THE PROTOQUEEN'S SACRED CONE?
IT'LL BE EASIER TO GET RID OF HIM ON "THE PUTRID MATRIX."
THE PROTOQUEEN'S CONE? HEY, GUYS, THEY'RE NOT SPIES; THEY'RE STUPID TOURISTS!
CAREFUL NOW! PREPARE TO BLAST HIM AT THE FIRST SIGN OF TROUBLE!
OKAY! WHAT DO WE DO NOW?
GET OUT OF YOUR SHIP!
HANDS UP!
AND NO WEAPONS!
FALSE ALARM!
I TOLD YOU -- TOURISTS!
IT'S JUST ANOTHER JONDIFF!
DON'T SHOOT!
IT WAS ONLY A JOKE!
SWITCH OFF THE DISIN-TEGRATORS!
PFF!
A JONDIFF? WHAT DID THEY MEAN BY THAT?
THEY'RE CRAZY! INCREDIBLE! THE BERGS HAVE ALL GONE CRAZY!!
MOEBIUS
2

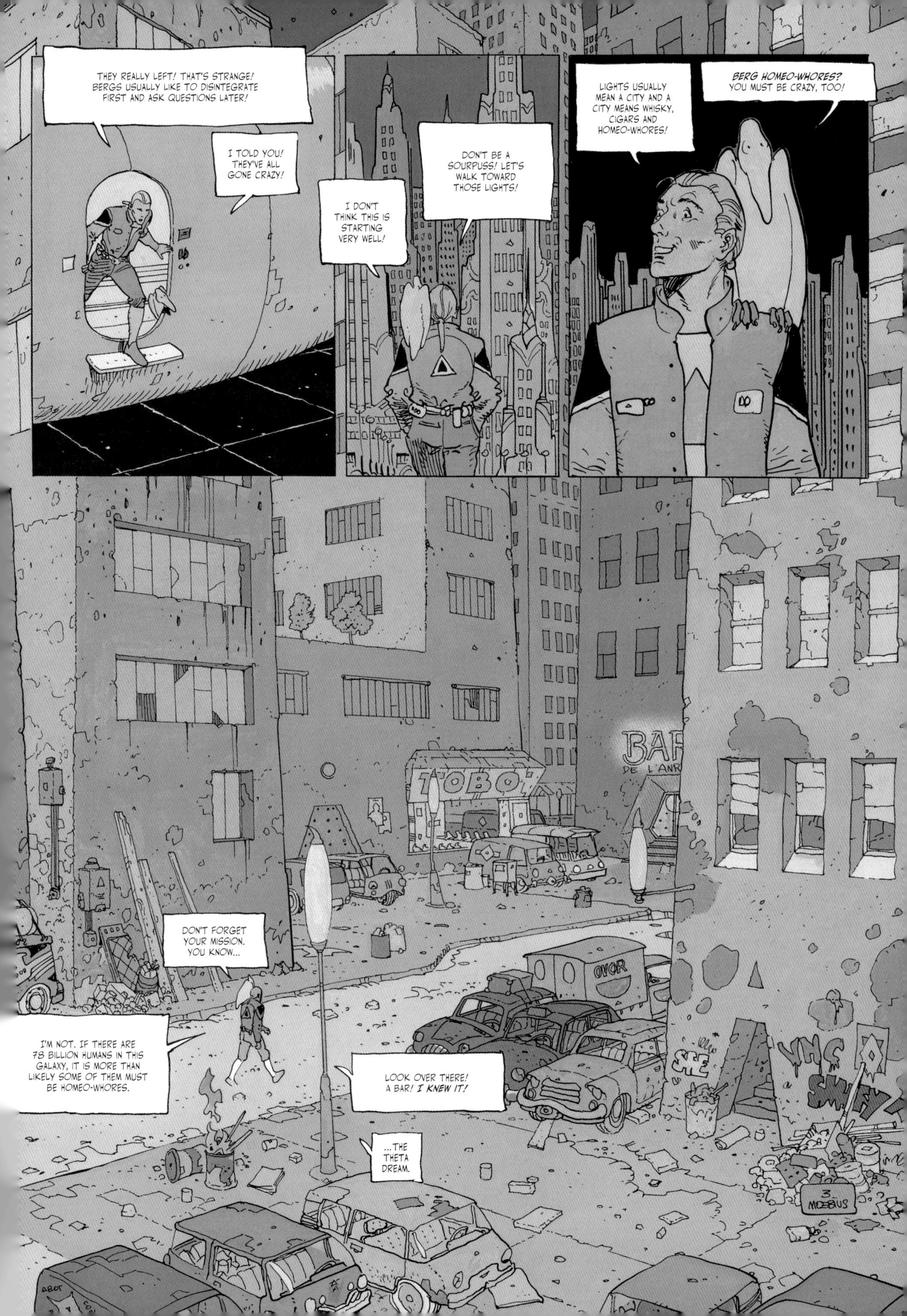
THEY REALLY LEFT! THAT'S STRANGE! BERGS USUALLY LIKE TO DISINTEGRATE FIRST AND ASK QUESTIONS LATER!
I TOLD YOU! THEY'VE ALL GONE CRAZY!
I DON'T THINK THIS IS STARTING VERY WELL!
DON'T BE A SOURPUSS! LET'S WALK TOWARD THOSE LIGHTS!
LIGHTS USUALLY MEAN A CITY AND A CITY MEANS WHISKY, CIGARS AND HOMEO-WHORES!
BERG HOMEO-WHORES? YOU MUST BE CRAZY, TOO!
BAR
DE L'ANR
TOBO
DON'T FORGET YOUR MISSION. YOU KNOW...
I'M NOT. IF THERE ARE 78 BILLION HUMANS IN THIS GALAXY, IT IS MORE THAN LIKELY SOME OF THEM MUST BE HOMEO-WHORES.
LOOK OVER THERE! A BAR! I KNEW IT!
...THE THETA DREAM.
3
MOEBIUS

THE CRIMSON CIRCLE BAR! AND SPELLED JUST LIKE IN THE GOOD OL' FRENCH QUARTER. DON'T MENTION DREAMS ANYMORE, DEEPO. THIS IS REAL! I CAN SMELL THE HOMEO-WHORES FROM HERE!
BAR DE L'ANROUGE
JOHN...
...BE CAREFUL.
HE! HE! HE!
LOOK! HERE'S ONE! HUMAN AND GORGEOUS! YOU SEE, I WAS RIGHT.
AHEM...
COME ON IN, PRETTY BOY!
...
IF I'M NOT YOUR TYPE, HANDSOME, JUST SAY SO. WE'VE GOT OTHER MODELS.
?!!
SO, WHICH ONE DO YOU WANT?
BUT...
MŒBIUS 4

WHAT?
HEY, BUDDY, BUZZ OFF; YOU'RE IN MY WAY!
WAIT!
!?
WHAT DA YA WANT, MAC? MY PICTURE? LEGGO OF MY ARM OR I'LL SMASH THAT UGLY MUG OF YOURS!
...
CRAZY!
IT'S IMPOSSIBLE!
GET LOST, YOU FAG!
BAR
DE L'ANROUG
I MUST BE DREAMING.
NO, I WASN'T DREAMING! THEY ALL LOOKED LIKE...
...LOOK LIKE...
OH, NO!
I'VE GOT TO FIND SOME...UH... SOMEBODY NORMAL!
WOW! MISSION IMPOSSIBLE!
LISTEN! WHAT'S THAT NOISE?
DOWN WITH JOHN DIFOOL! WHAT A BASTARD! PROTOFATHER IS A JERK! LOSER JONDIFF!
IT'S OVER THERE?
AAAH... PEOPLE AT LAST!
MOEBIUS

WHAT'S THAT THING THEY'RE BURNING?
CRAZY!
IT LOOKS LIKE A HEAD...
A BAS
TE
I BET I CAN GUESS WHOSE HEAD IT IS.
ODIO
VON
IT'S *YOUR* HEAD, JOHN! I KNEW IT!!
BUT... BUT...
NO!
MŒBIUS

DON'T YOU THINK YOU'RE OVERDOING IT A LITTLE BIT? EVERYONE'S BEEN GONE FOR AN HOUR! JOHN, GET UP!
WE DON'T HAVE ALL DAY! YOU'VE GOT TO FACE REALITY!
DON'T YOU EVER MENTION THAT WORD AGAIN!
WHAT KID OF CRAZY WORLD IS THIS, DEEPO? WHAT ARE WE GOING TO DO?
CONVERT 78 BILLION PEOPLE TO THE THETA DREAM. AND WE'VE GOT LESS THAN 33 HOURS TO DO IT!
DON'T YOU SEE? THEY'RE NOT PEOPLE! THEY ALL LOOK THE SAME! THEY ALL LOOK LIKE ME!!
HEEEEEKKK
WHAT'S THAT?
HEEEEKKK
?!
A BERG?!
NUTCASE!
GET OUT!
SLIMY CREEP!
MONSTER!
DIE! DIE!
!!
A CUL-DE-SAC!
WE'VE GOT HIM NOW!
PLEASE!
DON'T HURT ME!
WHY DON'T YOU GO CROAK ON THE DUMP!
YEAH! LIKE THE OTHER PARAKEETS!
WE DON'T WANT YOUR KIND IN TOWN ANYMORE! GOT IT!
MOEBIUS

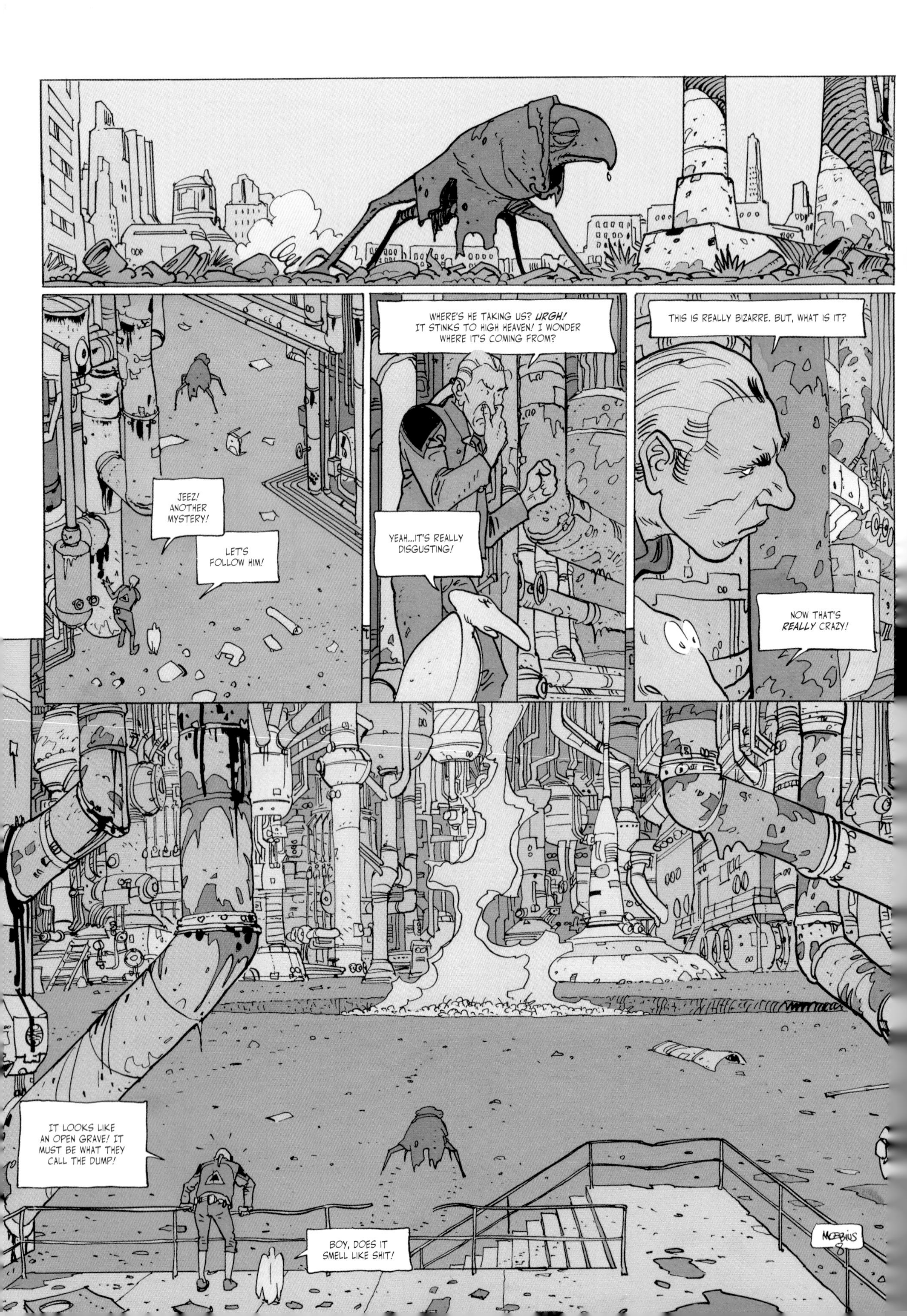
JEEZ! ANOTHER MYSTERY!
LET'S FOLLOW HIM!
WHERE'S HE TAKING US? URGH! IT STINKS TO HIGH HEAVEN! I WONDER WHERE IT'S COMING FROM?
YEAH...IT'S REALLY DISGUSTING!
THIS IS REALLY BIZARRE. BUT, WHAT IS IT?
NOW THAT'S REALLY CRAZY!
IT LOOKS LIKE AN OPEN GRAVE! IT MUST BE WHAT THEY CALL THE DUMP!
BOY, DOES IT SMELL LIKE SHIT!
MOEBIUS
8

O, BERGS! O, MY MARTYRED PEOPLE! SOON I'LL JOIN YOU IN THE ETERNAL VOID!
MILLIONS OF BERG BODIES SLOWLY ROTTING! NO WONDER IT SMELLED SO BAD!
LIKE I SAID, COMPLETELY CRAZY!
GO AWAY, JONDIFF! LET THE LAST OF THE BERGS DIE IN PEACE! GO BACK TO THE OTHER JONDIFFS!
?!
I'M NOT A JONDIFF! I'M JOHN DIFOOL! BY THE COSMOS, WILL SOMEONE TELL ME WHAT'S GOING ON HERE?
STOP MOCKING ME! WAIT! YOU SAID YOUR NAME WAS JOHN DIFOOL? JOHN DIFOOL! THAT WAS THE NAME OF THE PROTOFATHER!
HEY! WHAT? STOP!
I WANT TO SEE FOR MYSELF!
YOU DIRTY...
THERE'S NO DOUBT! HE'S TELLING THE TRUTH! HE HAS A NAVEL! IT IS THE PROTOFATHER! OOH! MY HEAD!
YOU SEEM TO HAVE SURPRISED HIM!
DON'T GO DYING ON ME! FIRST, YOU'VE GOT TO TELL ME WHAT'S GOING ON!
HEEEK!
TELL YOU? DON'T YOU HAVE EYES TO SEE? THIS IS THE GOLDEN AGE YOU LEFT US, A NIGHTMARE OF HATE! THE PROPHECY SAID THAT AFTER 24,000 IMPREGNATIONS, THE PROTOQUEEN WOULD GIVE BIRTH TO A RACE OF PERFECT BEINGS! 78 BILLION CHILDREN, ALL IDENTICAL TO THEIR ORIGINAL PROGENITOR!
CONGRATULATIONS, JOHN!
WHAT?!
MOEBIUS

THE PREVIOUS WINNER OF THE GREAT NUPTIAL GAMES WAS A BERG, TRILYS, A BIRD-LIKE SPECIES AND WE ALL SHARED HIS FEATURES! THEN YOU CAME AND FATHERED 78 BILLION BEINGS JUST LIKE YOU! BUT, BARBARIAH, OUR BELOVED PROTOQUEEN AND MOTHER, FELL IN LOVE WITH YOU IN A WAY SHE'D NEVER DONE BEFORE! AN ALL-CONSUMING LOVE!
IT'S NOT MY FAULT! I DIDN'T DO ANYTHING FOR--
AFTER YOU ABANDONED HER, THAT LOVE TURNED TO HATE! A HATE THAT GROWS WITH EVERY EGG SHE LAYS. SHE HATES HER CHILDREN BECAUSE THEY REMIND HER OF THEIR FATHER AND OF HIS BETRAYAL. YOUR BETRAYAL. THE CHILDREN THEMSELVES HATE HER AND MOST OF ALL THEY HATE YOU, WHOM THEY SEE AS THE CAUSE OF THEIR MISFORTUNE!
WAIT A MINUTE! I DON'T SEE WHY I SHOULD BE HELD RESPONSIBLE FOR--
WE, THE BERGS, SHOULD HAVE BEEN ALLOWED TO PEACEFULLY PASS AWAY AND JOIN THE GREAT COSMIC ALL, LIKE EVERY GENERATION BEFORE US DID. BUT, INSTEAD, BEHOLD OUR END! GARBAGE AMONG THE GARBAGE!
I'M REALLY SORRY, BUT HOW COULD I HAVE KNOWN THAT--
YOU'VE BEEN A CURSE TO THIS GALAXY, JOHN DIFOOL! YOU ARE A MILLION TIMES C-CURSED...EEEEK!
HE...HE'S DEAD!
ALIN
LISTEN! ALL OF YOU LISTEN TO ME!
?
LOLOS
MOEBIUS
10

MY...MY BROTHERS! OPEN YOUR EYES TO THE LIGHT! THE LIGHT IS DYING!
WHO IS THIS JONDIFF?
IS HE A NEW PROPHET?
THE LIGHT'S DYING? MAYBE YOU NEED GLASSES!
THE DARKNESS THREATENS US ALL! ONLY THE THETA DREAM CAN SAVE US, MY....ER...BROTHERS!
THE THETA DREAM?
WHAT?
?
I'VE HEARD OF THAT! IT'S BEEN ALL OVER THE HOLOVID BROADCASTS FROM THE HUMAN GALAXY!
IT'S A LOT OF BULL!
WE'RE IN THE JONDIFF GALAXY! WHO CARES WHAT HAPPENS IN THE HUMAN GALAXY!
BUT, THE WHOLE UNIVERSE IS DOOMED!
THE DARKNESS WILL DESTROY EVERY PLANET WHERE LIGHT AND LIFE COEXIST! THE HUMAN GALAXY HAS ALMOST SUCCUMBED! SOON, IT'LL BE...ER...OUR TURN!
STUPID PROPHET!
GET AWAY!
SHUT HIM UP!
MY BROTHERS!
GO DREAM SOMEPLACE ELSE!
GO AWAY!
SHUT UP!
ENOUGH!
CLEAR OUT!
THE POLICE?
WHO'S CAUSING THIS DISTURBANCE?
IT'S HIM, SIR!
A PROPHET!
GO PREACH SOMEPLACE ELSE! IT'S FORBIDDEN TO DO IT DOWNTOWN! GO AWAY!
GO TELL THE BUMS!
OOCH!
OUCH!
HALF A DAY'S ALREADY GONE AND NOT A SINGLE SUCCESS! HOW CAN I CONVERT 78 BILLION PEOPLE IN THE TIME WE'VE GOT LEFT?
YOU'VE GOT TO PERSEVERE UNTIL THE LAST SECOND, JOHN! THE INCAL SAID ONLY ONE MAN COULD DO IT AND THAT MAN IS YOU!
OKAY, LET'S TRY THE BUMS THEN!
MOEBIUS
11

GET LOST, YOU STUPID PROPHET!
GO AWAY!
CRAZY!
SPREAD YOUR LIES ELSEWHERE! TRY THE SLAVES! THEY'RE DUMB!
THE SLAVES? THEY'RE OVER THERE CLEANING UP THE SHELLS! MOST OF THEM ARE MUTANTS!
I KNOW THIS PLACE! IT'S THE PROTOQUEEN'S CONE!
THIS IS THE PITS! I DON'T KNOW IF I CAN DO IT!
ALL THE GREAT PROPHETS WORKED THEIR WAY UP FROM THE BOTTOM!
GO FOR IT!
THE GREAT DARKNESS IS COMING! THE LIGHT IS DYING!
DON'T WASTE YOUR BREATH, MAC! EVERYONE HERE KNOWS ABOUT THE GREAT DARKNESS AND THE THETA DREAM! NO ONE GIVES A DAMN!
WE'RE NOT HUMANS, WE'RE MUTANTS! WHY SHOULD WE CARE? SO SCRAM!
LOOK! THERE IT IS!
MOEBIUS 12

SPLRTTTTTT SHHHHH
?
IT'S THE LAST ONE!
FINALLY!
THE 78 BILLIONTH.
HURRAY!
THE LAST EGG! THE LAST JONDIFF! I GOT HERE JUST IN TIME.
OUR WORK IS FINISHED!
NO MORE PICKING UP SHELLS!
FFLIP
PPPRRRR
SLUPP
THE NIGHTMARE IS OVER! LET'S SEE WHAT HE LOOKS LIKE.
PLEASE. DON'T EVEN JOKE ABOUT IT.
I BET HE'LL BE AS UGLY AS THE OTHERS.
MOEBIUS 13

I HAVE AN IDEA. I'LL TALK TO HIM AS SOON AS HE LEAVES THE EGG. WAY BEFORE THE ENVIRONMENT CAN POLLUTE HIM. HE'LL BECOME MY FIRST DISCIPLE.
GOOD IDEA!
HERE HE COMES!
O, BROTHER! THE DARKNESS IS COMING! COME WITH ME AND LET'S MMPH...
GET OUT OF MY WAY, BUDDY! I NEED A GLASS OF WHISKY AND A HOMEO-WHORE ON EACH ARM FAST!
AND YOU, YA STUPID PROTOCOW! NEXT TIME TRY AND PICK A BETTER MATE!
!?
GEEZ, ALL OF THEM, ROTTEN TO THE LAST!
BITCH! WHORE!
PFFF!
CRAZY!
THIS TIME WE'VE ALL HAD IT. THE GALAXY HAS HAD IT! I'VE HAD IT.
THAT'S HIM. I RECOGNIZE HIM.
I'D BE ABLE TO PICK THIS BASTARD OUT OF MILLIONS! HE'S GOT THAT KIND OF SMELL OF SCUM!
HE'S THE BASTARD WHO CHEATED DURING THE NUPTIAL GAMES!
HUH?
WHERE ARE WE GOING, NOW?
I DUNNO! ANYWHERE AND FAR FROM HERE!
GORGO!
CATCH HIM!
KILL HIM!
BUT, THEN, HE'S THE PROTOFATHER!!
MOEBIUS

WHAT'S GOING ON?
PFF...HELP! PFFF...POLICE OFFICER!
DIRTY CHEAT!
POLICE...
CHIEF...
BASTARD!
STOP! GET BACK, YOU FILTHY MUTANTS! A JONDIFF IS ENTITLED TO SOME RESPECT EVEN IF HE'S A CRAZY PROPHET.
YEAH! TELL HIM I'M ENTITLED TO SOME RESPECT!
BUT, HE'S NOT A JONDIFF! HE'S THE ORIGINAL BASTARD WHO GOT THE PROTOQUEEN PREGNANT! AND BESIDES THAT, HE'S A CHEAT!
?!
THAT'S NOT TRUE!
YOU'D BETTER EXPLAIN YOURSELF.
I SHOULD HAVE WON, NOT HIM. THERE SHOULD HAVE BEEN 78 BILLION FOUL ONES! IT AIN'T FAIR.
WHAT'S HE SAYING? ARE YOU THE PROTOFATHER?
HE'S LYING. I'M A REAL JONDIFF. I CURSE THE PROTOFATHER. I SPIT ON HIS D.N.A.!
LIAR! IF YOU'VE REALLY BEEN HATCHED, THEN SHOW US THAT YOU DON'T HAVE A NAVEL!
YES, COME ON, BROTHER. OPEN YOU SHIRT. SHOW US YOUR BELLY.
ONE THING'S FOR SURE...
...HIS PROBLEMS HAVE JUST STARTED.
MOEBIUS

CROSS

DEAR JONDIFFS OF THE JONDIFF GALAXY FROM JOHNSTOWN, HERE'S SOMETHING NEW THAT WILL SEND A JOLT THROUGH 78 BILLION HEARTS.
WKL
JOHN DIFOOL, THE PROTOFATHER, WAS NOT DISINTEGRATED DURING THE ASSAULT ON TECHNOGEA AS HAD PREVIOUSLY BEEN BELIEVED. HE WAS ARRESTED THIS MORNING AS HE WAS LEWDLY WANDERING ABOUT THE SACRED CONE.
MY GOD, IS THIS TRUE OR IS IT ANOTHER TRICK TO SELL US APHRODISIAC YOGURT?
AND HERE IS...HIS NAVEL!
THIS SORDID PICTURE PROVES BEYOND A SHADOW OF A DOUBT THE IDENTITY OF THIS ARCHITECT OF OUR MISFORTUNE.
THE TRIAL OF THIS CRIMINAL IS CURRENTLY IN PROGRESS IN THE BERGS' FORMER HALL OF JUSTICE.
BEURAK!
IT IS OBSCENE!
THAT'S A NAVEL?
WHAT A GROTESQUE THING!
SILENCE! OR I'LL HAVE THE COURT CLEARED.
AND NOW THE VERDICT! HE! HE!
THIS TRIBUNAL UNANIMOUSLY CONDEMNS JOHN DIFOOL, A.K.A. THE PROTOFATHER, TO BE CASTRATED IN THE CITY'S CENTRAL SQUARE, BEFORE BEING DELIVERED TO THE RIGHTEOUS WRATH OF THE POPULATION.
DEAR JONDIFFS, THE TRIBUNAL'S VERDICT IS ABOUT TO BE ANNOUNCED. IT WILL HAVE BEEN THE SHORTEST TRIAL IN THE YOUNG HISTORY OF OUR GALAXY.
FOR "JOHNSTOWN NEWS," HOW DO YOU FEEL ABOUT YOUR RETURN?
AND SEEING ALL THE SHIT YOU CREATED?
DIE!
YOU GAVE US THE WORST OF YOU.
WE'RE GONNA CUT OFF YOUR BALLS, BUDDY!
ACCUSED, YOU'VE REMAINED SILENT DURING THE DURATION OF THE TRIAL. DO YOU NOW WISH TO SAY SOMETHING?
YES.
I HAVE SOMETHING TO SAY.
HE HAS SOMETHING TO SAY?!
CLIC FLASH CLICK
FIRST, DOES ANYBODY KNOW WHAT TIME IT IS?
?!
FIVE AFTER TWELVE.
SO THERE IS ONLY FOUR HOURS LEFT BEFORE THE DARKNESS DESTROYS THE HUMAN GALAXY. MY CHILDREN, ONLY THE THETA DREAM CAN SAVE US.
BOOOOOO!
AGAIN?
BEUARK!
YOU SUCK!
DIE!
BASTARD!
SHUT HIM UP!
CUT OFF THE SOUND!
MOEBIUS 16

LET JUSTICE BE DONE! TAKE HIM AWAY!
GUARDS!
BUT...BUT, LISTEN TO ME!
NO!
BOOO!
GET OUT THE SCISSORS!
CUT 'EM OFF!
DIE BASTARD!
THIS TIME IT LOOKS LIKE HE'S REALLY HAD IT.
IF ONLY HE STILL HAD THE INCAL IN HIM LIKE LAST TIME.
NOOO!
WAIT A MINUTE. I JUST GOT AN IDEA.
YES! HA! HA!
THE INCAL INSIDE. THE INCAL INSIDE HIM.
SEE! THEY'VE COME FOR THE PARTY IN YOUR HONOR! HA! HA!
THIS IS A NIGHTMARE.
THE INCAL INSIDE HIM!
OF COURSE!
THAT'S IT. I'VE GOT IT!
I KNOW HOW TO SOLVE THIS MESS. BUT, IT'S GOING TO TAKE A FEW MINUTES. HOLY CONCRETE! I HOPE HE DOESN'T RUN OUT OF TIME BEFORE I CAN TAKE CARE OF IT.
BASTARD!
DEVIL!
OUCH!
HEY!
MONSTER!
TAKE THAT! JERK!
MOEBIUS 17

THERE. THE PROTOQUEEN'S CONE.
BUT, THE HOLE IS CLOSING!
FASTER!
CUT 'EM!
JUST IN TIME!
SHLOP
WHO DARES DISTURB THE PEACE OF THE SACRED CONE. JUST AS I AM ABOUT TO ENTER MY FIVE THOUSAND YEAR SLEEP.
GREAT CONCRETE! SO THAT'S THE PROTOQUEEN?
5000 YEARS? IF I'M WRONG I'LL HAVE PLENTY OF TIME TO REGRET THIS, UNTIL THE LAST FEATHER CRUMBLES INTO DUST.
YOU STUPID BIRD! YOU DON'T THINK I'M GOING TO WAIT 5000 YEARS TO TURN YOU TO DUST?
PLEASE! I BRING YOU GREAT NEWS! JOHN DIFOOL, YOUR LOVE, IS ALIVE. HE IS HERE! HE HAS COME TO SEE YOU.
CLAC
WHAT?!
IS THIS YOUR GREAT NEWS? HA. IT'S THE WORST NEWS YOU COULD HAVE BROUGHT ME. I HATE JOHN DIFOOL WITH EVERY FIBER OF MY PROTOPLASMIC BEING!
BUT, I HAVE THE PROOF THAT YOU'VE MADE A MISTAKE.
A MISTAKE? HAVE YOU SEEN WHAT HAS BECOME OF MY GALAXY? WHAT WAS SUPPOSED TO BE THE LONG-PROPHESIED GOLDEN AGE HAS TURNED INTO A NIGHTMARE. THE WORLD IS INHABITED BY 78 BILLION JERKS THAT ALL LOOK LIKE JOHN DIFOOL. I'D RATHER SEEK REFUGE IN SLEEP.
MOEBIUS 18

NOW, I'M GOING TO...
PLEASE, BARBARIAH! I CAN PROVE TO YOU THAT YOU WERE NEVER IN LOVE WITH JOHN DIFOOL.
WHAT?
FOR INSTANCE, WERE YOU ATTRACTED TO HIS PHYSICAL FORM?
HOW COULD ONE SUCH AS I LOVE THAT DULL, MONOFORM SHAPE OF HIS?
DID YOU ENJOY HAVING SEX WITH HIM?
PFF! I BARELY HAD TIME TO ENJOY IT! NORMALLY MY ORGASMS COULD WELL LAST CENTURIES.
SO, YOU LOVED HIS FEELINGS FOR YOU?
DON'T BE SILLY. HE ONLY LOVED THE IMAGE OF THAT ANIMAH WOMAN. PFFF!
ERR...HIS INTELLIGENCE MAYBE?
DON'T MOCK ME, BIRD! HE HAD NONE.
OKAY! OKAY! THEN WHAT EXACTLY DID YOU FIND IN HIM TO LOVE?
HIS SOUL! THERE WAS A SUBLIME LIGHT INSIDE HIM. AN ALMOST INFINITE FORCE OF DIVINE BEAUTY.
BUT, BARBARIAH, YOU WERE IN LOVE WITH THE INCAL, NOT JOHN DIFOOL!
THE INCAL?
YES! THE INCAL WAS INSIDE HIM AND IT WAS IT WHO SEDUCED YOU. SO, SINCE YOU NEVER LOVED JOHN, YOU CAN'T HATE HIM.
YOU'RE RIGHT, LITTLE BIRD. THIS CHANGES EVERYTHING. WHAT DO YOU WANT FROM ME?
CUT OFF HIS BALLS!
CUT 'EM! CUT 'EM!
NO!
CLIC CLIC
THROUGHOUT THE JONDIFF GALAXY...
CLIC CLIC
CUT 'EM OFF!
SERVES HIM RIGHT!
JERK!
CUT 'EM! CUT 'EM! CUT 'EM!
?
HEY! LOOK UP THERE!
?
OOOH!!
THE PROTO-QUEEN!
WHAT NOW?
!???!
OOH!
THE MOTHER!
?
MOEBIUS
19

RELEASE THIS MAN!
ERR, I MEAN, BARBARIAH. I'D LIKE TO CLEAR THE AIR BETWEEN US ABOUT THIS UNFORTUNATE MISUNDERSTANDING WE HAD IN THE PAST AND--
ANIMAH!
DO NOT WORRY, JOHN DIFOOL. I HAVE FORGIVEN YOU. BECAUSE OF YOU I HAVE KNOWN THE ECSTASY OF THE INCAL.
THE PROTOQUEEN! SHE'S SO BEAUTIFUL.
TOO BAD SHE HATES US!
HOW SHE GLOWS...
BITCH! ERR...
HUSH!
YOU WERE BUT A CHANNEL OF EPHEMERAL MATTER THROUGH WHICH I DISCOVERED THE SUBLIME AND ETERNAL BEAUTY OF THE INCAL.
?!
?!
YEAH, YEAH! I WAS BUT A CHANNEL. BARELY A DITCH!
NOW, I ADDRESS MY BELOVED CHILDREN WHOSE FORGIVENESS I BEG. I WAS BLIND. I CURSED YOU WHEN YOU WERE THE TRUE SEED OF OUR FUTURE GOLDEN AGE. THE MIRACULOUS CHILDREN OF THE INCAL!
HUH???
WHAT?
WHO? US!?
IS SHE TALKING ABOUT US?
SOMETHING'S STIRRING IN ME...
WE FORGIVE YOU!
MOTHER, WE LOVE YOU!
BOOHOOHOO, MOMMY!
WE FORGIVE YOU, MOM!
WE LOVE YOU!
AMAZING!
I DON'T GET IT.
HUG US!
OH, MOTHER DEAR!
SHINE FOR US!
OH, MOTHER...
BOOOHOOO! SNIFF!
I FEEL ALL WARM INSIDE.

NOW WE CAN ALL JOIN TOGETHER IN THE INCAL'S DIVINE PLANE AND YOUR FATHER WILL SHOW US THE WAY.
WHAT? THE PROTOFATHER?
NOT HIM! GRRR!
BE QUIET. MY CHILDREN, CLOSE YOUR EYES.
HUSH!
LISTEN TO WHAT OUR MOTHER IS SAYING.
SO, JOHN, WHAT ARE YOU WAITING FOR? IT'S YOUR MOVE NOW. GO FOR IT!
HUH? OH, YEAH, THE THETA DREAM.
OKAY! ERR...RELAX AND EMPTY YOUR MINDS. NOW THINK OF A SINGLE RED LIGHT.
THE LIGHT GROWS...IT BECOMES ORANGE, YELLOW, GREEN, BLUE, INDIGO, PURPLE... NOW COUNT SLOWLY WITH ME: 9...
8...7...BREATHE DEEPLY... 6...5...SLOWLY...4...3... DEEPER...DEEPER...
YOU SINK EVER DEEPER... 2...1...YOU'RE ASLEEP.
ZZZ.
ZZZ.
ZZ
NOT ME!
YOUR THETA DREAM MAY BE SWELL, DIFOOL, BUT IT'S FOR HUMANS, NOT US.
WE'RE MUTANTS FROM THE LOWER DEPTHS. GARBAGE EATERS! BORN AMONG HUMAN FILTH...LOATHSOME MONSTERS!
GORGO THE FOUL!
HIM AGAIN?
ZZZ

THE THETA DREAM IS FOR EVERYONE.
STOP PUTTING OUR OWN KIND DOWN, GORGO. YOU CAME FROM INNER EARTH? SO WHAT? THAT'S WHERE THE INCAL WAS BORN. AMIDST THE GARBAGE.
YEAH, BUT I'M GORGO THE FOUL. EVERYONE FINDS ME DISGUSTING!
I DON'T, GORGO.
?
DON'T I DISGUST YOU?
I KNOW YOU. YOU WERE ALMOST MY MATE. MANKIND IS NOT A MATTER OF GENES, COLOR OR EVEN SMELL. IT'S A MATTER OF HEART AND YOURS IS BIG AND PURE.
NOW, COME. JOIN THE INCAL WITH YOUR BROTHERS.
WELL, OKAY, SINCE I'M HUMAN INSIDE. MAYBE I CAN DREAM, TOO.
GOOD-BYE, BARBARIAH.
THEY'VE ALL ENTERED THE THETA DREAM. I, TOO, SHALL GO BACK TO THE SACRED CONE. BUT, MY BELOVED INCAL WILL BE WITH ME. IN ME. GOOD-BYE, DEEPO. GO IN PEACE.
I'VE WON! I'VE WON! HA! LOOK AT HOW THEY SLEEP.
STOP PATTING YOURSELF ON THE BACK. THERE'S ONLY THREE HOURS LEFT BEFORE ZERO HOUR.
HE! HE! TO THINK THEY WANTED TO CUT OFF MY BALLS.
ZZZ
AND WE STILL HAVE A GOOD HOUR OF SUBSPACE AHEAD OF US.
I KNOW!... AH! HERE'S OUR SKIFF.
WHERE IS THIS THING PROGRAMMED TO TAKE ME NEXT ANYWAY?
I THOUGHT YOU KNEW? WE'RE GOIN TO TER21 TO FIGH THE DARKNESS ITSELF.
HELLO, PLANET OF GOLD? DEEPO HERE. I HAVE TOTAL SUCCESS TO REPORT! JOHN DIFOOL? I HAD TO GIVE HIM A SEDATIVE! HE BROKE DOWN WHEN HE FOUND OUT WHERE WE ARE GOING.
HE WAS TRYING TO TEAR OUT HIS NAVEL, POOR GUY. I'M ENTERING SUBSPACE RIGHT NOW.
22 MOEBIUS

THE CIRCLES OF NIGHTMARE

THE SUN'S ALMOST DEAD!
IT IS THE NIGHT.
GOOD TO SEE GOOD OL' TER21 AGAIN...
BUT, WHY DO WE HAVE TO GO BACK INSIDE THAT HOLE?
THAT'S THE INCAL'S CRADLE. THAT'S THE ONLY PLACE HE CAN FIGHT THE DARKNESS.
LET'S HURRY! THERE'S ONLY 17 MINUTES LEFT TO ZERO HOUR.
OOOH! LOOK AT ALL THOSE CHILDREN.
THEY'RE ASLEEP AND LEVITATING.
THEY ACHIEVED PERFECTION WITHIN THE THETA DREAM.
THE INCAL MUST RETURN TO HIS BIRTHPLACE, THE SUN-CORE OF INNER EARTH.
IT MUST BE DYING, TOO.
I THOUGHT IT HAD EXPLODED.
SO, WHAT ARE WE WAITING FOR?
THE ARAHTS. THERE THEY ARE. THEY WILL GUIDE US.
JOHN, ***WAKE UP!*** I WONDER HOW WE'LL FIND OUR WAY. EVERYTHING HAS CHANGED SO MUCH.

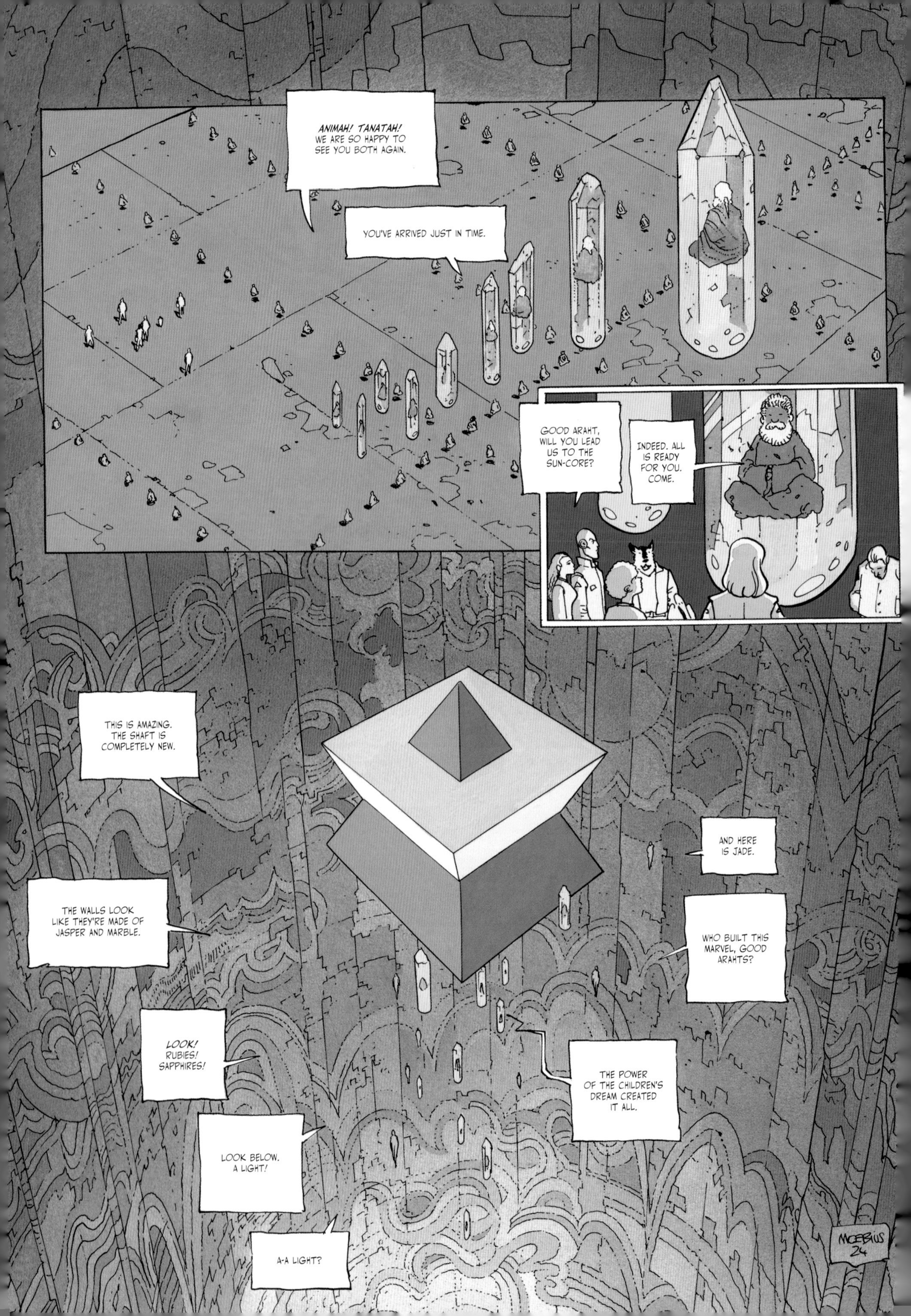
ANIMAH! TANATAH! WE ARE SO HAPPY TO SEE YOU BOTH AGAIN.
YOU'VE ARRIVED JUST IN TIME.
GOOD ARAHT, WILL YOU LEAD US TO THE SUN-CORE?
INDEED. ALL IS READY FOR YOU. COME.
THIS IS AMAZING. THE SHAFT IS COMPLETELY NEW.
AND HERE IS JADE.
THE WALLS LOOK LIKE THEY'RE MADE OF JASPER AND MARBLE.
WHO BUILT THIS MARVEL, GOOD ARAHTS?
LOOK! RUBIES! SAPPHIRES!
THE POWER OF THE CHILDREN'S DREAM CREATED IT ALL.
LOOK BELOW. A LIGHT!
A-A LIGHT?
MOEBIUS 24

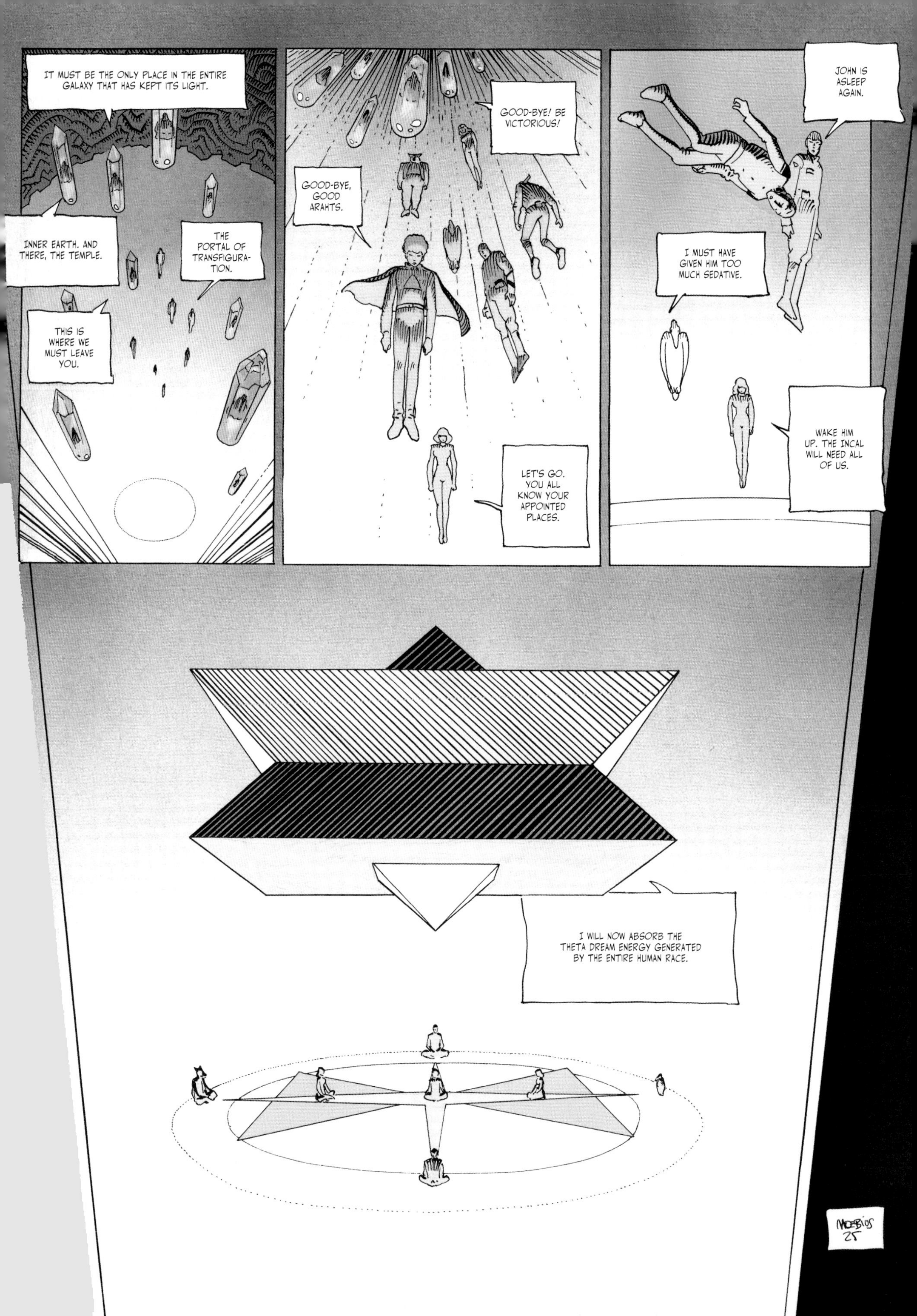
IT MUST BE THE ONLY PLACE IN THE ENTIRE GALAXY THAT HAS KEPT ITS LIGHT.
INNER EARTH. AND THERE, THE TEMPLE.
THE PORTAL OF TRANSFIGURATION.
THIS IS WHERE WE MUST LEAVE YOU.
GOOD-BYE! BE VICTORIOUS!
GOOD-BYE, GOOD ARAHTS.
LET'S GO. YOU ALL KNOW YOUR APPOINTED PLACES.
JOHN IS ASLEEP AGAIN.
I MUST HAVE GIVEN HIM TOO MUCH SEDATIVE.
WAKE HIM UP. THE INCAL WILL NEED ALL OF US.
I WILL NOW ABSORB THE THETA DREAM ENERGY GENERATED BY THE ENTIRE HUMAN RACE.
MOEBIUS 25

WE'VE DONE IT!
THE STAR VESSEL HAS BECOME ONE WITH THE PORTAL. WE ARE NOW ENTERING THE THETA DREAM ITSELF.
YOU MUST DREAM. EMPTY YOUR MINDS OF ALL THOUGHTS. DIVE DEEP WITHIN YOURSELVES. DREAM *INSIDE* YOUR DREAM.
I AM NOW IN FULL CONTROL OF THE PRANIC ENERGY OF ALL THE THETA DREAMERS! WE WILL NOW ENTER NULL-TIME AND NULL-SPACE TO CONFRONT THE DARKNESS ITSELF!
MŒBIUS 26

WE ARE ENTERING THE FIRST CIRCLE OF THE NIGHTMARE. WE'VE ALL MADE CONTACT WITH THE GREAT DARKNESS!
WHAT? WHERE ARE WE? WHAT'S GOING ON?
BE ON YOUR GUARD. THE DARKNESS WILL STRENGTHEN YOUR INNER MONSTERS TO BETTER FEED ON YOUR TERROR.
?
ARRGHHHH
MOEBIUS

MY EAR! ARRGH!!
NO!
TANATAH! HELP ME!
METABARON!
IT'S...IT'S HORRIBLE!
BUT...
YOU MUST RESIST! THE ATTACK OF THE NIGHTMARES HAS BEGUN! RESIST!
WHAT'S-WHAT'S HAPPENING TO ME? AM I GOING MAD?
HELP ME!
GOD-MOTHER!
I AM EVIL!
NO!
TANATAH! STOP!
IT'S YOUR OLD EVIL SELF RESURFACING FROM WHEN YOU WERE AMOK'S QUEEN!
ACCURSED DOG!
MOEBIUS

ZZZ
GRRRRRAH
STOP TIME...
GRRRR
GRRR
GRRRRR
GRRRRRRR
GRRRRR
GRRRRRRR
WHAT'S...WHAT'S HAPPENING?
HOLD! CONTROL YOUR MONSTERS! CONTROL YOUR MONSTERS!
TIME!
STOP...
TI-T-
TIME.
MŒBIUS

SOLUNE! NO!
MŒBIUS 30

CON YOUR MONS S!
INCAL! WHAT'S HAPPENING?
STOP!
STOP THIS MADNESS!
GRRRR
NOOO!
NOT...
GRRR
ARRF
GRRRRRRR
...REGRESSION!
CROOOT
CROOTTT
GRRRRRRRR
GRRRR
CROT!
GRRRR
RRRRR
MOEBIUS
31

WHAT ABOUT ME? HOW COME I DON'T HAVE ANY NIGHTMARES?
YOUR EXPERIENCE WITH THE PROTOQUEEN HAS MADE YOU IMMUNE. YOU MUST AGAIN BECOME MY CHANNEL.
OKAY...I'LL DO IT. GO ON. DO YOUR THING.
STOP FIGHTING THE NIGHTMARE MONSTERS! ACCEPT THEM! THEY ARE ONLY THE PARTS OF YOURSELVES THAT YOU ARE AFRAID TO FACE. TRANSFORM THEM.
EVERY HORROR CONTAINS A POSITIVE SEED. A NIGHTMARE IS BUT A GIFT IN DISGUISE.
METABARON, YOUR BIONIC EAR IS NOT EVIL! IT RECREATES THE HARMONY OF THE MUSIC WITHIN YOU!
TANATAH, YOUR INNER VIOLENCE IS ONLY A REFLECTION OF YOUR PRIMORDIAL CREATIVE ENERGIES!
KILL, YOUR BEAST-LIKE NATURE MERELY ENABLES YOU TO BETTER MASTER REALITY.
SOLUNE, YOUR SUDDEN AGING IS THE SYMBOL OF A TRANSITION...
...FROM A SHORT-LIVED INDIVIDUALITY TO A TIMELESS TOTALITY.
ANIMAH, YOUR DECAYING BODY SYMBOLIZES THE SEED OF THE NEW LIFE. IT ALSO MARKS A TRANSITION FROM THE EPHEMERAL TO THE ETERNAL.
MŒBIUS
32

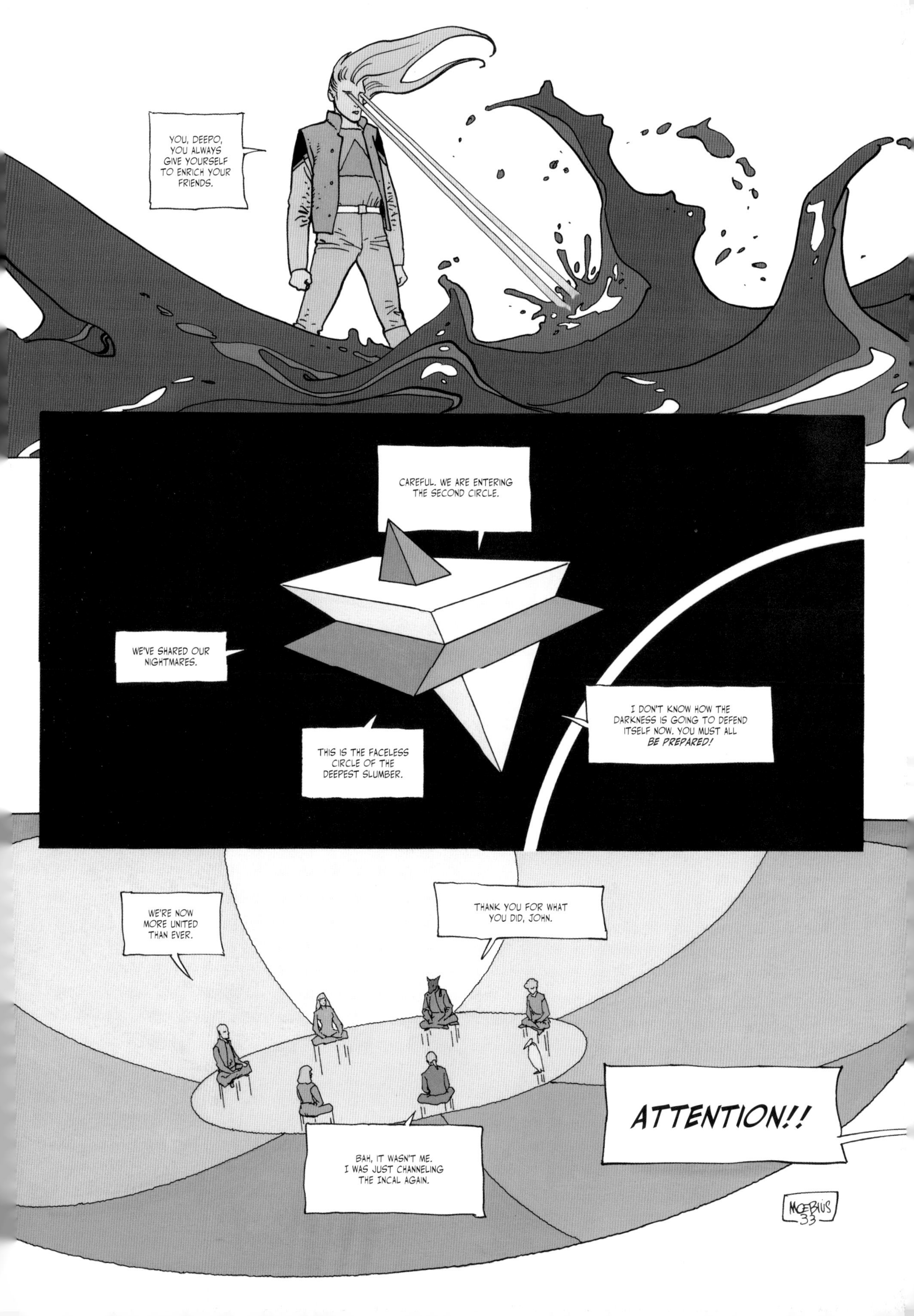
YOU, DEEPO, YOU ALWAYS GIVE YOURSELF TO ENRICH YOUR FRIENDS.
CAREFUL. WE ARE ENTERING THE SECOND CIRCLE.
WE'VE SHARED OUR NIGHTMARES.
THIS IS THE FACELESS CIRCLE OF THE DEEPEST SLUMBER.
I DON'T KNOW HOW THE DARKNESS IS GOING TO DEFEND ITSELF NOW. YOU MUST ALL *BE PREPARED!*
WE'RE NOW MORE UNITED THAN EVER.
THANK YOU FOR WHAT YOU DID, JOHN.
BAH, IT WASN'T ME. I WAS JUST CHANNELING THE INCAL AGAIN.
ATTENTION!!
MOEBIUS 33

AGAIN?
THIS TIME, THE DARKNESS HAS DIRECTED ITS *ATTACK AT ME!* YOU MUST CONCENTRATE AGAIN!
I NEED ALL YOUR *ENERGIES*. YOU MUST DIVE DEEPER THAN THE THETA DREAM. DESCEND INTO THE UNKNOWN. INTO THE *DAATH DREAM.*
JOHN, KEEP YOUR FEARS LOCKED INSIDE.
THE DAATH DREAM? I DON'T KNOW HOW TO DO THAT.
HE'S RIGHT, WE--
THE DARKNESS IS ATTEMPTING TO TAKE CONTROL OF THE DARK INCAL. THE DARK SIDE OF MYSELF IS REBELLING.
HELP ME!
DON'T THINK! LET THE INCAL GUIDE YOUR THOUGHTS.
THE INCAL'S VOICE IS GROWING FAINTER AND FAINTER!
MY LIGHT IS *DYING!*
OFFER YOURSELF TO ME.
HEY! THE LIGHTS ARE GETTING LOWER.
I OBEY.
I OFFER MYSELF.
ZCHZMMFFFF
BUT, INCAL, *WHAT ARE YOU DOING?*
I AM WILLING, TOO.
I OFFER MYSELF.
METABARON! NO!
34
MOEBIUS

NO! NOT YOU TOO! TANATAH!
SINCE IT'S NECESSARY, I OFFER MYSELF, AS WELL.
IT-IT'S MONSTROUS!
STOP!
I AM YOUR FAITHFUL SERVANT.
ANIMAH! NO, NOT YOU! I NEED YOU TOO MUCH. I LOVE YOU!
I OFFER MYSELF!
INCAL! STOP IT!
FLAM
DEEPO...
NOT YOU... DON'T LEAVE ME ALONE...
DAMN! YOU'RE NOT GOING TO LET THAT CRAZY MACHINE BLAST YOU TO CINDERS. DEEPO, NO! NOT YOU!
MOEBIUS
35

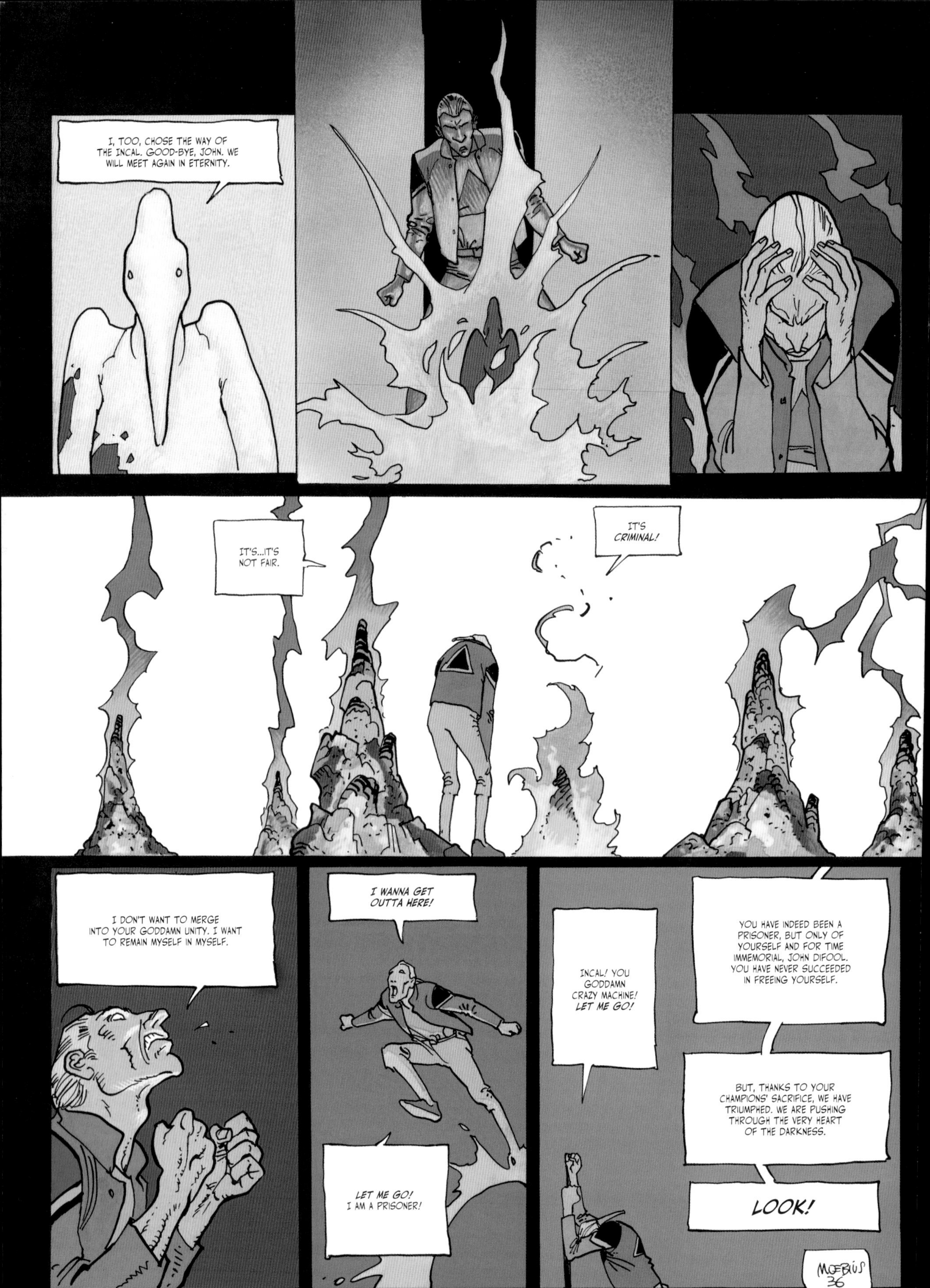
I, TOO, CHOSE THE WAY OF THE INCAL. GOOD-BYE, JOHN. WE WILL MEET AGAIN IN ETERNITY.
IT'S...IT'S NOT FAIR.
IT'S CRIMINAL!
I DON'T WANT TO MERGE INTO YOUR GODDAMN UNITY. I WANT TO REMAIN MYSELF IN MYSELF.
I WANNA GET OUTTA HERE!
LET ME GO! I AM A PRISONER!
INCAL! YOU GODDAMN CRAZY MACHINE! LET ME GO!
YOU HAVE INDEED BEEN A PRISONER, BUT ONLY OF YOURSELF AND FOR TIME IMMEMORIAL, JOHN DIFOOL. YOU HAVE NEVER SUCCEEDED IN FREEING YOURSELF.
BUT, THANKS TO YOUR CHAMPIONS' SACRIFICE, WE HAVE TRIUMPHED. WE ARE PUSHING THROUGH THE VERY HEART OF THE DARKNESS.
LOOK!
MOEBIUS 36

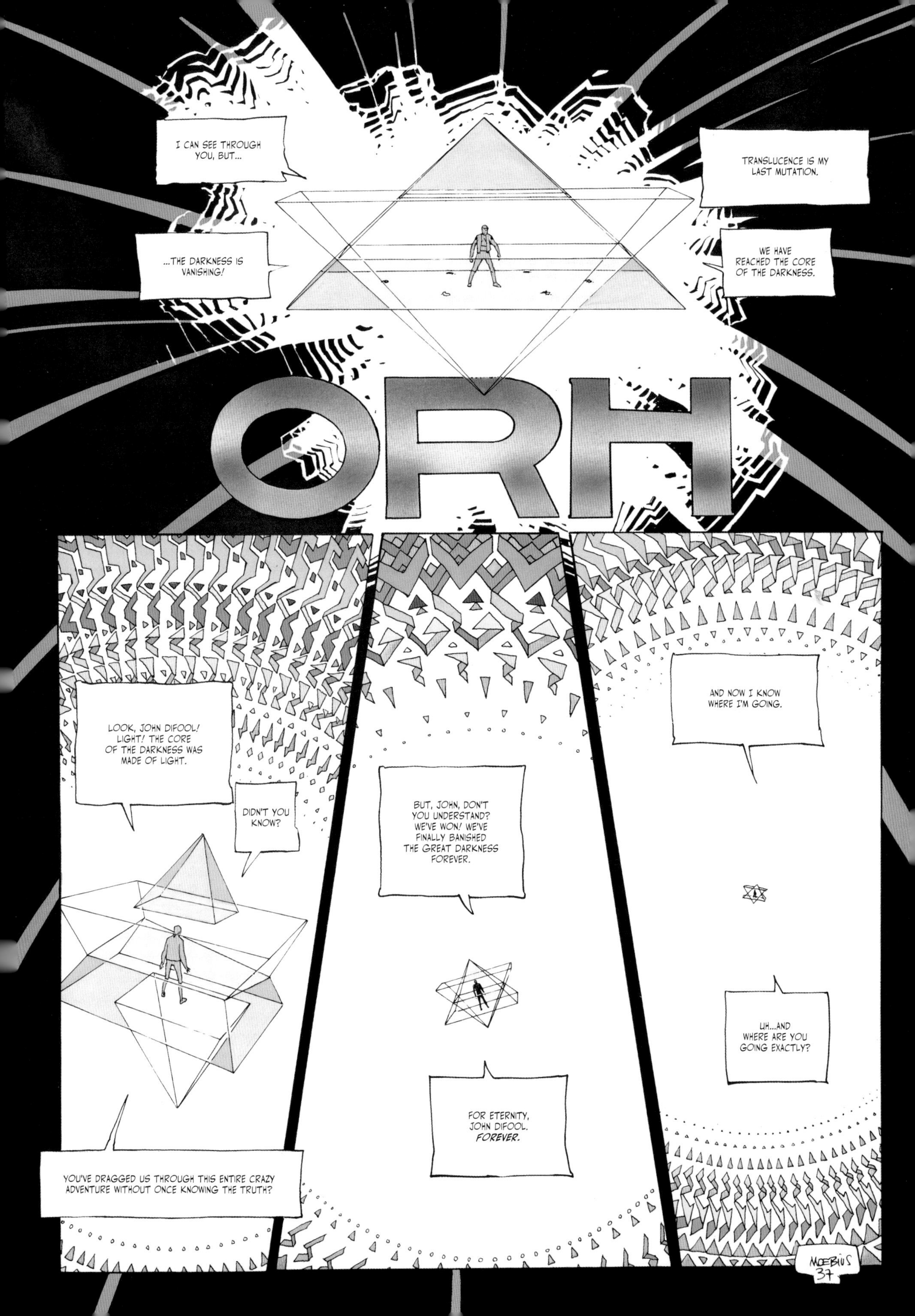
I CAN SEE THROUGH YOU, BUT...
TRANSLUCENCE IS MY LAST MUTATION.
...THE DARKNESS IS VANISHING!
WE HAVE REACHED THE CORE OF THE DARKNESS.
ORH
LOOK, JOHN DIFOOL! LIGHT! THE CORE OF THE DARKNESS WAS MADE OF LIGHT.
DIDN'T YOU KNOW?
YOU'VE DRAGGED US THROUGH THIS ENTIRE CRAZY ADVENTURE WITHOUT ONCE KNOWING THE TRUTH?
BUT, JOHN, DON'T YOU UNDERSTAND? WE'VE WON! WE'VE FINALLY BANISHED THE GREAT DARKNESS FOREVER.
FOR ETERNITY, JOHN DIFOOL. *FOREVER.*
AND NOW I KNOW WHERE I'M GOING.
UH...AND WHERE ARE YOU GOING EXACTLY?
MOEBIUS

TOWARDS THE TRUTH. BE *PREPARED!*
PREPARED FOR *WHAT?*
TO BE ILLUMINATED, JOHN DIFOOL!
!!!
MOEBIUS
38

MOEBIUS
39

OHHH!

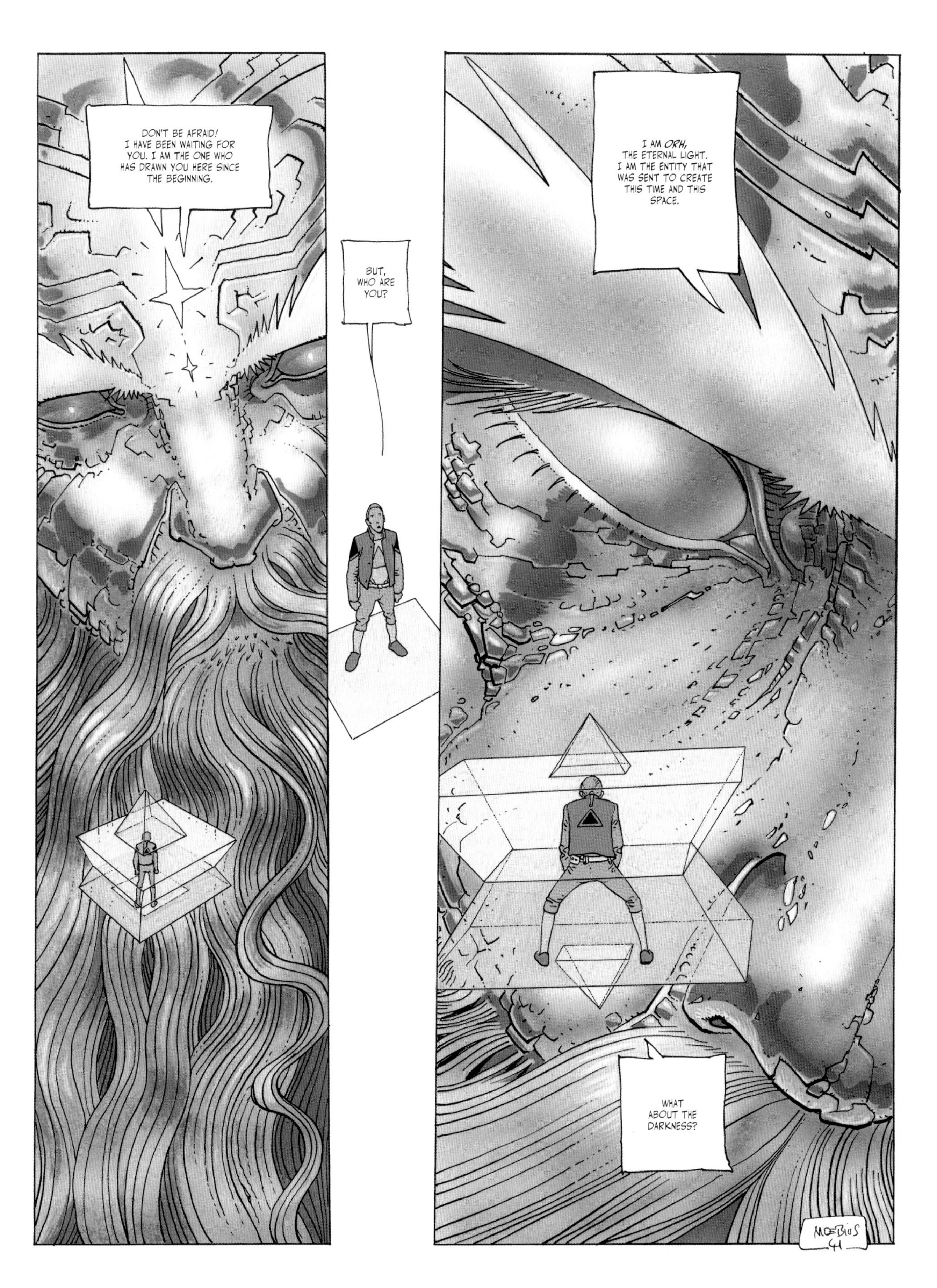
DON'T BE AFRAID! I HAVE BEEN WAITING FOR YOU. I AM THE ONE WHO HAS DRAWN YOU HERE SINCE THE BEGINNING.
BUT, WHO ARE YOU?
I AM ORH, THE ETERNAL LIGHT. I AM THE ENTITY THAT WAS SENT TO CREATE THIS TIME AND THIS SPACE.
WHAT ABOUT THE DARKNESS?
MOEBIUS 41

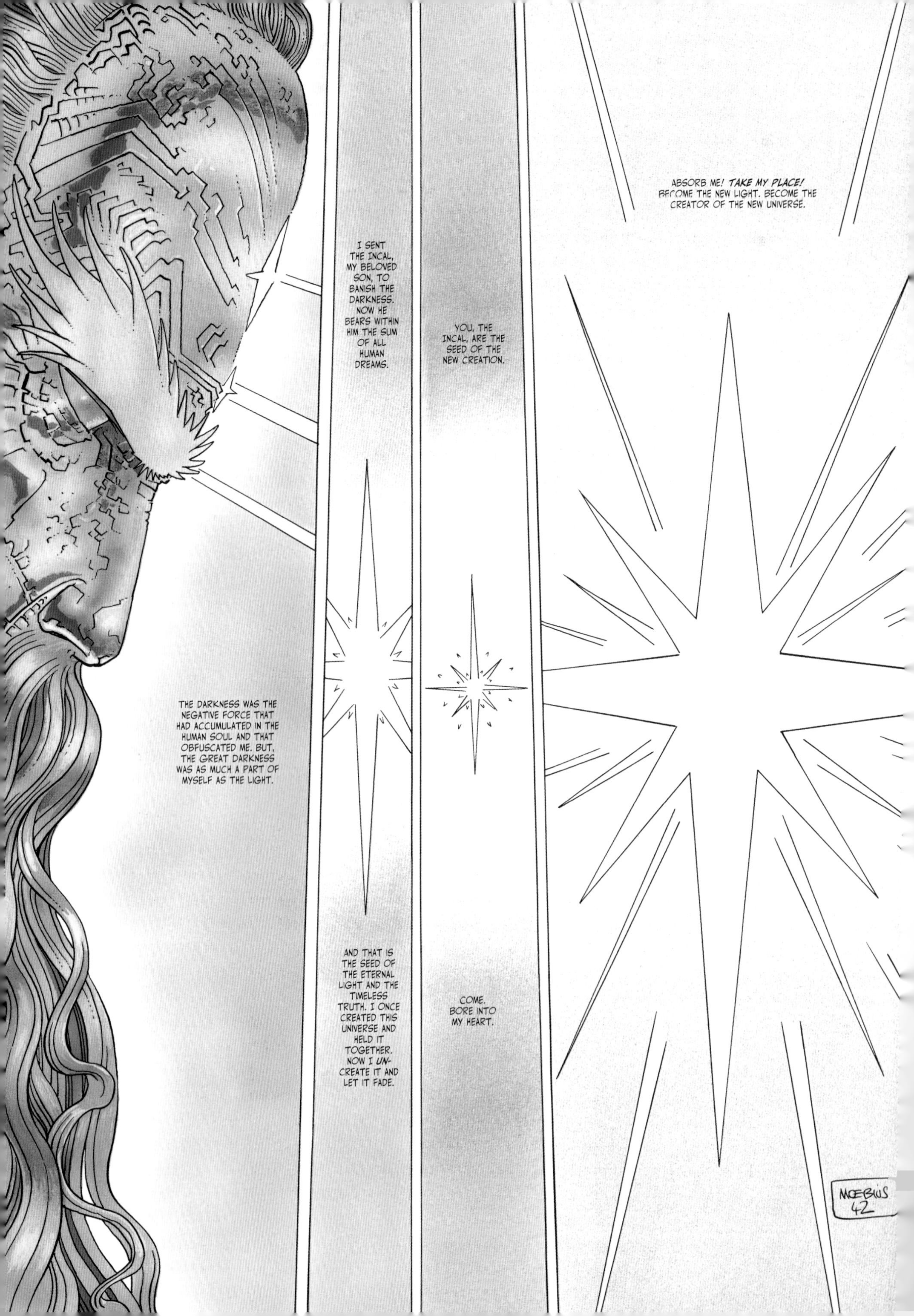
THE DARKNESS WAS THE NEGATIVE FORCE THAT HAD ACCUMULATED IN THE HUMAN SOUL AND THAT OBFUSCATED ME. BUT, THE GREAT DARKNESS WAS AS MUCH A PART OF MYSELF AS THE LIGHT.
I SENT THE INCAL, MY BELOVED SON, TO BANISH THE DARKNESS. NOW HE BEARS WITHIN HIM THE SUM OF ALL HUMAN DREAMS.
AND THAT IS THE SEED OF THE ETERNAL LIGHT AND THE TIMELESS TRUTH. I ONCE CREATED THIS UNIVERSE AND HELD IT TOGETHER. NOW I *UN*-CREATE IT AND LET IT FADE.
YOU, THE INCAL, ARE THE SEED OF THE NEW CREATION.
COME. BORE INTO MY HEART.
ABSORB ME! ***TAKE MY PLACE!*** BECOME THE NEW LIGHT. BECOME THE CREATOR OF THE NEW UNIVERSE.
MOEBIUS 42

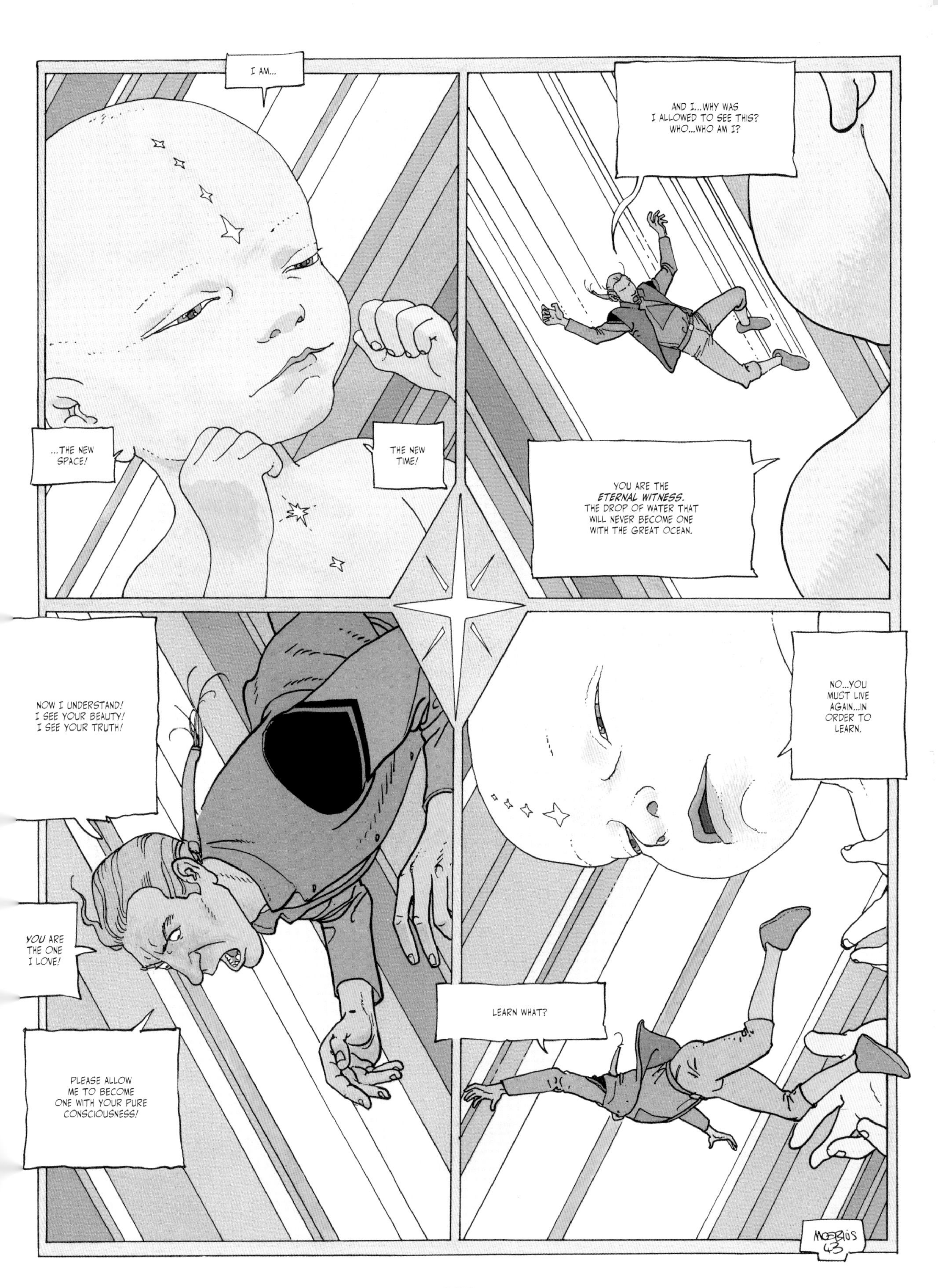
I AM...
...THE NEW SPACE!
THE NEW TIME!
AND I...WHY WAS I ALLOWED TO SEE THIS? WHO...WHO AM I?
YOU ARE THE *ETERNAL WITNESS.* THE DROP OF WATER THAT WILL NEVER BECOME ONE WITH THE GREAT OCEAN.
NOW I UNDERSTAND! I SEE YOUR BEAUTY! I SEE YOUR TRUTH!
YOU ARE THE ONE I LOVE!
PLEASE ALLOW ME TO BECOME ONE WITH YOUR PURE CONSCIOUSNESS!
NO...YOU MUST LIVE AGAIN...IN ORDER TO LEARN.
LEARN WHAT?
MOEBIUS 43

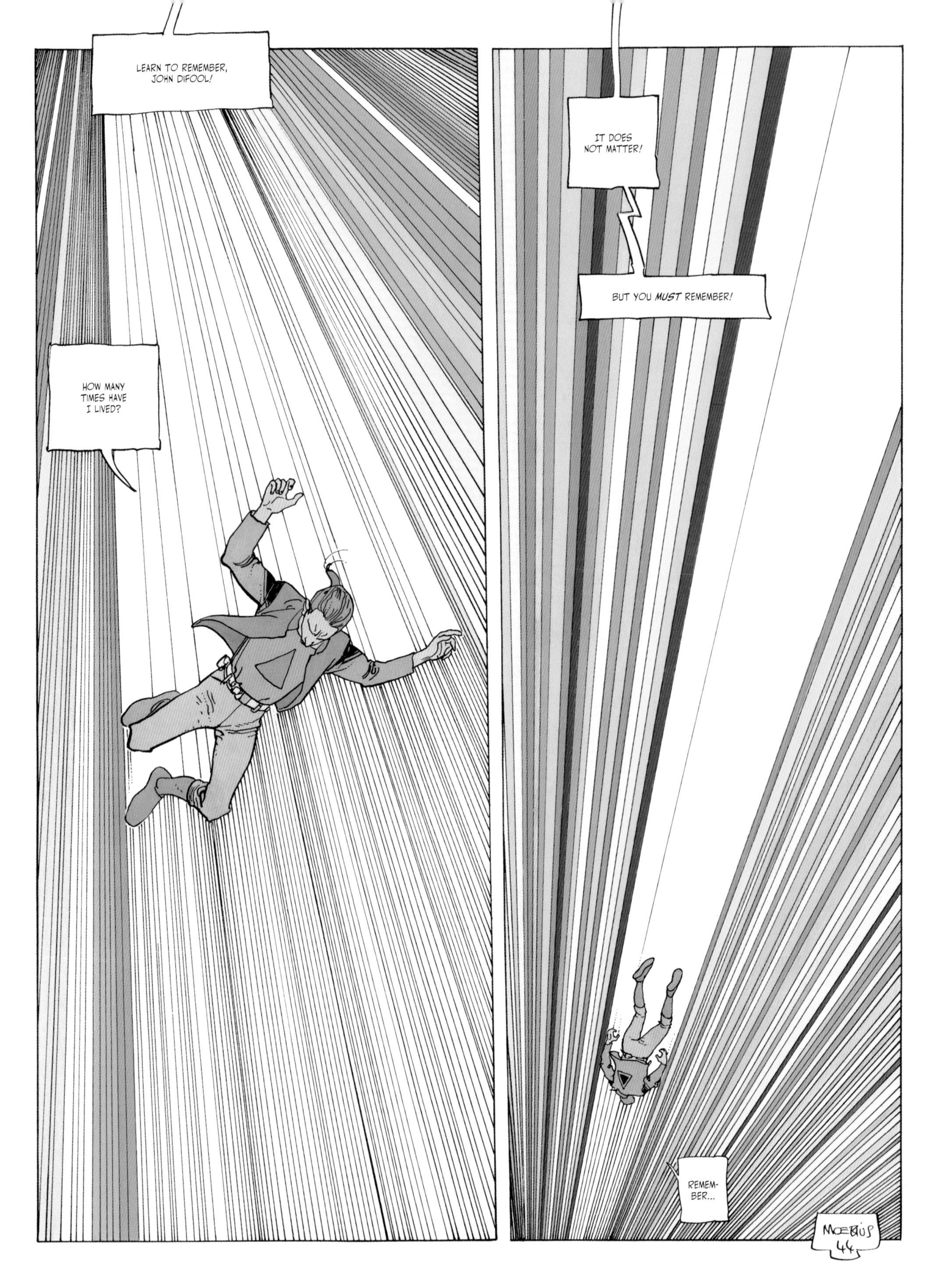
LEARN TO REMEMBER, JOHN DIFOOL!
HOW MANY TIMES HAVE I LIVED?
IT DOES NOT MATTER!
BUT YOU MUST REMEMBER!
REMEM-BER...
MOEBIUS 44

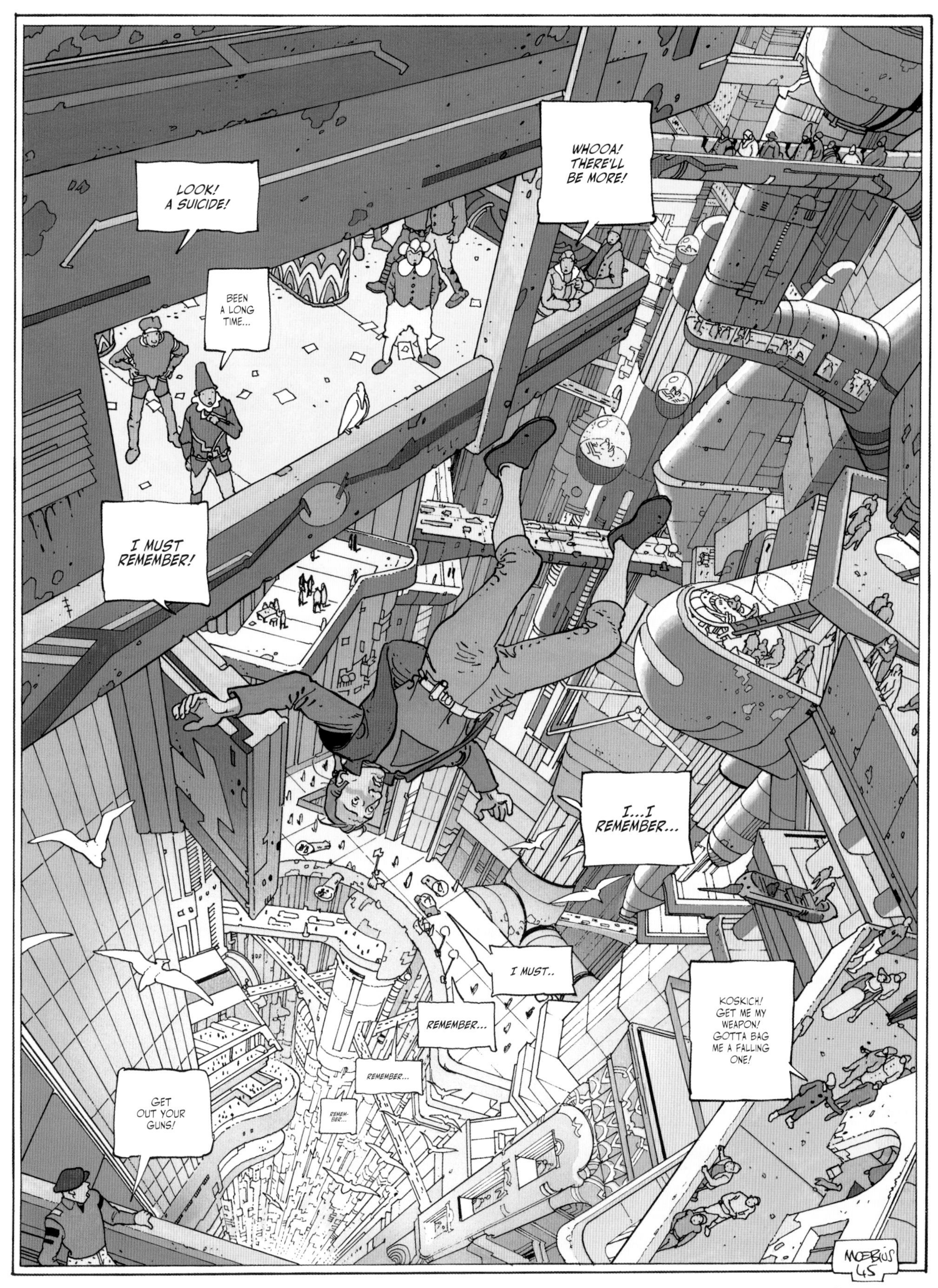

END OF "THE INCAL"

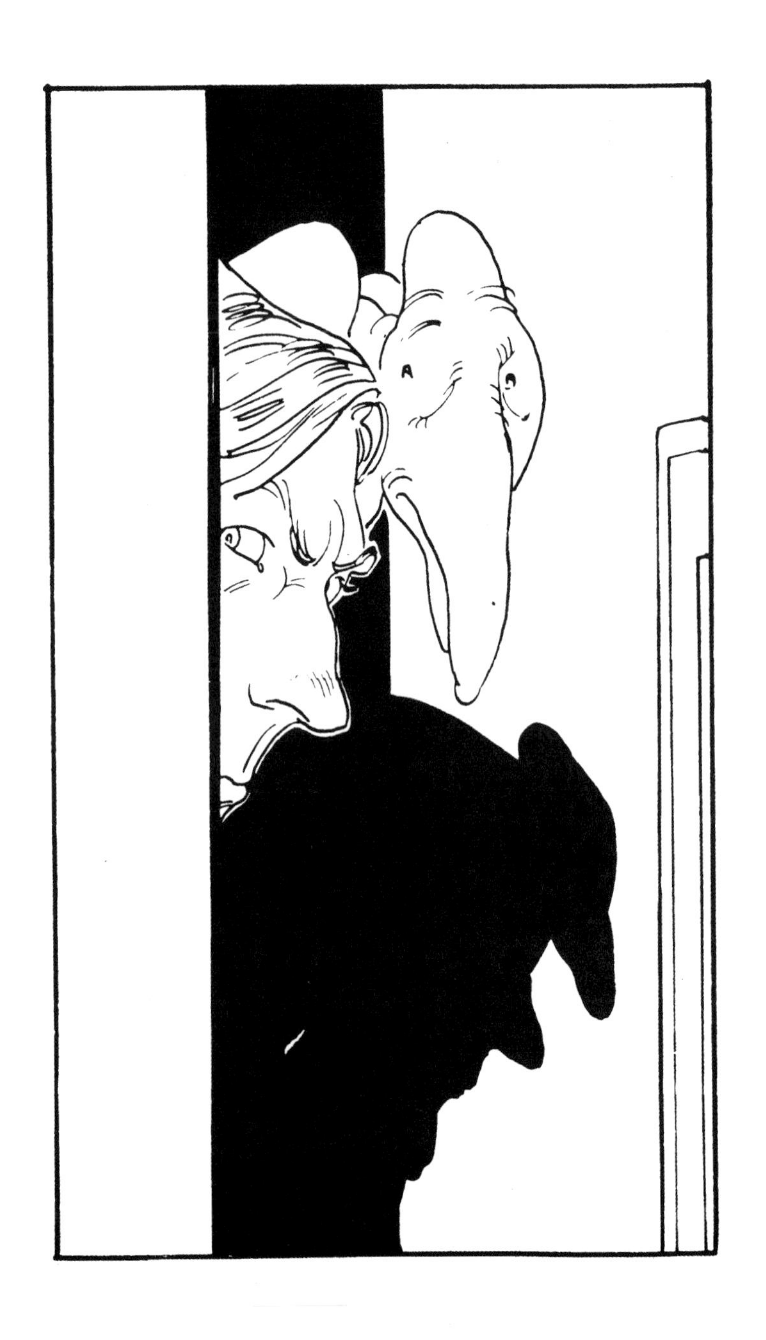

BONUS

IN THE HEART OF THE IMPREGNABLE METABUNKER

In 1989, while he was working on the original edition of what would become *Deconstructing The Incal,* Alejandro Jodorowsky was asked to pen a companion short story to *The Incal* that he and Mœbius had just wrapped up the year before. But what could have been seen as an easy task for the prolific author became a real challenge: how to add a new story when the series' entire concept is a loop, where the last page is inevitably…the first?

Enter the notorious "second thoughts"—the frequent feelings any author can experience after the completion of their work. What more could they tell with those characters, or what holes could they fill in in their backstories? (This was before the creation of *The Incal*'s ultimate prequel and even later, its sequel….) Jodorowsky suddenly remembered a key element from his and Mœbius' saga that is only briefly touched upon in the series (precisely page 21 of Volume 3, page 121 of this edition).

So, with Mœbius, for an encore they created a short tale that would come to play a vital role in the lives of John Difool and his friends. Further, a story that would plant the seeds for another great saga to come: *The Metabarons.* But that is…*another story*.

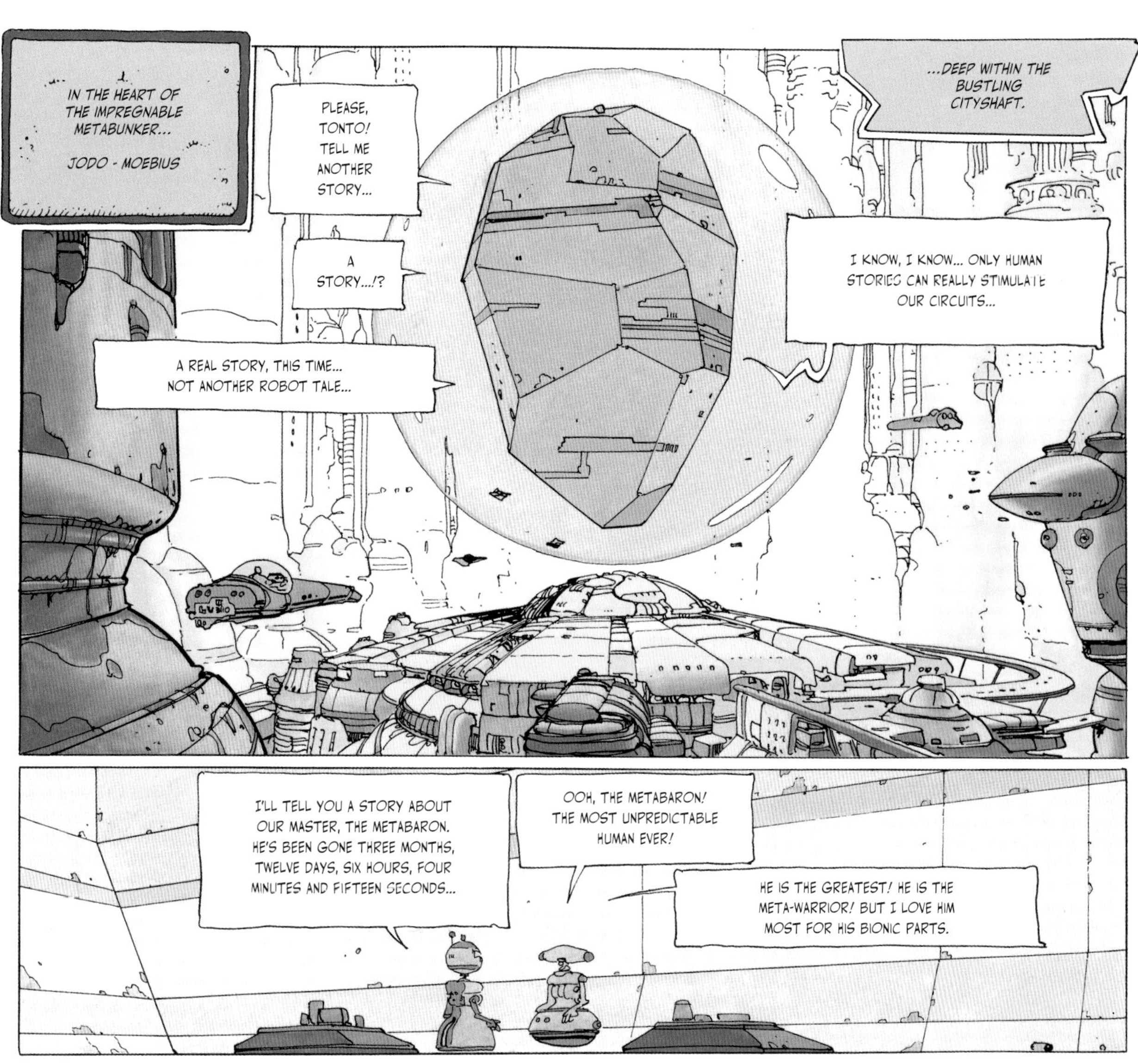
IN THE HEART OF THE IMPREGNABLE METABUNKER...
JODO - MOEBIUS
PLEASE, TONTO! TELL ME ANOTHER STORY...
A STORY...!?
A REAL STORY, THIS TIME... NOT ANOTHER ROBOT TALE...
...DEEP WITHIN THE BUSTLING CITYSHAFT.
I KNOW, I KNOW... ONLY HUMAN STORIES CAN REALLY STIMULATE OUR CIRCUITS...
I'LL TELL YOU A STORY ABOUT OUR MASTER, THE METABARON. HE'S BEEN GONE THREE MONTHS, TWELVE DAYS, SIX HOURS, FOUR MINUTES AND FIFTEEN SECONDS...
OOH, THE METABARON! THE MOST UNPREDICTABLE HUMAN EVER!
HE IS THE GREATEST! HE IS THE META-WARRIOR! BUT I LOVE HIM MOST FOR HIS BIONIC PARTS.

WELL, MOST HUMANS HAVE BIONIC PROTHESES...
TRUE... BUT JUST ACCESSORY ORGANS, POOR HUMANS... BUT THE METABARON HAS A BIONIC EAR AND BIONIC LOBES IN THE RIGHT HALF OF HIS BRAIN... AND I'M NOT TALKING "TOPAZ" CHIPS!
TOPAZ CHIPS! HA HA! BUT TONTO, HOW IS THAT POSSIBLE? WAS HE BORN LIKE THAT?

HA! HA! OF COURSE NOT, YOU FOOL! ROBOTS TEND TO FORGET THAT HUMANS ARE BORN JUST FLFLFLESH AND BLOOD!

NO, IT HAS TO DO WITH WHAT MY ABSENT MASTER ONCE CALLED THE INITIATORY TRADITION OF THE MATE-WARRIORS. LISTEN! I WILL TELL YOU THE STORY AS I KNOW IT...

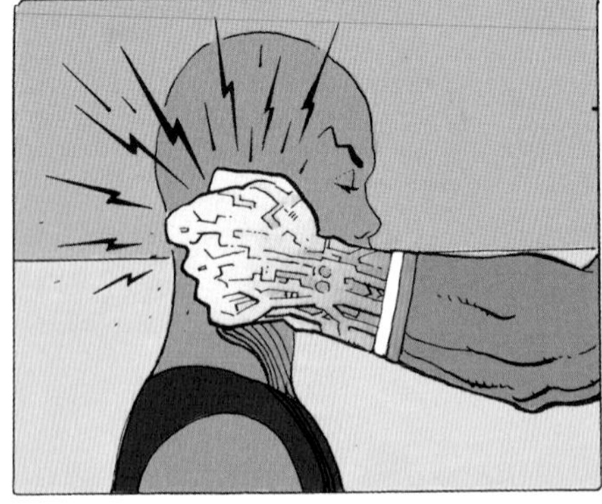

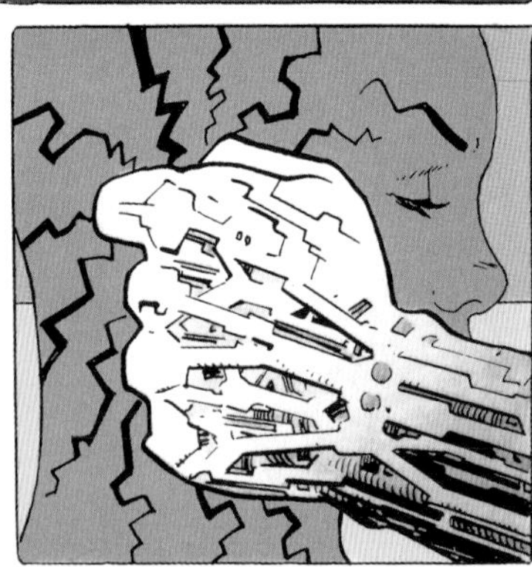

YOU AREN'T CRYING!
AND YOU, FATHER? DID YOU CRY DURING YOUR INITIATION?

I REMAINED IMPASSIVE, JUST LIKE YOU... BUT I COULDN'T PREVENT A TEAR FROM ESCAPING...

YOU MEAN-BEEP! TO TELL ME THAT THE METABARON'S OWN FATHER DESTROYED HIS SON RIGHT EAR AND PART OF HIS BRIN!
YES! AND THE FATHER HAD HIS LEFT HAND CUT OFF BY HIS OWN FATHER BEFORE THAT. THIS HAS BEEN THE TRADITION OF THE META-WARRIORS SINCE THE DAWN OF TIME.
AT 000
MOEBIUS 2.

I'M NOT SATISFIED WITH THAT ABSURD STORY TONTO. I THINK I'D PREFER A GOOD ROBOT TALE.
WAIT, THAT'S JUST THE BEGINNING! YOU'LL SEE, WHAT HAPPENS NEXT IS MUCH BETTER.
I HOPE SO I ALMOST FRIED A DIODE.
IT HAPPENED JUST AFTER HIS BATTLE ON THE WEST CONTINENT AGAINST THE POST-VANDALS...
THESE MASSACRES ARE TOO EASY...
I'VE HAD ENOUGH!
HE NO LONGER HAD ANY FOES WORTH OF HIM...
HIS ONLY CONTACT WITH HUMAN BEINGS WAS THEIR CRIES OF AGONY AND TERROR.
THIS TIME, I'M FINISHED. I'M RETURNING TO THE METABUNKER--
--AND NEVER COMING OUT FOR ANYBODY!

I'LL NEVER HAVE A CHILD, TONTO.
NEVER!
AN END TO CRUEL INITIATIONS, MASTER.

CRRRRRRRRRRRRRRR
WHAT'S HAPPENING?
WHO'S THERE?
MOEBIUS83

QUICK, TONTO! THE PROTECTIVE SHIELD!
THE SHIELDS ARE UP... ALL OF THEM! THIS IS INCONCEIVABLE!

A RAT!
MY SENSORS SHOW THAT IT'S AN ILLUSION, MASTER!

HOWEVER, THE DAMAGE TO THE FLOOR IS REAL!
LOOK! IT'S DISSOLVING!

A FIGURE IS APPEARING! SOMEONE MANAGED TO PENETRATE THE METABUNKER!
THAT'S IMPOSSIBLE! NOBODY CAN--

TONTO-- IS IT REAL?
MY SENSORS SAY IT IS, BE CAREFUL, MASTER.

WHO ARE YOU?
ANSWER, OR I SHOOT!
YOU HAVE NOTHING TO FEAR FROM US.
A HUMAN!
MŒBIUS 4

A WOMAN!
I HAD NEVER SEEN SUCH AN EXPRESSION CROSS THE METABARON'S SOBER FACE...

WHO ARE YOU? WHAT IS YOUR NAME?
I AM ANIMAH!

ANIMAH... YES. THAT NAME... IS FAMILIAR TO ME--

ANIMAH... IT'S YOU... SOMEONE I KNOW FROM LONG AGO.

STAY HERE! DON'T EVER LEAVE ME AGAIN...
MY PLACE IS NOT HERE...

I AM POWERFUL... VERY POWERFUL... I CAN CONQUER THIS CITY, THIS WORLD, AND OFFER THEM TO YOU.
COMMAND, AND I WILL OBEY.

IN THAT CASE... I COMMAND YOU TO TAKE THIS CHILD... TO BE HIS GUARDIAN, AND HIS TEACHER!
?!

HE IS CALLED SOLUNE... AT HEART, HE IS THE SACRED ANDROGYNE... RAISE HIM, TO BECOME THE NEW META-WARRIOR!

YOU ASK ME TO BE... HIS FATHER?!
NEVER!
YOU SAID YOU WOULD OBEY... THIS IS MY COMMAND.
MOEBIUS 5

NO!
?!
I CANNOT!
YOU TOLD ME YOU WERE POWERFUL.

I WANT TO--

--BUT I CANNOT!

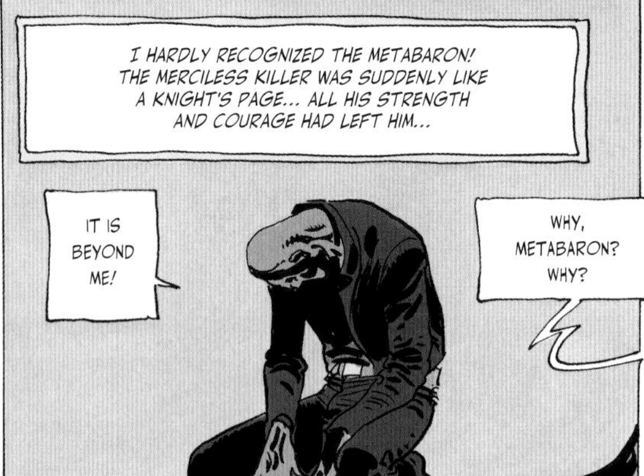
I HARDLY RECOGNIZED THE METABARON! THE MERCILESS KILLER WAS SUDDENLY LIKE A KNIGHT'S PAGE... ALL HIS STRENGTH AND COURAGE HAD LEFT HIM...
IT IS BEYOND ME!
WHY, METABARON? WHY?

ANIMAH, YOU DO NOT KNOW WHAT YOU ASK... LISTEN... I WILL TELL YOU WHAT...HAPPENED ON THE DAY I TURNED SIXTEEN... MY FATHER BID ME RETURN TO THE METABUNKER WITH WEAPONS READY, FOR THE FINAL TRIAL OF MY INITIATION.

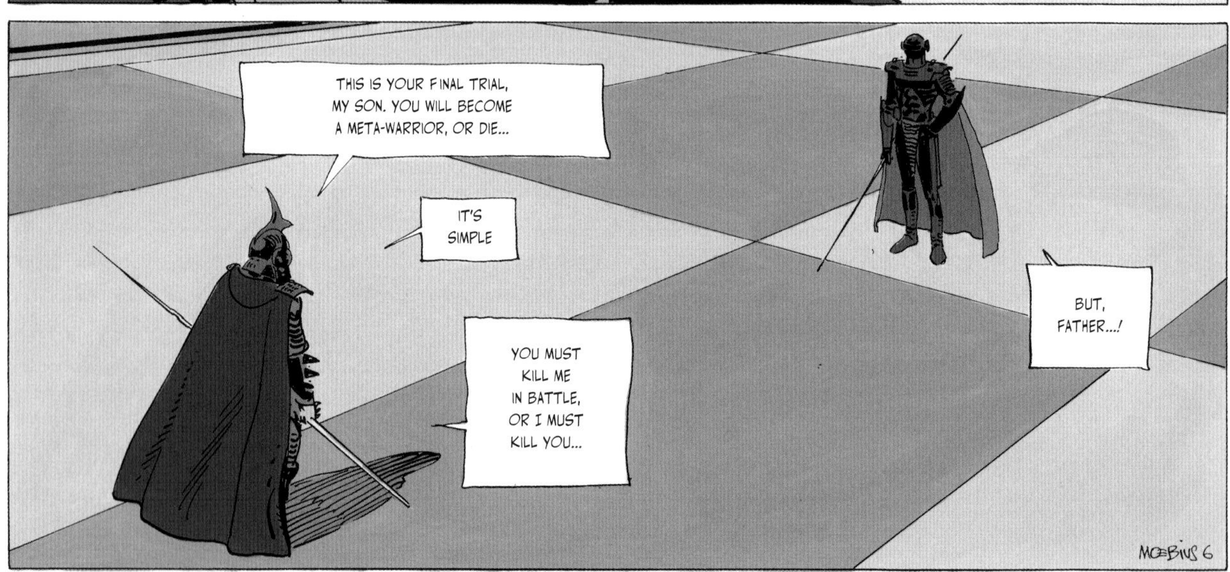
THIS IS YOUR FINAL TRIAL, MY SON. YOU WILL BECOME A META-WARRIOR, OR DIE...
IT'S SIMPLE
YOU MUST KILL ME IN BATTLE, OR I MUST KILL YOU...
BUT, FATHER...!
MOEBIUS 6

I WILL COUNT TO THREE, THEN DEAL THE FIRST BLOW!
ONE--
FATHER! NO!
TWO--

THREE!
THE DUEL WENT ON FOR TWO DAYS... UNTIL...
AAAA
NOW YOU UNDERSTAND, ANIMAH, WHY I CANNOT CARE FOR THIS CHILD. FOR HE WOULD NEVER BE ABLE TO DEFEAT ME.
YOU'RE MISTAKEN, METABARON. HE CAN ALREADY DEFEAT YOU.
DO YOU HAVE A DAGGER?

GO ON... TRY TO KILL HIM! PIERCE HIS HEART!
VERY WELL...

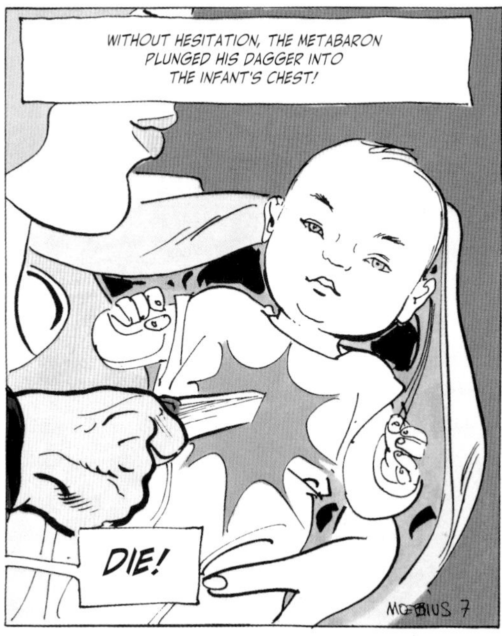
WITHOUT HESITATION, THE METABARON PLUNGED HIS DAGGER INTO THE INFANT'S CHEST!
DIE!
MOEBIUS 7

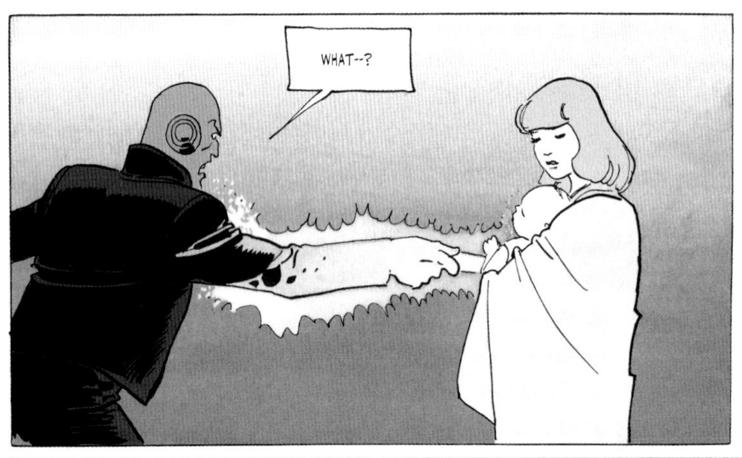
WHAT--?

THIS IS... INCRE-DIBLE!
HE IS NOTHING, AND YET.

I HEARD HIM--
HE SPOKE INSIDE MY MIN--

I'LL TAKE HIM!
WHAT DID HE SAY?

HE SAID: "TAKE ME AND NOURISH ME!"
IT WAS MY COMMAND--
BUT HIS DESIRE!

SHE DISAPPEARED, AND THE METABUNKER'S GAPING FLOOR CLOSED ITSELF OVER HER...
SHE LEFT WITHOUT A TRACE

A REAL TECHNO-MYSTERY!
I WAS ONCE THE BRINGER OF DEATH, BUT NOW I WILL BE THE BRINGER OF LIFE... WE WILL WAIT FOR YOU, ANIMAH, I KNOW YOU WILL RETURN.

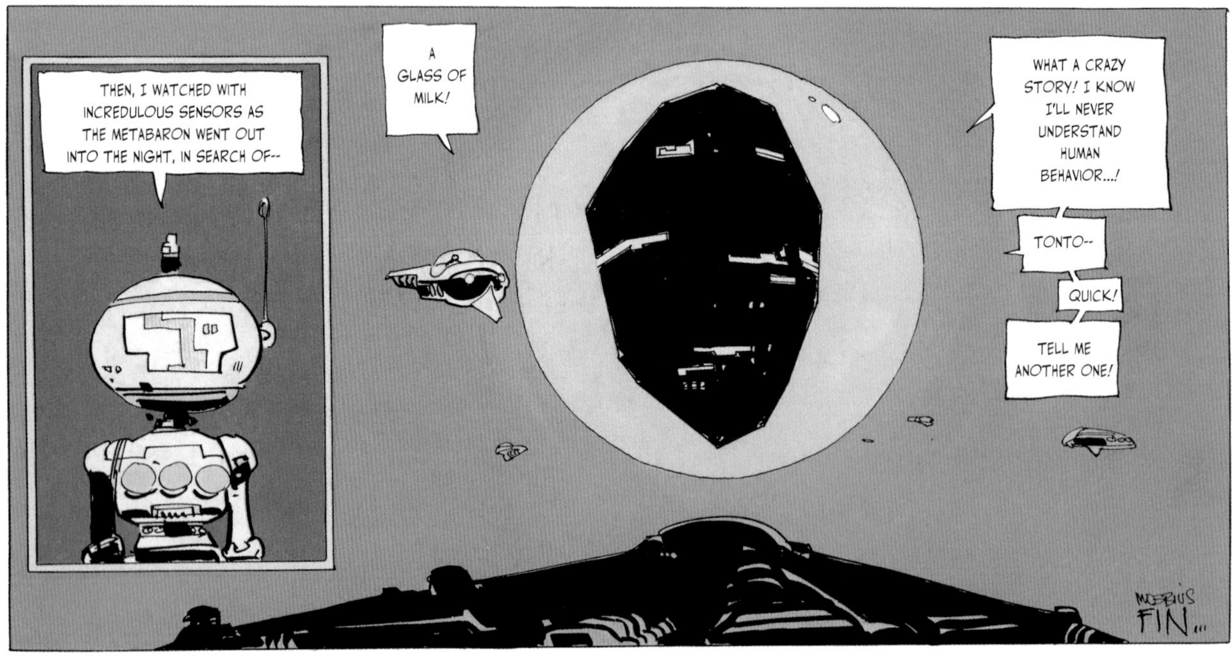
THEN, I WATCHED WITH INCREDULOUS SENSORS AS THE METABARON WENT OUT INTO THE NIGHT, IN SEARCH OF--
A GLASS OF MILK!
WHAT A CRAZY STORY! I KNOW I'LL NEVER UNDERSTAND HUMAN BEHAVIOR...!
TONTO--
QUICK!
TELL ME ANOTHER ONE!
MOEBIUS
FIN...